George Herbert Powell

Excursions in Libraria

Being Restrospective Reviews and Bibliographical Notes

George Herbert Powell

Excursions in Libraria
Being Restrospective Reviews and Bibliographical Notes

ISBN/EAN: 9783337077419

Printed in Europe, USA, Canada, Australia, Japan

Cover: Foto ©Andreas Hilbeck / pixelio.de

More available books at **www.hansebooks.com**

EXCURSIONS IN LIBRARIA
BEING RETROSPECTIVE REVIEWS AND BIBLIOGRAPHICAL NOTES BY G. H. POWELL

" For books, we know,
Are a substantial world."—*Wordsworth*.

NEW YORK
CHARLES SCRIBNER'S SONS
153-157 FIFTH AVENUE
1896

Of the papers which follow the first is reprinted from *Macmillan's Magazine* ("A Discourse of Rare Books," July, 1893), and the last, in part, from the *Pall Mall Magazine* (February, 1895), with the kind permission of the respective proprietors. Both articles are here presented in a revised and enlarged form, the latter, in fact, having been entirely rewritten.

PREFACE

SOME apology may be necessary for offering to the public, so abundantly supplied of late years with "books about books," another volume which can hardly help falling into that category. The present work, however, addresses itself (with all the misgivings of a first venture) rather to the humane interests of the general reader, than to what may respectfully be called the refined curiosities of the bibliophile, to the collector of books, that is, as books, and not as antiquities or objects of exoteric *virtù*,[1] in fine, to the bookbuyer who is also, and by virtue of his office, a "voracious" reader, even if he be not one of those

> " *Biblio*phagi, or men whose heads
> Do grow beneath their shoulders"

from excessive application to study. "Excursions," in Libraria or elsewhere, do not profess to be explorations, or to serve any serious industrial demand, although (within their inevitable limits) the *notes de voyage* of one tourist may have a certain use and interest for others. This is the only excuse

[1] See Ch. I., pp. 15 and 31.

for publishing a selection of those "marked passages" and "marginal (or flyleaf) notes" which accumulate during the unconscious labour of love expended in years of book-collecting.

Two or three of the chapters that follow might be described as sketches of "periods" or of "lost points of view," illustrated from 'contemporary sources of the fourteenth, the sixteenth, and the eighteenth centuries respectively. The *Gascon Tragedy* and the *Pirate's Paradise* rehearse more or less well-known romances of history. In the longer essay on memoirs, and in those dealing with rare books (or rather the principles which govern the practice of book-buying), and with early mythological literature, a conscientious if misguided attempt has been made to present—in an inevitably discursive fashion, but with some sense of proportion—a general survey (from the point of view of the practical reader and collector), of a larger province of that "world of books" which, if not always as "pure and good" as the poetry of Mr. Wordsworth, is at least always human.

The insertion throughout the latter chapters of so many dates and parenthetical details will, I hope, be excused by readers who have these things at their fingers' ends, in consideration of those who, like the author, hanker after chronological landmarks along the highroads of—

"The dusty travelled past."

With regard to the criticisms and descriptions of books (old or modern), which occupy almost all the notes and a great part of the text of this volume, I need only say that the works familiarly cited and quoted are almost all in my own possession. These comprise possibly a few "out of the way" books, and one or two such as are commonly called "rare," and might not be found even in reputable libraries. But I have not, except in the first chapter, referred to any work except on the ground that it was (to persons debarred from purchasing a more modern or more expensive edition) at least worth having, for reasons more fully diagnosed in the text.

In estimating the importance of form and typography as affecting the question whether the average individual is likely to read a book with pleasure or profit, or even to read it at all, and the considerable proportion of "old books" periodically in danger of being slighted or forgotten by all but their actual custodians, there is sometimes a danger of confounding *human* (that is historical, or literary) and merely "bookish" interest. In regard to the former, I have spared the reader no reference to any original work likely to rouse his interest or curiosity, though I fear I cannot add—his envy or regret.

Notes and references have thus, in spite of every desire to exclude vanities and repetitions, swelled to such a bulk, that the only excusable addition seemed an index, which is offered as an apology for the digressions of which several chapters are largely composed.

The "we" of the retrospective reviewer, inextricably embedded in the one long bibliographical article which has already appeared in print, has been allowed to permeate the text with no further idea than that of associating the reader in an amicable "voyage autour d'une bibliothèque choisie," of which imagination and the proximity of Bloomsbury have slightly extended the bounds.

Of the ornaments, devices, etc., with which my publishers

have illustrated the more specially bibliographical chapters of the book, the greater part are taken from works, chiefly of the sixteenth century,[1] in my own collection.

To these memoranda of cherished possessions and respected printers may be added the woodcut on p. 40, the "brasse plate" from Pagitt's *Heresiography*, and a portrait of Voltaire, with which I hope some readers may be unacquainted. For the more remarkable reproduction from the *Directorium vitæ humanæ* (1480), which forms the frontispiece to the chapter on mythology, and the exquisite little woodcut from the *Dyalogus creaturarum* of the same date; as for those taken from the (equally rare) Vérard edition of the Comte de Foix's *Book on Field Sports*, and the plate from Exquemelin's *Buccaneers*, recourse has been had to the treasure-house of the British Museum, and to the unfailing kindness and courtesy of its officials.

G. H. POWELL.

2 THANET PLACE, STRAND,
September 5th, 1895.

[1] See pp. 36 and 77.

TABLE OF CONTENTS

LIST OF ILLUSTRATIONS

The Initial Letters of the Chapters are reduced from the Froissart printed by Jan de Tournes (described on p. 49), all but that prefixed to Chap. IV., which is from the *Dialoghi piacevoli di N. Franco* (as to whom see p. 22). Gioliti : in Venetia. 8vo. 1542.

I.

THE PHILOSOPHY OF RARITY.

Woodcut of scholars in a library (exhibiting the early method of arranging books) from a very rare edition of Sallust, sm. 8vo. Lyons, s. a. (1509), discovered for me by the kindness of Mr. Pollard, of the British Museum. (Grenville Library, C. 8, f. 14.)

THE PHILOSOPHY OF RARITY.

" He peeped into a rich bookseller's shop,
    Quoth he, ' We are both of one college ' !
For I sate myself, like a cormorant, once
    Hard by the tree of knowledge."

Coleridge.

THE noble industry and royal sport of book-hunting
may safely be asserted to be as old as literature—
as literature, that is, inscribed upon any material
more portable than that of the Rosetta stone.

It would be difficult to feel sure that the earliest
papyrus ever marked by human hand was not immediately afterwards
destroyed by the rivalry of would-be proprietors, and as soon as the
first "book" came into existence nothing short of a military despotism can have preserved it in the possession of a single owner. The
gossiping Aulus Gellius has handed down the tradition of Aristotle's
extravagance at the sale of Speusippus, and Plato's unjustifiable
purchase (so severely criticised by Timon) of a particular work of
Philolaus the Pythagorean. Such collectors truly held to the motto
of our own philobiblical Richard de Bury (to whom the story of the
Sibylline leaves suggested a moral for the auction-room) " Libri non
libræ." The passion, growing by what it fed on, raged desperately

B 2

in the middle ages. Pope Sylvester II. had, in the tenth century, to borrow so simple a work as Cæsar, in return for eight volumes of Boethius on Astrology, and three hundred years later Roger Bacon complained that he could not get even a minor work of Cicero for love or money And it reached a triumphant crisis at the dawn of the Renaissance, when one of the most immortal classics might be looked for and found "at the bottom of a disused well" (or wherever it was that Bracciolini discovered the Quintilian), and his learned rival Aurispa could return from a single book-hunting expedition laden with 238 ancient manuscripts, containing all the works of Plato, Xenophon, Arrian, and Diodorus Siculus, the Geography of Strabo, and the Poems of Pindar.

Such were the "rarities" of those golden days; and comparing them with the works, or rather things, most sought after in our own, we might be disposed to think that the age of true "book-hunting" was no more; nay, when we contemplate catalogues crowded with really classical items (ancient or modern) labelled *selten, rarissimo, introuvable*, and *unique*, we may be moved to ask indignantly, what has posterity—the posterity of the fifteenth century—done, since that date, but lose or damage the works it should have taken most care of?

But this would be a harsh judgment, for posterity, including the nineteenth century, has had so many more things to think about.

And though we can never hope to make such "finds" as did the agents of Lorenzo the magnificent, the process of discovery, and re-discovery is as eternal as the art and mystery of losing books.

Thus the "Philosophy" we here struggle to expound is but the craft and "venerie" of the book-hunter.

It is hardly necessary to observe that as the mere unfrequent occurrence of a phenomenon is no index of its importance, so the fact that a particular book, or any other given chattel, is seldom to be seen is no evidence of its intrinsic value—should in fact be rather the reverse, proportionately to our belief in the intelligence of mankind, although the rarity of a book, again, must be distinguished from the difficulty of obtaining it.

This whole subject is excellently treated in the "Axiomata Specialia" prefixed to that interesting and not very common work of reference, Vogt's *Catalogus Historico-Criticus Librorum Rariorum* (fourth enlarged edition, 8vo, Frankfort, 1793). Prefacing the discussion with the remark that rarity is by itself no proof of value (some of the worst and some of the most worthless books being the most difficult to procure), he and his editors classify "rare books" under a copious variety of headings which we shall not here attempt to exhaust.

First and foremost in any such attempted classification would, of course, be ranked early works dating from the invention of printing to about 1520 or 1530. The casual reader may here be reminded that what is commonly believed to be the first book printed is the magnificent edition of the Vulgate known (since its rediscovery in the Mazarine Library by De Bure in the last century) as the 42 line "Mazarine" Bible, the "Hopetoun" copy of which (Sir John Thorold's brought £3,900) was recently sold to Mr. Quaritch for £2,000, and is duly described in his catalogue as produced at Maintz *before* 1456. It has indeed been assigned to 1450, or 1454; and a copy is to be seen among the specimens of early printing in the British Museum. From the conclusion of the aforesaid period every decade that one recedes the volumes pertaining thereto naturally rise in price by something like geometrical progression, and to go back further, "Block-books," which flourish from 1440 to 1480 or thereabouts, and do not trouble the bibliophile much upon his daily rounds, must all be described as tolerably rare, since only about 100 are known to exist.[1] Yet of recent years, owing to the dispersal of so many large libraries, books of the fifteenth century have been at times almost a drug in the market. A folio volume bound in such

[1] Gordon Duff, *Early Printed Books*, 1893.

pigskin as the invaders of Italy loved to use for saddles (the feelings of the *cinque-cento* war-horse are not recorded), comprising a splendid and spotless specimen of printing dated 1475, wrought with such ink and paper as men make not now, was purchased retail by the writer of these presents for only 20s. Works of the last two decades of that century are comparatively easy to procure, not seldom for a few shillings apiece, where no interest but the date of production attaches to them ; while anything printed between 1460 and 1470, when the first enthusiasm for the invention produced such superlative workmanship, still keeps a high value.

As to the question of interest (humane, that is, and literary), the early printed book is as a rule very deficient in this respect. Apart from the classics (and it is amazing how many Latin authors[1]— Hallam gives a list of them—were reproduced before 1500), Bibles, Theology, and Hagiology, are the chief and certainly the most artistically beautiful products of the press at this period, not that the collector anxious to possess an "incunable" of real literary and intellectual value need hesitate to squander £50 or £100 on such a work as the first edition of Augustine's *De Civitate Dei*, fol. 1467 (without name or place). Next to the absolutely earliest specimens of printing we may put the most celebrated editions of Latin and Greek classics and other authors published by the most famous printers (also in many cases their own editors) during the whole period of the Renaissance. The art of printing, originally born at some yet disputed date between 1450 and 1460, as well as of what may be called publishing, experienced a sort of chronic regeneration in one direction or another, in the matter of type, size, or some other detail, at the hands of the celebrated representatives of the Giunta, Aldus, Estienne, and Gryphius families. The Plantin establishment at Antwerp is equally famous, retaining its excellence during all the

---

[1] Among these a special interest attaches to the very early and valuable first edition of Tacitus (folio, circum 1468) wanting *the first five books of the Annals*, which are described in the edition of 1515 as " nuper in Germaniâ reperti.'

latter half of the sixteenth century. The first privilege was granted in 1554, and in the half-century that followed probably no press in Europe turned out a larger proportion of useful books.[1] In the

Device on last leaf of Sadoleti Epistolæ ap. Sebast. Gryphium. 1554.

VIRTVTE DVCE, COMITE FORTVNA.

LVGDVNI,
APVD ANT. GRYPHIVM.
M. D. LXXXV.

Macrobii Saturnalia. 12mo. 1585. (Device on title.)

[1] Of the " Plantins " in my possession I should be inclined to give the palm for practical neatness and legibility to the pocket edition of *Boethius*, 18mo, 1562, and the *Epistolae Clenardi* (" raræ, caræ, præclaræ," as an ancient authority calls them), 8vo, 1566. In the *Boethius* the device appears in a very simple form—with

catalogue of the museum at Antwerp,[1] which occupies the original premises of this press, it is stated that its founder (Christopher Plantin) produced on an average fifty works a year, and about fifteen hundred in all. It would be interesting to know what proportion of these are now in Great Britain. A large number, and still more of those published by Balthasar Moretus I. (1610–1641), are elaborately illustrated.

But for modern days, and for London, where incredibly immense stocks of second-hand books are now collected, the second

Cum Cæſ. Maieſt. gratia & priuilegio ad decennium.

Device of Jo. Oporinus (J. Herbst, ob. 1568) of Basle.

axiom must be confined to earlier work. Classics, ancient and modern, however excellent their execution, having vastly declined in value since the beginning of the present century, are now much more easily met with. The Stephanus Editio Princeps of Appian (folio, 1551), a very creditable piece of printing, is commoner than

the legs of the compass not twenty-five degrees apart. In the *Jornandes*, 8vo, 1597 (also an excellently printed work), they have expanded to twice that distance.

[1] *Catalogue du Musée Plantin-Moretus*, par Max Rooses, Conservateur. 2me ed. Anvers, 1883.

Device of Plantin-Moretus press, a late specimen (17th century, date mislaid.)

Device on title of Clenardi Epistolæ ex off. Christophori Plantin. 1566.

many English productions of the nineteenth century. The first, spendidly executed edition of Cardinal Bembo's Historiæ Venetæ —a work of quite insignificant historical value—bearing the same date, cannot be called rare, and excellent specimens of the Plantin-Moretus press can be unearthed with surprising facility at almost any second-hand shop. This remarkable state of things is only to be accounted for by that avidity on the part of English collectors of the last century, which had attracted the notice of earlier bibliographers than Vogt. The private libraries, and consequently the booksellers' shops of this country, have for long been probably much better stocked with literature of the fifteenth and sixteenth centuries than any others equally distant from the great printing centres of the Continent.

We have already remarked that a book is not necessarily very rare because it is seldom seen in the market, since it may, in stock-broking language, be "well held" in many quarters. Again, a book may be merely so rare that you may spend a dozen years looking for it, without being so much rarer that every known copy is, so to speak, the cynosure of all neighbouring eyes. One ought further to distinguish books which have become rare because, in bibliographical phrase, *recherchés*, and those which, being naturally few in number, or, from their nature, calculated only to survive in a few copies, have become sought after for that reason. It is obvious that the former will include all rare, old, or early printed works which present intrinsic attractions to the intelligence or antiquarian interest of book-lovers, and the latter such books as are valued chiefly as a source of curious vanity to the happy possessor, and of vexation of spirit to his rivals.

Some books are, it would be simpler to say, "born rare, some achieve rarity" by their merits or demerits, "and some"—of which more anon—"have rarity thrust upon them."

Andreini's *Adamo*, 4to, 1613, would perhaps never have become even a moderately rare book, but for its "ex post facto" connection with Milton's *Paradise Lost*. Similarly the work of "Erycius Puteanus" (*i.e.* Henry Du Puy 1574-1646), entitled *Comus sive Phagesiposia Cimmeria, Somnium*, first published at Louvain in 1611 (and reprinted at Oxford, 1634), may, for all we know, have been rarified by students anxiously verifying the numerous passages, borrowed thence by the English poet.

The texts of other works—none obtrusively common—infected by the same interest, such *e.g.* as Taubmann's *Bellum Angelicum*, 1607, and Valmarana's *Paradisus*, 1627, will be found in Lauder's *Delectus auctorum sacrorum Miltono facem prælucentium*, or "Selection" if we may so translate it, "of Sacred Authors who could hold a candle to Milton," 8vo, Londini, 1753, itself an out-of-the-way volume of considerable interest, even if it fails to prove, in the words of the fanatical author, that—

> " Had Milton not plow'd with his Neighbour's fair Heifer,
> Fam'd *Paradise Lost* had not been worth a Cypher " (!)

Similarly the "Tesoretto" of Brunetto Latini,[1] in itself merely a singular piece of doggerel, derives a shade of importance from the details (of scenery, &c.) which it certainly seems to have suggested to Dante, who during his exile attended Latini's lectures at Paris. The process is of course as often reversed. Had the "Divine Comedy" been a perfectly worthless production, it might have been treasured because it preserved a few phrases of some rare or perished original. Just as—to illustrate the case of a *precedent* interest—a certain folio Psalter of 1516 is highly priced on account of the long account of Columbus which is employed to illustrate a particular Psalm. This is the case with numerous works on miscellaneous topics published about the date of such episodes as the discovery of the New World. And, in general, details of a day long gone by have often served to preserve trivial or worthless works enshrining them, which would otherwise have long since been as extinct as the Dodo.

It would be idle to add that there are many old and good books which well deserve to be *recherchés* and in consequence rare,

---

[1] First printed with certain other mediæval poems, 1642 (a collection, reprinted in 1750). The "Tesoretto" appeared by itself in 1824. 8vo, Milano.

but are not, perhaps through some accidental ignorance on the part of booksellers, possibly because no ingenious critic of established reputation ever provided that worthy fraternity with one of those concise testimonials which we find reprinted in small type in catalogue after catalogue, year after year. Do not these do something to rescue a volume from dirt-commonness? or does no one purchase Hooft's *History of the Netherlands* because an eminent judge once observed that its perusal would repay anybody the trouble of learning Dutch?

Volumes of, so to speak, a native rarity, are those printed in relatively remote places, in small quantities (either owing to the expense of production or peculiarity of the subject, or merely for the sake of the consequent rarity), or at private presses.

The collector who values books according to the locality of their origin will do well to have at his fingers' ends the various dates at which printing was introduced into the different capitals and countries of the world, the degrees by which Italy, France, the Netherlands, Spain, and England fall behind Germany, and even the pettier distinctions between Oxford and St. Albans, and London and Westminster. Oxford, Mr. Gordon Duff tells us in his recent monograph on the subject of Early Printing, produced so far as is known, only two volumes in the fifteenth century, while St. Alban's boasts at least eight! and poor Cambridge lags a dozen years behind Edinburgh and York.

More distant countries, the East, America, come of course later still; and for all these the standard of rarity on account of place and date has to be proportionately shifted. No one, not entirely ignorant of history or devoid of the commonest human curiosity, would pass by a book printed in Mexico, or at Constantinople, early in the sixteenth, or in the Engadine valley, or the Scilly Isles, let us say even in the eighteenth, century. Specimens of English printing of the earlier time,—the excellent work of Wolf, Tottel, Newberie, Henry Binnemann, and others,—are common enough, though by no means

devoid of interest and value.   A Scotch production of similar date
(not a foreign tract, bearing the fictitious stamp of "Edimburgi")·
will be far more precious, and it is a singular fact, of which a
recently published catalogue of "Cambridge Books" supplies no
explanation, that there does not appear to be extant a single volume
printed at that University town (whose first specimens, perhaps·
illegally produced, date from 1521) between 1522, and 1584, when
the University itself began to print.

The products of private presses though occasionally exhibiting an
excellence (more often a magnificence) unattainable by the merely
commercial printer, as a rule appeal chiefly to curiosity.

Appended to Lord Hardwicke's *Walpoliana* is a list ("copied in
Mr. Walpole's presence") of the books printed at Strawberry Hill.
They do not exceed thirty works, averaging about three or four
hundred copies apiece, though Gray's odes reached eleven hundred.

The fashion of producing certain books in small quantities, as
Bodoni of Parma printed *Marriage Odes* for aristocratic families of
178-, and as modern publishers produce sumptuous "éditions de
luxe" upon that "large paper" which has become the handmaid of
minor poetic art, is a concession to the pursepride of the despotic
collector, who in these days must (it is hardly necessary to
observe) be as rich as Crœsus.   First and foremost among
works which, though produced in plenty, have been reduced to
rarity by recent demand, come those celebrated first editions of
modern romances which have of late years formed the chief big
game of London booksellers.   The title-page of an English book,
the impression of a date, the width of a margin, are matters
intelligible to the least learned among the trade.   There is therefore here a free competition, the results whereof throw a startling
light upon the amount of money in the hands of persons who
seem hardly to know how to dispose of it; though it must not be
forgotten that the personage typified as "the Chicago Pork-butcher,"·
has of late years been the mainstay of the West End bibliopole.

The following prices, however, culled from catalogues of the last few years, surely deserve to be placed on record; and let it be remembered that none of these books are printed on vellum, that "original cloth" does not refer to cloth of gold, and that banknotes will rarely be found among the "uncut" fly-leaves. *The Ingoldsby Legends*, three vols., £30; *Jane Eyre*, three vols., £15 15s.; *Sketches by Boz*, three vols. (one with the two extra plates, £9 10s.), £38 17s. 6d.; Thackeray's *Second Funeral of Napoleon* (with etching by the author), £52 10s. This last item might alarm a timid buyer, but another work of Michael Angelo Titmarsh is quoted at the more moderate figure of £18 18s. Mr. Surtees' well-known sporting romances, with, it must be noted, illustrations of peculiar excellence, average from eight to twelve guineas; a very good copy of *Handley Cross* is quoted at fifteen. *Master Humphrey's Clock* (in wrappers) may, or not long ago might, have been bought for twelve guineas; Walpole's *Mysterious Mother* for nine; Mr. Swinburne's *Queen Mother* for fifteen; and, to conclude, Byron's *Poems on Various Occasions* (in a perfectly phenomenal "state" purged, as it were, of all the grossness of earthly matter) for £60. As to condition, it may be noted that there are divers volumes attended from birth with some serious defect, the absence of which gives sometimes a high value to specimens so distinguished. Thus a copy of the *Gesta Dei per Francos*, fol. 1611 (*quels gestes de Dieu*, slily observes a French historian, *que ces actes de barbares!*) the pages of which were not the colour of strong tea, would, *ipso facto* attract any collector's attention. A similar hue pervades our *Anastasius de Vitis Pontificum*, Moguntiæ 1602, involving in a congenial darkness like that of London fog, the Annals of the early Pontiffs "from St. Peter to St. Nicholas the First." Something it seems went wrong with German (and Swiss) paper about the date of these volumes. If all the cheap literature and journalism of our own day, now encumbering the British Museum, should in another two centuries share a like fate, posterity need not experience either surprise or regret.

But to return to modern works, which are seldom "browned throughout" as yet, though sometimes "foxed"—there are persons who would grudge the above prices even for edges *absolument non rognés*, unturned by the binder's plough, and protected by the finest handiwork of Bedford or Zaehnsdorf—who would in fact decline to give £60 for Lord Byron himself in the flesh and all his works. But such persons are not book-collectors in the true and exclusive sense of the term. On the other hand it must be admitted that these latter gentlemen undoubtedly do get hold of the "best editions" of such works as are above enumerated, although the price paid for them may cause the hair of the impecunious to stand on end. George Eliot observes of one of her famous characters that, "He was not above the vulgarity of thinking that nothing but the best [furniture] would do for him." Perhaps it is a vulgarity to crave the best editions. "Every one," whispers the acutely democratic conscience, "*cannot* have them." But some one *must*, and there they are; and who shall say the best edition is not pleasant to read, at least if of a work in any form worth reading, which is of course another question? A volume (which few booksellers have seen) of suppressed juvenile effusions, entitled *Poems by J. R.*, changes hands (so we have been informed by an expert) at some £40 to £50; and generally speaking, works deemed worthless by those who should know most about them, are toiled after, as few men toil after virtue, by the ravening book-hunter, whose chief joy is to add "rarity to rarity" that he may be "alone in the world." One need hardly refer under this head to the "*Poems by two Brothers*, none of which have been reprinted" (1827), interest in which has to all appearance reached its financial apogee since the lamented death of the last Poet Laureate. It is astonishing, by the way, what large sections of the public, who seem to have neglected an author's works while he was alive, have their curiosity suddenly awakened, as many publishers could testify, by the news of his decease; as though this unavoidable concession to the fate of all mankind were the first evidence he had displayed of genius or originality. But this is a digression.

Whatever the reason, there seems hardly any limit assignable to the price which a first edition, in the finest state, or indeed a "tall" or spotless copy of a moderately out of the way work *in a superb binding*,[1] may not fetch, even in the auction room, to say nothing of unrecorded investments by eccentric private purchasers.

Artistic beauty, of any kind, is inevitably at a premium. Comparatively few modern productions, even when printed by hand upon hand-made paper (excepting those perhaps of the Kelmscott press, which, however, will scarcely regenerate popular taste until they are obtainable at more "democratic" prices) can

---

[1] In his exceeding regard for "outsides," the modern collector doth but revert to mediæval fashion. In the fifteenth century, for example, as we learn from the Catalogue of the Orleans Library in the Château of Blois (A.D. 1427), the *binding* of a book and its ornamentation were what seemed most worth describing, (and, indeed, with more reason than exists nowadays) while the contents are sometimes so cursorily mentioned as merely to arouse an unquenchable curiosity. Most of the Orleans books were, and for that matter still are, "bound in stamped leather" red or green, or in figured or embroidered silk, and many are adorned with miniatures (*histories*) and illuminations. Also their age and style of writing (" letter of form " or " running hand,") are carefully noted. One of the most remarkable—*videlicet* the Abbé Bonnet's defence of Valentine (Visconti), Duchess of Orleans against the charge of having caused the madness of Charles VI. —is described as " bound in red leather, written in French, *in rhyme* " (it was called the *Apparition of Jean de Meung* and still exists in the Bibliothèque Nationale), " with miniatures *half finished* (*historié à mi*) quite new, with two clasps —*apparently* (this in a later hand) of silver-gilt—with the inscription *Ave Maria*." No. 12 is a real rarity—nothing less than the lost poem of Froissart ! *Le Dit Royal* (black velvet, with miniatures, quite new), and No. 80, the last item, a (duplicate) Golden Legend, illuminated and bound in red stamped leather, is described as "re-covered by Simonette, lady's maid to the younger Madame d'Orléans." M. Le Roux de Lincy, the editor of this intensely interesting relic, not only identifies most of the books, but also discovers the names and charges of the binders, and traces the history of many a MS. volume, compared with which the rarest printed book seems but poor game. It is with difficulty that we tear ourselves from the perusal of *La Bibliothèque de Charles d'Orléans*. 8vo. Paris : F. Didot. 1843.

claim to be distinctly ornamental.   In earlier days the commonest
manual or treatise was more picturesquely attractive than a volume
of *Belles Lettres* turned out by Clark of Dunedin, or Whittingham of
Chancery Lane.   Sure many a youth of the fifteenth century must
have been attracted to the study of grammar by the mere title-page of

Title page of *Constantini Lascaris de octo orationis partibus.* 8vo. Nic. de Sabio. Venice, 1539.

Nicolas de Sabio's edition of the great work of Lascaris; the first edition of which (fol. 1476) was, by the way, the first Greek book printed.

If, however, we compare the above prices of modern classics and
romances with the early editions, for example, of Shakspeare (which
certainly have not their attractions in respect of typography), a
certain decent proportion will be found to be preserved.   In the

remarkable sale of Mr. Birket Foster's library, in June 1894, the
"first folio," though with the usual imperfections, brought £255
A perfect copy would, it is presumed, command four or five times
that figure. The second folio (1632)[1] fetched but £56, but the third
(most of the impressions of which were burnt in the Great Fire)

Last leaf of *Constantini Lascaris de octo orationis partibus.* 8vo. Nic. de Sabio. [Venice,
1539, with autograph of Estienne Baluze (Scholar, Antiquary, and Colbertian Librarian,
1630—1718).

reached £130. Single plays moreover—genuine and spurious—
fetched high prices.

The Midsummer Night's Dream, 1600 (large copy), £122.

[1] Lord Orford's copy (of the second folio) has just beaten all records by selling
June, 1895) for £540.

The Merchant of Venice, 1600, £146 (the last copy previously sold went for £99 15*s.*).

Sir John Oldcastle, 1600, £41.

King Lear, 1608, £100 (recently sold for £29 8*s.*). And the first collected edition of Shakspeare's Poems, 1640, with portrait inlaid, fetched £40.

At the same sale a first edition of the *Compleat Angler*, 8vo, 1653, fetched £150.

But what is money? Mere dross. Is not John Major's excellent reprint of Walton and Cotton's *chef-d'œuvre*, which is to be found, with portrait, plates, and woodcuts, in the library of all families of any social standing, an infinitely preferable one to read? . . .

We have referred to the kind of rarity which, being the result of what one may call an artificial, or at least an excessive demand, is in modern days a somewhat fanciful and fluctuating source of value. That which is produced by artificial diminution or destruction of the supply, is on the whole of a more solid historical interest. We say artificial, for the accidental or blindly malevolent destructions by fire, invading armies, and such like calamities, are of less intrinsic importance, although their undesigned consequences were often more serious.

The librarian of King Osymandias, whose collection was formed, we are told, " less than four centuries after the Flood," [1] might have been able to tell us something of the literature already known to be destroyed at that date. This first of libraries possibly possessed some priceless relic which the Brunet of the day would have described as " Ouvrage assez ancien ; Exemplaire portant l'autographe de Japhet ; *Quelques feuilles mouillées par le Déluge.*" But the earliest of historic destructions is the plunder of the Pisistratian collection by Xerxes, of which Seleucus probably returned only the duplicates.

[1] See the entertaining preface of Fr. Fournier's invaluable *Dictionnaire portatif de Bibliographie*, 2nd ed., Paris, 1809, containing 23,000 articles and catalogues of Aldine, Elzevir, Didot, and other editions. After many years' use (of the late William Bury's copy) I can testify to the generally reliable character of this work, which deserves to be better known.

The burning of one half of the Alexandrian library by the soldiers of Julius Cæsar, and of the other half, some seven hundred years later, by the Khalif Omar, and of Domitian's library in the Capitol (in the time of Commodus) ; the ravages of Goths, and of the French, Spanish, and German invaders of Italy, with scores of other mediæval calamities, down to the destruction by fire of some 8,000 valuable Arabic MSS. in the Escurial Library at Madrid in 1671, and that of the monastery of St. Germain des Prés (containing priceless private collections of books, MSS. and *papyri*) in 1794—the Bibliothèque Nationale was barely rescued from the Communist incendiaries in 1871—all these accidents and crimes have swelled the tale of valuable books which are no more, or exist only in such quantity as to be practically *introuvable*. Yet again there is a destruction which means but excessive popularity. Bunyan, Walton, the "Pastissier François" (exhibited in the Long Gallery at the British Museum and one of the rarest of Elzevirs, the Orford copy of which has just sold for £540), and the famous *Contes de ma mère l'oye*, are found "worn to rags" (as a kindly reviewer in the *Daily News* reminds me) "by anglers, devout women, cooks, and children." A seventeenth century edition of Bodenham's *Politeuphuia* (first published 1598, and frequently reprinted at the instance of N. L(ing) and others), which I purchased the other day, is thumbed almost into illegibility—a striking evidence of the dearth of humour when such a mere endless collection of truisms and platitudes could pass muster as *Wit's Commonwealth !* But confining our attention to the deliberate suppression or destruction of particular volumes, the presumption is in such cases perhaps rather in favour of the persecuted work possessing some human interest, creditable or the reverse.

It is far from being always so ; here again bibliomania is rampant, perhaps to a less degree than formerly ; for one must not hastily assume that high-priced catalogues or auction-duels terminating in rounds of applause are things belonging only to the nineteenth century. We have August Beyer writing, in the preface to his bibliographical *Memoriæ* (Dresden, 1734), that he had long noticed the "astonishing prices (*inexpectata pretia*)" commonly assigned to certain little known booklets. "Greater still was my surprise to see English, Dutch, French, and German buyers (he puts our countrymen first) engaged in a sort of tacit mutual conspiracy to secure them, and unwearied in their expenditure for this object, though I was unable to conjecture any motive, except the mere vanity of ostentation, why, for example, educated men, with some taste for real learning and only distinguished for their literary studies, should prefer rare books to good ones." Works of well-known merit, he goes on to say, by learned and capable authors, very seldom vanish at once from the public view, unless indeed (and the exception brings us to our next subdivision of the subject) they chance to be unsuited to the genius of the age, their author having been so ill-advised as, in historic phrase, to enter the world "before his time."

Without speculating where this hypothetical date could have been fixed in the case, for example, of such a person as Huss or Galileo, one may admit that the majority of works summarily suppressed appear rather to have deserved their fate. It is in the limited class of cases where reactionary authority, bigotry, or high-placed corruption has with more or less success endeavoured to stamp out some publication indicating the high-water mark of the free thought of the age that rarity becomes of most significance to the student.

With the mass of works suppressed as *contra bonos mores* we need not then here concern ourselves, though they will always attract the attention of certain curio-mongers ; but it must be borne in mind that the distinction is not always easy to draw, indecency and an outrageous disregard of orthodox *convenances* being so often, as notably in the case of Rabelais (whom no one succeeded in suppressing), and in certain of the Protestant Reformers, such as Beza (not to mention Luther himself), one effective edge, so to speak, of the

newly-forged weapon of free thought.   Few writers have contributed
more to this class of rarity than the celebrated Pietro Aretino, commonly known as "the Scourge of Princes," though it would rather
appear from Mazzuchelli's interesting life of this indefatigable libeller,
that his self-interest was at least equal to his candour.   Half a dozen
editions of the comedies and rhymes of Messer *Partenio Etiro* run
up the whole gamut in Gamba from *assai raro* to *rarissimo*, and are
in fact almost as difficult to procure as the censor of morals would
desire.   Perionius, an eminent Benedictine, addressed a singular
petition to the princes of Europe in 1551 (a rare piece) begging the
authorities "To remove so horrible a monster from among them
(*ut tam horribile monstrum de medio tollatis*)," a proposal which could
hardly be made with regard even to the most unpopular of satirists in
our own day.   The "monster," however, remained, alternately insult-
ing Charles V. and Francis I., and died at a mature age leaving six
volumes of correspondence.   With Nicolo Franco (1505–1569), the
rival both in obscenity and scurrility of Aretino (whom he spent half
a lifetime in abusing), but a writer of undoubted ability, the case
was different.   Pope Pius V. by way of effective reply to certain
other libels directed against a former Head of the Church, *lo fece pub-
licamente appiccare*.   His *Rime contra Pietro Aretino* (8vo, 1548) are
nearly as rare as the Elzevir edition of the latter's *Ragionamenti*.
The dialogue of the *Carte Parlanti*, even in an expurgated form,
was retained in the ecclesiastical black-book in the seventeenth century.   For ourselves, we are not perhaps sufficiently grateful to the
sedulous amateur who, in Edward Cheney's copy of the Venice edition of 1650, has restored all the most objectionable passages, in
M.S.   Improper works, suppressed with more or less rigour, may of
course be found at any date ; and a few examples suffice, since from
Petronius Arbiter to M. Claude Prosper Crébillon, the supposed
author of the fictitious *Pompadour Letters* (*Londres*, 1774), this class
of literature admits no very rich variety.

It is necessary to distinguish, alas ! as we approach the darker ages between the cause of religion and that of morals. Probably from its very nature, persecution, dealing with minute points of doctrine, has exhibited throughout history more single-minded enthusiasm than any divergence of opinion (which has perhaps seldom been very great) upon merely moral questions.

One of the rarest books in existence is, according to general opinion, the tract of Servetus (Dr. Michel Révés, that is, who, at the

Venetijs apud Antonium Gardane.
M D XXXXII.

From "Le pistole vulgari di M. Nicolo Franco." 8vo. Venice. 1542.

instigation of his former friend Calvin, was burnt alive at Geneva in 1558), entitled *Christianismi Restitutio* (8vo, 1553), of which only one copy is known to exist, viz. that sold at the Lavallière sale for something over £150; and next might come the same author's three tracts on the Trinity (printed in italics, 1532) *prix arbitraire*. A more common topic of bibliographical gossip is the *Treatise of the Three Impostors* (*Liber de Tribus Impostoribus*), of which the first chapter is headed " De Deo "; a work once attributed without the slightest foundation to Servetus, but which, according to Fournier, is erroneously dated 1598, and belongs, as indeed is obvious from the allusions to Descartes and to the philosophy of the seventeenth century, to a hundred years later. Endless research has been expended on the history of this publication, or another of the same name now lost, but said to have been in existence early in the sixteenth century. For this the curious reader may be referred to the notes of La Monnoye and others in the French version (a common book of the last century), to Burton's *Anatomy of Melancholy* (that wondrous collection of "sweepings from the Bodleian "), where the leading idea of the work is ascribed to the Emperor Frederick II. who died in 1250; the authority given for this statement being a curious passage in Matthew Paris which we find on p. 685 of our folio edition of 1571. Sir Thomas Browne, in the first part of his *Religio Medici*, also speaks of the work, or rather of a work of this name (without explicitly saying that he has seen it) as a " miscreant piece," but of the author as one who was "not a positive atheist." Browne's anonymous annotator (and this brings us to another illustration of our subject) remarks that the piece was "by Ochino."

And so many people once thought, and doubtless with some reason. For the works of Bernardino Ochino " of Siena," who passed through several religious phases and finally died a Socinian in 1564, fill several pages in bibliography, and are almost all "very rare"; the rarest perhaps being, after certain sermons printed in 1541, *A Dialogue of Purgatory* (8vo, 1556), and an attack on the errors of the "Sinagoga del Papa " (Geneva, 1554), a " Dialogue of the unjust and usurped primacy of the Bishop of Rome, and the just abolishing thereof" (London, 1549). It is hardly necessary to say that these were all suppressed with conscientious care.[1] Ochino, like so

[1] I have before me the original edition of his *Catechismo overo Institutione*

many others, had something to say on the then popular subject of Antichrist. The work of Huss bearing this title (never printed till the sixteenth century, a 4to volume of *Opuscula* with no date) was the immediate cause of his destruction. It was not always found possible to suppress the obnoxious author; but an inevitable epithet in the description of the lucubrations of early Protestantism, is the phrase *fort rare, supprimé par la cour de Rome*. Another work, which was the occasion of about as much literary fuss as the *Three Impostors*, is the *Cymbalum Mundi* (8vo, Paris, 1537), of which only two or three copies are said to be known. Every kind of shocking impiety was long attributed to the author, till at last it occurred to one eminent bibliographer of the last century to read the book, which he accordingly did, and found it of quite depressing propriety. A more important example of a very rare book which, though its author suffered years of martyrdom for his advanced opinions, was not suppressed, is the *Scelta d'alcune poesie filosofiche di Settimontano Squilla* (s.l. printed in Germany) *nell' anno* 1622. This title conceals no less important a work (to the student of History in Literature) than the sonnets of Campanella (1568–1629), the famous author of the *De Monarchia Hispaniæ* (24mo, Elzevir, 1641), which were published with a valuable preface by his friend and contemporary Adami. They were reprinted at Zurich in 1834, and have been translated (with those of Buonarroti) by the late Mr. J. A. Symonds.

The most select catalogue of books "ordered to be burnt by the common hangman" would exhaust our space, even if the subject had

---

Christiana, a pious and sensible work addressed "alla chiesa Locarnese che è hora in Zuricco"—8vo, in Basilea, 1561; and the *Dialogus de Purgatorio*—which is an ardent, and more entertaining polemic—Tiguri, apud Gesneros, 1555. These works have no high market value at the present day, though by no means worthless in the hands of a theological bookseller. The "Cymbalum" is easily accessible in Prosper Marchand's edition, Amsterdam (Paris), 1732. I could find nothing in it the least worthy of attention, except perhaps one mild reflection on the Catholic religion.

not been recently handled by Mr. J. A. Farrer in a curious little work wherein he advocates the revival of the custom, we dare not say upon insufficient grounds. But nowadays we do not achieve any destruction more discriminative than an occasional conflagration in Paternoster Row.

During all the interesting period of the revival of learning and thought, the discrimination was all in one direction, until ecclesiastical damnation came to confer upon the volumes it honoured a sort of hall-mark of excellence, or at least of candour and originality.

Wiclif's Dialogues (a handsome 4to volume of 1525 with a fine wood-cut title-page), and especially the fourth book reflecting on the Roman Sacraments and those unfortunate donations, were rigorously suppressed by Rome. All Wiclif's works were ordered to be burned by Archbishop Arundel. Francis I., the orthodox ally of the Grand Turk, once went so far as to prohibit printing, for fear of Protestant publications, but apparently without success. To the fate of Huss and Servetus we have already referred. In such a context one could not omit all mention of the unfortunate Giordano Bruno of Nola, a philosopher who, having been much persecuted in his own day, has perhaps been unduly praised in our own. His *Spaccio della Bestia trionfante*, etc., 12mo, Paris, 1544 (London, 1584), dedicated to Sir Philip Sidney, is one of those volumes occasionally described as "rarity itself." "I would not have it thought," writes Bruno, "that I aimed either directly or incidentally at opposing the truth or at attacking what is good, useful, natural, and consequently divine"; and he then proceeds to inveigh against various current forms of superstition. But authority could not accept this view of the case, and the usual process of rarification was applied to the *Bestia*, a copy of which was sold for £28 at a London auction in 1711 and at a later date for £50.[1] We dare say few readers have seen the

---

[1] See an interesting review of this book in the *Spectator*, No. 389, (where it is characterized as "a short fable with no pretence to reason or argument and a very small share of wit") and the editor's note.

English version, *The Expulsion of the Triumphant Beast*, of which a few copies were printed in 1713. The original work, together with a vast number of others, some of which not even bibliographers have seen, was rigidly suppressed; the author was burned in effigy, and afterwards, as is well known, *in propriâ personâ* (A.D. 1600) at Rome.

The case of one Pallavicino, not the Popish historian of the Council of Trent, but the author of the *Divortio Celeste* (the divorce, that is, of Christ from the Romish Church) and other satirical works, a volume in 12mo dated Villafranca, 1643, which for some reason is quite common in London at the present day (though Hallam says he had never seen it), is a parallel to that of Franco above mentioned. Ferrante Pallavicino thought he had got off scot-free, but was treacherously entrapped and beheaded by Pope Urban VIII., while his book was, we may presume, selling like wildfire in the Protestant market.[1]

Satirists had indeed to be very careful (see *Le Danger de la Satire, ou la vie de Nicolo Franco*, a nice little book printed at Paris in 1778); and not only satirists but booksellers. As to the general sense of oppression under which they laboured, we can hardly do better than cite a precious passage from the letters of Paolo Manuzio, not those formal and laboured *Lettere Volgari* which he issued from the Aldine press in 1556 and 1560, and which enjoyed so much popularity among the stylists of the Renaissance, but the real homely business and domestic communications first published by Renouard with the sumptuous excellence that marks his productions, in 8vo. *papier vergé*, Paris, 1834. Under date Rome, February 28, 1570, the worried but ever industrious and hopeful Manuzio writes to his son, "As to your books (*quanto a tuoi libri*, p. 181) they are in a safe place, in cases carefully secured, as you left them." The anxious collector had been previously assured of this in a letter of May of the preceding year: "I don't know if there is any-

[1] *v. Naudæana & Patiniana*, 2nd ed. 1703, p. 323.

thing forbidden or suspect among them. I have no wish to touch or look at them, lest I should have happen to me what happened to an *employé* of mine, who has had five months in prison and risk of the rope, though without his fault, only for being mentioned by one who professed to have read to him, here in the house, some pieces of Franco's, a writer whose mere name (he was hanged, by the way, only a few months before the date of this letter) is enough to send to prison any one who has so much as conversed with him— not to say read any of his works." And this reflection the respected and privileged Manuzio thought too audacious even for a private letter, without a saving clause, and so he adds: "The Tribune is most severe, but most pious (*rigorosissimo ma santissimo*), and *we must praise its every act* for the benefit of this Holy Throne so much attacked by the perverse reasoning of heretics."

Yet more praiseworthy seems the connoisseur who during these troublous times preserved for us in *luogo sicuro* and *casse ben legate* or perchance (a practice rightly condemned by Mr. Gladstone) at the back of shelves of other volumes, as school-boys conceal illicit romances, the very things we are now most anxious to read. The tyranny of lay authority was perhaps not equal to the ecclesiastic, or was less often provoked; but it had to be reckoned with. Candid historians, such as the prudent and impartial Guicciardini, needed often to deny themselves the glory of publication in their own lifetime for fear the powers that be should show too keen an interest in the production, and in fact "take up" the whole issue with such ardour as modern booksellers do the last work of the popular author of the hour. It was almost more exasperating when they took to editing or "Bowd-lerising" the work. Interest, rarity, commercial value, may be found dancing around these apparently trifling bibliographic details. Bruto's History of Florence (4to, 1562) is an excellent specimen of the Giunta press. The book was so far successful that the Grand Duke ordered all the copies there were, sold or unsold. "Es ist überaus rar" a German commentator tells us; but "extraordinarily rare" or not, the history exists, lies before us in fact, as we write. It is only brought up to the year 1492 (the death of Lorenzo the magnificent) and unfinished. The preface is such a scathing review of certain historians (Giovio in particular) who had reflected upon

Con vna nuoua tauola copiofiffima del medefimo, per maggior commodità de' Lettori.

IN PARMA.
Appreffo Seth Viotto. 1 5 7 2.

From title page of *Francesco Guicciardini, gli ultimi quattro libri,* ed. Papirio Picedi (not a common edition), ap. Seth Viotto. Parma. 4to. 1572. These last four books were first published in 1564.

Florence, that it was reprinted under the title of a "defence of the Florentines" (in Italian), 4to, 1566. On the other hand the text of Platina's celebrated *Lives of the Popes* was seriously corrupted in the editions of the sixteenth century. The ingenuity with which the passage in the life of Pope Cletus, "uxorem habuit in Bithynia" was altered in some versions into "uxorem *non* habuit in Bithynia," is a solitary and startling anticipation of nineteenth century humour. In our own copy, formerly the property of M. Estienne Baluze, and bearing his bold autograph,[1] the damaging expression is omitted altogether. And there were other alterations, more pernicious though less amusing.

Textual corruption, in fact, in ages of unlimited monarchy, stalks abroad, becoming almost a rule, not an exception. Holinshed's Chronicle, we all know, was altered to please Elizabeth : and Camden, a better annalist than antiquary, hit on the device, as Disraeli recites, of handing over to De Thou the passages which he dared not entrust to an English printer.[2] There is a more curious modern example in the case of Huet's memoirs of his own time (*Commentarius de rebus ad eum pertinentibus.* Amsterdam, 8vo, 1718 : "*ouvrage curieux*"), certain passages of which (see p. 36) are, apparently on theological grounds, omitted in the French translation of 1853 !

It is in these matters that the bibliographer is most needed ; in his columns are collected the test-passages, nay, the very words and printers' errors by which the genuine work is to be discerned from the counterfeit, the historical justice from the imperial or ecclesiastical thief. A score of important original records suffer from this malady, quite apart from the inaccuracy intrinsic to the genesis of so many early texts, and the casual buyer discovers in time, through the pain which Æschylus tells us is divinely associated with learning, that the commonest are the worst affected.

In a treatise which is nothing if not philosophical we have not thought worthy of notice such rarity or singularity as results either

---

[1] See p. 18 *ante*. He signs his surname *Baluze* on the Platina.

[2] This fact will be found in the *publisher's* preface to the *Annals* (I quote the 8vo ed. Elzevir, 1625), and not in the author's, which, however, gives some interesting details on the relations of the two historians.

from the ignorance or stupidity of a printer or from some fancy or fad of a former possessor. Books have been treated in strange ways. The great Charles Darwin, when encumbered by the weight of a bulky volume, thought the shortest way of getting through the same was to cut it in two.

Anatomically he was of course right, nor, in the case of a modern Science-book (probably in the odious garb of " Publisher's cloth ") need the destruction be regretted. But the tremendous actuality of such a pursuit of wisdom would send many a dilettante "bookman " into wild hysterics.

An eminent Shakespearean scholar, now deceased, is famed for having ruthlessly torn out of volumes in his possession all the matter which he considered of insufficient interest. Here again enthusiastic and indefatigable fatuity will be found pressing hard upon the tracks of eccentric genius. There are, or were recently at large persons bearing all the outward semblance of sane humanity who purchased these half-plucked volumes at comparatively high prices. To such truly was the "half more than the whole." It is not so usually, or we should not hear of so much happiness depending on a millimètre more or less of seventeenth century paper, with nothing on it. Etymologically, of course, a "tome" is that which has been cut. A collector, however, is the slave of an "*atomic* theory" which has nevertheless little to do with science or learning of any kind, and does not tend to the preservation of books, which should always have their top edges cut and gilt, and their sides shaved smooth (at least if any one is going to turn over the leaves) as soon as possible.

To return to Bibliography proper (which is not occupied with "curiosities "),[1] not only should the systematic bookbuyer read his

---

[1] " A taste for books," says the great Gibbon—a dictum naturally popular with the trade—"has been the pleasure and glory of my life."

To humbler collectors the pleasure is more obvious than the glory.

Perhaps this latter may be thought to be dawning when an individual whom you do not know writes from a distant locality requesting an exchange of Bookplates ! *Should these lines meet the eye* of the " Ex-Librarian " in question (" Ex-Librist "

tomes in a manner respectful to their matter, but he should study those
" externals" which are really material, to wit styles, introductions,
dedications, nay, even typography and " get-up," in order to facilitate
the rapid discernment of a "book" from a mere " volume," even in
the best French morocco—to distinguish not only the air and "je ne
sais quoi" of colouring and appearance that sometimes give a sort of

is a term one would not apply even to a political opponent), let him know that
while their author does not as yet either possess a bookplate himself or require
that of any one else, he has discovered (?) and preserved a really interesting
specimen in that of the Marquis of Macciucca (*littérateur*, 1699–1785), comprising
besides a conventional crest and monogram, *fifteen printed rules* expounding the
principles on which the books in his lordship's library were lent out.

This document, of which a description was printed in the *Athenæum* not long
ago, I first found in a copy of the *Lettres Fanatiques*, 8vo, 1739 (now in the
British Museum), and again in Alciati's *Tractatus contra vitam monasticam*, &c.,
4to, 1740. It seems to comprise the whole duty of a book-borrower, and can
hardly be a common specimen. The original, of which the text is here appended,
was exhibited in 1894 by the " Ex-Libris " Society.

Leges, Volumina ex Bibliotheca nostra commodato accepta, lecturis, secundum
auspicia lata Lictor Lege agito in Legirupionem. Mas vel Fœmina fuas, hac tibi
lege, Codicis istius usum non interdicimus.

I. Hunc ne Mancipium ducito. Liber est : ne igitur notis compungito.

II. Ne cæsim punctimve ferito : ostis non est.

III. Lineolis, intus, forisve, ducendis abstineto.

IV. Folium ne subigito, ne complicato, neve in rugas cogito.

V. Ad oram conscribillare caveto.

VI. Atramentum ultra primum exesto : mori mavult quam fœdari.

VII. Puræ tantum papyri Philuram interserito.

VIII. Alteri clanculum palamve ne commodato.

IX. Murem, tineam, blattam, muscam, furunculum absterreto.

X. Ab aqua, oleo, igne, situ, illuvie arceto.

XI. Eodem utitor, non abutitor.

XII. Legere, et quævis excerpere, fas esto.

XIII. Perlectum, apud te perennare ne sinito.

XIV. Sartum tectumq., prout tollis, reddito.

XV. Qui faxis, vel ignotus amicorum albo adscribitor : qui secus, vel notus
eraditor. Has sibi, has aliis præscribit leges in re sua, ordinis Hyeresolimitani
Eques Franciscus Vargas Macciucca. Quoi placeas annue, quoi minus quid tibi
nostra tactio est ? Facesse.

"gamey" flavour to a genuine "find," but the differences, so often discovered too late, between volumes entitled indeed alike but radically different in essential qualities.

The *Commentaries* of Sleidan, one of the most valuable authorities on the time of Charles V., are to be consulted in the rare first edition, folio **1555**. In later issues he is gravely suspected of having toned down certain trenchant reflections on the Catholics ; while the anxiety he expresses in his preface to please all parties if it could be done, is as obvious as that of any Broad Church theologian. Bernardo Segni's *History of Florence from* 1527 *to* 1555 (not printed till 1723), and at least one other Italian history, have, in complete copies, scandalous passages printed and inserted on a separate slip. Similarly almost all copies of the Aldine edition of the Poems of Lorenzo de' Medici are found in a mutilated state, the eight leaves of one whole "gathering" (O) having been reduced to four, an alteration effected by Paolo Manuzio during the printing of the work. This appears from the fact that the "register" was altered, as the bibliographer Gamba first pointed out, to suit the omission. It does not seem clear why Manuzio did this, since two of the poems thus withdrawn from publication were of a religious nature. But any one can understand why Trissino, during the impression of the "original and only complete edition" of his great epic poem, withdrew from some copies of the work (those which were intended for circulation in high places, or all that there was time to alter after he had realised the danger of their publication ?) about thirty lines of prophetic invective against the Papacy and the Church. The wonder is rather that they were ever printed. But very possibly many an author who in such days enthusiastically committed to paper, in a veiled or poetical form, an indictment of existing abuses, was struck —as what authors are not often struck ?—by the difference in lucidity and directness between manuscript and "copy."

Let the purchaser, then, of the *Italia liberata dai Goti* (3 vols. 8vo, Venice and Rome, 1547-8), undistracted by the curious Greek type

scattered about Trissino's pages, look carefully at the 131st page of
the second volume.

Again the first edition of Burnet's History of his own Time is very
common. A bookseller would not stoop to pick it up in the streets.
It appeared in a much garbled form ; so did that of Clarendon, and
numerous others. So, for different reasons, did most of the precious
correspondence of Madame de Sévigné, of which the Rouen edition of
1720 is extremely rare ;—and the dearth of MSS. has made their perfect reproduction at the present moment almost impossible. This corruption of the very springs of our knowledge of the past is a constant
and endless source of exasperation. Better to be burned out once
for all, to have to buy back the charred remains of your manuscript,
as the historian Paolo Giovio did from a tipsy Spanish soldier engaged
in the sack of Rome [1] (and at what we may assume to have been a
prix arbitraire), than to be coolly edited with scissors or blacking-
brush by a Roman Catholic divine, as Russian censors in our own
day treat the revolutionary *Punch*, or prepared for the intelligent
student of politics by some one-eyed and unlettered partisan. The
great De Thou—who, by the thoughtless emission of such expressions
as *Rupisfulcaldius*, involved his countrymen in the compilation of
dictionaries wherewith to translate his valuable history—is said to
have refused the request of James I. that he should alter therein the
text of a certain passage. Yet the Pattisson folio edition of 1604 is
counted rare for the containing of *certains endroits* which, in the
words of the poet, are not met with elsewhere. When Alexander
Gordon, in the eighteenth century, published his interesting History,
he could only quote the suppressed passages in Guicciardini's fourth

---

[1] Two officers—to speak quite correctly—found the MSS. in a box also containing money. Those on paper were thrown away, but the parchments restored
for a price, to wit Holy Orders (!) conferred on the plunderer by the Pope at
the tearful request of the author. See *Jovii Opera, fol. Basileæ.* 1578, I. 151.
In the same passage we are told that the last six books of the first decade were
those destroyed, but that the author hopes to restore them from memory and
notes.

book from such surreptitious publications as the little volume entitled *Thuanus restitutus, &c.* (12mo, 1663), one of the numerous historical opuscula printed in Germany and burnt in France. Nor was the work correctly printed until 1820, the date of Rosini's edition.

The memoirs of Sully (like, for that matter, the first edition of Lambarde's *Kent*) contained reflections upon certain noble families. Gui Patin, in a letter dated February 28, 1650 (ed. 1692, vol. i. p. 94), speaks of a recent edition (Rouen, 1649?) considerably mutilated at the request of " M. le Prince."

We do but glance here at a few of the casual elements in what may be called the philosophy of rarity, which, indicating as they do difficulty of acquisition and necessity of research, may recall to the buyer of books, as books, how many snares and pitfalls beset those who go forth to the chase unequipped with the requisite information. It is only necessary to add that in these peaceful days of international communication, where manuscripts subsist and have been reprinted, old and early editions, however rare, tend to fall into discredit. What has been done by French editors for such great classics as Joinville, Froissart, and Saint-Simon, and by the late Dr. Luard and other no less trustworthy scholars for Matthew Paris and an immense number of our own early Chronicles, is well known. Nevertheless, though an "old edition" of the *Historia Major* may be bought for very little, it must not be imagined that the magnificent black-letter first editions of the great French Chroniclers published at the close of the fifteenth century are not (even when far less correctly printed than the above) both valuable and uncommon.

Early histories, it has already been observed, were sometimes found better, at least safer, for a little keeping. But the interest attaching to a book being a matter of so many and divers influences, it is equally true that contemporary editions of records of important events may be supposed to possess both rarity and interest. A letter from Columbus announcing the so-called discovery of America (of which a perfect copy was only recently discovered, dated 1493), Vespuccio's account of his explorations (1503–4), the *Summarie and True Discourse* of Sir Francis Drake's West Indian voyages, and the early editions of Marco Polo, whose original (*French*) text was, as we learn from Mr. Quaritch's instructive catalogue, only published in 1824,—these are the very models of rare and invaluable historical monuments.

It is a mere platitude to observe that the men of action who discovered the New World were fortunate in being among the first who found developed and ready to hand the greatest force ever known for the celebration and recording of great deeds. Previous explorers, conquerors, thinkers, historians, had had to wait, often at great risk.

From the invention of printing it became possible for every human memorandum to be at once committed to a form which in its multiplicity and durability was practically indestructible. But the sixteenth century was, like our own, an age of enthusiastic and on the whole tasteful reproduction. Few more attractive books have ever appeared than, to take examples at haphazard, the Silvian edition of Gulielmus Neubrigensis (8vo, Antwerp, 1567) ; Wolf's first edition of Matthew Paris (fol. Lond. 1570); the "Various Letters" of Cassiodorus (fol. Augsburg, 1533 : "*assez rare*"); Morel's beautiful rubricated Gregory of Tours (8vo : 1562) ; or, again, the valuable and excellently printed collection of *Epigrammata and Poematia* (Paris: Duval and Gilles, 12mo, 1590: "*rare et recherchée*") edited by Pierre Pithou. And the Monstrelet of P. Mettayer (3 vols. in 2, fol. 1595) is unquestionably one of the finest large-type library editions that ever left the press.

Device of Guillaume Morel (1562).

In estimating the interest of such productions an allowance must be made for a sentiment which is not perhaps devoid of historical value. If it seems to a common child of Adam more natural to read such writers as Gregory and Cassiodorus (unique sources of mediæval history) in what, though separated from them by some nine and a half centuries, still strike us as " old editions," how transcendent must be the interest attaching to a volume which, so far as chronology is concerned, might have been read by the author himself ! Did Savonarola by chance actually handle this " spotless copy " of the " Compendium," as he called it, of his *Revelations* printed for him by Buonaccorsi in Florence three years after the death of his arch enemy and three years before his own ?

Persons living in that age have clearly a special interest for all students of history as recorded in the " printed book." How difficult to shake off the impression that one somehow reads between the lines of such an " original " more than can be conveyed to the circulating-library student of our day by, let us say, the modern English version, if there be one, cheaply printed in double columns ![1]

But, again, it must in justice be remembered that in ever so many cases, which only special knowledge and experience enable us to discern, the *old book*, in spite of its rarity, beauty, and antiquarian interest, is not, after all, the thing itself, but only an inaccurate or fraudulent perversion of a text printed, perhaps, last year " from the original MSS.," preserved—happily we have not often to inquire where ? But the reader who would shake off the " idols " of the Book World need but cross the threshold of a modern manuscript department or " Record Office " and tremble ! He may, indeed, bitterly console himself with the reflection that many " originals " are hopelessly lost

---

[1] Perhaps a better example of a rarity concerning " Frate Hieronymo " would be the unique (?) quarto volume containing the "*canzona d' un piagnone pel bruciamento delle vanità nel Carnevale del* 1498," printed at the time, and reproduced in a superb edition on hand-made paper—Firenze, 1864 (160 copies, of which mine is No. 143)—together with the contemporary account of a " burning of vanities," by Benivieni, the friend and supporter of the unfortunate Savonarola, for a glimpse of whose half-mystic attitude see the *Compendio delle Rivelationi* aforesaid (1495). There were two Carnivals, those of 1497 and 1498 (Florentine style, 1496-7) at which Savonarola preached (*vide Romola*) the destruction o " vanities and abominations," which, as carried out by bands of fanatical youths, " weepers," or *piagnoni* in the singular manner here described, formed part of an enthusiastic but ephemeral crusade against luxury.

or preserved only in a translated or secondary form, which it is impossible for the most ardent research, in legal jargon, to " go behind."

" Mais, pour suivre notre route" (as even Montaigne once observes), hardly a ray of the "contemporary" interest can be said to touch the first editions of Greek and Roman Classics. When we contemplate the magnificent folio Virgil (1468 or 9) which in 1780 was sold in an imperfect state for £164, and in 1889 (the Hopetoun copy) for £590, we do not think of Virgil, but of Conrad Sweynheym and Arnold Pannartz, the importers of printing into Italy, and of the enthusiasm attending the revival of letters.

Far different, for example, is the " local colour," historically speaking, attached to a volume, bearing on its very back evidence of the feeling of a dead and gone generation. Here, for example, is a small 8vo of 1763, lettered in bold type "*Poison for the Scotch.*"

" What is its title ? " would be a fair question to a candidate for Honours in Bibliography. Several copies (*at least*, to be perfectly accurate, my own and another) of the *North Briton* (this edition, by the way, is "unknown to Lowndes") were so lettered.

There exist of course volumes combining every element of interest connected with date, place, printing, authorship, "proprietary" binding, and autograph—as there be perfect eggs of the Great Auk. As a rule, however, specimens of early printing are rather to be classed as historical curiosities. The "six copies known" of the aforesaid Virgil are, where such things should be, in public libraries. An old book, which is also a contemporary monument, which marks an epoch in history or belongs in its genesis to that epoch, is the most intrinsically valuable of books; and a keen perception of this (though deranged by odd and variable fancies) will be found to govern much of the forces of research now at work and with which the book-buyer must needs do battle. With regard to the pursuit of the "first edition," the case of a volume differing from another (even to expert eyes) by no more than one figure on the title-page (a defect which the bookseller of mediæval morals may sometimes

remedy for himself) is not to be compared to that in which the first
edition bears in general character and typography the stamp of a long
past and widely different age. A genuine first edition is in its small
way a monument of history. In fact Allan Ramsay's poems (published in 1728) were even called in to prove an important point of
law, and settled a family dispute.[1]

The studious plutocrat will therefore do not altogether foolishly to
buy the first edition of the first part of *Don Quixote* (4to, Madrid,
1605) for, let us say, £140, if it were only to fix an important date

Woodcut from *Amadis de Gaul*, trad. par Ant. Tyron. 4to. Lyon, 1574.

in his mind. When he has read therein as far as the highly
unfavourable review of existing romances of chivalry contained in
the famous sixth chapter, he will be interested to learn that the
original edition of *Amadis de Gaul* (in folio black-letter, Saragossa,
1508) may be valued at a still higher figure, although the author is
believed to have died early in the fourteenth century. To explain
this (if the reader has not already been provided with sufficient
theories from which to choose) we may add that the copy is unique.

---

[1] See *Memoirs of Dr. Somerville* (cited p. 152, *post*). Ramsay's *Elegy* was
also accepted as evidence of the death of the infant Lord Carnegie without issue.

Until it was discovered in the present century at Ferrara, the best
and oldest of chivalric fictions (as the Curate and the Barber agreed
in calling it) was chiefly known in a charming illustrated edition,
complete in twenty-seven volumes, when you can get them, ranging
between 1570 and 1590.   We confess to having long since determined to rest content with a single one, the fourteenth, translated by
Antoine Tyron, and dated 1574, the woodcuts of which are capital,
and crowded with incomparable dragons enough to stock all Mr.
Andrew Lang's new and blue Fairy Books.

Bibliography, to be more than a vain curiosity, must of course be
studied as a material part of history.   Many indeed are the books
whose appearance marks the accession of something far more important than king or queen, nay of that which is often apt to destroy
kings, queens, and existing conventions generally, to wit a new idea;
of which we are thus provided with the most congenial *memoria
technica*.   Not less significant than the first edition of *Don Quixote*,
for example, is the publication of Galileo's *Nuntius Sidereus*, his
Message from the Stars, in 1610; or of those *Lettres écrites par Louis
de Montalte à un Provincial de ses Amis* which make the year 1657
an epoch in the history of French literature.

The final ripening of scientific conclusions, the impatient outbursts
of long shackled humour and good sense, the explosions of oppressed
suffering, and the exultant happiness of peace and secured civilisation—all these leave their mark in the records of bibliography, and
are more important and more interesting than all the official Acts of
Sovereigns and States.

Yet of the latter Herr Vogt, whom we have almost forgotten,
makes a special class, as things not generally entrusted to "the
trade," nor indeed concerning the general public who had but,
in earlier ages, to pay or fight as they were told.   Under this head
come the numerous swarm of Edicts, Declarations, Articles, Ordin-
ances, Petitions, Requests, and Resolutions of Most Christian Kings,
Illustrious Princes, and the representative bodies of which they from

time to time invoked the assistance. The student of French history would not leave on the shelf a 12mo volume, let us say, in nice old red morocco, entitled *Traitté des droits de la Reyne très Chrèstienne sur divers estats de l'Espagne* (1667). Rather would he look further for a very similar volume to put by its side—*Vérité défendue des*

Last leaf of a *Déclaration du Roy*. Printed by Antoine Estienne. 8vo. 1631.

Sofismes de la France etc. à la Sphère (1668); and should he find both, might return with great content to study the tremendous question of the Spanish Succession. The complete reports of the States-General of 1614, printed in handy form by Morel and others, might a few years ago have been found "lying about" within a mile of the spot on which we write. So, for that matter, was the *Official List*

of all " Conspirators " guillotined by the Revolutionary Tribunal up to
the fourth year of the one and (except in the matter of heads)
indivisible Republic—the original French text, that is, although
some twenty years before the eleven numbers uncut sold at Messrs.
Sotheby's for six guineas.

A good example of the strictly historical Tract would be the
mysterious-looking, poorly printed—and there is a certain poor and
rough badness of typography and paper which is to the expert eye
more appetising than the "largest" glories of the mediæval or even
the Kelmscott Press—the poorly printed thin 4to, we were observing,
hight *Squitinio della libertà Veneta*, &c., printed at Mirandola in
1612. This severe attack (by a Spanish diplomatist, as the learned
Bayle tells us, *Lettres Choisies*, p. 133 ; *sed?*—the authorship seems
to be undecided) upon Venetian independence of the Empire, was
rigorously suppressed—"every copy," an old-fashioned bibliographer
writes, "having been impounded by the Signory" Yet *one* fell into
our hands but the other day, disguised as the work of one "S.
Quitinio,"—and we have our (other) eye upon a second—it skills
not to say where—the volume is not worth half a green Pickwick
wrapper.

But of ephemeral literature the greatest is not the historical tract,
but the pamphlet, the free and inevitable contribution of individual
opinion. It need not be pretended that all pamphlets are interesting.
For utter weariness of the flesh those of our own seventeenth
century have no rival. Who knoweth not those "Horrid pictures of
Popish treachery," "Bundles of rods for the Back of this, that, or
the other Ungodly," varied by "Warning Cries," "Trumpet Calls,"
and endless "Brief Displays" of other people's Iniquity, Ambition,
and Tyranny? Anything more awful to contemplate in the mass
than the thirty thousand leaflets which, historians tell us, issued from
the English press in the twenty years or so following upon 1640, the
biblical imagination boggles at. The very paper and print of these
things afflict the experienced eye with that atmosphere of dull, stale,

jaded and pedantic controversy from which the uproarious license of
the Restoration was perhaps the only way of escape. Yet here too
occasional oases of interest, political or religious, may be marked
amid deserts of dulness; though the reader should not purchase
such works, even by the stack or cart-load, for the sake of finding
"rarities," like needles in a bottle of hay.

In truth there is many an uncommon book which, as we once
heard a cynical bookseller observe to a would-be vendor, is "almost"
yet not quite "as rare as the buyer."

The best in this kind after all are but dry dust and drivel to the
productions of that true age of libels, the sixteenth century, and, in
particular, of the dark and stormy period of the religious-civil wars in
France, France the home of the fiercest of passions, the mistress of
spiritual *épanchement*, the inventress of the pamphlet, and the
memoir. From the most abstract theory of Society down to the
latest amour of Henri Quatre, from the mysteries and iniquities of
the Papacy, to the most scurrilous personalities and the most
abominable crimes, every topic may be found discussed *ad nauseam*,
in the literature of this excited age, and discussed in most cases at
white heat.

The *Franco-Gallia* of Francis Hotman (1573), the "*contrat social*,"
as one historian has called it, "of the sixteenth century," the *Appeal
against Tyrants* ("Edinburgh," 1579) of Stephanus Junius Brutus,
alias Hubert Languet, the correspondent of Sir Philip Sidney—the
discourse on *Voluntary Slavery* of the enlightened Estienne de la
Boëtie,[1] the admired of Montaigne—these mark some of the higher

---

[1] The important tract of La Boëtie (1530-1568) *Le Contr'un ou Discours de la
servitude volontaire* (see Montaigne, *Essais*, II.) appeared in an imperfect form
in the *Mémoires de l'Estat de France* (see p. 254), 3 vols. 1578, which by the
way contain a large number of celebrated pamphlets of the time, the *Hist.
ragique de Marie Royne d'Escosse*, the *Discours merveilleux de la Vie de Catherine
de Medici* (usually attributed to Estienne), and various political ephemerides.
For an account of the treatises of Barclay, Buchanan, Mariana (*De Rege*, 1599,
rare), see Hallam, who points out what a store of constitutional arguments and

levels of thought. The *Alarum of Frenchmen*, the *De Furoribus Gallicis*,[1] are more immediately concerned with actual history, while of the literature of the "League," the *Histoire au vray du meurtre de M. le Duc de Guise* (1589, with a woodcut of the Duke lying on the ground pierced with five poniards), and the *Banquet du Comte d'Arête* (1594), a ferocious attack by the turncoat Louis d'Orléans upon "the hypocrisy of the King of Navarre, and the morals of him and his companions"—would be fairly typical specimens. The first editions of such opuscula are not only rare, but, in a chastened intellectual sense, of considerable value. But of all Tracts for the Times (and such times!) none rivals in interest (or in bulk, for brevity is not *essential* to the nature of a pamphlet) that celebrated miscellany of iniquity, half concealed under the mask of an erudite commentary, the immortal *Treatise of Wonders*, or *Apology for Herodotus*, from which scores of modern authors have drawn such priceless materials. The original edition of this work (1566), containing passages afterwards mutilated and suppressed, is a historic rarity.

Estienne's *Apology* is pre-eminently a social tract, as much so as Young's *Centaur not Fabulous*. Of the political and religious outbursts of this period, the greatest beyond doubt is the little volume of the *Satire Menippée* (1593), in which the awakening common sense of distracted France found an antidote to the venomous drug of "Spanish" fanaticism, and quenched in torrents of ridicule the dying ashes of the League.

---

precedents (utilized to some extent in the political struggles of the seventeenth century) were accumulated during this period.

[1] The *Reveillematin des Francois & de leurs voisins*, par Eusebe Philadelphe (Theod. Beza?) Edimbourg (Genève?) 1574, is tolerably rare. The only copy for sale, which I know of, is priced about £2 5s. The *first part* of the work, is merely a translation of the Latin *Dialogus de Cœde Hugonottorum*, &c., excudebat Adamus de Monte. Oragniæ, 1573,—a little volume by no means equal in interest to Hotman's *Vera et simplex narratio* (of the massacre of St. Bartholomew) auctore Varamundo Frisio, 12mo, Londini (and elsewhere), 1573.

The intensity of feeling expressed in a publication varies, as a rule, —if one may hazard the axiom—inversely to its bulk : and great is the amount of passion and enthusiastic ratiocination compressed into the pamphlet, from an *Invectiva* of Poggio on the poetry of Lorenzo Valla (6 pp. black letter, 148—), to *Tract* 90, or even the latest threepenny ebullition on Bimetallism or Fair Trade. Moreover, since it is only bulky and pig-skinned volumes that preserve themselves, we can seldom be surprised at the rarity of a tract which we may happen to want for any of the diverse reasons above discussed, since the material life of such frail things is but the matter of a day. Like flies, indeed, have they multiplied at all epochs of excitement, and like flies they perish, unless stored in the *recueil factice*, that precious repository of the rare, the forgotten, and, very often, the unknown and consequently uncatalogued.

Hence the practical collector will keep open for such volumes— obscurely lettered, imperfectly indexed in MS.—an eagle eye. His library will contain scattered among its memoirs and histories a dozen or a score of such ephemera as indicate the high-water mark, so to speak, of the tidal waves of feelings which have at various periods disturbed the stream of History. Small quartos for the "Civil War Tracts" and sermons reflecting on Kings and Commonwealths ; octavos for all the brood of the "Higuiero Infierno" above mentioned, and the conciliatory literature that followed them ; duodecimos for the exciting appeals of a century later, *L'Europe esclave si l'Angleterre ne rompt ses fers*, 1678, *La France sans Bornes*, &c., all which the candidate in history should be asked to "date approximately." Opuscula thus clearly entitled, and even perhaps *Proposals for Reviving Christianity* may explain themselves, but not so *Loose Meat for the Pigs*, even with year and full title given.[1]

---

[1] At the end of an 8vo volume containing the political works of Fletcher of Saltoun, 1732, *The Memoirs of Voltaire*, the (violently anti-religious) "Chapter on Dreams" from a *MS.* part of Paine's *Age of Reason*, and a few other items, I find T. Spence's rare and curious Satires upon the House of Hanover—(1795).

But *facile princeps* of all pamphlets of the age when, as Arthur Young tells us, every morning produced a new swarm (and that is, surely, of all pamphlets in history), stands that introductory handbook to the French Revolution, the famous *Qu'est-ce que le Tiers État?* of the Abbé Sièyes.[1] We do not know that this work—a thin volume in large octavo, dated 1789—can be called rare or *recherché*, even in the first edition, but it is certainly not common, and quite worthy of pursuit for its own sake.

For it is not "rarity" alone or in chief that has been here considered, but the reasons which have produced it, or should "if men were wise," produce it. And on the shores of this vast and trackless ocean of "Ephemera," almost all rare and *mostly*, we may surely say, of little worth, further research even of the lightest and most irregular kind is easily deterred. Here, then, with a tardy regard for the reader's patience, shall this all too common Discourse of Rarities be brought to a close.

One verse of its truculent poetry, which belongs to a past age and may be usefully contrasted with that, for example, of Mr. Eric Mackay, runs as follows :—

> " Gruntum, snorum
> In terrorum
> Let us keep de Schwine O !
> 'Twill save from chip chop
> Our stout wig-block
> By de Guillotine O ! "

In vain would the collector look nowadays for such publications at the " Hive of Liberty " in Holborn ! Some dozen 12mo reflections upon the dangerous greatness of France, the duty of Great Britain, &c., fill a dumpy little volume dated 1670 to 1700.

[1] 3me edition, s.l. 1789. A work containing many original and striking reflections, which are as interesting to-day as they were a century ago. The lengthy anonymous quotation on the title-page—" Tant que le Philosophe n'excède point les limites de la vérité, ne l'accusez pas d'aller trop loin," &c., might serve as a compendium of French idealism. The work was written during the assembly of notables in 1788, and first appeared in January 1789. The " Three Questions " with which it opens have become historical—

1°. Qu'est-ce que le Tiers Etat ?—Tout.
2°. Qu'a-t-il été jusqu' à présent dans l'ordre politique ?—Rien.
3°. Que demande-t-il ?—*A être quelque chose.*

II.

A GASCON TRAGEDY
(14TH CENTURY).

From De Foix's *Deduicts de la Chasse des bestes,* &c. (1507). Vérard. (*Brit. Mus.*c. 31, m. 2.)
See Note on p. 53 *post.*

A GASCON TRAGEDY.

VERY late on the evening of St. Catherine's Day (Nov. 25), in the year 1388, Jean Froissart, Canon and Treasurer of Chimay, accompanied by a friend, rode into the little town of Ortais (some twenty miles from Pau), and dismounted at the hostel of the "Moon," a small inn still in existence and known to modern travellers as "La Belle Hôtesse."[1]

Having sent word of his arrival to the castle of the Comte de Foix, whom he had come to visit (with the view of acquiring information at first hand of the wars in Gascony and Spain), the historian, who bore letters of introduction from his patron, the Comte de Blois, was at once received with every hospitality, and remained as his lordship's guest, so he expressly tells us, for more than twelve weeks.

Ortais, or Orthez as it is now spelt, was once, as we may learn

---

[1] *Chroniques de France, Angleterre et d'Espaigne.* Reveu par Denis Sauvage de Fontenailles-en-Brie. Fol. Jan de Tournes, Lyon, 1559-60-61 (Bk. III., ch. 8). This admirably printed edition (the first *edited* Froissart, "peu commune . . . très belle—infiniment supérieure aux précédentes," *Brunet*), which bears upon its title the device reproduced on the next page, is by no means to be despised for the purposes of the general reader : who should moreover possess T. Johnes's *Memoir, &c., of Froissart* (translated *with additions* from the French of Ste. Palaye) 8vo, Lond. 1801. The complete text of the Chronicles is now accessible in the twenty-five volumes published by Baron Kervyn de Lettenhove. Brussels, 1870, &c. The story here rehearsed will be found in vol. xi.

E

from modern guide-books, a place of considerable importance, and the residence of the Princes of Bearn, until, at the close of the fifteenth century, they removed to Pau.

Of the "Castle of Moncada," built after a Spanish model by Gaston de Foix in 1240, and dismantled by Cardinal Richelieu, but one stately tower and a few ruined walls remain.

QVOD TIBI
FIERI NON
VIS, ALTERI
NE FECERIS.

The associations of the place seem, curiously enough, to be mostly of a sanguinary cast. On the heights above the little town (Feb. 27, 1814) we defeated the French army under Soult in a bloody engagement, the only one in which the Duke of Wellington was ever injured.

From the Gothic Bridge, or rather from the tower in the centre of it, the Calvinistic soldiery, who took the tower by assault in 1569, are said to have precipitated into the river the Roman Catholic priests found with arms in their hands, who refused to abjure their religion.

Lastly, the castle—more particularly the tower—was the scene of unparalleled crimes during the life of the brutal Gaston Phœbus, who filled its dungeons with the victims of his unbridled passion ; among whom were his kinsman, the Viscomte de Chateaubon, Pierre Arnaut, the faithful Governor of Lourdes,[1] *and finally his own son and only child, whom he killed with his knife here in the dark cell in which he had caused him to be immured.* " Blanche de Navarre," we are further told, " was poisoned here " by her younger sister, the Comtesse de Foix. That was in 1466.

The place was in fact a complete mediæval Chamber of Horrors, and the brutal " Gaston Phœbus," Comte de Foix, has been handed down in history as a monster of profligate iniquity in a period when such celebrity was no trifling achievement.

[1] The horrid murder of Pierre Arnaut is described in detail (*Chronique*, iii. 6) by the Chevalier d'Espaing du Lyon, whose store of anecdotes beguiled, as well they might, the long ride from Pamiers (where Froissart had met him) to Ortais. The Count, his relative and liege lord, having invited the Governor of Lourdes to a parley, adjured him to give up the citadel. The latter declined, with profuse apologies, saying he was in honour bound to the King of England, who had placed him there. On this De Foix, in mortal rage, drew a dagger, and crying " Ha, traitor ! ' No,' sayest thou ? By this head it shall not be for nought ! " stabbed him fiercely in five places. " Oh, my lord ! " cried Arnaut, " you do no knightly deed to send for me and then murder me ! " " But stabbed he was whether he liked it or not " (*toutefois il eut ces cinq coups de dague*) is the singular comment ; and the Count ordered him to be thrown into the castle ditch, where he shortly afterwards died. *But not a knight nor baron dared stir a finger to prevent it.* . . . De Foix's " neighbours," the kings of France and England, were, the same informant tells us, a perpetual source of diplomatic anxiety to this " sage prince," who was careful never to offend unnecessarily any *great lord*. He could levy any day more men-at-arms than either of the kings of Aragon and Navarre. In response to Froissart's cross-examination, his companion was going on to recount the fate of young Gaston, but it was too late for so long a story, as the travellers were just then arriving at Tarbes, where they made themselves very comfortable at the " Star."

During the fourteenth century the feudal system was at the height of its power; and the tremendous forces inevitably developed within itself by European society for dealing with a chronically recrudescent chaos, seemed only too often—in their independence of any public opinion—to act in the direction of unmixed evil.

The despotic defiance by feudal lords (the ideal "wicked barons" of later romance) of the conceptions of right and wrong, law and outrage, which were in an irregular way beginning to leaven society, is a thing peculiar to the age when the power of the former, already at its zenith, had yet no cause to fear extinction from the new influences of gunpowder, the printing-press, and general enlightenment.

This is one of the great sources of interest attaching to the period of history illuminated for us by the brilliant colouring of the greatest of born chroniclers.

Froissart in his history seems to live for the purpose of accumulating information on every subject which might interest posterity. Inconsistent, inaccurate, as he often is, heartless (*qui pis est*) as he often seems, as to his capacity for telling a story there can be but one opinion; and nothing in his whole work forms a more complete, instructive, and dramatic episode than that briefly and incorrectly abstracted in the passage we have quoted from Mr. Murray's "Guide."

The genealogy of the Counts of Foix and Bearn, according to the *Art de Vérifier les Dates*, extends, with but one break of the direct succession, from the tenth century to the end of the fifteenth, where it merges in the royal house of Navarre; and of all who bore the title none was more famous, or infamous, than the particular Gaston III., called "Phœbus," in the annals of the De Foix family cited by Denis Sauvage; whether on account of his long and flowing hair, his general personal attractions, or of his passion for the chase, seems not quite certain.[1]   Certainly no one would con-

---

[1] See a note in De Lettenhove's edition.

jecture, from Froissart's description, that the gentleman who, on this November evening, in the year of grace 1388, received the chronicler into his magnificent château, and there "made him good cheer" for some three months, was identical with the "monster of iniquity," the brutal tyrant whose cold-blooded murder of his only son brought to an end the long generations of the ancient barons of Foix.

For Froissart, who indubitably saw the ogre in his castle, and knew him, as we might say, "at home," was, it may fairly be presumed, disposed to take people, and especially the rich and powerful, as he found them, with perhaps no special care as to how they treated their other fellow-beings.

The Count was at this time, he tells us, about fifty-nine years of age. "I tell you I have seen in my time many knights, kings, princes and others, but never none have I seen so handsome, so tall, so well built," as the Count Gaston Phœbus. He was so perfect in all respects *qu'on ne le pouuoit trop louer*—an Admirable Crichton, in fact, as we are shown by the detailed portrait that follows.

A splendid figure of a man, brave, beautiful, accomplished, munificent, with a bright colour, a winning smile, and *green eyes*, from which darted now and then an amorous glance.

A sage statesman, and a wise ruler, a skilful and daring warrior (for had he not fought in all parts of Europe, slaughtered the "heathen" in Prussia, engaged, on his own account, the Powers Spain, England, Aragon, and Navarre, and even defied the King of France himself, with tolerable success?), "he loved what should be loved, and hated what should be hated." Most regular in all religious observances, *il disoit planté d'oraisons*, with every night a "Notturne" of the Psalter, Hours of our Lady, The Holy Spirit, and the Cross, with Watches for the Dead; and every day five florins given in small change to the poor, and alms at the gate for all comers. The Count was also an ardent sportsman, and even an *author* upon his favourite subject,[1] fond of dogs above all animals—we are told

[1] The book is entitled *Miroir de Phébus des déduits de la Chasse des bestes*

elsewhere that he kept several hundred—liberal and hospitable. At midnight, the dinner hour, twelve varlets carried twelve torches to light him and his numerous guests to the dining hall, where a plentiful banquet was daily spread *pour souper qui souper vouloit.* None spoke to the Count (who, by the way, was particularly partial to *fowl,* especially the legs and wings) unless first addressed. At other times he was approachable by any one, and spoke them fair and "lovingly," though his answers were brief and presumably to the point.[1] The castle was, of course, thronged with knights and squires from all quarters; it was a great centre of news, and there was much talk of "love" and "feats of arms," the principal "news" in the good old days of Jean Froissart.

Then there was music. The Count was well skilled in the art, and had many a song, rondeau, and virelet sung before him of an evening. These fanciful forms of verse were just becoming popular.[2] Froissart, moreover—on such terms were the two—had brought the

---

Sauvaiges & des oyseaux de proie, and seems to have been first printed in black letter about 1505, and by Anthoine Verard (in 1507) with woodcut illustrations, of which two editions copies are in the British Museum. De Foix is cited as a great authority on sport by Jacques de Fouilloux in his *Venerie,* 4to. 1585. Froissart, who brought the Count four greyhounds (called Tristan, Hector, Brown, and Roland) from England, was himself, as he travelled on horseback with his portmanteau behind him, always accompanied by one of these animals. (See Sainte-Palaye's *Mémoires sur l'ancienne Chevalerie, la Chasse,* &c., 3 vols. 8vo, 1781; a work containing several valuable original texts.)

[1] *E.g.,* on the critical occasion of the defection of d'Armagnac, when others thought of retreat. "As we are here, my lord," said De Foix to his father, "we will fight your enemies," and he started off with 1,700 *men at helm,* and 6,000 foot, killed 11,000 Spaniards, and chased their king out to sea, bringing his son and brother home as prisoners. The Count was then quite a young man.

[2] Massieu (*Hist. de la Poésie Francaise,* 8vo, 1739) says that Froissart did much to bring them into vogue. Of the poems composed by the worthy canon himself, Estienne Pasquier (*Recherches de la France,* Book vi., ch. 5) gives a list taken from a volume of the same which he had seen in Francis I.'s library at Fontaine-bleau. One of these pieces, cited by Sainte-Palaye (*Memoirs of Froissart*), was a pastoral in honour of Gaston Phœbus—a truly Arcadian subject!

Count a precious volume written out by himself at the request of King Wincelaus of Bohemia, Duke of Luxemburg and Brabant, and containing all that "gentle Duke's"[1] poetical works. Every night after dinner was Froissart requested to read this book aloud (it was called, he tells us, " Meliader "), and during the reading no one dared to utter a sound, so anxious was the Count that it should be heard properly; but such literary points as occurred to him he would himself discuss with the reader, "*not in his native Gascon, but in good French and fair.*"

In truth, De Foix was quite an ideal host, and with all the lavish munificence of his court (no visitor departed without a handsome *douceur*), a careful and strict man of business. He kept a safe in his private room. Twelve agents managed the estates, under a controller, who had to show vouchers for everything to the Count himself; and there were four copying-clerks who *had to be ready (bien convenoit que fussent prests)* when the master of Foix stepped hurriedly out of his study to read and answer letters.

This last detail of the accounts has a touch almost of Gilbertian burlesque when we consider that after a successful foray among the Armagnacs[2] or other relatives or neighbours, the popular form of rural visit in the fourteenth century, there would frequently be a dozen or a score of distinguished prisoners in the dungeons at Orthez. The "bag" made at Cassières in 1362 alone (*d'une seule prise*),

---

[1] The Royal balladmonger is no other than the Wincelaus, King of Bohemia, Emperor of Germany and son of Charles IV., known to history as "the drunkard," whose cruelties and debauchery earned him the name of the " Nero of Germany." He succeeded his father in 1378, and having been born in 1359, must now have been in his thirtieth or thirty-first year. His sister married the unfortunate Richard II., and became the "good Queen Anne" of the fourteenth century, who protected the Lollards, and introduced the side-saddle into England.

[2] The endless quarrels of D'Armagnac arose from the claims of the latter (who had been disinherited by his father for not appearing in arms against the Spaniards, *v.* note, p. 54) to certain rights then conferred upon the hero of this story.

as described in a previous chapter, which included the Count D'Armagnac (husband of De Foix's eldest sister) himself, and many inferior nobles, brought in a sum total of 1,800,000 francs, doubtless duly apportioned on the credit side of the "roolles & livres escrits" aforesaid, minus the expense of each prisoner's board and lodging. For the Count "never loved wild debauch, nor *foolish extravagance*, but would know each month what became of his property." His economy is exhibited in an anecdote related elsewhere, but which, as Froissart himself is so fond of saying, is not *altogether* out of place here, although it chiefly illustrates the popular practical joke of the fourteenth century. One Christmas night, when the house was crowded with guests, an intimate friend and neighbour, one Ernauton d'Espaigne (a gentleman of remarkable physique), happened to be in the great gallery, to which you go up by twenty-four steps, where there was a *chimney*, and sometimes, when the Count de Foix was at home, a very small fire—such was his rule—and on other occasions none at all, however cold it was. "Lord, what a wretched fire," exclaimed the cheery D'Espaigne, who had probably been out hunting all day, "for such a frosty night!" and without more ado he tripped off down the gallery and steps, and out into the courtyard, where, as he had noticed from the windows, there chanced to be a number of donkeys standing laden with wood. Promptly seizing the biggest, he carried it upstairs on his shoulders, and threw the animal, feet uppermost, wood and all, upon the fire, amid roars of laughter from De Foix and the company. This was on a festive occasion, and neither ass nor wood belonged, as it happened, to the Count. But to return to our serious narrative. . . . "And well as any did he know whom to trust, and *how to take what belonged to him*"—without, we may be sure, waiting to be asked. Nor need we wonder that he was continually amassing treasure against a rainy day; for even so great a lord was anxious, we are reminded, as to the future.

But with all this external splendour and prosperity there was a skeleton in the cupboard, a death's head at the nightly banquet.

The Comte de Foix and Madame his lady were not on good terms, nor had been for a long time : and their only son was, alas ! no more. On this latter point Sir John, as we know, was curious. He had probably too much tact to ask De Foix himself how the death (of which he had heard from his fellow-traveller D'Espaigne) had occurred. The green eyes might have replied with a flash of something different from love. So he discreetly inquired of an ancient and notable " Esquire " of the House, and heard and recorded for our benefit the whole " piteous tale."

It is far from being the only tale, the only family scandal recorded by an indefatigable chronicler, who, if he lacked depth of feeling and perception, was at least singleminded in his industry. For some forty years, as we know, he never rested—travelling, inquiring, exploring records and documents, and sparing no expense (which his own or a patron's purse could supply), and nightly noting down the results of his labours. And even had he deliberately gone aside to falsify the personal character of an important personage in history, he might have given good politic reasons for it. Suppose the account written—nothing is more likely—during the early part of his stay at Orthez, and that the gentle Count had asked him one evening to read aloud his own work instead of those eternal rondeaux and virelets of the " German Nero," nay, even insisted on despatching one of his ready " clerks " to fetch the MS. : how then ? And, to take the least danger, fancy quarrelling, on account of a few private peccadilloes, with a man who had such priceless information to give relating to every war of the last twenty years ! Doubtless Froissart acted for the best. The probability is also that his hasty and brilliant portrait was perfectly sincere. In any case it forms an admirable introduction to the tragedy that follows. If it is difficult not to smile at the after-dinner eloquence of Froissart's account of his noble host ; nothing more natural was ever penned by any easy-going and uncritical visitor entertained in so sympathetic and sumptuous a style.

The Count and his lady—so said the ancient esquire in private conference with the Canon—were not, "truth to tell," on good terms. The reason was simplicity itself. The Countess was the sister of the King of Navarre, by whom the Sieur d'Albreth had been "pledged" with the Count, for the sum of fifty thousand francs.[1] He was kept in one of the dungeons at Orthez by his uncle Gaston. The latter knowing the King of Navarre to be "crafty and malicious," was unwilling, in spite of the entreaties of the Countess, to trust his brother-in-law for this large amount, and the event seems to show that he here exhibited the prudence for which Froissart gave him credit.

But the lady was bitterly wroth. "My lord," said she, "you do but scant honour to the King my brother when you will not trust him for fifty thousand francs. *If you never got more out of the Armagnacs and Labrissiens*[2] *than you have had already*," she continued, treating the Count's commercial warfare with his relatives as one might an abuse of their hospitality, "*that should suffice you ;*" and she concluded with a clinching argument. Fifty thousand francs was the precise amount of the marriage settlement which her lord, as she reminds him with some asperity, was bound to hand over to Monseigneur her brother, presumably in trust for her. To which the Count Gaston Phœbus replied curtly, "Madam, you say truth. But if I thought the King of Navarre would so reckon the sum, the Sieur D'Albret should never leave Orthez till I had been paid the last penny. But since you ask it, I will let him go, not for love of you, but of my son."

---

[1] Compare the figures given above (p. 56). These were *gold* francs, first coined in 1360, and called *francs à cheval* (from their bearing a mounted figure of the king) as distinguished from the *franc à pied* introduced by Charles V. Silver francs do not appear till 1575. Chéruel, *Dict. des Institutions, &c.*

The franc d'or may be roughly valued at about £1. The ransom of King John when captured at Poictiers in 1356 was 3,000,000 crowns, or something between one and a half and two million pounds sterling. But the fluctuations of money values in the fourteenth century baffle calculation. *Vide* Michelet, *Hist. Fr.*

[2] Those of Labreth, otherwise called Albreth. *Sauvage.*

And at this point we may conjecture how the speaker "parted with huge strides among his dogs."

So, however, the matter was arranged.[1] D'Albreth gave a bond to his highness of Navarre (who became De Foix's debtor) and went back to France, where he married the Duke of Bourbon's sister. Before that, however, he had repaid "at his ease" the sum due to the King of Navarre. But it was never forwarded to De Foix. Therefore he suggested that the Countess should pay a visit to her brother and explain that the Count took it much amiss that he was not paid "what was his." The lady readily consented to do so, and went off to the court at Pamplona to her brother, who received her gladly. The Countess gave him her message straight to the point. But the King (who also had a genius for saying what he meant) replied, "My fair sister, that money is yours; De Foix owes it you for dower, and *long as I have control over it never out of the Kingdom of Navarre shall it go.*"

"Nay, my lord," quoth the Countess, "that will be to make too great hatred betwixt myself and the Count. If you hold to your word

---

[1] The business-like manner in which these affairs were conducted may be seen from the case mentioned in another chapter (III.). The ransom of the Count d'Armagnac amounted to 260,000 francs. The Prince of Wales ("The Black Prince") on one occasion, being requested to beg him off, replied (with that royal tact and good sense to which we are still accustomed) that, "all things considered," he could not undertake to do so. "You were taken," he replied to D'Armagnac, "in fair fight, and our cousin De Foix risked his person and men in adventure against you, and you must abide the result. Neither my royal father nor myself would like to be asked to give up what we have lawfully got." In fact, they inclined (as no one has told us better than Froissart) rather to the opposite course. . . . The Princess approached the subject in the kindness of her heart, with feminine artfulness, by asking vaguely for *a gift*. But the noble Gaston Phœbus, *qui en ses besongnes assez cler veoit*, was too many for her. He was, he said, a poor knight in quite a small way ("petit home"), who could not make expensive presents; he had many outgoings, *castles and towns to build* (the magnificent château at Pau, famous as the birthplace of Henry IV., was in fact then in course of reconstruction); and he only consented, as a great favour, to knock off the odd 60,000 francs.

I shall not dare return to my lord. He will slay me. He will say I have deceived him."

"I don't know," concluded her royal brother, "what you will do (*ie ne say que vous ferez*), whether you will go or whether you will stay : but I am master of this money to take care of it for you, and it will never go out of Navarre."

So the Countess also stayed, for she did not dare return to Foix ; and the Count, who had been on good terms with her before, began to be consumed with hatred against her, though she was in nought to blame, for not giving his message (he knew the malice of the King) and returning to him. And thus matters remained. Now the young Gaston, son [1] of my lord, was grown to a fine youth, tall and handsome, very like his father in build. Being now some fifteen or sixteen years of age, he was married to a young lady, the daughter of the Comte d'Armagnac, "sister of the present Count"; and it was hoped that this alliance would heal the feud between the two families.

And the fancy took him to pay a visit to his uncle and his mother in Navarre ; and he went, and stayed there some little time, and then took his leave. But he could not, by any means, persuade his mother to return with him. For she asked, *had the Count, his father, specially charged him to bring her back?* and the boy could only say, No ; there had been no special mention of that at his departure. So she dared not come. For she knew her husband to be cruel (this and the remark of Arnaut's quoted above are the first suggestions that he was anything but "gentil"), at least, in matters where he found cause for displeasure. So Gaston went alone to take leave of his uncle the King at Pampelune.

---

[1] Only son born of the Countess. He had two others, of one of whom we hear presently. On the death of the Count, Yvain, here described as ill-disposed, made an attempt to seize the inheritance. The Count had expressed a wish after the death of young Gaston to prefer his illegitimate offspring to the legitimate heir, Chateaubon, of whom he had a poor opinion.

The King of Navarre received him hospitably, and gave rich presents both to the young Count and to his attendants, and kept him there ten days.

Just before their departure, Gaston's uncle drew him aside and gave him a little purse full of powder, and said, "Fair nephew, you must do as I tell you. You are aware that the Comte de Foix is wrongly enraged with your mother and my sister, which I much regret, as doubtless do you. Now, to bring them on good terms again, as soon as you have opportunity, take a little of this powder (be sure no one sees you) and put it upon his food : and as soon as ever he has eaten it, his one desire will be but to have your mother again with him, and they will love one another and live together in peace : which you must surely desire. But be sure to tell no one."

And the boy believed every word, and replied he would gladly do it : and so went home, and was gaily received by his father, and showed him the presents—all but one.

Now in the De Foix mansion it was usual for Yvain, the bastard, to share the chamber of Gaston, and they loved one another from children like true brothers ; and being much of one size and age they even wore each other's coats and clothes. And it happened one day, as will with boys, that their clothes got mixed up, and that Gaston's coat got upon the bed of Yvain, and the latter, a mischievous boy, noticed the powder in its little bag, and asked Gaston, "What is this thing that you wear at your breast?" Of this word Gaston had no joy at all, but cried "Give me back the coat. It has nothing to do with you." And Yvain threw it him, and Gaston put it on, and was more thoughtful than ever before, that day. And it happened (as God would, to save the Comte de Foix) that three days later Gaston quarrelled with his brother at fives, and boxed his ears. And the boy Yvain, angered and sulky, went crying to the Count's chamber, where he found him, having just heard a mass.

" What do you want, Yvain ? "

"God's name, my lord, Gaston has beaten me, but he deserves a beating more than I do."

" Why so ? " said the Count, who at once became suspicious.

" My faith ! since he came back from Navarre he carries at his breast a little bag all full of powder, but I know not what use it is or what he will do with it : but that he has told me once or twice that my lady, his mother, will soon be in your good graces more than ever before."

The unconscious Yvain was dismissed with the strictest injunction to hold his tongue.

The Count, we are told, then spent a long time in thought, till the dinner-hour, when he entered the hall and took his seat as usual.

According to the feudal custom of the day, the son Gaston waited upon his father, handing him the successive courses, and tasting each one himself.

He had no sooner placed the first dish before the Count, when the latter, with a quick glance, detected the strings of the mysterious purse hanging at the boy's vest.[1] *Le sang luy mua*, and that not for the first or second time, in Froissart's brief account of one who never forgave an injury and whose wrath was dreaded like the plague by even his adult and powerful enemies.

"Gaston," he said, "come here. I would speak with you privately."

Deathly pale, trembling and confounded, the boy stepped forward, feeling that he was undone, as the Count, fumbling at his breast, seized the fatal purse, drew it out, and taking a knife from the table cut it open and found the powder.

---

[1] The similar discovery described in Shakespeare's *Richard II.*, Act v. Sc. 3 (a drama representing the same period as Froissart's story), will recur to many readers. In Aumerle's case the seal " that hangs without his bosom " betrays to his father, the Duke of York (by what seems an extraordinary piece of carelessness), his possession of a treasonable document.

Putting some of it on a slice of bread, he called a dog and gave it him to eat. The dog no sooner tasted it than he rolled his eyes and lay dead on the floor.[1]

The wrath of Gaston Phœbus broke all bounds, and in a moment his son would have fared like Pierre Arnaut, but on this more important occasion knights and esquires rushed in between the two, imploring the Count at least to inquire further into the matter. But his first cry was, "What! Gaston, caitiff! *For you and the heritage that should be yours have I had war and hatred against the Kings of France, England, Spain, Aragon, Navarre, and held my own against them, and now you would murder me!* You shall die for it." And he rushed from the table with his knife and would have killed the boy. But friends and retainers fell on their knees in tears before him. "Ah, good my lord, for God's sake, mercy; slay not Gaston. You will have no other son. Let him be put in ward, but wait and judge of the matter, for belike he had no guilt in the deed, and knew not what he brought."

"Away with him, then," cried the enraged Count, "to the tower." And there was the boy imprisoned. Of the companions that had attended him to Navarre many were arrested, and many prudently "departed." But fifteen were put to death "most horribly"; for the Count did not see how he could do otherwise, since they were in the secrets of his son. And this, we are told, did move some to pity, for they were as pleasant and well-looking esquires as any in all Gascony. But they had never told of young Gaston's wearing the fatal purse (perhaps they never knew), and for that they died "most horribly." The news of these tragical proceedings spread soon over the whole country: and the feeling which they aroused seems to

[1] Of the King of Navarre—Charles II. "the bad" (1347-86)—it may be observed that he had attempted, in a similar manner, the lives of the two unpopular uncles of Charles VI. of France; but he employed an English agent who bungled the matter. (See Chapuy's curious *Hist. du Royaume de Navarre*, 8vo, 1596, where this story is told with a few variations.)

show the Comte de Foix in a pleasing light. There can be no doubt that he was a popular landlord in the feudal sense. He looked after his own and protected them with the strong hand, as with a strong and merciless hand he had suppressed the terrible rising of the "Jacquerie." Knightly adventurers who returned with great plenty of plunder and prisoners from forays in other quarters, dared not touch a thing on the De Foix property without paying for it—for they might not "abide" his wrath : and not the precipitous pass of Lagarde, where half a dozen might hold a host at bay, could keep back Gaston Phœbus when "greatly desirous to get by" that way, to succour his people at Pamiers.

So the nobles and prelates, the estates of Bearn, in fact, gladly assembled to *intercede* for the imprisoned youth. For when the Count briefly expounded the crime and his fixed intention of putting his son to death "as he deserved," they, without argumentation, all with one voice expressed their particular desire, "saving his good grace," that Gaston should not die. By these entreaties the Count, it is said, was seriously moved. He bethought himself, and meditated punishing the boy by a term of imprisonment, then sending him for three or four years' travel, till change of air had cured the inherent viciousness of his disposition. And with this assurance he sent the company away. But those who knew him best would not leave without a positive promise of mercy,—*tant aimoyent l'enfant ;* and the Count promised, and they all went. No one seems to have thought of consulting the boy himself, who remained shut up in the Tower of Orthais, in a chamber "where there was little light." In similar apartments, as we know, other relatives of the Count had been detained for periods varying according to their financial circumstances. Among others, his own heir, Chateaubon (a young "coward," in whom the Count could not be expected to take much interest), had spent eight weeks there, and paid for such sumptuous lodgings at the rate of 5,000 francs a week. Yet the young Gaston, imprisoned only for ten days, seems to have taken it more to heart.

Confined, "as he was," and in his clothes (a thing, we pathetically read, he was not used to), he grew even more melancholy, and cursed the hour when he was born. He would not eat, and when the servants brought him his food (and we are specially told what nice servants they were) and said, "Gaston, here is your dinner," he would only say, "Put it there," and took no further notice.

The event had been so noised abroad that Pope Gregory XI. sent a Cardinal from Avignon [1] to try to accommodate matters; but the Cardinal was stopped half-way by the news that it was too late.

"Having told you so much," says the ancient esquire as if Froissart would have let him stop there, "I may as well tell you the end." And thus it was. A servant having informed the Count that Gaston would not eat, and that his food lay there all untasted, and implored him to take thought for his son, the indignant father strode upstairs to the tower, trimming his nails the while, as ill luck would have it, with a small knife. The prison door being opened, he went up to the boy standing in the corner (consumed with we know not what innocent indignation, faint with hunger, and trembling before the wrath of his father), and, angrily asking him what he meant by not eating, the baron, with his right hand, in which the knife was covered, "all but the size of a gold piece," "jobbed" him, as one would say, roughly, in the neck, and went downstairs again. The blade, it seemed, could hardly have touched the flesh,.

---

[1] This shows that the death of Gaston must have taken place in 1377 (when Gregory XI., who died the next year, restored the Papal seat to Rome) or earlier, *i.e.* at least eleven years before Froissart's visit to Orthez. The bastard Yvain grew up a likely and handsome youth, went to Court, and was a great favourite of the young King Charles VI. During a "mummery" (at the Hôtel de St. Pol. in Paris, *mardy avant le Chandeleur*, 1382), in which the latter and several of the young nobility dressed up as "savages," the Duke of Orleans, by holding a torch too near, accidentally set their inflammable costumes on fire. From this accident Yvain lost his life, and the king himself ran considerable risk. —*Chroniques*, IV., 52.

F

anything to speak of; but by ill fate it chanced upon a vein, and under the circumstances that was enough. Poor young Gaston, the hope of the De Foixs, "turned aside" from this trying world of alchemist-uncles and suspicious cut-throat fathers, and then and there died.

When the Count heard of it (he had only just got back to his room, and would not believe the news at first, till he had *sent some one to see*) he was taken with one of his chronic attacks of indignation, mingled, we may believe, with some serious regret that he had not been more careful.

"Ah, Gaston," was his exclamation, "an ill chance this for me and thee. I shall never know such joy again as I had before. Woe worth the day thou wentest to Navarre;" and he sent at once for his barber, and then ordered mourning for himself and his retainers.

There was a grand funeral, of course, and much weeping and wailing, and that was all.

And thus did God preserve the gentle Comte de Foix from the wiles of his royal relative But it was not for very long.

Three years later we find Gaston Phœbus in the woods of Sauveterre—after a long summer morning devoted to his favourite pastime of hunting—they had just killed and cured a bear—riding with a party to the little village of Riou, where lunch had been prepared.

It was "deep noon" (*basse nonne*)[1] and very hot, and the room had been nicely decorated with refreshing and sweet-smelling greenery. The Count sat down and called for water. Scarcely had he dipped his fingers (which were "long and fair") in the silver bowl held by two squires, when his face turned white, his feet trembled, and with one cry, "Lord God, have mercy on me, I am dead," he fell back senseless; and though they applied bread, water, spices, and such

---

[1] The only trace of the ecclesiastic about Froissart is his chronology, expressed in the terms *prime, tierce, vêpres,* and *nonne,* modified by the epithet *haute* or *basse.*

mediæval restoratives, he was gone in half an hour, gone—shall we say ?—to meet Pierre Arnaut, Gaston, and other known and unknown victims of his lust and cruelty. His domains the disappointed tyrant had devised to the French crown, but they were sold by the Duc de Berri to Matthew, son of Bernard II., Vicomte de Carcasonne.[1]

The well-known Court doctrine as to the damnation of a "man of quality" applies with far more point to a feudal tyrant, who was also at least a stark man of action, than to his enfeebled descendant of the Revolutionary period.

To deny heroism, nay, romantic grandeur, to the former, would be absurd. But life, under their *régime*, assumes somehow an undeniably sombre hue.

The mere recurrence in Froissart's description of words expressive of rage and ill-temper is such as to strike the eye. Someone is for ever becoming *courroucé, enfelonné,* &c., as a prelude to someone else being *décollé, décapité,* or, in some other form, *occis.* Eternal freebooting, "chevauchées," burning villages, outrages, and piteous deaths teem through the volumes. Indeed, were every description of bloodshed in these pages printed in a congenial red, not the most brilliantly illuminated mediæval missal would compare with their flaring hue. The thing does not seem matter for melancholy to the parties chiefly concerned. With a light heart do they join the frequent fray, "fighting and cleaving one another so well it was wonder," with as sincere joy as any hero of Mr. Rudyard Kipling's.[2] Even to

---

[1] *Biographie Universelle.*

[2] See in particular the detailed description of a perfect fight (almost the best the Chevalier de Foix, who described it to the chronicler, had ever known), Bk. III., ch. 6. After three hours' hard work, when the "battle-axe" stage had been reached, those of the combatants who were out of breath and had been "roughly handled" retired to a ditch or stream, and took off their "bassinets" for a moment's refreshment. Ernauton de Ste. Colombe being very hard put to it and almost discomfited, his "varlet," a stark man of his hands (the "varlets" as a rule took no part in the combat, being presumably unarmed), came up and

Froissart as spectator, and much more to the warriors themselves, did it appear that there was nothing else half so well worth doing. To those who were otherwise employed, matters appeared, we know, in a very different light. .

The Comte de Foix assured Froissart while complimenting him on his history, that more remarkable things had occurred in "the last fifty years" than in three hundred before them. Oddly enough, this is just what most of us think at the present day. But from his point of view, in which "feats of arms" were the chief events of interest, he was not altogether wrong. It was certainly an age of unbridled violence, of moral and intellectual stagnation; the earth full of triumphant iniquities; righteousness, it would seem, scarcely venturing to look down from heaven; the hearts of men (of the few who had leisure or peace to reflect) failing them for fear and for looking after those things which were coming upon the world, where so faint and far glimmered the dawn of a better day. The misery of the common people was everywhere terrible, and of all countries perhaps France suffered most. The Seven Years' War of Burgundy and Ghent, which ruined half the north of Europe and "was deplored by Turks, Pagans, and Saracens"—"you may judge," confides the chronicler, "how it affected adjoining countries." To the calamities of the English invasion were added the devastations of the Black Death. Charles V. "stifled," as a French historian tells us, "all spirit of liberty." The crushing burden of taxes was yearly increased. The experiment of a permanent *taille* was coupled with the universal imposition of the

took his axe from him, saying "Ernauton, you sit down and rest a bit; you don't know how to fight," and himself with a blow of his master's weapon proceeded to knock his antagonist "silly." When the latter recovered himself the varlet dodged his return blow, and threw him, threatening to take his life "*unless you surrender to my master.*" "Who is your master?" "Ernauton de Ste. Colombe, with whom you've been fighting all this time." The esquire, as the varlet knelt on him, presenting a dagger at his throat, agreed to this compromise—"to appear at Lourdes in fifteen days, rescue or no rescue."

more odious *gabelle,* which had first become a regular crown monopoly in 1342. In 1357 the Parisian Bourgeoisie under Estienne
Marcel had inaugurated a civil war, in their demand for the reformation of abuses. And the next year burst forth the blind, wild-beast fury
of the Jacquerie ; stamped out in turn by the fierce reprisals of indignant feudalism, assisted by the very Comte de Foix of whose heroism
we have heard so much. Yet this was but an item of calamity to
the chronic invasions of the English, whose kings and princes well
seem to have spent their leisure time, seldom interrupted by a "rain
of stones" from heaven, in careering (*chevauchant*) up and down the
harried and mangled provinces of what, by a curious irony, they
called their own country.

In a special "digression" upon the character of the Gascons and
the English (III. 22), Froissart tells us that he once heard the
Sieur d'Albreth at Paris make a singular observation, of which he
(the chronicler) made particular note. D'Albreth meeting a Breton
knight, the latter inquired how his country fared, and *how he managed*
(this was after D'Armagnac, D'Albreth, and others had been won
over by the kindness of King Charles V. "of blessed memory"—
Gascons could only be led by tact and kindness) *to keep French*
(*comment il se savoit contenir à estre François*). "Thank God,"
replied D'Albreth, "I am pretty well. But I had more money, and so
had my people, when I made war for the King of England. Why,
on every foray we chanced on some rich mercer of Toulouse, Con-
don, Riolle, or Bergerath : and scarce a day but brought us some
good booty—*dont nous étions frisques et jolis.*" On which the Breton
gentleman laughed and said, " Ah, that's the way with you Gascons
—always after plundering your neighbours "—and the chronicler
made a mental note that the Sieur D'Albreth probably repented that
he had "turned French." Other of his countrymen, we learn,
dissatisfied with the "kindness" shown them at court, went back to
their own country and their allegiance to the English crown.

It is quite a pathetic reflection that the only proposed "invasion

of England " (1385) was, like several of later date, a miserable and
ruinous failure, ridiculed by Froissart with such scathing details of
English contempt as French historians, otherwise given to citation of
that author, do not like to reprint.[1]   And while a return of the black
death decimated the population, whole countrysides were often, by
the forays of the nearest resident nobility, swept of the better class
of inhabitants, whose ransoms had to be ground out of a starving
peasantry, only left behind for this useful purpose. The condition of
the latter, at the close of the fourteenth century, may be studied from
the nude in the bald and agonising "Plaint of the poor commoner
and labourer," preserved for us by Monstrelet.[2]

It was also an age of peculiar and frantic extravagance among
the upper classes. The chronicler of St. Denis goes so far as to
attribute the defeat of his compatriots at Crecy (1346) to their
ridiculous and impossible style of dress. While the upper clothing,
made of the most expensive materials and elaborately embroidered,
was so tight that to take it off "was like *skinning* a person," and

---

[1] The chapter (III. 36) is headed : "*Of the useless expenditure on the French
Navy and of the good preparations of the English to resist them.*" English men-at-
arms mocked at the proposed invasion, and insolvent free companions comforted
their debtors, saying, "The florins that shall pay you are now a-coining in
France."

[2] After ch. cclxiv. of the first book "s'ensuit" without any introduction "la
complaincte du poure commun, et des poures laboureurs de France."

> "Helas, helas, helas, helas,
> Prelats, princes et bons seigneurs,
> Bourgeois, marchands, et advocats
> Gens de mestier grans et mineurs,
> Gens d'armes, et les trois Estats
> *Qui vivez sur nous laboureurs*
> Confortez nous d'aucun bon ayde :
> Vivre nous fault, c'est le remède," &c.

And the numerous verses that follow appeal with cogent logic, but as yet
humbly enough, to each of the above classes in turn. *Chroniques d'Enguerran
de Monstrelet contenant les guerres civiles*, &c., qui suyvent celles de Fr oisrart.
Chez P. Mettayer. 2 vols., fol. Paris, 1595.

required assistance, the sleeves were so long that they almost swept the ground. At the date of Poictiers, ten years later, French knights and nobles went about laden with gold and jewels. The Duke of Orleans, brother of Charles VI., wore, embroidered upon his sleeves, "at full length," the ballad "Ma dame, je suis plus joyeux." The *notes of the tune* were represented by *five hundred and sixty-eight pearls !*

The contrast of such barbaric luxury with the appalling misery of the labouring classes appeared even to the latter to be part of a natural law. The lower orders, ill-fed, neglected when not oppressed, fell in thousands, as a contemporary Latin poet tells us, "before the lightest breath" of the destroying plague.[1] "But fierce Fate spared princes, nobles, knights, judges, gentlemen ; of these few die, because the life allotted them is one of enjoyment." "*To the poor life is more cruel than death.*" The pleasures of life, under such a *régime*, seemed strictly reserved for the upper classes.

Upon the phenomena of unrestrained individual conduct we have in this sketch specially dwelt. France was not the worst governed of countries at a period when every Italian city, as Sismondi summarises the matter, had its tyrant, every tyrant was stained with the blood of his kindred, and atrocious crime seemed the recognised avenue to political power. King John, by no means a bad specimen of a king, after raising 600,000 florins by the sale of his daughter Isabel, aged eleven, to Galeazzo Visconti, Duke of Milan—she was the affianced bride of Gian Maria, afterwards celebrated as the most ferocious monster that ever sat on a throne, who hunted men in the streets of his capital and cast them alive into ovens[2]—escaped from the burden of his national and feudal re-

---

[1] Cited from a French MS. in Wright's edition of Piers Plowman.

[2] See *Corio, Istoria di Milano, & Giovio, Vite de' Visconti* (8vo, 1632, p. 162). Poggio Bracciolini (1380–1459), a contemporary, merely says, "ipse nonnullos vivos lacerandos canibus edendosque objecit." *Historia Fiorentina*, 4to. 1715, p. 160 (sub. anno 1403). Giovio gives the name of the Huntsman.

sponsibilities to the Paradise of—London, where, as we commonly
read, he ate himself to death in 1364. Charles VI., torn in pieces
by the unchecked fury of every evil passion—bloodthirsty and
other—found a different refuge—assisted, it was thought, by the
machinations of sorcerers—in insanity. Had there been a few more
monarchs like Pedro the Cruel, we should never have heard ill of
the Comte de Foix. It is but for one trait that we recall this tyrant,
who in any museum of the moral monstrosities of the age would
occupy a class by himself.

When at the suggestion of "a trusty Jew" (whose fair daughter
he loved) Pedro had despatched a "sergeant" to strangle his wife
(sister of the King of France), he revoked the order two days later,
thinking that the murder of a virtuous lady *of such high lineage*
might run counter to some dimly discerned ethical convention.
It was, unfortunately, too late. The sergeant, wearying of the
"pretty orisons" which she had leave to say first, had stifled the
queen with a cushion ; and thus the whole force of Pedro's repent-
ance was diverted upon the Jew. The man of money was beguiled
awhile by the redemption of his teeth at 100,000 crowns apiece,
which (according to the biographer of Du Guesclin) *seriously
impoverished him.* But to Pedro it seemed but poor fun. The
wicked Jew was accordingly tortured in true mediæval fashion,
blinded with hot irons, &c., &c., *écartelé*, and finally hanged.[1] A
catalogue of the awful crimes of the century would fill many
volumes. It is yet more appalling to think to how many an individual,

> Pinned to earth by the weight
> And persistence of hate

of the *instans tyrannus*, death itself, as the poet above quoted tells

---

[1] *Chronique de Bertrand du Guesclin* (1314-1380), ed. Fr. Michel (with
portrait and facsimile of Bertrand's signature), sm. 8vo., Paris, 1830, where the
whole story is related. This excellent and entertaining little history is one of
those that call themselves "Romances" in the linguistic sense of the word.

us, must have been welcomed as a relief. Justice, though assisted by the revival of torture, did but feel in the dark after minor wrong-doers, without affording peace or security to the average harmless and industrious citizen. True, there was the cloister. But that nothing may be wanting to complete the picture, even religious ties and hopes were enfeebled. The Papal Court of Avignon[1] was a very sink of iniquity; and in 1378 came the great ecclesiastical schism, shaking men's religious convictions, and undermining their allegiance to the Church long before Reform had attained shape or power to replace it.

Mediævalism, in fact, with all its fierce chiaroscuro of blood-stained splendour, is at its apogee, on the very verge of the precipice down which are doomed to slide all human institutions and types of society against which human nature itself comes to rebel.

And through the whole scene, past pillaged house and wasted land, in gay converse with robber baron, knight, and esquire, good queen and wicked prince, ever goes "gallivanting" the cheery Froissart, Canon of Chimay, and *soi-disant* Canon of Lille (for the reversion never fell in), recking as little of Church preferment as of the unpaid tavern bills in his parish at home—filled with but one thought, the splendour of his age and the magnificence of the portrait of it which he would leave behind, and "well knowing," as he avows with his usual frankness, that "when I am dead and rotten this grand and lofty history shall be known far and wide, and all noble and worthy folk shall therein take great pleasure and profit."

[1] De Sade, *Mémoires pour la Vie de Fr., Pétrarque* (3 vols. 4to, 1764), i. 60 & *passim*. Poisoning, we learn, was much in vogue, but rivalled by *magic*, in particular the use of waxen "*imagines*" of the person or persons to be removed, which, in order to accomplish this object, were pricked and burnt. See Christina Rossetti's eerie ballad of "Sister Helen."

From De Foix's *Deduicts de la Chasse, &c.* See p. 53 n.

III.

A SHELF OF OLD STORY-BOOKS.

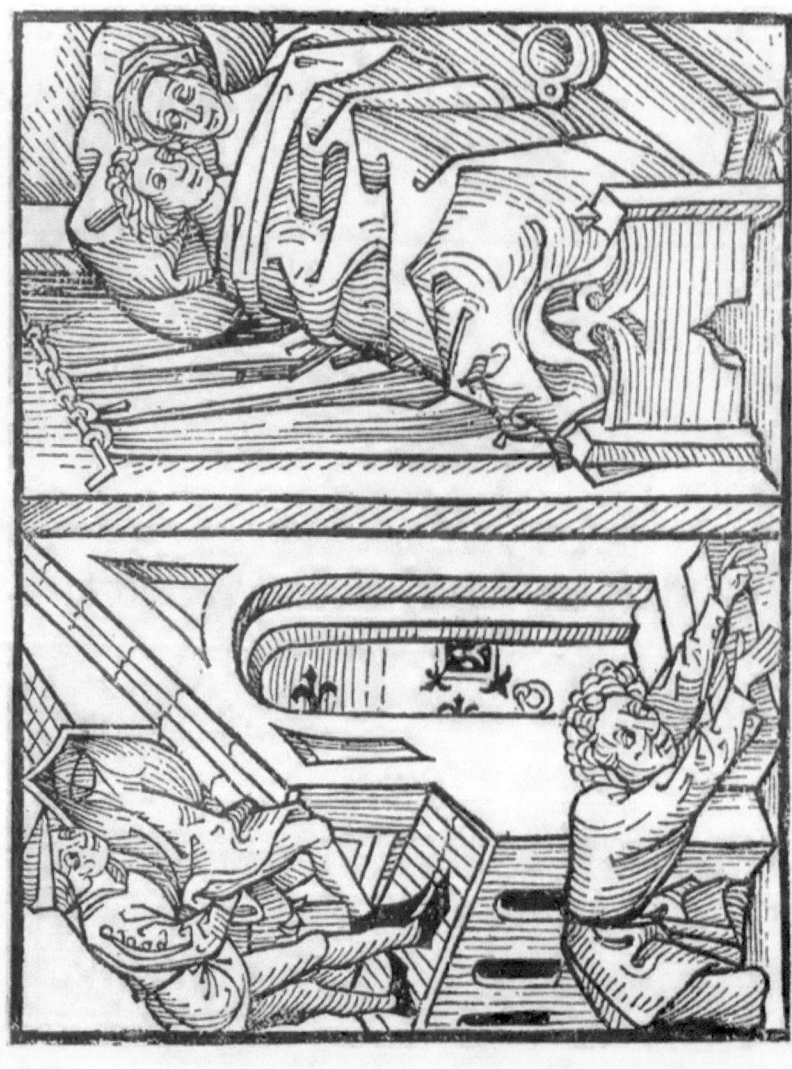

Woodcut to the "Fable of the Robber and the Moonbeam," from the profusely illustrated *Directorium humanæ vitæ alias parabole antiquorū sapientū* [verbum Johannis de Capua post palpationem ritus Judaici divina sola inspiratione ad firmum verum statum orthodoxæ fidei revocatij] 1480. See p. 87 n. and p. 88, *post.*

I.—THE HUNTING OF THE MYTH.

YTHOLOGY, comparative or other (though a positive mythology seems hardly conceivable), has in modern days become a science so vast and serious as to be quite terrifying to the casual reader. Scarcely may he peruse the fairy tale that charmed his childhood without being reminded of its " variants " current in Kamschatka or Timbuctoo : and a school of instructive and destructive criticism which has descended upon old-fashioned literary conventions as the Goths and Vandals descended upon the smiling plains of Italy, has shaken to its foundations that last stronghold of self-satisfaction—a faith in the independence of our own national and local " ideas," and in the originality of our favourite authors.

That the field of such a science should be vast in both dimensions of time and space is, however, not to be wondered at. We have but to consider the number of deliberate story-tellers in any age, to add thereto the proportion of persons incapable of reporting exactly what they have seen or heard, to multiply this' sum total by the quantity of credulous individuals for ever anxious to hear some new or apparently new thing, and to allow for the increase of the product by a sort of geometrical progression during any given number of centuries, and the matter becomes statistically obvious.

The realm of inquiry, then, being not only immense, but misty in outline, and roughly co-extensive with the history of mankind, the principal danger for the inexperienced tyro is, that he should wander aside from the faintest of tracks into that arid and pathless desert where wild specialists chase one another for ever through the dusty void.

Kept within reasonable and humane bounds, the pastime of myth-hunting has as decided and satisfying a charm as any other sport. Nor should the bibliophile be precluded from dallying therewith, after his fashion. In fact, it is with a view to encourage him in so doing that this chapter has been written.

The invaluable M. Le Roux de Lincy, at the end of his excellent edition of those *Cent Nouvelles Nouvelles*, which amused the youthful exile of Louis XI. (a work first printed by Antoine Vérard in 1486) appends a most interesting genealogical table, showing (1) where the original form of each story, if known, is to be found; and (2) what more recent authors have imitated or worked it up into something different, and (to all, perhaps, but the expert in these studies) new and strange.

Thus, if we take, for example, Novel No. 50 contributed by Antoine de la Salle (the supposed author of the *Quinze Joyes de Mariage*), the "original" is to be found in the *Facetiæ* of Poggio Bracciolini (1380–1459) who probably had it from some obscure Latin source. An imitation, on the other hand, appears both in the "novels" of Malespini and in *Tristram Shandy*. No. XIV. again, which one may read in Marmontel, and in the *Contes* of La Fontaine, is given chapter and verse in Josephus.[1] "Origin," of course, can only

---

[1] Professor Morley, in his popular edition of the *Confessio Amantis* of John Gower (1327-1408) has noted in a similar manner the many and various sources from which that author drew the famous collection of stories which he has loosely and pleasantly arranged under the headings of the "Seven Deadly Sins." Josephus, the "Thebaid" of Statius (96 A.D.), Justin's Epitome of Trogus Pompeius, the Books of Daniel and of Kings, these—besides other mediæval and classical works —are among his materials, of which Ovid (especially in the Metamorphoses) sup-

be a comparative expression for a large proportion of such cases. Mediæval stories deal largely with questions of conduct little affected by changes of man's environment. The *Cent Nouvelles Nouvelles* are no more new than they are "proper," and Barbazan's fascinating three volumes of *Fabliaux*, though containing a few incidents that border upon decency,—may all be described as primitive, especially in their morality ; and many of them might, from their general drift, have been confided to Eve by the old serpent, about the date of the Fall of Man.

European man, however, experienced a sort of second fall during the "dark ages," and the true mediæval story has not the healthy simplicity of an early classic myth, but presents the appearance, like certain old books, of having been not only thumbed and handled, but repaired and perhaps fraudulently "hocussed-up" by successive hands. Homer, on the other hand, and Æschylus, and the Eddas, so complete is the Scandinavian rejuvenescence, recall the virgin splendours of an unsullied "original impression."

plies as much as all the remaining authors put together. Then the curious tale of the adder, which *stops its ears* (a feat still puzzling to many a juvenile reader of the Psalms) *with its tail*, is taken from the " Etymologia " of St. Isidore, of Seville (570–635), author of a Chronicle of the Goths printed with that of Jornandes, (8vo, 1597).

And the story of "Alexander and the Pirate" (in Bk. III. *Wrath;* ch. 5, *Homicide*) is assigned to Augustine, *De Civitate Dei*, and the Gesta Romanorum. Prof. Morley does not, however, give its original source, which may be found in a curious note to Jannet's edition of Villon. François Villon, who recounts the anecdote in a good ballad, assigned it to Valerius Maximus.

> " Valère pour vray nous l'escrit
> Qui fut nommé le grand à Romme."

But it is not in the " Dicta et Facta Memorabilia " of that author, and it *is* in the fragment of Cicero's treatise *De Republicâ*, preserved by Nonius Marcellus, a grammarian of the sixth century, and will be found on p. 558 of the Plantin Edition (8vo, 1565) of his *De Proprietate Sermonum*, under the word " Myoparo," which means a pirate boat. The story was apparently unknown to Quintus Curtius and to Arrian.

Few myths indeed can boast a pure and authentic genealogy; nevertheless the tracking of this curious and cross-bred game, up hill and down dale, so to speak, across the wilds of history soon becomes quite an exciting occupation.

Soon also the reader finds that to follow it with comfort and satisfaction he must surround himself with such a portentous pile of volumes as would attract attention even in the rotunda of the British Museum.

With modern fiction and the leading dramatists we may presume him to be well supplied. La Fontaine, Don Quixote, Boccacio, Chaucer (with Tyrwhitt's introduction to the *Canterbury Tales*), the *Cent Nouvelles Nouvelles* already referred to, the *Heptameron* of the Queen of Navarre (1575) and other such standard works do but represent the "cover" in which the sport is ordinarily carried on. But in case of a bare "idea" breaking back in the direction of antiquity, we must have ready all the ancient classics—Homer, Hesiod, Herodotus, Plato, Aristotle, the Æsopian fables (including those of Babrius and Avienus), and of course Virgil, Ovid, and the Latin classics, through which so much of Greek myth (notably in relation to Purgatory) filtered into the mind of the early theologian. The ancient classics, we say, assuming that the reader's shelves are lined with respectable Dindorfs and Hermanns, Oxford and Cambridge texts bound in academic "russia," and profusely annotated with the *obiter dicta* of some distinguished lecturer now dead and gone. But supposing that to the original text he should prefer a comprehensive "crib," there is none better than the splendid *Bibliotheca* of Apollodorus the Athenian; who flourished in the second century A.D., late enough to safely include the whole of classical mythology in his handy and very readable compendium. Heyne published an excellent edition of this work, which contains elaborate genealogies of gods, demigods, and heroes (2 vols. sm. 8vo, 1782-3) and Thomas Gale collected in a *rare* (but unfortunately very incorrectly printed) volume, the works of Apollo-

dorus, and four other early mythologians, including the " Transforma-
tions" of Antoninus Liberalis (cir. 150 A.D.). These *Historiæ
Poeticæ Scriptores*—8vo, London or Paris, 1675 (with copious
index)—are worth adding to our list. Theology, again, will be represented by the Bible, the Koran,[1] Augustine, the *Sentences* of
Petrus Lombardus,[2] and a few of the more conversational fathers,
of whom more anon. Next let us pass to rarer works, firstly
the series known as the Italian novelists, noting the editions
which it is desirable to secure. Almost a contemporary of
Boccacio is Sacchetti (2 vols. 8vo, 1724), and in the sixteenth century
appear quite a galaxy of famous collections, almost all of consider-

---

[1] The Koran of Mahomet, it may here be observed, represents, according
to modern researches (see Gibbon, vol. VI., and the profusion of variorum
notes), a mere compilation, by the hysterical fanatic whose name it bears, of the
religious doctrines of the Arabians of the seventh century, edited in no particular order by his successor, Abu Bekr. The details of Arabian life and
manners, and the fictions, even the grotesque parodies and perversions, embodied
in the work give it a great historical and mythological value, in spite of the re-
volting artificiality of its style. "*All this stuff*," says the judicious Sale (who,
unlike certain modern Orientalists, is not altogether *désorienté* by the intoxicating
influence of "the East") "*seems to be a confused recollection of the Beast in
Revelations*"—a remark which many a Christian is moved to repeat, *mutatis
mutandis*, of other flowery passages in that tiresome imposture.

[2] The classical *opus magnum* of Pietro Lombardo (1100–1164), hight
"Master of the Sentences," a work said to have produced more commentaries
than any other known to history, is, as Hallam observes, a "magazine of arms"
drawn from the works of all the Fathers, for the use of scholastic disputants, a
compilation of immense labour, somewhat in the form of a legal text-book. It
deals with such abstruse questions of theology as, where the Creator abode before
creation—whence Satan fell and how far—why Adam and Eve did not become
immortal, and why the latter was made from a rib—whether the Israelites were
guilty of theft in spoiling the Egyptians, &c., &c.

"On all these points and points obscure as these," among which lurk the germs
of many a later myth, we can only refer the reader to the copious indices appended
to the excellent edition of the "Magistri Sententiarum Libri IV. 8vo. P.
Landry, Lugduni, 1594." Peter the Lombard was Bishop of Paris, and an
appendix to the work contains a catalogue of the opinions condemned during the
two following centuries by the authorities "in England and at Paris."

G

able rarity, the *Cento Novelle Antike* (probably compiled in the thirteenth century) 4to, Bologna, 1525; the better known *Novelle* of Bandello, of which three volumes appeared at Lucca in 1554, the fourth at Lyons in 1573; and those of Nicolo Granucci, an extraordinarily rare work, of which a fuller description may interest some readers. It is curiously entitled—*Di Nicolao Granucci di Lucca L'Eremita, la Carcere e 'l Diporto* (Prison Diversions); *opera nella quale si contengono Novelle, et altre cose morali; con un breve compendio de Fatti più notabili de' Turchi* (Turkish history, manners, and customs were at this date the subject of indefatigable curiosity), *sin' a tutto l'anno* 1566. Lucca: Busdraghi. 8vo, 1569. His *Piacevol Notte e lieto Giorno, opera morale* (what the Renaissance novelist did for morals it is difficult to estimate!) in Venezia: 8vo, 1574 ("volume assez rare," *Fournier*) is better known. Granucci was born in 1530.

Next might follow the perhaps equally rare *Notti Piacevoli* of Straparola da Caravaggio (1550 and 1553), the common volume of *Facetie* edited by Domenichi and the rarer *Recreations* of Ludovico Guicciardini, nephew of the great historian, which appeared at Antwerp in 1585. Of the fifty stories of Giovanni "Fiorentino," published under the title of *Il Pecorone*, Milan, 1558, an edition described as "rarissimo," the wretched counterfeit dated "Milano, 1554" (*i.e.* Lucca, 1740) is to be avoided. The *Prima e Seconda Cena* (with one story from the third) of Anton Francesco Grazzini, *Il Lasca*, may be purchased in the octavo edition, London (*i.e.* Paris) 1756. Last, but most indispensable, come the *Duecento Novelle*, above mentioned, of Celio Malespini (2 parts in 1 vol. 4to, Venice, 1609), a precious collection, which fetched £3 12s. at the Pinelli sale. If we add two curious little duodecimo volumes, the *Facezie e buffonnerie del Gonnella e del Barlacchia e diversi*, Florence 1616, a decidedly out-of-the-way work, and *L'Arcadia in Brenta, ovvero la malinconia sbandita*, Colonia 1667, this will do by way of Italian literature for the present. The *Arabian Nights'*

Entertainments in twenty odd volumes, with copious index, will please us then, the *Fables* of Bidpai, the *Hitopadesa*, and one or two modern handbooks to Oriental literature.

The great Flemish satirical "Beast-Epic" *Reynard the Fox* (Van den Vos Reinaerde),[1] will often be useful for reference, in either of the modern editions containing the original text.

To turn to our own country, there is one work of an absolutely unique interest, and from which, in the words of a modern editor, "all our great vernacular poets have drawn the materials for their noblest works of fiction," to wit, the celebrated *Historia Britonum*, composed or translated (from sources now lost or unknown) by Geoffrey of Monmouth before the year 1147, and containing the complete and orthodox legendary chronicle of Britain from Æneas to King Arthur, in what is apparently its most original accessible form. This work, of such immense popularity in the Middle Ages. and upon which in our own days volumes have been and will continue to be written, the reader will possess in Dr. Giles's useful edition, 8vo, 1844, which also includes the abridgment by Ponticus Virunnius.[2]

But there is something almost sacrilegious in the suggestion that any "bibliophile" would care to study this subject in a modern text loosely covered with green cloth. We therefore proceed to give him a selection of more artistically interesting "early printed" repositories of anecdotes and fiction, which, since all the volumes

---

[1] With the Latin Isengrimus, German versions, and kindred minor pieces. Ed. Jacob Grimm. Berlin, 1834.

[2] Published, together with the first edition of the Welsh Itinerary (1188 A.D.) of Giraldus Cambrensis in a small 8vo, ap. *Henr. Bollifantum, Londini*, 1585 (edited by David Powell). My copy has the inscription "J. H. Newman, given by G. H. Exmouthiæ, Aug. 1842." The history of Merlin is contained in the *Historia Britonum*, but the volume of "Prophecies" published by Michel and Wright in 1837, is assigned to another author. Geoffrey of Monmouth is severely handled by his contemporary, William of Newburgh (d. 1208): "Gaufridus hic dictus est, *agnomen habens Arturi*, quod fabulas de Arturo ex priscis Britonum sermonibus sumptas, et *ex proprio auctas*,...historiæ nomine palliavit."

are worth having, and their typography will be found to assist an appreciation of the mediæval frame of mind, he should at once—to save trouble—order of the nearest bookseller.

Any such a selection, to whatever length it be extended, must of course begin with that unique storehouse of pious fiction, the Golden Legend,[1] or, properly speaking, the *Legenda Sanctorum, aureum opus Jacobi de Varagine*, a work, which from its nature, has required constant re-editing to keep it up to date. Next would come the *Gesta Romanorum, cum applicationibus moralizatis*, folio (cir. 1473); the *Dyalogus Creaturarum moralizatus* (and illustrated with woodcuts), Goudæ, 1480, a work which reappears later under the title *Destructorium Vitiorum*; the *Speculum Historiale*, &c., &c., of Vincent of Beauvais (ob. 1264)—in the fine edition by Mentelin of Strasburg, fol. 1473,—a cumbrous volume within whose oaken iron-bound doors, one cannot call them covers, lies a perfect storehouse of

---

[1] This wondrous compilation, put together by the original author about 1290 A.D. (and called after him by an eighteenth-century critic, a "*vorago Fabularum*"), was originally also known as the "Historiæ Lombardicæ," a title which properly belongs, as Fabricius points out, to the "Life of S. Pelagius." In the small folio edition printed by Nicholas Petit (black letter, Lugduni, 1535) which lies before us, the work is entitled "Legenda—opus aureum, quod Legenda Sanctorum vulgo nuncupatur," &c., but the colophon is "Explicit legenda aurea sive lombardica histori(c)a." The life of S. Pelagius forms ch. 177. The author takes it, as he tells us, from the History of the Lombards of Paul Warnefrid (730–796 A.D.), where it will duly be found, *De Gestis Langobardorum*, 8vo. Plantin, 1595 p. 95, &c. Legend 176 contains the history of Prince Josaphat and the monk Barlaam, abridged from that of Joannes Damascenus. (v. *post.*)

The "additions" by subsequent editors comprise St. Lazarus, St. Anselm, St. Louis, and St. Thomas Aquinas, of whom the first at least might, one would think, have been mentioned before. After the Ascension, we here learn that the persecuting Jews put Lazarus and his sisters and a number of other Christians into a boat without oars. By Divine assistance, however, they succeeded in reaching Marseilles, of which city the Saint became the first Bishop, bequeathing at his death the usual quantity of relics.

The epithet "golden" is, it need hardly be said, frequently applied, by authors themselves, throughout the Middle Ages and the Renaissance to describe what in modern times would be called, as this certainly is, an "indispensable" work.

obscure and impossible mediæval lore ; and the *Directorium vitæ humanæ*, fol. s.a. (1480) which is easier reading in the Latin translation than in the original Arabic—a work of unique importance, of which a word shall be said presently. Scarcely less indispensable would be the *Speculum Exemplorum* of Thomas Cantimpratensis (1200–1270) folio, Strasburg, 1487 ; and the *Sermones de tempore* (or occasional discourses) with the *Promptuarium Exemplorum*, composed by the Dominican Herolt, about 1418, and published under his *nom de plume* of "Discipulus" in Nuremberg, 1475 (and elsewhere 1481, 1484, &c.), and the extraordinarily rare *Novellino of Massuccio Salernitano* (who wrote in the fifteenth century and in the Neapolitan Dialect) which first appeared in folio at Naples 1476, but was reprinted some half-dozen times in Italy alone before the close of the century. The first edition is to be preferred. To conclude, the last three works upon our little list shall be perhaps the most famous, or singular of all : to wit the *Historia Alexandri magni regis Macedonie de preliis*—a moderate-sized volume—first printed at Cologne, 1480 ; the *Book of St. Barlaam and of Josaphat King of India* (1st ed. cir. 1470) of which an Italian fifteenth-century text was published by Bottari, 8vo, 1734 ; and the wondrous legend of the "Seven wise men of Rome," otherwise known as *The Historia Calumniæ Novercalis*—folio, 1475, a volume by common account, of great attraction, although the White Knights copy only sold for £10 15s.

Of the substance of this last romance, an admirable specimen of its kind, we may here add a word, premising that we draw it from an Italian source, the *Libro de' sette Savi*.[1] The framework of the stories is familiar enough. The phenomenally clever youth instructed by the seven sages is each morning rescued from execution (to which his father the Emperor sentences him, at the instance of the jealous young stepmother, whose amorous overtures he had re-

---

[1] Printed from a fifteenth-century MS. in dialect, alla Libreria Dante, 8vo, Florence, 1883.

jected) by a judicious apologue interposed by one of the wise men, and, to balance this diversion, the wicked stepmother tells her royal husband every *evening* a fable embodying an exactly opposite moral. This ingenious mechanism, it will be seen, provides a sort of double self-acting Arabian Nights' (and Days') entertainment, which but that the number of wise men is limited, and that none were apparently heard twice, might have revolved round the axis of one monotonous situation for evermore, or at least as long as the central character, the auditor, was simple enough when confronted by the vaguest precedent to go on inquiring "How—or why was that?" It lasts a week, which is quite enough, and then the wicked stepmother is burnt, on which the reader feels a distinct sensation of relief. Through the dim atmosphere of this confused fable the modern student may discern as in a fog the uncertain outline of the remorseful Llewellyn and the faithful Gelert, Joseph's dream and reception of his brethren in Egypt (?), and other less familiar legends. The oddest thing in the book is perhaps the decision by the Pharaoh of one narrative (assisted by the newly arrived Joseph, whose wisdom enabled him of course to understand bird language) of an extremely doubtful question in the law of divorce and maintenance (!) raised by three *crows* who pestered the monarch, for what reason no one could tell, until, upon the above explanation, he delivers a judgment which they accept as final. The Italian is translated more or less from an earlier Latin version (particles of which still adhere to the "vulgar" text). Both this, and the variant of the thirteenth century attributed to "Dam Jehans" of the Abbey of Hauteselve, in which the king is known as Dolopathos,[1] and Virgil is the principal wise man, are translated or imitated, as authorities tell us, from the Hebrew work known as the *Parables of Sandebar* (first published in

[1] See Brunet and Montaiglon's preface to Jannet's "Elzevirian" edition of *Li* vast and tiresome *romans de Dolopathos*, where the uncertain relations of the *Hist. of the Seven Sages, Dolopathos*, and the *Fables of Sandebar* are discussed. Inasmuch as the (so-called) *Fables of Bidpai* have (in the opinion of some editors)

a collection ; of opuscula, printed at Constantinople, 4to, 1516, and at Venice 1544, 1568, and 1605), and the said Parables are again derived from a Persian translation or imitation of—and here we reach the usual terminus of such research—an "ancient Indian work."

obtained a wider circulation than almost any known work, the following genealogical sketch of the principal imitations and translations may interest the reader.

ORIGINAL SANSKRIT.

The *Pantcha-Tantrum*, or "Five Collections," ed. Kosegarten, Bonn, 1848.
This, the earliest existing text, is said to be a "second redaction."

PEHLVV (*i.e.* Ancient Persian version) by Barzuyeh, physician of Nuschirvan (6th century A.D.), with additions and introduction, and entitled *Fables of Bidpai.* (See *Gibbon's Rome*, V. 186, ed. 1872, and editor's note.)

THE HITOPADESA. A collection later in date and more corrupted than the Pehlvy version.

HEBREW. Attributed to the Rabbi Joel, containing two chapters not in the "Calilah and D." "Bidpai" is here metamorphosed into "Sandebar" v. *Silv. de Sacy.*

ARABIC VERSION. By Abdallah Ibn Almokaffa, 9th century A.D., entitled *Calilah va Dimina* (names of the two interlocutors). Ed. Silv. de Sacy, 4to, 1816. Engl. by Knatchbull. Oxford, 1819.

LATIN VERSION. By John of Capua (13th century A.D.). Sub. tit. *Directorium Vitæ Humanæ.* First printed 1480, and source of innumerable modern versions, *e.g.*

DONI. Filosofia morale (1552, 4to).

SIR E. NORTH'S VERSION. Reprinted, ed. Jacobs, 1880. Shakspeare, &c.

1ST (mod.) PERSIAN VERSION. By Abou'l Maali Nasr Allah cir. 1137 A.D.

SPANISH (?). Utilized by Raimond of Béziers in his Latin version, cir. 1300 A.D.

GREEK VERSION. By Simeon Seth, cir. 1081 A.D., translated in *Specimen Sapientiæ vet. Indorum*, Berolini, 1697.

2ND PERSIAN VERSION. Recast in a modern and popular form by Hosain baez Caschefi, cir. 1530 A.D., in his *Anvari Sohaili*, or "Lights of Canopus" (The Emir "Sohaili" being compared to the favourable star Sohail=Canopus).

3RD PERSIAN VERSION. By Abou'l Fazl., 1621 A.D., entitled *Eyari Danisch* (Touchstone of Knowledge).

TURKISH VERSION. A mere reproduction of above, by Ali Tchelebi, cir. 1540. Dedicated to Solyman the Great. Sub. tit. *Homayoun-Nanieh* = "Royal Book."

FRENCH. Of Galland and Cardonne : *Contes Indiennes de Bidpai, &c.* 2 vols. 1724.

FRENCH. Of David of Ispahan, or rather of Gilbert Gaulmin (1585-1665), *Livre des Lumières des Rois.*

ENGLISH. *Instructive, &c., Fables of Pilpay.* London, 16—, 7th ed., 1775, w. plates.

Similarly the "Directory of Human **Life**" above mentioned is a Latin translation by one John of **Capua**, also of the thirteenth century, the genealogy of which is almost equally complicated. The Greek text is drawn, through the **Fables of** Bidpaı, from the early Sanskrit "*Pantscha Tantrum*," or "**Five Collections**," the source of the once ancient esteemed collection of **Fables** known as the *Hitopadesa*, and indeed the well-spring of Fabular Fiction.

The reader who does not keep an original *Directorium*, may perhaps be able to lay his hands upon the *Specimen Sapientiæ Indorum liber ethico-politicus pervetustus*—an edition of the Greek and Latin together, published at Berlin, 8vo, 1697.

It will naturally be inferred that but few of the black letter folios enumerated above represent original work. They are at best Latin versions, for European circulation, of what thus became the popular light literature distinguished by its more or less "improving" drift and moral, from the merely idle romance of chivalry of the fifteenth and even the sixteenth century.

The *Vita et res gestæ S. Barlaam et Josaphat Indiæ Regis*, above mentioned, is a translation into the vulgar tongue probably made by the Papal Librarian Anastasius in the ninth century, of the "mystic" Greek romance, as Brunet describes it, attributed to the ascetic S. John of Damascus (who died in 754 A.D.), and abridged, as has been said, in the Golden Legend. This last-mentioned divine, the author of a tract against the Iconoclasts (printed by Aldus in 1554) was a wealthy and noble Christian holding high office under the Khalifate at an early period in the development of Arabian literature.

"East is East and West is West," sings a modern bard, but the rise of the Saracen power and the Mahometan invasion of Europe represent, as far as concerns modern literature, the most distinct point where "the twain *do* meet," though how far the distinctive Oriental and European imagination and taste, are ever capable of amalgamating is another question. Of the immense popularity of the works drawn from such sources there can be no possible doubt. Their very strangeness gave them a vogue. To take for example the Romance of Alexander, to the subject of which we shall presently return,—of the Latin text four fifteenth century editions are well known. Cologne, 1480 ; "*à Albi, en Savoie,*" 1480 ; Strasburg, 1486 and 1490. Of the *French* translation *three* editions were printed at Geneva, 1492, 1494, and 1498, one at Paris (n.d.) in 4to, and another undated 4to at Lyons, which recently sold for nearly £20. A *German* edition ("*Hienach volget, &c.*") black letter Augsburg 1472, is described as extremely rare. A *Dutch* version appeared in 1483. A *Spanish* 4to, 1530 and 1583. Finally an *English* translation (of the first edition of which the British Museum possesses only an imperfect copy) was printed by Wynkyn de Worde, apparently in 1520, and by Copeland of Flete Street, somewhere in the fifteen-fifties. Lastly, the romance appears at Edinburgh in "Scottis meter," 8vo, 1575 ;—and that, we trust, will satisfy the reader. Of the "Seven Wise Men" and the "Book of Barlaam" the editions are simply innumerable.

To return from the rehearsal of these prosaic details to our list of "hundred best books," for the study of humane fiction in general. Of French works perhaps too little has been said, but then so many of them are well known. Besides the great satirical hotch-potch of Rabelais—a work which invites an unlimited amount of learned editing (though why any one should attempt to translate it into modern English passes our comprehension)—there are two important original collections of floating fact and figment to be mentioned (and curious facts, it must be remembered, often repeat themselves in successive ages), to wit, firstly, that great repository of sixteenth century scandal, the *Apologie d'Herodote*.[1] A volume or two of the "free sermons," of which Estienne gives such entertaining extracts, may be thrown in ;[2]

---

[1] See note on p. 44.

[2] *E.g.* Michel Menot's *Sermones Quadragesimales olim Turonis declamati*, 8vo. black letter, Paris, 1525. These discourses, in a jargon of French and Latin, are highly entertaining, and throw some light upon the history of manners and morals. Estienne, by the way, does not cite this volume (the Tours sermons), but those preached at Paris—"volume moins rare "—8vo, 1530.

and secondly, the still more singular but less serious production of
Beroalde de Verville, so ambitiously described as "*Le moyen de
parvenir, ouvrage contenant la raison de tout ce qui a été, et sera.*"
Then if we add the *Nugæ venales*, a little volume frequently reprinted
during the seventeenth century, and the Duc de Roquelaure's
Roger Bontemps (1670), all the modern story (or fairy) books red,
blue, or green that we know, *Dunlop's History of Fiction, Ducange's
Glossary*, and a couple of dozen other standard works of reference,
we might, in a leisurely fashion, get to work, at least upon some
of the less abstruse mythological exercises. One may, of course,
take up the research either in the middle (with M. Le Roux de
Lincy) or at one end, if it can be found, as is not always the case.

We are reminded of this when we approach that most famous of
all mediæval fictions—for their supremacy seems to be quite unquestionable—the immortal *Arabian Nights' Entertainments*. As is
the case with so many collections, their origin is provokingly obscure.
Perhaps, indeed, the extreme popularity of a work which is imitated
and translated by a score of hands, as soon as it is known, naturally
augments the difficulty of tracing the original.

The earliest mention of what is believed to be the "archetype" of
the *Thousand and One Nights* was discovered by the learned Von
Hammer, in the chronicle of a well-known Arabian historian writing
about the year 945. This author, whose names are too long to rehearse, in a casual reference (of which he can little have foreseen the
importance) to certain current stories of the time, remarks that
educated people looked upon them as mere inventions, "*like the
' Thousand Fanciful Tales.'*"[1]

The earliest history of Arabian literature (*cir.* 987 A.D.) assigns the
said work, which was regarded in the tenth century as a "corrupted
collection of silly (literally cold or tame) narratives" to a Persian

[1] See the critical review appended to Lane's English version of the "Thousand
and One Nights." Ed. E. Stanley Lane Poole. 3 vols. 8vo, 1883.

origin. *An* Arabian version existed as early as the twelfth or thirteenth century; and it seems to be agreed that the work, as we
know it, is an Arabic compilation, made and augmented at various
dates from perhaps the tenth or eleventh up to the sixteenth century,
and chiefly in Egypt, for while the fame of Haroun El Raschid, to
whose reign most of the stories purport to refer, extended far from
Bagdad, all the MSS. contain frequent and exact descriptions of
Cairo. In a word, the *Thousand and One Nights* is, modern com-
mentators tell us, "as much an Arabian work as Virgil's *Æneid* is a
Latin."

Their original source, or sources, it is in most cases impossible now
to discover or disentangle. The task might literally in judicious,
that is, in sufficiently learned, hands

"Extend from here to Mesopotamy"

and embrace, as Von Hammer remarks, even Homer himself in an
early Syriac version. But then Homer, we know, in spite of Mr.
Andrew Lang, was himself probably "put together" from earlier
materials in the eighth century B.C., and who really wrote him no one
precisely knows. How far, then, must the wearied student look
backwards for finality? Scarcely, it seems, shall he find it in
the grand simplicity and primæval calm of a Vedic hymn !

But to take up the matter (of the *Arabian Nights*) from its other
chronological end, no existing text is known to be earlier than 1548,
the date which chanced to be inscribed upon the imperfect MS. from
which Galland worked, which MS. by the way does not contain
eleven of the most famous of the tales, including "Aladdin and
the Wonderful Lamp," and "Ali Baba and the Forty Thieves." It
was never discovered until the other day, after near two centuries of
doubt, wonder, and suspicion, *whence* Galland had obtained these,
and all that we now know, from an entry (March 25, 1709) in the
translator's journal recently unearthed (1888) in the Bibliothèque
Nationale, is that he derived the eleven tales from one "Hanna,

a Maronite of Aleppo." But who was Hanna? and where did he get them? No one seems to know. Such are some of the broken threads which make up the vast tangle of comparative mythology.

The delightful French version of Galland (first published 1704–1717) many of us know and love better than later and completer editions. Indeed the dimensions of the great Burton translation[1] are almost terrifying; they recall too realistically the original conception of an endless serial which never stopped even with a Christmas number. "Half-hours" of light fiction pass very well, but who can face "Ten Hundred Sleepless Nights with the Best Authors"?[2]

Incomplete is a mild expression for the first instalment of the Tales, which embraced, as the translator himself tells us, only one thirty-sixth part of the stupendous whole. Yet Galland, though a deliberately loose translator, in the opinion of many good critics, really improved on his original by the omission of many of those ornamental absurdities which jar upon a European ear. Arabian fiction has been said to be characterised by a certain "coarse broad humour, and a terrible and gigantic sublimity," which inevitably trenches now and then on the ridiculous.[3] Moreover a certain

---

[1] A new and but slightly abridged "Library" edition is now announced in twelve volumes at the price of £6 6s., of which critics seems to agree that it will probably be quite "complete" enough for the average reader of moderate means, and rather too much so for the subscribers to the original extra-complete and curiously annotated Burtonian text, of which it might well have taken the place.

[2] "Frappée de la clarté du jour qui commencait à paraitre Scherazade ne dit pas davantage." *Mille & une nuits, passim.*

[3] See a most interesting work (cited repeatedly by Lane), *Remarks on the Arabian Nights, the origin of Sindbad's Voyages, &c.,* by Richard Hole, LL.B. 8vo. Cadell, 1797. "An excellent little book" (Lowndes), which figured in the Fonthill and other catalogues. "Ouvrage fort bien fait," adds Brunet, "et qu'on ne retrouve plus facilement." (*Même dans la boîte à six sous où nous venons de le déterrer.*) In this volume the relation of Sindbad's adventures to the actual experiences (and erroneous inferences) recorded by European and Oriental explorers of India, China, and Japan, and to the professed fictions of earlier classic writers

artificiality of form, and in particular a passion for reasoning by
way of question and answer—as the reader will presently see—serve
to identify the genus.

But it is rash to dogmatise from such sensations, in regard to any
particular episode or story. To tear off the original environment of
the hero, and to clothe him in bran new vestments of another place
and time is, to an able mythologist, the work of a moment. Thus,
to return to Antoine Galland, who, besides the *Mille et Une Nuit(s)*,
the *Contes Indiennes de Bidpai et de Lokman* (2 vols. 8vo, 1724), and
other works, also published a celebrated collection of Anecdotes and
Maxims,[1] one would never have guessed that perhaps the most
familiar of all British schoolboy anecdotes—that, to wit, of the

is discussed with considerable learning. Sindbad is of course frequently in accord
with Marco Polo and other travellers. Lucian, in the second century A.D. had
already produced a rival to the Roc "as big as twenty vultures" (*Vera Historia*,
Bk. ii.). The "Old Man of *the Sea*" (a mistaken address) is really a well-ascer-
tained Ourang-outan; and Benjamin of Tudela, who travelled late in the twelfth
century, either borrowed from or furnished to Sindbad his method of escaping, *by
the assistance of an Eagle*, from the Valley of Diamonds. (v. *Benj. Tudelens's
Itinerarum.* 8vo, Antwerp, 1575, p. 98.)

[1] *Orientaliana ou les Bons Mots des Orientaux, &c.*, selected from various
original sources, including unpublished MSS., with copious notes and index,
8vo, Paris, 1701. The story of the inquisitive man is on p. 35. The work first
appeared under another title, "*Paroles Remarquables*," &c., in 1694, and an
English translation in 1695. The volume contains a great deal which is historically
interesting in a very readable form, but it must be admitted that the stories are
not as a rule what would now be called amusing. A son and heir is asked if he
wishes his father would die. "No," he answers, "I wish some one would kill
him, that I might have the blood-money as well as the inheritance." *Quel bon mot!*
A Persian poet reads his second-rate verses to a person of taste. "They were
composed on the spot," he urges. "I should think so," answers the critic, "they
smell of it." (Nothing is said of the insanitary nature of their subject.) *Quelle
plaisanterie!* The stories mostly break off—they can hardly be said to conclude—
with the rudest and inanest of platitudes. Some are mildly amusing, such as the
answer made to the proud author of a poem in which the letter Aleph had never
been used: "Why not omit all the others?" The majority reflect a strange and
to most temperaments somewhat uncongenial frame of mind.

inquisitive Irishman who looks over the shoulder of a gentleman writing a letter, and by an indignant denial of the reflection therein made upon his impertinent curiosity, inadvertently convicts himself —was to be found in such a work, from which, however, we have doubtless borrowed it.

With regard to fiction in general, in spite of the maxim that there is nothing new under the sun, competition seems to run distinctly in the direction of antiquity, and "latest authorities" are commonly employed in knocking century after century off the age which certain classic works have successfully claimed in less critical days.

Associating, as one inevitably does, a certain rude vigour with a quite "primitive" antiquity, probably many readers are surprised to find that the mythological Eddas as we know them, for example the ballads first popularised by Gray,[1] are only to be assigned to about the same date as the "silly and corrupted narratives" of the *Arabian Nights*. The question is, of course, one of independent and very diverse racial developments. At the date of the genesis of the Eddas, the Northmen, as we have good reason to know, carried all before them, and bullied the feeble and struggling infancy of the France and Europe of the dark ages. But (up to and of course

---

[1] Now easily obtainable in Dr. Finnur Jónsson's edition of the *Gedichte Mythologischen Inhalt's* (text, critical notes, and glossary). 8vo, Halle, 1888. See p. 69. The oldest MS. of the Eddas dates from about 1250. Snorro Sturleson's work was published by Rask in 1818.

In Gray's time the Eddas seem to have been accessible only in the chronicle of Torfæus, and in the valuable and somewhat rare *mélanges* of T. Bartholinus— "Antiquitates Danicæ—*de causis contemptæ a Danis adhuc gentilibus mortis*," with engravings, 4to, Hafiniæ, 1689, from which Gray's translation (or rather imitation of the Latin translation there given) was made. The editor of the Poems (Scatcherds' ed., with portrait and front. by Burney, 8vo, 1779) wonders why Gray omitted the first five stanzas of *Odin's Ride*. Probably because Bartholinus does not give them. The "Antiquities" include a large selection from unpublished texts, and should be added to the list of useful books abovementioned.

excluding Mr. Henrik Ibsen) what have they since produced that rings in our ears like the last lines of Odin's ride? The secondary and artificial period sets in with the prose Edda attributed to Snorro Sturleson (1178–1218). "*D'abord le chant*," as M. Xavier Marmier puts the matter, "*et puis l'analyse*." [1]

The *Arabian Nights* in which, as has often been remarked, there is hardly any mention of war, is the expression of an already corrupt and, indeed, as we now know, a profligately immoral civilisation. Not a trace of Saracen vigour is to be perceived in the luxurious and enervated "mercantile" society from which its characters are drawn. The fiction, for a work of what Europeans call the dark ages, presents to us quite a surprisingly modern and conventional artificiality. But the utter dearth of moral and spiritual energy makes this society more trying, in a sense, more puzzling to the modern, or at least to the Teutonic mind than the violence of Odin and Thor, or the mysticism of an Æschylean chorus. These things seem to us to correspond to something either in the forces of nature, or in our own intelligence or aspirations. But the Oriental imagination (which for this if for no other reason we can hardly expect to understand) [2] is

---

[1] *Lettres sur l'Islande*, 1837, containing an excellent abridgment of Scandinavian mythology.

[2] But if in the best known Oriental literature there are aphorisms and witticisms and rhetorical ornaments of which we do not appreciate the point or force, that is but a natural and trifling uncongeniality. For genuine mediæval obscurity, nay, for blank head-splitting unintelligibility, we need look no further than the nearest Celtic *chef d'œuvre* of the dark ages. Take for example Dallan Forgaill's celebrated elegy in praise of St. Colomb (*Amra Choluim Chilli, &c.*, edited from the MS., with literal translation and notes, by J. O'B. Crowe, Dublin, 1871) composed late in the sixth century.

"*He cried*," sings the poet (c. 21), "*a melodious lion in a snow's new meeting*;" and then follows the explanation (infinitely more trying in each case than the text): "Like the roar of a melodious lion in snow in a new meeting is the praise of the strong one, that is, Colum Cille ; for when the lion gives his roar out of him, all the animals come at it *until he gives a coil of his tail around them, so that there die in that place a flock of rats and of foxes* (!). The hunter comes to

distinguished, as a French critic observes, "by an abuse of the imagination and intellect" and a contempt of "nature."

To trace the kinship between the North and the East, we must
in fact go back to the literature of early India. Take, for example,
the immensely striking idea of the "*Churning of the Ocean, in order
to recover Amrit, the lost drink of Immortality,*" which occurs in that
colossal epic the *Mahabhàrata*,[1] and is probably seven or eight
centuries older than the Eddas, which it at once recalls.

---

him then until he gives nets about him afterwards, so that he dies. Thus Colum
Cille." We trust the reader follows the analogy. "Dignity of mind," we read
elsewhere, "came for the cleric." Such language, which is no obscure jest of the
translator's, sounds like something out of the *Star* newspaper (1894), and brings
a stifling crowd of burlesque associations about the reader's brain. "Thou hast
leave," says the cleric, "*to be on a craneing on which thou art.*" "Thou hast leave,"
says the cleric, "to be on a craneing" (*sic*)—so that it is then she "was turned
into a crane"! And Englishmen wonder that they cannot understand the people
whose ancestors, to the number of many hundreds (see *Forespeech*), wrote such
poetry as this, until—and here a ray of comprehension dawns upon us—they
were "banished for their burdensomeness." The Life of St. Patrick in the Book
of Armagh (Irish Antiq. Researches, Dublin, 1827) is far more readable fiction.

[1] A lucid analysis of the two great epics, the *Mahabhàrata* (which contains
100,000 stanzas) and the *Ramayana*, will be found in ch. 1 of Marshman's History
of India. These stupendous works, composed a century or so before Christ, and
referring to events—the careers respectively of Krishnu and Ramu—of about
1,000 years earlier, may shortly be said to embody all the earliest traditions of
India (thickly overlaid, especially in the case of the Ramayun, with supernatural
mythology and Brahministic doctrine), and to be the sole sources of Indian History
before the Mahometan invasion. The earliest literature of India is now accessible in Prof. Max Müller's *Sacred Books of the East*, Oxford, 1879, &c.,
translated by various Oriental scholars. The Hymns of the Rig-Veda, "the most
ancient literary monument of our Aryan race," of which *the existing text dates
from the sixth century B.C.*, have just been published in English with a popular
commentary (Benares, Lazarus, 1894. See *Athenæum, No.* 3502) by Mr. Ralph
Griffith, the translator of the Ramayun, whose "Specimens of Old Indian
Poetry" (produced so long ago as 1852) contain selections from the Vedic Hymns,
the larger poems, and the Law of Manu, in a convenient form. The *Questions of
King Milinda*, a work of great importance, and a cardinal text on Buddhism, is
translated, in the series above-mentioned, by T. W. Rhys Davids, Oxford, 1890.

In fact the golden age of Sanskrit literature, so much of which has of late years been brought within reach of all English readers, appears to coincide with the beginning of the Christian era, and what is described as the only artistic prose work of ancient India—the *Questions of King Milinda* (*i.e.* it is supposed, "*Menander*, one of the kings who carried on in Bactria, the Greek dominion of Alexander the Great") was composed about that date, and conveys the didactic ethics of its age in the form of a historical romance.

Apart, however, from rude and vast primitive fancies bearing the stamp of "ancientry," scores and hundreds of simple stories of human and animal life, more or less ethically applied in the example, as the Spanish call it, or fable, are, beyond doubt, of great antiquity, though it is not always traceable, and the number of these imported at one date or another from the East is enormous.

Pour "passer au déluge," to omit that is the common stock of simple (and largely agricultural) ideas which the "Indo-European group" inherit from their parent race an early Oriental idea may arrive at the modern English reader either by the main line, so to speak, through Greek, Latin, and Italian, or French ; or indirectly, as will be seen presently, by a more or less tortuous Aryan or Semitic route. Again an incident or fancy traceable to an Arabian source (whether original or borrowed from India) may have been indirectly imported through Byzantine Greek or late Latin in the Middle Ages, or directly during either the Moorish invasion of Europe, or the European crusades into Palestine.

From the catalogue above suggested—the outlines of which the intelligent reader can fill in for himself—it will be seen that an adequate Library of Fiction, properly indexed, should enable him to stop or tap any given figment, by whatever route or channel it approaches or departs, and whether it be a complex chapter in some elaborate "cycle," or the simplest human incident, of obvious

H

"moral," and world-wide application. Thus to take the common-
place story (cited by Richard Hole from *Beloe's Miscellany*) of *The
Man* (it should be "two men"), *the Lion, and the Serpent,* which is
apparently foreign, but affords no exact evidence of date, one might
easily speculate as to when it was imported. As it happens, however, we know that it came in in the twelfth century, since the
whole story is printed at length in Matthew Paris. That author—
who, by the way, has a good deal to say about the "Fables" of the
heretic Mahomet—tells us (*sub anno* 1195, on page 241 of the folio
edition of 1570, cited above) that Richard Cœur de Lion, who it is
presumed brought the legend home from the Crusades, used to
repeat it to his courtiers to enforce the moral of gratitude to
benefactors.

The tale is not a striking one, but reads comically in the Latin
of St. Alban's. The King's real object was to persuade more of
his courtiers, and especially those upon whom he had conferred
honours, to take service in the Crusade demanded by Pope Celes-
tine III. With this aim he himself "turned preacher," and taking
up his "parable" told the company of one Vitalis, a wealthy Venetian, who one day wandering in a wood fell into a pit artfully prepared
for lions and serpents, and indeed already occupied by two of those
intelligent animals, who, however, as Vitalis "fortified himself with
the sign of the Cross," allow him unmolested to "howl and yell"
for a day and a night. Then arrives on the scene a poor charcoal-
burner, who, on a promise of half the rich man's fortune (500 talents).
rescues him and also the lion, which plays about and wags its tail,
and the snake, which "squirms" and "hisses softly" with delight.
The lion subsequently brings the poor man a kid, and the serpent
finds him a precious gem ; but the wealthy Vitalis, on his safe return
to Venice, forgetful of solemn oaths and promises, declines to pay.
The charcoal-burner insists on having the law of him, produces the
gem, and conducts witnesses to a personal interview with the lion
and the snake, whose exhibition of delight, though clearly only evi-

dence against the beasts themselves, satisfies the judges of the truth
of the whole story !

Thus King Richard, by way of reflection upon the ungrateful.   It
may be presumed that some of the "circumsedentes," who knew
nothing of comparative mythology, must at once have handed in their
names as volunteers.   The parable was already at least 300 years
old, being drawn from that inexhaustible Oriental source, the
Calilah va Dimnah, alias the *Fables of Bidpai, or Sandebar*.[1]

Under the title of ***The Story of Bardus the Fagot Gatherer***, it was
popularised by Gower (Book V., ***Avarice***, chap. 6, *Ingratitude*), and
duly re-appears in the ***Gesta Romanorum***.

[1] See note to p. 86.

Woodcut from the *Dyalogus creaturarum*, printed by Gerard **Leeu. Goudæ.** 1480. (*Brit.
Mus.* C. 38, h. 3.) The typography and illustrations of this **famous volume** are of peculiar
excellence.

CHRONOLOGICALLY and naturally enough the mention of Richard I. suggests the subject of a certain *chef d'œuvre* which we had intended shortly to review, after concluding the above prefatory remarks, and which seems never to have been printed in complete form until the present century, though it may very possibly have been read by Cœur de Lion, or have served to distract the mind of the suffering King John.

The *Disciplina Clericalis* of Petrus Alfonsus, a Spanish Jew, baptized in the year 1106, at the age of forty-four, is one of the most famous collections of its kind. Under another name (and especially under that of the French version, *Le Castoiement d'un Père à son Fils*, published by Barbazan in 1760) this pious composition is well known to every student of early modern literature. In fact the notes and cross references appended by the learned F. W. V. Schmidt to his edition of the Latin text (8vo, Berlin, 1827) seem to embrace the whole literature of mediæval thought, to say nothing of the fiction of some twenty centuries. From Aristophanes to Hans Sachs, from Eginhard to Muratori, all the past is laid under contribution by an editor, who, not content with printed books, quotes long passages from priceless and out of the way manuscripts, and Greek translations of obscurer Æthiopian originals.[1]

[1] The celebrated and highly apocryphal *Book of Enoch*, which has been since published (3rd ed. revised and enlarged, Oxford, 1838; translated from the

To the unprejudiced reader the expression *Disciplina Clericalis* is at first sight an unattractive title, no more suggestive of a mine of anecdote than is *A Lover's Confession*. Looked into more closely we see that it only means the education, religious as well as intellectual, of a gentleman and a scholar, at a period when this was not such a serious business as it is now-a-days.

But it was no simple matter even then. "There are," we read (chap. vi. 6), "seven arts, seven probities (*probitates*), and seven industries. The seven arts are dialectic, arithmetic, geometry, physics, music, astronomy; *about the seventh philosophers differ;* some say that it is 'science,' some 'grammar,' which one would have thought, as literature is not mentioned at all, would have come before the other six.

"The seven prowesses are riding, swimming, shooting with the bow, boxing, fowling, *playing chess* (!), and writing verses.

"The industries (*i.e.* virtues, and no such bad name for them,) are not to be greedy, drunken, luxurious, violent, mendacious, avaricious."

The mastery of chess may be a prowess, but it seems strange that "versification" should go in the same class with boxing.

In that precious monument of typography, the *Summa quæ vocatur Catholicon* of Joannes de Januâ (alias Giovanni Balbi, ob. 1298), the "seven arts" of mediæval education are more methodically and, sensibly defined. I. The *Trivium* (a triple road to eloquence) grammar, dialectic, and rhetoric. II. The *Quadrivium* (the fourfold road to wisdom), arithmetic, music, geometry, and astronomy. Those who took up No. I were called "Triviales," those who preferred the second "Quadriviales." "Trivialis" is, of course, quite independent in meaning, though not in origin, of "trivial," nor can we positively describe the "trivials" as a sort of "poll"-men, though they

---

Ethiopian MS. in the Bodleian Library by Archbishop Lawrence) is a unique source of history upon the period immediately preceding the Deluge, an account of which by Noah (who, according to Tertullian, at least revised the work) occupies chapters 64 to 67.

obviously would fall into an inferior class. Gregory of Tours, in the sixth century, alludes to these seven branches of learning, in the celebrated *Apology* for his own defective style appended to the *Historia Francorum*, and incidentally explains that *Rhetoric* meant a mere knowledge of metres, and Matthew Paris, seven hundred years later, speaks of an educated man as one "*in trivio et quadrivio excellentissimus.*"

To return to the *Disciplina Clericalis*. We are clearly informed how and why Petrus Alfonsus wrote the work. The Almighty had endowed him "with manifold wisdom," which he did not think it right "to hide under a bushel." But considering the frailty of human nature, he had endeavoured to convey his instructions in an entertaining and not too tedious form. "Accordingly," he tells us, "I have compiled this little book partly from the proverbs of philosophers and their counsels (*castigationes*), partly from Arabian proverbs and counsels, and fables and verses, partly from similitudes of beasts and birds. In fact there would seem to be very little really original matter in the book. The greater part is either purely Oriental, or what has filtered through some Eastern channel from an earlier European source.

All that is strangest in incident in early European fiction, we are disposed to assign, by virtue of that uncongeniality which has been discussed already, to an Oriental origin. On the other hand, the "mediæval mind" is itself a strange thing which requires some understanding; a childish intelligence, it often seems, darkened by suffering, and deranged by moral and intellectual disease, yet with intervals of singular and sometimes hysterical mirth—little more intelligible to us than its terribly materialist attempts to pigeon-hole all human intelligence, and its verbose confusions of names, numbers, and things.

Thus the stories of the pious Petrus Alfonsus interest us chiefly as part of the history of civilisation, and are mostly, as we say, "in an atmosphere." In the first place, and in spite of the author's assurances, their subject-matter hardly strikes one as moral.   Like most other mediæval fictions, they treat very largely of the infidelity of the fair sex, a subject popular with Boccacio, and hardly yet exhausted ; and in the second place, while giving unquestionable advice they darken counsel strangely.   Familiar characters appear, but pursue their ends in an oddly *blasé* or topsy-turvy manner.   The most celebrated personages of antiquity come upon the scene, yet somehow they are not quite as we remember them.

Virgil, the poet and the country gentleman, is an individual of whom we naturally feel that we know something.   Yet his character passed very early into the realm of the supernatural, being almost worshipped, if only as a genius, soon after his death.   Perhaps he would never have sung of magic, and charms potent

cœlo deducere lunam (Bucolics, Ecl. 8),

and would even have denied Æneas the pleasure of a visit to the infernal regions, could he have foreseen how such diversions would be misunderstood by subsequent generations.   At any rate Virgilius, schoolmaster, necromancer, and mesmerist—Virgilius the wooer of the "Sodan's daughter of Babylone," the builder of Naples on a foundation of eggs, the inventor of innumerable and highly dangerous automatic toys, including the wondrous "coper man and horse" (the historic if not etymological equivalent of the modern "copper"), which kept the streets of Rome from "theues and nyght-ronners "—this Virgil is perhaps the most refreshingly novel and entertaining figure in the whole world of fiction, especially in the English text "emprynted in the cytie of Antwarpe," with woodcuts, by John Doesborcke.[1]

But the conduct of Aristotle is more seriously trying to the unsuspicious modern student.

He leaves the venerable Stagirite gravely discoursing of the "excess" and "defect" of dignity ("hightonedness," as Americans

---

[1] *One copy known*, from which Utterson reproduced sixty in 1812, all presumably "well held" at the present date.

perhaps translate it) and such virtues, or asserting, with ever so little
of a grin, that it was ridiculous to talk about courage "at sea."
Returning late in the Christian era he discovers the philosopher
—to his horror!—*saddled and bridled*, capering skittishly about
an Oriental garden with a young lady in scanty clothing, the mistress
of Alexander, upon his back! To the cultivated mind this is a
severe shock. The learned Pope Pius II., better known as Æneas
Sylvius, took it seriously to heart. "What are we to say of philosophers," he asks, "when they do such things?" What, indeed?
But we soon find out that it is not Aristotle's fault at all, since
Aristotle, and, for that matter, Alexander the Great and Socrates, and
Virgil, and Joseph of Arimathæa, and numerous other celebrated
individuals [1] are only, as Mr. Lewis Carroll might put it, "persons
in the dream" of the mediæval mythologer.

As the editor of the *Disciplina* explains in a lucid and interesting
note, there are in fact—in myth rather—if the startled reader can
believe it, no less than *three Aristotles.*

For firstly, there is the "here altogether to one side laid"
Aristotle of *History*, who died in 322 B.C., and upon whose works—
which are nearer akin to the modern mind than any mediæval
lucubrations—our university professors continue to lecture.

The second is the corrupted and perverted Aristotle celebrated in
the literature of his time, as the fountain head of "Scholastic"
Philosophy and Theology, in the form in which he appears from the
time of Boethius (say 500 A.D.), but who only takes a definite
position in the Christian literature of Western Europe through

---

[1] The "Lyfe of Virgilius" (a fiction of Italian origin) will be found in the
admirable selection of "Early Prose Romances," edited by Prof. Morley (*Rout-
ledge's Carisbrooke Library*, *No. IV.*), who points out its relation to the "Seven
Sages." Of "Joseph of Arimathie or the Romance of the Holy Grail," an
"absolutely unknown poetical version," and others printed in the sixteenth
century, were published by Skeat (Early Eng. Text Society), 1871. On the vast
and obscure subject of the Saint-greal, see a very learned work recently published
by Mr Alfred Nutt.

Arabian translations, and corruptions of his works.[1] Thus the conventional attitude of the mediæval mind towards the great philosopher is strongly affected both by ignorance and prejudice—as may be inferred, indeed from the allusion in Hans Rosenplüt's Play of the *Seven Masters*, or wise men, composed about 1450;

> " Hie vindt man *loyca* mit irer list "

(Logic, that is, and its cunning)

> " Die lert was falsch und unrecht ist
> Ir meister heisst Aristotiles."

Poor man !

His third impersonation—and the one with which we are here concerned—is the purely mythical Aristotle evolved by the Oriental imagination out of Jewish and Arabian traditions, and made the subject—one cannot say the hero—of various strange tales.

Of these, the most famous is that embodied in the French Fabliau (see the collections of Barbazan [2] and Le Grand d'Aussy) and entitled in the former *Le Lay d'Aristote*, in which the philosopher, having warned the youthful Alexander against the excessive and degrading servitude of love, is himself subsequently victimised by the fair charmer and exposed to the ridicule of the conqueror of the world in the painfully absurd position above mentioned.

---

[1] Cf. Hegel, *Geschichte der Philosophie*, ed. 1844, iii. 119. The historical interest of the Arabian acquaintance with and predilection for the works of Aristotle lies in the fact that for many centuries " all that the Western world knew of him was derived through this channel "—that is, through Arabian versions, selections, and commentaries, some of which were but vaguely related to the original —re-translated into Latin (*with sometimes a Hebrew version between the two*) by Spanish Arabs and Jews in Africa, Spain, or Portugal. During the early Middle Ages the study of Greek was, it will be remembered, *almost unknown* in Christian Europe. Very few writers of the time have a first-hand acquaintance even with Homer. As their philosophy was for long drawn from Arabian sources, so their Greek mythology was almost exclusively derived from Ovid and his low Latin imitators.

[2] *Fabliaux & Contes des poëtes François des* 12e, 13e, & 14e *Siècles* (original texts and glossary), 3 vols., sm. 8vo (or rather 18mo large paper, well printed in good-sized type). Paris, 1756. See vol. i., 155.

It is obvious that ninety-nine hundredths of this story which, though once so popular, would hardly amuse the present generation, is Oriental fancy.

A Bishop of Ptolemais who spent the closing years of his life at Rome, Jacobus de Vitriaco, imported the fiction into Europe early in the thirteenth century in his famous *Historia Orientalis et Occidentalis.* It enforces a moral concerning women in Herolt's *Promptuarium Exemplorum,* mentioned above. A French author works it up, as we have seen, into a lengthy *Fabliau,* and Hans Sachs into a comedy (of the year 1554)—*Persons, the Queen rides the philosopher Aristotle, and has five acts.*

From Aristotle we naturally turn to his distinguished pupil.

That a strange and rich web of fiction should weave itself about the name of Alexander the Great was natural enough. The real magnitude, and the distance from Europe, of so many of his exploits (which recalls Mr. Hume's argument concerning miracles) rendered such a result inevitable, human nature being what it is. " Alexander died," as Hamlet tells us, " Alexander was buried " about the year 323 B.C. But the first real history of his astonishing expeditions—and a most excellent and readable one it is—which has come down to us is that of Arrian, the Nicomedian, who was Governor of Cappadocia in 134 A.D.

Arrian is a most conscientious writer ; and while he pins his faith to the two contemporary historians (Ptolemy and Aristobulus) where they agree, he is constrained to observe upon the remarkable differences in the various accounts given of the life of his hero.

" These things I mention," he tells us at the close of a chapter (vii. 27) containing various traditions as to Alexander's death, " rather that I may not appear to be ignorant of what is commonly reported, than because I think them worthy of credit." But we may be sure that many of his readers, and many writers of bad Greek or " infamous Latin " failed to note the distinction.

What could be expected then, when Quintus Curtius, a rhetorician with a decided taste for the romantic, and imperfectly acquainted with Greek, takes up the tale, at an uncertain date in the first or second century? He refers indeed to "authorities" (which include already at least one romancer, Clitarchus), but, having a lofty contempt for chronology, repeats their diverse accounts of identical events "as if they referred to different things," a practice leading to confusion.

The modern German editor can discover "only three passages where he attempts to distinguish truth from falsehood." The dreadful result of all this being that Quintus Curtius, although a trifle flowery, produced, at this shockingly early date, what has been described as a "readable historical novel," which had undoubtedly an immense, nay, a fatal vogue. Any one can understand this who will take the trouble to turn to his capital chapters on the conspiracy of Hermolaus, and the death of Callisthenes the friend and biographer [1] of the monarch. A modern demagogue addressing a "capitalist" could not speak with greater frankness and prolixity than the unfortunate page expounding the attitude of an aggrieved military employé towards the despotic conqueror of the world. (Q.C. viii. 6–9).

The author indeed says elsewhere when relating wonders which Strabo, Ælian, Plutarch, and Pliny merely state as facts, "I transcribe more than I believe" (*De rebus gestis Alexandri*, ix. 1); which shows that, in spite of what has been said, some feeling for history still hung about him. Pausanias felt the same difficulty, and the

---

[1] Callisthenes, the nephew and disciple of Aristotle, was put to death by Alexander in Bactria, 328 (see Arrian, iv. 13), for his supposed connection with the conspiracy to murder Alexander in bed, which was only defeated by that monarch's fancy for sitting up all night

"drinking, drinking, drinking."

Callisthenes perished, but his ghost walked many centuries later, and the pseudo-Callisthenes furnished materials for almost all the later histories of Alexander, *except*, it would seem, the Irish version, which, like the Irish Odyssey, appears to be an "original compilation." See notes to Kuno Meyer's edition (and literal translations) of these works. (D. Nutt, 1886.)

same obligation to posterity. In the true Middle Ages, the question how much a writer or reader could believe soon became immaterial.

The first mediæval writer on the subject would seem to be Gaultier de Chastillon who, about 1180 composed a passable epic poem, the *Alexandreis* (8vo, 1541) in ten books, beginning

> Gesta ducis Macedum totum digesta per orbem
> Quam large dispersit opes, quo milite Porum
> Vicerit et Darium, &c., &c.
> Musa, refer.

in which one only observes a slight deficiency of "ear," and of grammar. But Gaultier whose work was in the thirteenth century preferred to the ancient classics, descends in a later passage to a miserable "play po' words," writing

> Forte Fortunæ pereo, si pareo ; mentem
> Non sinit insontem fortuna potentior esse.

Nor does he scruple at an atrocious pun.

> Hæc *secura* manet, in me parat illa *securim.*

Since then various poets have descanted in vulgar tongues upon the theme. Before the close of the twelfth century, Alexander of Paris became joint author of another famous epic (in lines of twelve feet, " *hence called Alexandrines,*" but after which Alexander it seems doubtful), recounting the "gestes" of the Macedonian monarch, lightly flavoured with early French history. The most celebrated of all these works is the immense "Poema de Alexandro" in 2,514 four line rhyming stanzas (" Alexandrines " of fourteen feet) which occupies the third volume of Sanchez's celebrated collection.[1] It was once attributed to Gonzalez de Berceo (1190–1266) but internal evidence assigns it to Juan Lorenzo Segura de Astorga, who probably was writing about 1200 A.D., and who refers with the

[1] *Coleccion de Poesias Castellanas anteriores al siglo XV°* (5 vols, sm. 4to, Madrid, 1779–90), an indispensable work. Vol. i. contains the "Poema del Cid."

profoundest respect to the *Alexandreis* of the above-mentioned Gaultier.

Without tracing further, then, the growth of this particular branch of Oriental-European mythology, whose ramifications extend over two hemispheres, the reader will see that the authors of romances, of chivalry, and Fabliaux, in the next two or three centuries, could suffer from no dearth of material, of a kind, concerning Alexander the Great.

But to return to the last mention of him in the *Disciplina*, which also occupies the last chapter of the *Historia Alexandri magni de prœliis*. His tomb was of gold, and a large number of philosophers assembled and heaped laborious epigrams upon it. Thus one said—

> " Alexander made a treasure of gold,
> Now things are changed, gold makes a treasure of him."

(The "Lyke" of Alexander supplies by the way another subject to the voluminous Hans Sachs). Another said—

> " Yesterday the world did not suffice him.
> To-day four ells of cloth are enough."

Another—

> " Yesterday he could free many from Death,
> To-day he could not himself escape Death's darts."

And another (the eighth) said—

> " Yesterday he had friends and enemies,
> To-day all are alike to him."

All which we read word for word in the last chapter of our *Historia Alexandri magni regis macedonie de preliis* (Argentinæ, 1486), in which work moreover it is asserted—a detail of more intense actuality than any here mentioned—that Alexander, when first feeling that he had been poisoned, "got a feather" (*quæsivit unā pennā*) and tickled his throat, but unfortunately to no purpose.

" But it would be tiresome (*memoriæ longum*) to rehearse all that

the *thirty-two* philosophers said of the most mighty king," especially
as they are rehearsed in so many other places.

For this relief the youth, whose powers of memory are being considered, should have been thankful ! The most ancient literature was
more refreshing than such originality.

Chapter xxiv. is a complicated variant of the Æsop's fable of the
countrywoman and the Wolf. In this version a ploughman says to
his oxen, when they would not go straight, "Wolves eat you up !"
Now when Brer Wolf heard this he lay low (*quod lupus audiens
acquievit*) ; but at evening, after the man had done ploughing, he
went up to him and said, "The oxen, please, that you promised me."
The ploughman answers that he had *said* so, but not sworn it. " But
you gave them me," said Brer Wolf, "and I ought to have them."
So they went to law about it.

But on the way they meet the Fox, who, having heard the dispute,
says, he can decide it for them as well as any judge. " But I must
first speak a word to each of you in private." And first he spoke to the
ploughman, "Give me a hen, and my wife another, and you shall
have your oxen." "Agreed," says the ploughman. Then he turns
to the wolf, " My good friend, for your singular deserts my eloquence
is bound to make every effort. I have so persuaded this country-
man that if you will let his oxen go scot free (*quietos*) he will give
you a cheese (what natural history are not fabulists responsible for !)
as big as a shield."

Then Brer Fox takes the deluded wolf off by a long and circuitous
route to a well, which they reach by moonlight, shows him the reflection of the *half-moon* in the well, and says, " There is your cheese, go
down and eat it." The wolf's cautious request that he, Brer Fox,
should go down first, is the cue for the celebrated well and bucket
trick, to which, moreover, the whole weight of the introductory
moral (belonging by rights to "The Dog and His Shadow") is
appended ; the rest of the story remaining as pointless as the
descriptive part of a Virgilian simile.

In Æsop, La Fontaine, and all orthodox fabulists, it is of course the goat upon which the fox exercises his ingenuity, in order to escape from an unpleasant predicament, and the original fable is said to have given rise to a popular phrase (see Plato, *Theætetus*, 165, B) descriptive of an embarrassing situation. Pulci (*Morgante maggiore*, ix. 75) appropriates the version here given.[1] The confusion and fatuity of many of these hybrid fables, the characteristic, it would seem, of a curiously indolent sort of ignorance, is something almost past belief. The writer seems to think that the orthodox postscript direction "Apply to sinner" (*applica ad peccatorem*) could give point to the most inconsequent ancedote.

For sheer inanity one might be disposed to give the palm to the following.

A coy young lady will not her heart incline to an amorous youth. The latter consults an elderly confidante (the one good and wise woman of whom the philosopher can remember hearing). This astute person has a little dog which she starves for three days and then feeds with bread and mustard, which makes it weep.

Followed by the weeping hound she pays a call on the coy one, who is struck by the melancholy air of the animal. "Why does the little dog weep?" she inquires. "O don't ask," replies the wise woman, "it is too painful a matter."

Finally, however, the necessary fiction is imparted to the maiden. "That little dog," says the confidante, "used to be my daughter, who

---

[1] In ancient fable, as in natural history, both ancient and modern, the fox maintains the reputation of superior astuteness. It would be interesting to know at what date, and among what Indian or African tribe, the rabbit developed the cleverness so constantly emphasised in the stories collected by Mr. Joel Chandler Harris. But the "Rabbit and the Lion" in the *Instructive, &c., Fables of Pilpay* (ed. 1775, p. 14, see note above) is identical with that given in *Uncle Remus and his Friends;* and the "Elephant and the Rabbits" shows another example of cunicular wisdom. Does the clever rabbit first appear in the Persian *Lights of Canopus* (1530), from which this English text is derived, through a bad French translation?

was passionately loved by a certain youth, but she was coy and refused to marry him. So she is now always weeping from remorse."
The young lady is taken in, without a struggle, expresses her terror
of becoming a little dog and weeping mustardy tears for ever more,
and, the tolerably obvious moral having been clearly driven home,
agrees to marry the rejected lover. This story is expanded and improved in the MS. text quoted by Schmidt from the Greek *Seven
Wise Masters*, itself a translation from the Syrian.

Side by side with such half-fairy tale fiction we find the serious
"modern instance." The following simple story occurs also in the
Gesta Romanorum.

A rich man wished to pick a quarrel with a poor young man, his
neighbour, and to obtain possession of his house which he would
not sell.

So he begged to be allowed to store in the courtyard ten barrels
of oil, offering to pay for their safe custody. The youth reluctantly
agreed. But the crafty rich man had filled five of the barrels *only
half full;* and when the time came for restoring them, complained
that the young man had robbed him of the oil, and brought him
before a magistrate.

The youth, in great straits, repairs to a certain philosopher in the
city known as "the Helper of the Needy," who takes up his case,
and being universally respected is invited to take a seat, we must not
say on the bench, but near the judge. Then, the plaintiff having
been heard, the philosopher makes a suggestion that they should
ascertain the exact amount of fine oil, and of sediment respectively,
in the full barrels. If the same amount were found in those only
half full, then clearly the oil had been stolen. If not, the young man
was innocent, as is accordingly demonstrated. The "*Auxilium
Egentium*" subsequently decides another abstruse case in a fashion
faintly recalling that of Solomon.

But few sages in the story seem to have made themselves so practically useful. In fact the quantity of pretentious wisdom distributed

about the book in small parcels of miscellaneous advice is appalling. Of the utterances of the immense staff of "philosophers" employed upon the task not more than a tenth part is really worth listening to.

One can well believe the anecdote recorded by Galland (*Orientaliana*, ed. 1701, p. 134) of the thousand camel-loads of literature—presumably of this class—which having been abridged and abridged by learned editors at the abject request of a monarch who, presumably, had to pay for the camels, was at last found to be condensable into four maxims concerning Obedience, Despotism, Health, and Womankind !

" Abide not in the city of a king whose expense is greater than his income," indicates an understanding of early finance ; and there is originality and point in the reflection upon injudicious effusiveness, " A counsel unspoken *you hold imprisoned*, once uttered *it imprisons you*."

The melodious bird which a man captures in his garden, advises him in a lighter vein. It declines to sing. "If you won't sing I'll eat you." "*How* will you eat me ?" says the bird, with curious nonchalance. "Boiled I shall be too small, and roasted I shall be smaller still, or not nice to eat. But let me go, and I shall bring you great advantage."

Cross-examined the fowl promises, in awful Latin, to show to the learner "*tres sapientiæ maneries*," and is set free. Then it begins : " 1. Don't believe everything that is promised or told you. 2. Keep what you have got, when possible. 3. Don't grieve over what you have lost "[1]—and retiring up a tree sings a joyful song, of which the tenor is, " Ha ! ha ! what a fool was the man to let me go when, if he had only known, I have a jacinth weighing a whole ounce in

---

[1] Literally translated in the *Chastoiement* :
  (1) Ne croi pas quanque tu orras.
  (2) Garde bien ce que tu auras,
    Par promesse nel' perdre pas.
  (3) Ne trop ne soies confondu
    Por nule riens qu'aies perdu.

I

my inside!" This of course sets the man off again, weeping and beating his breast, till the bird, resuming its lecture, asks, "Did I not tell you not to believe what you are told? How is it possible that I could have a jacinth of one ounce in my inside, when my whole body does not weigh so much? Further, I told you not to grieve over what was lost." And so on in a tiresome and self-conscious strain, which makes the reader long for the society of Brer Rabbit or the March Hare.

Yet mythologically this is an important and far-reaching apologue. It first appears in the book of Barlaam and Josaphat, where the bird by the way is a nightingale. The Latin translation is borrowed in the *Gesta Romanorum*, and other variants will be found in the *Golden Legend*, the French mystery *Du Roy Advenir* (see Parfait, *Histoire du Théatre Français*) in John Lydgate's *Tale of the Chorle and the Byrd* (1440), and Hans Sachs' *Three Good Useful Advices of a Nightingale* (1555). But this brief parable is a mere interlude.

To return to more serious literature. The *Story of the Robber and the Moonbeam* (in the *Fabliaux*, "*Du larron qui embraça le rai de la lune*") is more curious, if scarcely less absurd, than that of the weeping dog, and perhaps worth giving *in extenso*.

"1. It is told that a certain robber came to the house of a certain rich man with the object of stealing, and going up on to the roof to the opening (*fenestram*) by which the smoke went out, listened to find if any one was awake inside. And the master of the house observing this, said softly to his wife, '*Ask me aloud how I became possessed of my great wealth, and insist on my telling you.*' 2. Then she said aloud, 'My lord, how is it that you have so much wealth, when you were never a merchant?' And he answered, 'What God has given that keep and do your will of it, and do not enquire how I got so much money.' And she, as had been enjoined her, pressed more and more to know the matter. 3. At last, as if constrained by the prayers of his wife, the master said, 'See you reveal our secrets to no one. I was a robber.' But she replied, 'It is a marvel to me how you can have got so much wealth by robbery, since we have never heard any complaint or scandal about it.' 4. Then he said: ' A certain master of mine taught me a charm (*carmen*) that I used to say over when I climbed on to the roof, and going to the hole I took hold of a beam of the moon in my hand, and repeated my charm seven times, saying " *Saulem ! saulem !* " and so I went down without hurting myself, got together all the valuables in the house and took them. Then coming again to the moonbeam, and again repeating my charm seven times, I ascended with all that I had taken in the house, and carried off home what I had stolen. By such a device I am in possession of the wealth which I have.' 5. Then the woman answered, ' You have done right to tell me this story, for whenever I have a son I will teach him this charm to pre-vent his living in poverty.' And the master answered, ' Let me go to sleep for I am tired and want to rest.' A person acquainted with infantine histrionics hardly needs to be told that ' in order the more to deceive he began to snore.' 6. After hearing such a story the thief in great joy repeated the charm seven times, and taking the moonbeam in his hand, let go both feet and hands, and fell through the smoke-hole into the house, making a loud noise, and groaned aloud, having broken his arm and his leg. Then the master of the house, as if ignorant, said, ' Who are you who have fallen in this manner?'

" The robber answered, ' I am the unhappy thief who believed your deceitful words.' "

Poor thief! One can hardly think that he required such elabo-rate precautions. He would probably have fled at a menacing gesture, and certainly burst into tears at an unkind word. Yet the mediæval pupil is quite properly impressed. Thus—

" 7. The son answered, ' Father, blessed be thou who hast taught me to avoid crafty counsels." Which seems a very questionable asser-tion, but that the moralist in his introduction to the story, " Do not believe all the advice you hear, till you have tried it . . . . lest you fare like the thief who believed the advice of the householder," had rather emphasised the point of view of the criminal.

Then follows a sentence of obscure profundity. "8. A philosopher says, '*Beware of an unleavened counsel, till it be fermented.*'"

One wishes there were more counsels of this kind, but the greater part are distinguished by a distressing vapidity. What makes the volume rather difficult to read is that though divided into chapters, each containing a fable or story, and then a string of morals (with which the pupil is almost as well primed as the teacher), they mostly have very little point, and never a conclusion, generally finishing up with the familiar "And how (or what) was that, father?" Even when the last sentence appears to be a final statement of the matter, the next chapter begins with "for," and the weary reader finds himself off again upon another tack. The paragraph just quoted concludes with a curious piece of advice given by Aristotle in a letter to Alexander (the *Correspondence of Aristotle*, not to mention the *Works of Socrates*,[1] and Plato's astrological book on *The Cow*, were within reach of every mediæval writer, though hid from the scholars of our own day) which is not devoid of a certain coarse tact—

"Hasten not to repay a debt whether of good or evil; since your friend will court you, and your enemy fear you all the longer."

The story of the robber and the moonbeam will be found among those in the Sanscrit collection known as the *Hitopadesa* (which, as a collection, is probably not older than that of Petrus Alfonsus) but is very likely of great antiquity.

A very similar version appears in the *Directorium Vitæ Humanæ*, which again is literally translated in the German *Book of the Wisdom of the Ancient Sages* (Strasburg, 1529). On the other hand the ver-

---

[1] It is worth remarking that the pseudo-Socrates first appears in the *Capita Theologica, sive scite dicta atque electa ex diversis tum Christianorum tum externorum libris* of S. Maximus of Constantinople (ob. 662). Paris. 2 vols. folio. 1675. For the correspondence of *Joseph and Pharaoh*, &c., &c., see Fabricius Bibl. Med. and Inf. Latin.

sion in the *Gesta Romanorum*[1] is taken from the *Disciplina*, and the editor has added, out of his own head, that the thief was detained by the householder and hanged in the morning. We can hardly believe the householder capable of such an atrocity. Still more miserable is the said editor's "moralisation" of the story. The thief is the Evil One "*who by evil thoughts climbs up the roof of the heart, and makes an entrance*" (the original thief did not make an entrance, but found one ready made), "through evil compliance" (!) Therefore we should be watchful, &c., &c, Or, again, he is "Lucifer the beautiful, who with his whole might would ascend to be another God" (see Isaiah, chap. xiv.), "and he broke his legs, that is *lost his beauty* (!), which God had given him, and is hanged upon the infernal gallows, from which may He protect us who reigns for ever." If this application be not far-fetched, what is?

The teacher in the *Disciplina*, whose object is at once to amuse and instruct, maintains no high level of seriousness, and descends to details of common life. "Do not speak with your mouth full." "When you have washed your hands for eating, touch nothing but your dinner, till you do eat." (An extraordinarily involved way of expressing so simple a suggestion!) And after a page of weary prattling, the youth says to the old man, "When I am invited to dinner, what shall I do? Eat too little or too much?" The old man, avoiding the pitfall of "Neither," into which any modern instructor would have fallen, replies, "Too much. For if it be a friend who has invited you he will be glad [will he?], but if an enemy, he will be vexed." At which the boy laughed. Both parties were by this time getting rather feeble, and the sage gives a fillip to the flagging conversation by a few anecdotes of "Maymund the lazy," a celebrated domestic servant. An old man once asked him (old men in the middle ages seem to have made a business of this sort of aimless cross-questioning), "how much he could eat?" Maymund replied with a counter-question, "Of

[1] Ch. 136, where for "saulem" we read "fallax" (4to. ed. 1497).

whose dinner—my own or someone else's?" "Your own." Then
said Maymund, "As little as possible"; and there the colloquy
ended. But the boy was anxious to hear more about Maymund,
one of the most trying domestics ever known.[1] Maymund was too
lazy to get up and shut the house-door at night, when he was told,
but said that it was shut already. In the morning, when the converse question arose, he said, "I never shut it because I knew
you would want it open in the morning." Then when his master
hastily exclaimed, "Get up and do your work. It is daytime and
the sun is high." Maymund said, "If the sun is high let me have
my dinner." "Villain," cried the master, "do you want to eat in
the middle of the night?" "If it's the middle of the night, let
me go to sleep."

In a Teutonic story one feels sure that some brisk action would
here have followed. Indeed this is precisely that species of "nag-
ging" which in a modern slum causes the rude coster (as we
know from police reports) to throw boots and furniture at his wife.
But here nothing follows, and Maymund goes on. In the night
the master asks him if it is raining. Maymund whistles on the
dog who lay outside, and feels his feet. As they are dry he
answers "No, sir."

"Maymund, is the fire burning?"

Maymund calls the "mouse-catcher" (*murilegus*, in Latin *feles*,
Anglicé the cat), and feeling that puss's fur is cold, replies "No,
sir." Maymund's great *forte* was his loquacity. The chapter (No.
xxx.) illustrating this, may be found in a better form (entitled
The News) in a recently published collection of fairy tales.

Maymund's master is returning home from the market-place in
cheery mood, having made some good bargains. He sees his servant coming to meet him, and, knowing the latter's habits, enjoins

[1] See *Ellis's Early English Metrical Romances*, I. 140, the *Seven Wise
Masters*, and a volume of Fairy Tales recently edited by Mr. Jacobs.

him strictly to repeat no "evil reports." "Oh no," said Maymund, "but our little dog Pipella is dead." "How did she die?" "The mule got frightened, broke his halter (*chamus* or *camus*, a rare Greek-Latin word not found in all glossaries), and in running away trampled her to death."

"What became of the mule?"

"He fell into a well, and was killed." But the reader will observe that this question and answer might well be omitted, since it is immaterial to the chain of interrogatories, which should be unbroken.

"What frightened the mule?"

"Your son fell from the top of the house[1] and broke his neck, and that frightened the mule."

"What did his mother do?"

"She died of grief."

This reply also is clearly out of place, since it would have brought the colloquy to a natural termination before half the "news" has been imparted.

"Who is looking after the house?"

"Nobody, for it is burnt to ashes with everything inside it."

"How was it burnt?"

"On the same night the mistress died, a maidservant who was watching for her, left a candle burning;" and so on.

The conclusion is dull, and the dialogue clearly required a few more rehearsals. It should run, we believe, somewhat in this style—

"Who is taking care of the house?"

"Nobody, for it is burnt down."

"How did it catch fire?"

"Oh! from the flaring of the torches at your mother's funeral."

---

[1] *Solarium—i.e.* sunning-place (which in a northern climate would be the "balcony")—*Höchster offen liegender Raum des Hauses*, says Diez. *Wörterbuch der Romanischen Sprachen.* The word occurs in a curious passage (*Claudius*, x.) of Suetonius. See the Variorum note, ed. 1751.

" My mother ! what did she die of ? "

" She died of grief at your son's sudden death."

And so on, making a completely logical " Jack-to-fetch-the-mustard."

This might well be as interminable as the narrative of the royal story-teller, whom we all know, and who duly reappears in the *Disciplina*, this time with a story of a rustic who has bought 2,000 sheep, and has to take them across a river two at a time. So he takes two sheep, puts them in the boat, and rows across the river.

At this point the official *conteur* falls asleep. Awakened by the sleepless monarch and ordered to go on with the story, he adds, " Sire, the boat is small, the river wide, and the sheep innumerable. Let the man ferry them across, and when he has done I will finish the story."

This monarch, we feel, would have appreciated the Chinese comedy (described in Acosta's entertaining *History of the Indies*), which lasted ten days and ten nights, the actors working in shifts.

Perhaps, indeed, the clearest impression left by the great mass of the literature here considered is that of an intense and dragging boredom of existence, the vacuity of which was to be dissipated at all hazards, intellectual and literary.

A narrative of the serious kind last mentioned could hardly have been necessary to send the reader of the *Disciplina Clericalis* to sleep, the purpose for which most of us, like the poet Wordsworth, use to count imaginary sheep. Persevering would he be who remained awake so long as to hear the short and pithy sermon from a hermit, which brings the work to a close with an inevitable reference to the Day of Judgment, and (that which seems to have weighed so lightly upon mediæval story-tellers) the shortness of human life !

IV.

THE PIRATE'S PARADISE.

(1740)

Plate of the capture of Porto Bello (see p. 138 *post*), from the original (Dutch) edition of Exquemelin's *History of the Buccaneers*, sm. 4to, Amsterdam, 1678, p. 88. (The illustrations to this volume are poorly reproduced in the English translation of 1684.)

THE PIRATE'S PARADISE.

(1740)[1]

" He was the blood-thirstiest buccaneer that ever sailed—but I was sometimes
proud that he was an Englishman . . . . I've seen his topsails with these eyes
off Trinidad, and the cowardly son of a rumpuncheon that I sailed with put back,
put back, sir, into Port of Spain."—*Treasure Island.*

T is perhaps no matter for serious regret that from
the well-policed seas of the modern world, that
picturesque hero—the pirate—seems almost to have
vanished, or, in those remote corners where the
" Black Flag " still flies, to cut but a miserable figure
in the face of well-armed and civilized society—miserable alas!
because no longer surrounded by the halo of success.

But the pirate lives in story, and if we can seldom meet him except
by appointment, on the high seas, yet the locality of his former
haunts, of the true " Treasure Islands " of History is easily to be
gathered from the highly actual romance of Mr. Robert Louis
Stevenson. Is not the vessel called the *Hispaniola*? Does not
Squire Trelawney's remark (above quoted) sketch for us the haunts
as well as the habits of the ideal pirate in one dramatic sentence?

[1] This date is of course not that of the golden age of piracy, but of the point of
view from which it is regarded in the work here reviewed.

Moreover in what the historian has preserved of Flint's own log—
"offe Caraccas" is the location of at least one of that celebrated cut-
throat's undescribed deeds of blood.

The real "Treasure Islands" are of course the picturesque group
known—ever since poor Columbus just four hundred years ago
mistook one of the Bahamas for the coast of Japan—as the "West
Indies"—a name representing a concession on the part of Geo-
graphic Science to the foible of a great man. The sanguine explorer,
like the inexperienced Alpist who takes each successive "col" for
the longed-for summit, imagined that he had reached "India" before
his little flotilla had made half, or indeed, allowing for the non-
existence of a canal at Panama (of which more anon) even one third
of the way.

The singular ocean lake, shut in on the south and west by the
twisted half-broken strip that holds together the two Americas, and
protected on the north and east by the projecting arm of Florida,
the broken bar of Cuba and San Domingo (Hispaniola), and the
long curving sweep of the Windward Islands, appears from the first
glance at the map, as a little world shut off and secluded, remote, as
it still is, from any centre of civilization, which we might expect to
possess a beauty, a climate, and perhaps even a standard of morals
entirely its own.

The ardent prayer of Mr. Kipling's *blasé* hero,

> Ship me somewhere east of Suez where the best is like the worst,
> And there ain't no ten commandments, and a man can raise a thirst,

would have been answered early in the last century by a transporta-
tion to the fertile and beautiful Island of Jamaica, the very heart of
the sequestered nook just described. If the "West Indies" are not
exactly "east of *Suez*" (a point not very material to the navigator
of the eighteenth century) by the shortest route from Great Britain,
they would have supplied all the other essentials here demanded in
even more than satisfying quantity. So we infer from a series of

Letters from Jamaica, which have just reached us, although addressed to the public about 150 years ago.[1]

A mere "account of Jamaica" though dedicated to the Earl of Eglinton and Winton, is a thing one might throw aside after half an hour's after-dinner perusal. Dazzling beauties of Nature, sugar-canes, slaves (who chronically revolt with more or less awful consequences) hummingbirds that one shoots with sand, swamps, fevers, and rum—all these things, including the habits of the alligator so graphically depicted by Mr. Waterton, are familiar enough, and (except for the abolished institution of slavery) might be better described in a modern guide to the Island. But when we stumble in Letters IV. and V., on an authentic cameo of piratical history from the point of view of an inhabitant of the capital which was the centre of the buccaneering industry, the work arrests our attention at once.

To revert for one moment to the explorations of Christopher Colon is not to digress—a most objectionable practice—but merely to hitch on the details of Mr. Leslie's veracious romance to the course of general history.

It need hardly be remarked, to begin with, that Columbus no longer enjoys the exalted reputation which he once had. Of his seaman-ship and general ability we need not doubt, but in respect of avarice and bigotry he might have been a born Spaniard. Gold, the gold which he thought and wrote was a most excellent thing, which meant "mastery of the world, and could even bring souls into Paradise," constantly occupied his thoughts.

His motives therefore for the voyage to the "West Indies," though overlaid with a great deal of superstitious piety and indeed mysticism—for at one time he seems to have asserted if not believed that his discoveries were independent of all the material assistance derived from science and hydrography—were not very much better than those which inspired so many others and in particular so

---

[1] *A New and Exact Account of Jamaica*, &c. (by Charles Leslie). 3rd edition, 8vo, Edinburgh, 1740.

many Spaniards to betake themselves to a territory in itself inde-
scribably attractive, and inhabited by the most guileless of savages.
But this fact does not diminish the interest attaching to the Biography [1]

[1] *Vita di Cristoforo Colombo, descritta da Ferdinando suo figlio & tradotta
da Alfonso Ulloa* (the original text is lost), Dulau, Londra, 8vo, 1867 (a poorly
printed edition, but with conveniently large margins), supplies a most natural
and fascinating, if not perfectly reliable narrative. In the first expedition (1492)
the orders of the Admiral on leaving the Canaries were that after the fleet had
done 700 leagues of "westing," they were *not to sail during the night*, for fear of
collision with land. A velvet doublet and an annuity of thirty scudi had been
promised by their Catholic Majesties to the sailor who first sighted land, and
Columbus himself received this prize—having sighted some moving light on shore
from the deckhouse of his own *Caravel*—on the curious ground that he (the
Admiral) had discovered spiritual "light in darkness," *i.e.* surpassed the rest
in the religious fervour of his belief in himself, or in Providence, although a
mariner on the *Pinta*, which carried more sail, claimed the reward, apparently
with better justification. Ferdinand gives lively details of the voyage—the
singing of the "Salve Regina" every evening, the birds flitting about the
rigging, and the objects floating in the water that announced the vicinity of the
long-desired land.

The result of the discoveries of Columbus, and of Amerigo Vespucci was the
famous diplomatic contest between Spain and Portugal which cannot be better
summarized than in the words of Dyer (*Mod. Europe*, I. 320). "The
theory of the sphericity of the earth (see the entertaining arguments of
Lactantius, *Div. Inst.* III. 24), on which the discoveries of Columbus were
founded, and in accordance with which Spanish and Portuguese adventurers might
have come into collision in their new settlements, was an heretical notion which
could not for a moment be entertained by the See of Rome. Unfolding the
orthodox map of Cosmas Indicopleustes" (in his *Topographia Christiana*, composed 536 A.D., and published by Montfaucon 1707), "from which it appeared
that the longer the Spaniards sailed to the west and the Portuguese to the east,
the farther they would be separated from one another, Pope Alexander VI. drew
from north to south a line of demarcation passing 100 leagues west of the Azores
and Cape Verd. All to the east of this line he gave to Portugal, all to the west
to Spain (May 4, 1493)." The Bull was subsequently modified by another which
shifted the line of demarcation another 370 leagues westward—a trifling alteration
—in order to secure Brazil to the Portuguese, who by the way had previously
asserted a Papal title (derived chiefly from Eugenius IV., ob. 1447) to the *whole*
of the "New World," whatever it might turn out to include. See the interesting
chapter in Mariana—*Historia General de España* xxxvi. 3, *Del descubrimento*

which describes his voyages, and supplies the first chapter in the History of Europeans in the West Indies.

According to the account given by his son (chap. xxi.) Columbus first landed on Thursday, October 11, 1492, at the island of "Los Lucagios," which he afterwards tells us (chap. xxv.) was called by the natives Guanahani, and which *he* christened San Salvador ; but modern authorities, we believe, have decided in favour of *Mariguana*, now a deserted island.[1] He subsequently proceeded from one island to another, guided by the reports of their gold-bearing properties. It was at the close of his second voyage that leaving Cuba on the 3rd of May, 1494, he set sail for Jamaica, which had been reported to him as particularly rich. The natives at first made an unusual exhibition of hostility, but being soon awed by a few shots into quiet behaviour, came and exchanged victuals and other things for "any article offered them." The admiral did not land, but coasted round towards the west some way, before returning to Cuba.

The biographer records that a very young Indian came to Columbus and begged to be taken to Spain, and in spite of the supplications of his relatives that he would return with them, remained on board, orders being specially given that he should be kindly treated. The incident has quite a pathetic interest. Before this "very young Indian" had reached middle age, his compatriots at least knew all that they could desire of the avarice, tyranny, and cruelty of Castile, and must have cursed the day when the caravel of Columbus first hove in sight.

Columbus was the first of the long succession of gold-hunting adventurers—his later followers made no pretence of religion—to

de las Indias Occidentales. In spite of the "incredible activity" of Spanish explorers, "it has not yet been quite clearly ascertained" he tells us (writing about 1590) "whether Western India joins on to Eastern (*se continua con la Oriental*) or whether north of Cathay in China, and of Japan there is a stretch of sea which divides them"—the strait discovered by Vitus Behring in 1728.

[1] E. J. Payne, *History of the New World called America.*

visit these beauteous but ill-fated shores. In 1509 Jamaica and San Juan were thoroughly "settled" by the Spaniards, after their fashion. We turn to that most tragical of records, the *Short Account of the Destruction of the West Indies*, addressed to Philip II. in 1552, by the humane Bartolomeo de Las Casas, and under the brief heading which concerns these two islands, we read of dreadful outrages, crimes (it is a relief to hear) previously rehearsed, new and singular atrocities and barbarities, murdering, burning, *roasting*, torturing, hunting with wild dogs, forced labour in the mines, &c., of which the net result is that of "these unhappy innocents," of whom there had been 600,000 souls, there are now scarcely left 200! "and all died without religion or the sacraments."[1]

In such fashion was European civilisation and religion first imposed upon the simple and harmless inhabitants of the "West Indies."

To connect their career with the general history of Great Britain, Jamaica, as the veriest Jacobite would now admit, is a valuable possession conferred upon us (in 1655) by the enterprise of the usurper Cromwell. The leaders of the expedition, we all know, were on their return committed to the Tower, and Sir W Penn appears to admit to Mr. Pepys (*sub anno* 1663) that the failure to seize more than the one island of Jamaica was his own fault.[2]

At this date a company, established by royal charter, was under contract to supply the Spanish colonies in these parts with 3,000 slaves per annum. Indeed the business of importing negroes to the West Indies first inaugurated by Sir John Hawkins (whose profits were shared by Queen Elizabeth) in 1562, continued to flourish for some two centuries later. Yet Penn's acquisition was not thought much of at the time, and Oliver Cromwell, who ap-

---

[1] *Las Casas, Fr. Barthol. de* (1474-1566), *Breve relacion de la Destruccion de las Indias Occidentales* (Seville, 1552). 8vo, Londres, 1812.

[2] The original account of the expedition—*Journal of the English Army in the West Indies, by an eye-witness* (Harl. MS. VI. 372) is cited in Carlyle's *Letters and Speeches of Cromwell*.

pears to Mr. Leslie to have been a person not devoid of a certain
malign ingenuity, was even suspected of circulating too glowing
accounts of its attractions, in order to get discontented Royalists
to go there. Anyhow, "persons of desperate fortune" betook themselves in large numbers to Jamaica. After the Restoration, again,
this class was augmented by followers of the Republican party.
The "old grudge" disturbed even so distant a colony worse than
ever, Royalists being favoured, while Cromwellians, "*the only party
that understood the art of war*," were excluded from all places of
trust and profit. The Government party, therefore, in the island
found the encouragement of the already popular industry of
"Pyracy" to be "necessary," both to counterbalance the force of
these malcontents and to lure them into some profitable occupation. This simple policy, the reader will learn with interest,
was a complete success. The colony, whose population (placed at
20,000 in 1740) had, it is true, but little increased since Cromwellian days,[1] became "the resort of the Privateers, who made

[1] The "peopling" of Jamaica was effected in strange and dreadful manners.
First the Royalist, closely followed by the Cromwellian "malcontents," with
tribes of the desperate characters bred of a disturbed time. Secondly, one of the
most awful pages in Irish history is the correspondence of Henry Cromwell with
the Protector upon this subject. Mr. Secretary Thurloe writes that "a stock of
Irish girls and young men are wanting for the peopling of Jamaica"; and Henry
Cromwell answers: "Concerning the supply of young men, although we must use
force in taking them up, yet, *it being so much for their good*" (exactly how much
the reader may conjecture) . . . "it is not doubted that you may have such a
number as you think fit to make use of." He thinks also it were well to send
1,500 or 2,000 boys to the place mentioned. "*We can well spare them: and
who knows but it may be the means of making them Englishmen—I mean, rather,
Christians?*" . . . In reply Thurloe informs him that "the Council"—as a man
might order trout for the stocking of a stream !—"have voted 4,000 *girls and as
many boys* to go to Jamaica." It is not clear that they went. Some of these
passages may be found collected in Moore's *Memoirs of Captain Rock*. Moreover,
hundreds of the victims of Judge Jeffreys, after the Monmouth rising, were
despatched to the same place (1685). *See* the account given in *John Coad's
Memorial* (cited by Macaulay), published by Pickering, 1848.

K

Jamaica a kind of home." This "was no sooner known" than all persons with a distaste for the Ten Commandments, all who found "life too inactive,"—or law, we may presume, too active,—in Old England, eagerly transported themselves thither. Malcontents, Republican or Royalist, "soon found their account in joining with the Privateers, forgot their old murmurs, acquiesced in the administration, and in a short time all distinction of parties was quite lost." [1]

Such was the Arcadian state of Jamaica during what appears to have been the golden age of piracy up to the last decade of the seventeenth century. Governors and planters vied with each other in providing the necessary arms and vessels, expecting their return in the wealth which the successful buccaneer regularly squandered in the friendly port. The funds thus accumulated and dissipated became the life and soul of the colony. The gentlemen of fortune who actively engaged in the trade "had such surprising success as will perhaps scarce gain belief in succeeding ages." The author hardly knows how to describe them to us. He regrets, of course, that "the stain of Pyracy sullies their great actions, and *caused them to be regarded* as disturbers of mankind, and villains ;" but calling in the assistance of our venerable friend the "better cause," he assures us that "their fame *might* have equalled that of any antient or modern heroes." He "cannot tell whether it was bad policy, although it was certainly bad morality, to encourage these desperadoes," but is sure "that a summary of their lives will suggest a great many useful reflections" to the reader. And this it certainly does, the most obvious perhaps being the contrast between the weakness of what the author calls the "silly dastardly Spaniard " (whose monopoly of the West Indies, as we read in Mr. Green's history, was first broken up by our capture of Jamaica) and the increasing superfluous energy of Great Britain.

[1] It is moreover a curious fact that after the Act of Union in 1706, so many Scotchmen emigrated to the Island, that it was called, Dr. Somerville tells us, "the grave of Scotland."

But the first of the heroes here sketched by Mr. Leslie is a Portuguese, Bartholomew, the model, piratically speaking, of a self-made man, who started with nothing but "the courage of a lion." He begins life in a "leaky scooner (a small kind of sloop used for carrying sugars to Port Royal) mounted with four iron guns." His crew being "all brave and to be depended upon," they make no difficulty of attacking, off Cape de Corriente, in Cuba, a fine ship of twenty guns and seventy men, bound to the Havannah; are beaten off with loss, but, coming up with her again, renew the attack until she is glad to surrender. Taking to the prize, which they find "an excellent relief," they steer for Cape St. Antony, on the west side of Cuba, meaning to water, but, unexpectedly falling in with three Spanish coastguards, are, after a smart engagement, taken and made prisoners. As they had on board 120,000 weight of cacao and 70,000 pieces of eight,[1] this depressed their spirits exceedingly. The vessels, being dispersed by a storm, were driven to the port of Campechie (Campeachy, on the west coast of Yucatan), where the Pyrates were well known, and Bartholomew was "without much form or ceremony," condemned to be hanged. In the night, however, he stabbed his keeper, floated himself ashore upon two earthen jars, fled to the woods, and lived on herbs and fruits for many days, eluding the strictest search and hidden in a hollow tree. Thence, almost famished, he strikes out overland for some forty leagues; crosses a great river, being a poor swimmer, on an old board and a few boughs cut off by means of nails "sharpened with incredible pains"; and, after enduring calamities which one can well believe "nothing but his invincible daring spirit could have supported," arrives at Golfo Triste (Ascension?), and is welcomed by a crew of Pyrates then in the bay. Bartholomew did but ask a boat's crew of twenty men to return to Campeachy, "and be revenged on the

---

[1] As to the value of this coin we may refer the reader to a passage in *Pepys's Diary* (May 11, 1663), where he records his disputing with Sir G. Carteret whether the "piece of eight" were worth 4s. 5d. or 4s. 9d.

Spaniards;" a feat which he at once accomplishes, finding himself thus master of a fine vessel where he had lately been confined and condemned to be hanged, and also of a vastly rich prize, having on board much merchandise, besides what had been originally taken from himself—"a happy success," which gave the simple Pyrate "a great deal of pleasure." With the proceeds he proposed to make a "good deal" at Jamaica; but unfortunately his ship went ashore on the banks called the Jardines, near the island of Pinos, where she split; and Bartholomew and company, barely escaping with life, returned to Jamaica to seek their fortunes anew.

Brasiliano, the Dutchman expelled from Brazil at the Portuguese invasion, was another who, having taken refuge in the British colony, and being anxious to get on, "saw no way so likely to do it as by turning Pyrate," in which line he soon distinguished himself by the same qualities. "He feared nothing, avoided no danger, and always went upon the most difficult enterprises." This was indeed the golden rule of Pyracy which, accidents apart, invariably led to success.

Vessel after vessel did Brasiliano and his friends take, regularly returning to Port Royal to squander away their gold in every kind of debauchery. On sea or on land "nothing could withstand the valour of these desperadoes." They shrank from no encounter at any odds, and their victories were generally followed by "horrid cruelties with which they tortured the poor Spaniards after a manner shocking to relate," partly in order to get more money, partly, it seems, in mere wantonness of fury. Whatever they got was, however, spent in a very short time, the Pyrate being quickly reduced to beggary. "They have been known to spend 2,000 or 3,000 pieces of eight in one night." On these occasions wine literally flowed down the streets. The successful buccaneers insisted upon every one partaking of their hospitality; at other times they showered the beverage about the streets, wetting the clothes of passers-by, which seemed to them an "excellent diversion." Some persons objected, doubtless, but on the whole it was considered good for trade.

When poverty, on one occasion, drove Brasiliano to sea again, he, like Bartholomew, was captured whilst calmly "viewing the Fort" of Campeachy. The Governor determined to hang him and his crew; but their captain had the address to write a letter, *as from other Pyrates*, threatening horrid cruelties to any of the Spanish nation who should ever fall into their hands. And *this letter had the desired effect*, so well known were both the courage and cruelty of the pirate community.

Brasiliano and his friends were sent home in the galleys, from which we are not surprised to learn they shortly after escaped, and continued to commit "horrid barbarities" on the Spanish coast. Brasiliano had an inveterate spite against the race, and expressed it in a way which left no room for misconception. Some he roasted alive on wooden spits, others he tortured with lighted matches put under their armpits. In sober truth "those that died were the lucky ones." The Spaniards do not seem at the time to have provoked this conduct. It proceeded rather on the principle of *odisse quem læseris*, or took its rise in the deadly boredom caused by every interval of repose in a life of "battle, murder, and sudden death." Brasiliano continued thus, we read, for many years still successful in his attempts, and highly regarded by his fellow-villains, over whom he had such influence that in all his adventures there never was one mutiny, "which" (not the mutiny, but its absence) "is a rare thing aboard of a Pyrate ship."

It being remembered that these particular freebooters were but shining lights among the numerous throng of their fraternity, we are not surprised to learn that the effect on Spanish commerce was considerable. The greatness of Spain—a thing of scarce more than a century's apparent duration—had never very deep roots. It made much show while it lasted by an enormous extravagance and vanity, but was almost from the first eaten at the core by bigotry, fanatic blindness, cowardice, and cruelty, which the efforts of a score of Brasilianos could hardly have repaid as it deserved, for no deeds attributed to the worst pirate equal those recorded of his countrymen by Las Casas.

The contemporary records of the great Armada (introduced only recently to English readers by the late Mr. Froude) give an astonishing picture of material force and wealth nullified by the moral and physical incompetence of which so many examples are to be noticed in Leslie's narrative, and by a peculiar sort of sanctified stupidity.[1] The power of Spain, then at its height, after the destruction of the Armada and during the seventeenth century steadily declined, but she still had a practical monopoly of the West Indies.[2]

It is rather surprising, therefore, to be told that "the Spaniards found themselves so miserably harassed that they resolved to diminish the number of their trading vessels," hoping by this means that the pirates would leave off, finding they could get no good prizes! But the Dutch, it may be remembered on two occasions during the seventeenth century, "forbad trade" in order to save it from England. Another evidence of the straits to which the proprietors of the Indies were reduced may be noted elsewhere in the well-known account of Anson's voyages round the world. The solitary island of Juan Fernandez, where early mariners were in the habit of taking a rest after rounding the terrible Cape Horn, was also a favourite resort of pirates, for whom the native goats afforded a useful supply of meat. The *Centurion*, touching there in 1740, found several of these animals bearing the mark of Alexander Selkirk (who was taken off by Wood Rogers and Stephen Courtney, of the *Duke and Duchess* privateers, of Bristol, in 1709); but most of them had been driven up into the high ground by the "wild dogs" with which the Spaniards had stocked the island in order to render it less attractive

---

[1] See the account of the extraordinary religious apparatus brought in the Spanish Armada, coupled with the insufficiency of powder, shot, anchor-ropes, &c., also Dr. Sharp's well-known *Letter to the Duke of Buckingham* reporting the examination of the first Spanish prisoners taken. *Collection of original Letters* (2 vols. 1755), vol. i.

[2] See the passage cited from Montesquieu's Letters (*Memoirs*, p. 157, *post*).

to pirates. These dogs would even attack a man.[1] But to return to the West Indies. These concessions on the part of the merchant community to the organised forces of piracy produced quite the opposite effect to that intended. They were, in fact, but the beginning of piracy on a really extensive and wholesale scale.

For the buccaneers "were resolved to have money from them at any rate," and so, finding no ships of value upon the sea, they determined in this extremity to land and plunder the country. The proceedings of Lewis Scot, who first began this method of robbing, resemble closely those of the successful bushranger of thirty years ago. To use the Australian term, Lewis Scot "stuck up" the town of Campeachy, and did not leave it until he had exacted an enormous ransom. Mansvelt meanwhile captured the island of St. Katharine's and took everything that was valuable, extorting heavy ransoms from the prisoners.

But the name to conjure with at this time was that of John Davis, a native of Jamaica. His most celebrated feat was a successful attack upon Nicaragua with only eighty men.

Nicaragua lies some seventy miles inland from the Caribbean coast. The pirates, therefore, having hidden their vessel in a creek, and "using the night-time lest their black designs should be discovered," sailed in canoes up the river, which American engineers have since made part of a canal, and arrived at the town "on the third night." The sentry taking them for fishermen, they were allowed to land without question; and, knocking at the doors of the chief inhabitants, were admitted without suspicion, and at once

---

[1] One wonders if these were the dogs (*perros bravos*) which the Spaniards, at an earlier date, had trained to kill and eat the natives of the West Indian Islands. See Las Casas, *Relacion;* also *Colliber's Sea Affairs*, 1735, p. 295. *Voyage Round the World* (1740–1744) of George Lord Anson, Bk. II., ch. 1. "Anson," writes Walpole to Mann (June 18, 1744), "is returned with a vast fortune. He has brought the Acapulca ship into Portsmouth, and its treasure is computed at £500,000. He escaped the Brest squadron in a mist."

"began to exercise their wonted cruelties. Some they immediately murdered, others they bound and gagged"; and then proceeded to pillage, houses, churches, and everything.

The citizens, indeed, presently got together, but could do no more than the inhabitants of an Australian town surprised by the Kelly gang. The pirates, having secured all that they desired, retreated to their canoes and got back to their ships in safety, with "a great deal of riches" and many prisoners. The latter they compelled to beg provisions for them from the neighbouring plantations, and then stood out to sea; not, however, before 500 well-armed Spaniards appeared on the sea-side. But the pirates let fly several broadsides into them, which "put the party into no small confusion," and sailed off with the booty—50,000 pieces of eight—to Jamaica, where it was spent in the usual fashion.

"Davis grew famous. This exploit gained him universal esteem." The planters "were in love with his success," and nothing was talked of in Jamaica but his courage and conduct; and another fleet was soon provided, of which he was admiral, and with which he made a more distant expedition to St. Augustine, in Florida. The place was defended, if we can say so, by a castle with 200 men. But Davis stormed the fort, pillaged the town, "committed horrid murders," and retired without the loss of one man.

During this period, says the reflective historian, the colony was in its greatest glory, and money was so plentiful that Port Royal was reckoned the richest spot of ground in the world—and thus we are introduced naturally to the history of one "whose name is to this day a terror to Spain."

The bushranging associations above referred to will be recalled by the mention of the name of Morgan. Sir Henry Morgan, who was born in the principality of Wales, the son of a respectable farmer, might have been a Pirate of Penzance, so prosaic was the practical success of his career.

After running away to Bristol, where he bound himself as a

servant for four years, he was duly transported to Barbadoes and there sold. Having faithfully served his term, he shipped himself to Jamaica, determined to follow his natural bent in the direction of piracy, and at once found a satisfactory engagement.

His resolution and courage in several prosperous expeditions on the Spanish coasts were much admired, and having noted the ill effects of the extravagance and debauchery popular among his associates, he practised a thoughtful economy, "lived moderate, having vast designs in view," and soon invested his honest savings in a vessel of his own. Prize after prize did he bring into Port Royal, by rapid steps ascending the ladder of piratical success. His renown next attracted the attention of the veteran Mansvelt, above mentioned, who engaged Morgan as his vice-admiral.

With fifteen ships and 500 men they swept down upon the little island of St. Katharine's, on the "rich coast" of Central America, and made themselves masters of it, leaving a garrison in the place, which they intended to keep for their own use. The adjoining island they also pillaged, and a further attack upon the territory of Costa Rica itself was only cut short by the vigorous efforts of the Governor of Panama.

The island of St. Katharine's—which the Governor of Jamaica refused to occupy—not daring to give such open support to the pirates, was, shortly after Mansvelt had "ended his wicked life," retaken by the Spaniards.

Morgan, now an independent pirate king, soon found himself at the head of twelve ships and 700 fighting men. He first thought of attacking Havannah,[1] but decided to begin with a smaller enterprise upon the "fine inland town" of Puerto del Principe. Owing to the

---

[1] Havannah possessed a harbour capable of holding a thousand vessels, protected by two forts. It was taken in August, 1762, by Pocock and Lord Albemarle —one of the largest captures ever made, and the most important exploit of the war, the "bag" being thirteen vessels and near £3,000,000 in gold nd merchandise.

escape of a prisoner, the place got the alarm, and the Governor set ambuscades, blocked up the roads, and encamped with an armed force in front of the town. Morgan and his friends were "surprised," but could not think of retreating—it was indeed too late. They took to the woods, avoided the ambuscades, and soon reached the plain where the Spaniards awaited him. The usual result followed. "Nothing could stand against the fury of the Pyrates, who fought like so many madmen." After a regular engagement of four hours, in which the Governor and many others were killed, the Spaniards fled, and the town, after some defence, was taken.

The usual "horrible barbarities" followed; men, women, and children were shut up in the churches and almost starved, while the pirates plundered and devoured their property. Torture was freely practised on the same business-like principles. Enormous ransoms were exacted. Many unhappy wretches died of the torments, besides those that succumbed to famine.

Disturbed by the unseasonable piece of news that a force was coming to attack them from Santiago, the pirates at last decamped with all they could get. One painful incident marred the success of the expedition—an "unhappy division among the crew." An English sailor had stabbed a Frenchman! *C'était trop.* Morgan carried the criminal in chains to Jamaica and then "caused him to be hanged."

But the life of a successful and industrious, nay, virtuous, pirate was not unmixed bliss. The spoils of Puerto del Principe hardly paid the debts of Morgan's company in Port Royal. So they started out again—450 men in nine small vessels in the direction of Costa Rica. Not till they were well out at sea did Morgan confide to them his design of attacking Porto Bello, "one of the strongest places in the West Indies," and a great centre of commerce, with a population of "500 families." A few pirates objected. But Morgan pointed out that "if their numbers were small, their hearts were great," adding (with perhaps an imperfect recollection of Shakespeare), "the fewer men, the greater share of plunder." Thus con-

vinced, and guided by an Englishman who had been a prisoner in
the hands of the Spaniards, and who had chosen to "list a Pyrate,"
solely with a view to revenge, they sailed up miles of river, and
finally assaulted the place from the land. It was indeed a dangerous undertaking, and in the course of capturing *three castles*, armed
with artillery, Morgan came as near as ever to being nonplussed,
although his men took their aim so well that they never missed to
shoot the Spaniards when the latter came to load the guns. Both
parties behaved with equal courage. The attacking party applied
fireballs to the gates, but the garrison threw down huge stones and
flasks of powder. The "crafty Pyrate's" idea of employing the
monks and nuns taken from the monasteries to set up their scaling
ladders for them showed an extravagant reliance upon Spanish
orthodoxy, and was defeated by the resolution of the Governor, who
fired with the greatest fury, killing great numbers of the religious.
Fortunately, at such a moment of embarrassment Morgan observed
the "English colours" (a pleasing reflection for the nineteenth-
century Briton) "hoisted upon the other fort" which had succumbed
to another detachment of his forces. "This sight encouraged his
fainting troops to the attack," and shortly after the whole place was,
if one can say so, at their mercy. The Governor, with whom one
feels much sympathy, died at his post fighting and killing pirates
with his own hand to the last.

Every variety of outrage was let loose upon the wretched inhabitants. The pirates, sailing under the British flag, appear to have
carried about with them a whole arsenal of tortures worthy of the
Inquisition. Elderly gentlemen, "reported to be rich," were hung
up by the "thumbs and great toes" and roasted with a fire made of
palm-leaves, until they or their friends bid the required amount of
ransom, and, the business of barbarity being accomplished upon the
captives, "the Pyrates made game of their misery." This, indeed,
and the debaucheries of Port Royal were the only relaxations to the
sombre routine of their profession. One hundred thousand pieces

of eight was the required ransom, and some inhabitants vainly trusted to a rescuing party from Panama. But a hundred pirates soon disposed of the latter hope, "killing an incredible number," merely to show that Morgan was not to be trifled with.

That our pirates "were welcome guests at Jamaica" we can, after what we have been told, well understand. "The planters caressed Morgan," and the inferior sort—the tradesmen, we presume—"soon drained his associates of their money." The Governor of Jamaica gave Morgan a fine new vessel of thirty-two guns, and he soon found himself at the head of "1,000 brave resolute fellows." The vessel indeed chanced to blow up with several hundreds aboard, but, Morgan being fortunately uninjured, all the rest were soon replaced. Their next venture touched the utmost limit of audacity. To attack Maracaibo they sailed up an inland lake—a sort of sea, in fact, guarded at the mouth by a fort—forced their way in, reached the town, and after immense trouble (and the indefatigable employment of torture) succeeded in getting a fair amount of booty. The inhabitants indeed took to the woods, in a manner which exasperated Morgan, concealing the possessions which they dared not even attempt to defend, and had to be hunted out, the Spaniards on the coast having all the time thus occupied for repairing their defences and cutting off the pirates' retreat by blocking up the narrow passage. This, in fact, they did, and Morgan's party on their return, "tired," as we are pathetically informed, "with repeated rapes and murders," found the fort strongly garrisoned and provided with artillery, and, if that were not enough, three Spanish men-of-war guarding the entrance of the lake.

The reader will have inferred from the expressions of Mr. Leslie, which we have ventured to quote, the difficulty experienced by this gentleman in concealing or subduing his affectionate admiration for a class of persons to whom the happy British colony which he had made his home owed so much of its prosperity. Although recollecting himself sufficiently to exclaim now and again upon their wickedness and cruelty, this language may be significantly compared with what he says elsewhere of the barbarities exercised upon their masters by a few revolted slaves. But if the somewhat laborious attempt to whitewash Morgan from the charge of complicity in "horrid barbarities," of which it would be impossible to print a detailed catalogue, smacks of a patriotic partisanship, nothing showed up more clearly than the Maracaibo affair the sterling qualities of this prince of pirates.

He and his troop were practically done for—outnumbered and cut off, yet such was the respect inspired by the mere name of Morgan that the Spanish Governor proposed to let them pass if they would give up all the spoils and prisoners taken during the expedition. The pirates, instead of jumping at this proposal, regarded it as "shocking." " *The riches they had got* (as the Spanish Governor seemed not to understand) *they had exposed their lives to obtain ;* and they resolved to quit with life before tamely resigning what they had bought at so dear a price." Nor did they. Morgan's ready resource at once devised a fire-ship, which looked quite unlike one. Its portholes were fitted with counterfeit cannon, and there were imitation pirates, in picturesque attitudes on the deck, made of wood, and provided with "hats and Montera caps." This soon disposed of the first Spanish man-of-war. The second ran aground, the third fell an easy prey, and matters soon wore a different complexion. Indomitable courage and straight shooting shortly reversed the position of parties altogether. The pirates "*accepted of* 15,000 pieces of eight, and thereupon went quietly away" with twenty times that amount in jewels, merchandise, and slaves. What were the reflections of the Governor in his fort and of the captains and crews of the "three Spanish men-of-war" we are not told.

After a few minor successes Morgan, whose fame was now at its height, proceeded to the great exploit for which he is famous in history, to wit, the sack of Panama, perhaps the greatest feat recorded in all the annals of piracy.

The fort of Chagres—a preliminary step—was captured in a curious way. "One Pyrate happened to be wounded with an arrow; he pulled it out and wrapped a little cotton about its bloody point, put it in his musket, and fired it off to the Castle." The cotton ignited, and happening to alight near the enemy's powder magazine blew it all up. "This soon made them yield," and on August 18, 1670, Morgan started, at the head of 1,200 men, upon his last grea expedition.

We cannot here describe it in detail.

How the pirates marched for days through a country laid waste by the Spaniards (who had ample notice of their approach), enduring "every kind of misery," so that they were *forced to gnaw the leaves of trees*, until at last, when "the high steeple of Panama" appeared in view, joy filled every buccaneering breast, and they threw their caps into the air and shrieked aloud, we leave the reader to imagine. Parties of horse and foot came out to meet them, but "thought it not proper" to come within musket range. The great guns of the city, presumably ill-directed, played upon their camp; but "the Pyrates, who were used to such kind of musick, pulled out their satchels and fell to supper."

In the great engagement which followed, outside the walls, the Spanish Governor brought into the field 400 horse, 3,000 foot, 200 Indians, and—a curious detail—2,000 wild bulls, which proved of less use than the "Lucanian cows" of Hannibal.

Two hundred pirates indeed fell, but the town was taken.[1] An *incredible* slaughter (were anything incredible at this stage in Mr. Leslie's history) was made of the inhabitants. Finally, 7,000 houses, "mostly of cedar," were burnt down; in fact, the whole town was

---

[1] It is worthy of note that Drake's expedition (in 1595) had been altogether deterred from marching to the attack of Panama by *the newly erected fort*. They returned on board, and Sir F. Drake dying soon afterwards (Hawkins had died just before) went back home. Four hundred wild bulls had been tried on Drake at San Domingo (1585). *Colliber*, p. 72.

reduced to ashes. It is painful to learn that "the blame of this black and barbarous action" was generally laid on Morgan, although a justification of him was published by one of the parties actually concerned, alleging that the act had been done in his absence and without his orders, and the whole lamentable occurrence was rather to be attributed, in the author's opinion, to a certain nasty "revengeful temper" of the Spaniards, prompting them "to disappoint the expectations" of brave and industrious buccaneers. The latter, however, remained in this unhealthy spot some three months, unearthing "millions" of gold and silver from wells and cisterns, where it had been hidden, and extorting as much more by the processes already described, from such "unhappy captives" as they could get hold of. Returning to Chagres, we are told they "made a dividend," larger probably than that of any trading company of the date.

The profits of this kind of enterprise, which doubtless laid the foundation (in the seventeenth century and later) of many a great mercantile fortune, were certainly enormous; the most necessary form of capital being a high degree of moral (or immoral) courage and a hardy disregard of the finer feelings of civilisation. Commerce, the wasteful cultivation of the richest soils, was all very well. It was better to capture a mine, and occupy it—a tenant against will—for three weeks, while the forced labour of natives brought up eighty pounds weight of gold dust; but it was best and simplest of all to seize ready piles of coined gold, or merchandise packed for transmission and sale. The principle had been enunciated long before by Raleigh in his descent on St. Thomas. "This is the true gold mine, and those who think of any other are fools!" Morgan's company brought off from Panama 175 mules' burden of silver, gold, and other precious spoils. Each sailor received 200 pieces of eight, and "it seems probable" (a reflection in which we may respectfully concur) that Morgan, who, upon their mutinous demand for more, was glad to sail off privately with a few trusty friends, "reserved too large a share for himself." In any case, he reached Jamaica with 400,000 pieces in specie.

The fall of this great man from such a pinnacle of renown and fortune is a lamentable affair which recalls our attention to history.

The question whether piracy was to be encouraged or tabooed was the problem of home policy occupying the attention of each successive Governor, and there were eleven Governors in the course of forty-two years. The ceaseless agitation in favour of "local option" in this matter perhaps tried these officials as severely as the climate. To favour piracy was to be popular with "the trade," and with the enterprising inhabitants of Jamaica in general. To oppose it was to secure at least the formal approval of the authorities at home. In fine, "sharp memorials" from the Spanish authorities addressed at this period to the English Government had their effect, and piracy was discouraged for a while. Morgan, *who had never acted without a commission,*[1] refused to prosecute any further designs when the Governor recalled it. He was indeed threatened vaguely with punishment for his "pyratical courses" in the past, but "his money "—

"So useful it is to have money. Heigho !"

"saved him at that time." He purchased a plantation and settled down to a civil career, was made a councillor of Jamaica, and afterwards knighted by the King. He even became Lieutenant-Governor

---

[1] The editor of the recent new edition of Exquemelin's famous *History of the Buccaneers* (1893) seems to make a mistake, as pointed out by a reviewer in the *Athenæum*, in ignoring this important fact. The code of law in force in Jamaica since the governorship of Sir Thomas Lynch (1682) and abstracted in Leslie's account, made it a capital felony "for any person to serve in America in an hostile manner against any foreign Prince, State, or Potentate in amity with the King of Great Britain without special license under the hand and seal of the Governor." It should also be added that blasphemy and profane swearing were subject to a penalty of £20 for every offence, &c., &c. "You will observe," naïvely remarks the author, "that whatever bad character be given of this place proceeds not from want of good regulations, but from a neglect of putting them in execution."

of the island ; yet, nevertheless, he was called to account, like Raleigh, for actions sufficiently authorised in years long past, and sent a prisoner to England, where, unaccused and unheard, he languished and died, the victim of a " Court faction."

A detestation of everything Spanish is a characteristic feeling of the time and place.

In the good old days of Morgan, laments the author, " no *Spaniard* durst insult a *Briton*. . . . English colours struck terror into whole fleets. . . . Now (1738) our brave sailors work in the Spanish mines, our merchants' effects are seized. . . . We may complain, but, good God ! we dare not make reprisals."

Piracy, vigorously suppressed in 1689—Sir Henry Morgan died in 1690—revived at intervals during the eighteenth century, notably in the case of the famous "Blackbeard Teach," who seems by all accounts to have been the blood-thirstiest of all the buccaneers, and the true prototype of Captain Flint of *Treasure Island.*

Teach took to piracy in 1716. The peccadilloes of Morgan pale before his atrocious barbarities. When his crew grew too large he "marooned" half of them, by the ingenious artifice of a pretended wreck, upon a desert island, and sailed away with the more desperate remainder. At mess he laid his pistols on the table and fired at his officers (or those who had not taken the hint and retired) merely to maintain an atmosphere of discipline. When asked if, in case of his death, his wife or any one knew where his treasures were hid, he replied, " Only the d—l and myself know that."

Teach was killed a few years later in a hand-to-hand combat with a lieutenant of the royal navy. But privateering by no means ceased at his death.

The career of Port Royal was indeed cut short by the appalling earthquake of June 7, 1692, which seemed to many, as similar calamities had appeared to the pious Las Casas a century and a half earlier, the Providential punishment of the iniquity of the

L

inhabitants. As to that, Providence might have suffered from an *embarras de choix*. The wickedness of the West Indies was proverbial. Its historical record for the preceding two centuries had begun, as we have seen, with a catalogue of the most appalling outrages and barbarities known to history. Every spot, every settlement, named after all the saints and dogmas known to the Catholic religion, was stained with blood. The most horrible crimes of Brasiliano or Teach were child's play to the foul monstrosities which the *Brevissima Relacion de la Destruccion de las Yndias* disclosed to the civilised European world in 1552, especially as the latter were exercised upon the simple, innocent, and defenceless natives, the former against a well-armed, though cowardly and corrupt, race of Europeans, who, when they had the chance, retorted in kind.

The tone of colonial morals in the eighteenth century does not, however, quite satisfy the author from whom we have been quoting. His heart is indeed with the pirates,[1] which leads him, after singing

---

[1] The exact definition of "piracy" is a point of some delicacy to the English historian, these being matters which it is difficult to regard from a cosmopolitan point of view. The Spanish historian Mariana naturally speaks of Elizabeth's great admiral as "*el pirata* Drake." Sir Walter Raleigh's is of course the most interesting case, the practical decision of which turned on a sudden "exigency" of foreign politics, as is explained very clearly in two of James Howell's immortal letters. King James, who would perhaps have appeared as a sleeping partner in the gold-mine venture, *had it been successful* (James Howell regarded it as an "altogether airy and supposititious mine." "*Who would not promise mines, nay, mountains of gold, for liberty?*"), betrayed his plans for the descent upon the island of St. Thomas to the Spanish Governor of that island, in whose cabinet the document, *communicated by Raleigh to the King in the strictest confidence*, was afterwards found. Howell is convinced that the Royal Patent should have protected him. But the influence of the Spanish Ambassador was very strong, and "there was more than an overture at that time of a Spanish match." Gondomar (letter of March 28, 1618) "speaks high language," asked an audience of James, saying he had but one word to say; and, entering the Royal presence in a towering passion, "he said only '*Pirates, Pirates, Pirates*,' and so departed." "I believe he will never give him (Raleigh) over till he hath his head off his

the praises of Sir Henry Morgan, self-made man, buccaneer, statesman, and martyr, to a reflection which would otherwise appear un-
called for. "I would not have you imagine *that I look upon vice as
the origine of virtue.*" There was, indeed, room for a little misappre-
hension. The persons whose constancy, bravery, and other virtues are
here lauded to the skies by the patriotic colonist were more cruel and
bloodthirsty, more repulsive to humanity than the very alligators and
venomous reptiles of their adopted home, while the moral atmosphere
of the insular aristocracy, described as "haughty" in disposition,
leading the life of petty despots, and despising all intelligent industry,
was even more unhealthy than the climatic conditions which encouraged it. But when our author, carried away by an academic
indignation against the dead and gone buccaneers, exclaims, "No!
Such principles I look upon as base, and the *dazzling consequences* of
them I view with an eye of equal horror," we can hardly take his
assurance *au pied de la lettre.* The "dazzling consequences" were
highly profitable to Jamaica. The hero of Panama, whom John

shoulders." Raleigh was executed October 29, 1618, although Queen Anne of
Denmark wrote a special letter to her "kind dog" the Duke of Buckingham, to
intercede for him. (Dalrymple, *Memorials*, 1762, p. 58.)

It was funny, observes Howell, "that the same man should be condemned for
being a friend to the Spaniards, and lose his head, under the same sentence, for
being their enemy."

The richest of all Spanish mines—according to the author just quoted—*i.e.* those
in Potosi, only paid 6 per cent. about the middle of the seventeenth century. But
this fact only rendered the richly-laden Acapulco still more attractive. "Spanish
galleons not yet in sight" is the constant refrain of Anson and other pious
navigators of the eighteenth century, what time scores of "waggon loads" of gold
and jewels went up from Bristol to the Bank, and a large proportion of our
"Pyrates" must have found employment in more legitimate maritime enterprises.
Their irregular service had long been the best training school of an effective
marine. The first Van Tromp himself (Martin, 1597–1653) began as "cabin-boy
to an English pirate, who had killed his father, and taken the Dutch man-of-war
of which he was captain." See Samuel Colliber's *Critical History of English Sea
Affairs* (2nd ed. 8vo, 1739) a rare and valuable work compiled from French and
Dutch sources.

Evelyn (meeting him at Lord Berkeley's in October 1674) naturally compared with Sir Francis Drake, was the sort of person whom circumstances seemed at the time, and for long after, imperiously to require "to keep both the Spaniards and the French in awe." Their "insolence," especially the former's, exasperated a race conscious of superior ability, character, and physique. Nor had cosmopolitan theories of the immorality of a policy of "annexation" yet begun to influence the growth of the empire. Peace, therefore—not undisturbed by domestic trouble, for in 1735-6 the island had been in arms for nine months together against the rebellious negroes, finally conciliated by the humaner policy of Hon. Edward Trelawny, the last Governor mentioned—was often endured with impatience.

With 1739 came the destruction, by Admiral Vernon, of Porto Bello—when Commodore Browne fired 400 shots in twenty-five minutes against the castle—and with the recrudescence of war the spirits of the colony revived. Mr. Leslie concludes his little volume in a happier tone :—

"*The Privateers have had a wonderful success, and again (if the war continues) Jamaica will be the richest spot in the universe.*"

Tailpiece of Jacob Tonson's (1725).

V.

A MEDLEY OF "MEMOIRS."

Title-page from Rob. Gaguin's *Compendium* (of French History, from Pharamond, with the additions, to 1491)—*Impressit rursus diligens ac peritus chalcographus Anthonius bonemere in inclyto Parisiorum gymnasio . . . . . A.D. 1514. Sm. 8vo.* The text of this work begins "Franci (ut pleræque aliæ nationes) a Trojanis prodiisse gloriantur.'

A MEDLEY OF "MEMOIRS."

History is the great Looking-glass through which we may behold with ancestral eyes the various actions of ages past, and the odd accidents that attend time, discern the different humours of men, and feel the pulse of former times.

JAMES HOWELL.

Ayez les choses de la première main, puisez à la source ; les premiers commentateurs se sont trouvés dans le cas où je désire que vous soyez.

LA BRUYÈRE.

"ORIGINAL authorities" are things with the importance of which we have all of us, since the modern renaissance of criticism and scholarship, been made thoroughly acquainted.

In the ideal text-book of nineteenth-century education we walk, so to speak, upon a very mosaic of citations through galleries of genuine antiquities, carefully selected and arranged to give us the due proportion of contemporary feeling and local colour, while the mind of the historian of the higher order represents, one may respectfully presume, a sort of refined and concentrated essence of everything that was ever said or done in the period he has made his own, but lightly flavoured with his "personal equation."

This was not always so ; not, for example, in the more conventional days of the eighteenth century, during which history, even when composed by the "person of quality," was apt to become a mere réchauffé of respectable but scantily examined traditions, of the ideas which it was thought proper to hold of certain famous epochs and personages with whom the common world could not in due respect claim a very intimate acquaintance.

Gibbon, indeed, set a splendid example of telling us, with the sociable enthusiasm of a lover of books, where he got the materials used in building that great "bridge from the old world to the new," which is to most of us yet the main highway across the dark forests and dismal swamps of the early Middle Ages. But to many a historian of Gibbon's date, and still more to historians of a preceding generation, "authorities" were a mystery concerning only the learned author.

And their use was sometimes a matter of indifference, and sometimes of serious fraud. Did not Johnson himself, while sneering at the "verbiage" of Robertson and the "foppery" of Dalrymple, prefer Dr. Goldsmith's *Natural History* simply on the ground that (having been constructed, at the great lexicographer's own suggestion, without reference to facts) it more closely resembled a "Persian romance"? And even if "facts" and "authorities" were to hand, their treatment was not that to which we are accustomed. Thus when Archdeacon Coxe forwarded the Oxford and Townshend papers to Dr. Somerville, the historian of the reign of Queen Anne, the favour was coupled with a suggestion that the proprietors of the documents would be glad if he (Dr. S.) *could see his way, by their evidence, to justify the Whig Ministry for rejecting the terms of peace offered by Louis XIV in* 1707-9.[1] The conscientious historian came to a quite opposite conclusion, yet suppressed a note on the ground that it was indelicate to criminate statesmen upon evidence supplied by their descendants! This, at such a proximity of date, would be natural enough, but none the less delusive to posterity. But the truth is that in the eighteenth century, though the most casual of historians would probably have asked for a few "papers" to give an antiquarian flavour to his work—just as Goldsmith was on the point of studying *Natural History* until warned by the learned Doctor of the respon-

[1] *Somerville's Hist. of his own Time,* 8vo, 1861, p. 290.

sibility this would involve—the modern critical spirit, that which inspires the very latest German (or American) explorer into Venetian archives, was almost unknown, and though educated writers might know that "original authorities" ought to be "consulted," few persons in those days of imperfect communication had a very clear idea what or where those authorities might be.

Still, as the gentle reader in all ages craved for personal and domestic details, these had often to be supplied either from a traditional store of anecdotes, or out of the writer's own head. Hence the large space occupied by *negation* in the best and most authoritative modern histories.

Half the characteristics of the most famous personages of preceding generations, as we learnt them in our youth, have now to be remodelled or cast aside. For we are not only daily discovering new sources, new archives, rescuing priceless family papers, hitherto latent in lofts, from the perusal of "opici mures," cataloguing imperfectly examined volumes, and arranging neglected libraries, but daily correcting the errors and imperfections of the vast mass of older literature which (sometimes because it is so much better written) we still find it difficult not to read.

Thus even in an epitome,[1] the most wondrous with which we are acquainted in an age of handbooks and abridgments, we are obliged to be told that Otto II. never fought at Basentello, nor Lucullus at Artaxata, that Cleon was not a tanner, but a capitalist and owner of factories (this sounds rather too much like a modern political "explanation"), and that Sulla (not Sylla) did *not* die of the *so-called* Phthiriasis. The individual reader may be driven to exclaim, "I never said he *did*." It is no matter, others have. And these notes

---

Professor Karl Ploetz's *Epitome of History, Ancient, Mediæval and Modern*, translated by Professor Tillinghast, of Harvard, U.S.A., with a magnificent index, carries the reader with perfect safety but almost terrifying rapidity, from the earliest Pyramids to the new Japanese constitution of 1882! An invaluable work, with references to the best modern authorities.

do not mean that recent research has unearthed the private accounts of " Cleon and Co.," or that Sulla (like the late Mr. Henry Matthews, or Montaigne in Italy) left behind him the *Diary of an Invalid*, just printed at Oxford or Berlin.   It only means that, owing to the intellectual renaissance aforesaid of the so-called nineteenth century (the hackneyed phrase itself surely indicates our attitude of " Historic doubt "?) we now know, like Socrates, *that we do not know* a great deal which our ancestors, in the dark ages and even the last generation, believed with scarcely an effort.

But in these more enlightened days all such darkness and even a good deal of doubt has been chased away, and every *Geschichtliche Quelle* rendered as accessible as possible to the thirsting student.

How vastly moreover is our positive knowledge increased by the publication of the "original text unabridged," or, as in the case of the very latest version of the Journal of Mr. Samuel Pepys, *almost* " unabridged edition."

" We knew already," writes a serious reviewer of the first instalment of this work, which in truth seemed to contain no new fact of much greater importance than this, " that on January 4, 1659-60, ' It snowed hard all the morning, and my nose was much swelled with cold,' *but the entry at the close of the day was wanting. ' Home, and so to bed, but much troubled with my nose, which was much swelled.' "   Specialists in English history then, who have during fifty years been tormented with doubts as to whether the Secretary of the Admiralty did or did not go to bed on the evening of " January 4 1659-60," may now seek their respective couches in peace.   Nay, they know more, as much as any courtier could have wished to know of the Grand Monarque, that a nose swelled on that eventful morning continued—so little change have two centuries and a " new style " wrought in human nature—to trouble its methodical owner until nightfall !

Yet we have not *all* the Diary of Mr. Pepys—of Mr Pepys who

occupies half a page in telling us that a man told him nothing on
April 7, 1664—even yet, for though much that is questionable has
been printed, "*certain grosser improprieties have been left out,*" (!)
and the reader is still a victim to the harassing anxiety, pathetically
referred to by the reviewer, that "something is being kept from
him." Alas! many things ; but oh! how full of hope and promise
for the higher education of the future is this passionate appetite for
a fulness of knowledge. Or shall we admit that even with regard
to "complete" texts, the sagacious maxim sometimes holds good,
"*Magnæ immo maximæ sapientiæ est quædam æquo animo nescire
velle*"?

The general reader of the nineteenth century, among his other
inestimable advantages, lives in a very atmosphere of editorial
comment. There is not a great classic that might not be buried
under a mountain of works written upon or round about it, any one of
which some expert or other will generally assure the tyro that he
ought to read, and with all of which the critical "authority" of the
day must, we fear, be presumed to have a "bowing," or at least a
"dagger-drawing," acquaintance. Thus the popular exposition of even
the most famous of highly intellectual works is apt to become more
appreciated than the "original." But it is not so with the best samples
of the "original memoir." As a species of "reading," this literature
stands by itself. It goeth down like an oyster, and sticketh in the
mind like the scandal of which—such is human nature—it is so
largely composed. It has, indeed, important advantages, not only
over obscurer "original works," but over the history which is specially
addressed by moderns to moderns.

In our appetite for "private views" of life, for familiar letters,
notes, journals *et hoc genus omne*, is expressed a primæval human
instinct—the ardent desire to know the affairs of other people as
distinguished from things which the historian is anxious to tell us—
rather ostentatiously—for our good. And, mere curiosity apart,
uncorrupted humanity retains a deep suspicion of all the prepared

stories, concocted explanations, analogies, and apologies often disguised as histories.   Does not Mr. Thackeray tell us that he believed
no autobiographies but those of Robinson Crusoe, Mariner, of York,
and his kind, and that fiction (here spoke the novelist) carried most
"truth in solution"?   But almost the earliest works of our Aryan
ancestors were concocted with a religious and political purpose, and
even modern historians sometimes have prejudices.   "So," it may be
rejoined, "has the memoir writer."   Most true ; but the prejudices of
the modern are too " more than kin and less than kind " to our own
to be, yet, of great interest to us.   While, of original writers (who are
not thinking about us) even the contradictions, as Bolingbroke says,
are instructive.[1]   Their awfullest lies convey more striking truth than
the platitudes of a writer of our own generation.   Moreover, to grasp at
a deeper reason, man, even nineteenth-century man, is by nature as
profoundly diffident as he is gregarious.   He may " talk tall " among
a dense population of his contemporaries, but the fact is that just as
the simple-minded "masses" delight to learn, by means of the interviewer, that their wealthy, learned, and high-born contemporaries
resemble them in divers otherwise insignificant particulars, so the
most cultured and independent agnostic of us all is, in his secret
heart, vastly reassured by the knowledge that Charlemagne took an
apple and a glass of water and went to sleep after luncheon ; or that
Petrarch walked about the streets of Avignon in painfully tight boots,
fearing lest the wind should blow his hair out of curl.[2]   We like to
know that other people are not really different from, nor (*sotto
voce*, be it said) much better than, ourselves , and the detailed

---

[1] Bolingbroke's notes *On the Study and Use of History* (8vo, Cadell, 1779),
which also embrace a valuable memoir of his time, have, one is glad to see, been
recently reprinted in a cheap pocket edition.

[2] The Abbé de Sade's " copious, original, and entertaining" *Mémoires p. s. à
la Vie de F. Pétrarque* (3 vols. 4to, Amst. 1764), so freely utilized by Gibbon, is
an old-fashioned labour of love, and genealogical pride (though the portrait of Dr.
Sade's ancestress, Laura is not such as to rouse admiration), collecting a mass of
original matter to which he should have added an index.

evidences of these simple truths are just what the memoir-writer preserves for us, whether he writes about himself or about other people.

The memoir, again, as distinguished from the history, which is the sublimated essence of all such *Quellen*, gives us, when judiciously studied, what lawyers call a *case-knowledge* of history, a thing different in kind from the grasp of "general principles," but within its range more satisfying and reliable. Take, for instance, an original letter—and letters (not letters like those in which Mrs. Chapone strove to form the character of the "young person") are often but a detached and more instantaneous variety of memoir—·take several typical examples which chance to be at hand,—the Emperor Julian's angry mandate for the exile of St. Athanasius;[1] Charles IX.'s official explanation of the "regrettable" events of August 24th, 1572;[2] Montesquieu's passing remark on the decay of Spanish and the growth of British empire;[3] Maximilian the Great's confidential and ungrammatical communication to Margaret of Austria, announcing his intention to reform, and, if he could raise the necessary funds, *run for the Papacy*;[4] Theodore Beza's instinctive apology for the destruction of a

[1] *Juliani Imperatoris Opera*, 8vo, Parisiis, 1583, p. 157.

[2] Appended, with other documents, to Hotman's account of the massacre (see p. 44). *A propos* of the same episode, it is in the Letters of the famous Cardinal d'Ossat (p. 687 of the 8vo ed., Paris, 1627) that we find recorded the historically invaluable remark of Cardinal Alessandrino—on hearing the news of the massacre —"*Loué soit Dieu, le Roy de France m'a tenu promesse!*"

[3] "Que dites vous des Anglois? . . . . c'est une grande baleine :
     ' Et latum sub pectore possidet æquor.'
La Reine d'Espagne a appris à Europe un grand secret, c'est que *les Indes qu'on croyoit attachées à l'Espagne par cent mille chaînes, ne tiennent qu'à un fil.*"— Montesquieu, *Lettres Familières* (ed. par l'Abbé de Guasco). 8vo. Florence. 1767. P. 15 (Mar. 6, 1740), and see p. 134.
     In another passage, the author of the *Esprit des Lois* refers in a light-hearted manner to the improbability of kings reading his book, which Voltaire, he tells us, "was too clever to understand."

[4] *Lettres et Mémoires de Louis XII.* &c. &c. Ed. Godefroy. 4 vols. 8vo. 1712. (IV.)

heretic, "*exustus est sane, sed sero*" [1]; or the picture of a very pretty literary quarrel, handed down by the Cavalier Marino.[2] Do not these photograph for us with inimitable effect, an attitude, an atmosphere, a stage of civilisation, a striking scene never more to be recalled, and only now realisable through that wondrous telescope—the printed book ?

The memoir is of course not to be too nicely distinguished from the history. The "Memoirs" of Philip de Comines range from intimate personality to the profoundest diplomacy of the time. Duclos's invaluable *Mémoires Secrets sur les Règnes de Louis XIV. et XV.* (library edition, 2 vols. 1791) represent rather the collected notes and reflections of a serious historian upon the fearfully interesting period during which ripened and matured "the red fruit of an old idolatry."

The genuine memoir is intensely, if not grossly, personal, and does not aspire to the "dignity of history." But what is the "dignity of history"? The late Mr. Charles Kingsley thought it could not be denied to his account of the poaching affray in *Yeast* (itself a fictitious memoir carrying a good deal of "truth in solution") by "any gentleman who had had his head among the gunstocks for a few minutes." If not, one felt that one could get on without it. The early chronicler did, and, since his chronicle is also as often as not a memoir, must here have a kindly word. In ages when the flame of thought burned but dimly, and writing for pleasure was apparently unknown, we owe all that we have to this well-meaning and laborious person. He has been lightly accused of a "crude voracity for fact" because forsooth he has not always nicely weighed the proportionate interest of a complicated political crisis and the alleged birth in some remote county of a puppy with three heads, or because the Saxon chronicle sums up the national affairs of a twelvemonth long preceding what is known

---

[1] *Epistolarum Theologicarum, Liber unus.* Genevæ, 8vo, 1573. p. 10. This is a rare and interesting volume.

[2] *Lettere gravi argute e familiari,* 12mo, 1673.

as "the Oxford Movement" in the brief and pithy sentence—"No one went to Rome this year."[1] A more serious charge is the heavy burden that lay upon these our first historians of "totalling up" in a lengthy compendium all that they believed to have happened from the creation to the beginning of their own experience. The estimable Gregory of Tours has indeed given us a unique and priceless picture of the Merovingian courts, but why did the Bishop, unlike our own Venerable Bede, stuff his precious little volume with so much that would have been better included in one of his hagiological works? Sanguinary and horrible anecdotes, too, are their bane. Saxo the grammarian (who did not, as the eminent Shakespeare-Bacon controversialist supposed, write in Danish!), however he may fall short of historic "dignity," leaves us in no doubt as to how the Prince of Denmark (Amloda—the madman, or Amleth, as the chronicler calls him, though "we," as Mr. Podsnap would explain "say *Hamlet*," putting the "h" at the other end) disposed of the body of Polonius. It was given to the pigs; but that is another, and a painfully mediæval, story.[2] Let us begin at the beginning. Has any one yet published a

---

[1] On looking back to this entry I find that I had slightly underrated its importance. The full text is "*An.* 889. This year no one went to Rome, *except two couriers whom King Alfred sent with letters* (!)."—*Chronicon Saxonicum.* Ed. Gibson, 4to, 1692, p. 90.

Severe weather distinguishing any particular year is constantly noted by the early annalists: and a liberal amount of space, as we should expect, is usually given to remarkable phenomena of natural or supernatural history. See the entertaining account given by Matthew Paris—the best and most instructive of our chroniclers—of a tremendous and unheard-of conflict between whales and other marine monsters on the east coast (*an.* 1240), where eleven huge dead carcases were cast up by the sea." Finally an enormous whale made up the Thames estuary, and with difficulty got between the piles of London Bridge. It was pursued by a large number of sailors in boats as far as a certain "manerium Regis quod *Mortelac* dicitur," where there was an exciting finish, and the monster was killed with some difficulty. A minor poet of the day wrote a jocose epigram on the subject in Leonine verse. Matt. Paris, *Historia Major*, ol. 1571, p. 733.

[2] *Saxonis Grammatici Historia Danica.* Ed. Müller und Velschow (a superbly printed edition), 4to, Hafniæ, 1839, p. 138, et seq.

list of the "best hundred books" of the kind we are here considering?

The deservedly respected, if occasionally tiresome, Xenophon[1] would
appear to be one of the first of European memoir writers. Soldier,
sportsman, and *littérateur*, his writings include all interests military,
social, and political. In his *Memorabilia* he plays the part of a
more dignified Boswell to the greatest man of his age, the martyred
philosopher by whose side he fought at the Battle of Delium in 424
B.C.; and his only too well-known *Anabasis*—for all its monotonous
breakfasts and "parasangs"—can only be compared to the accounts
by La Baume or Ségur of the more disastrous Napoleonic retreat
from Moscow.[2]   Julius Cæsar's memoirs of his own campaigns were,
we know, the favourite reading of the French Emperor, and the commentaries of both monarchs are unreliable, where they are so, for
very similar reasons, since, as a sage critic has remarked, a knowledge of the truth does not always imply a desire to tell it.   To omit
classic historians who have been the model of all subsequent ages,
the *Lives of Emperors* by Suetonius (68—116 A.D.) form a series
of priceless historical cameos the suppression of which would
certainly have left human nature higher than it now stands in public
estimation.   The letters of the younger Pliny (belonging to the same
period) supply, quite incidentally, unique materials to history.   In

---

[1] Thucydides is, of course, the prototype of the dignified historian. In Herodotus,
on the other hand, there is more of the digressive story-loving Frossardian
chronicle, and of the true " Memoir of my Life and Times." " Imagine," says
a modern French historian, " Marco Polo, Joinville, and the Arabian Nights mixed
up and thrown into the form of a prose Odyssey, and you have the History of
Herodotus."

[2] Eugène La Baume (whose account is less known than that of Ségur) appears
in his preface (*Relation Complète de la Campagne de Russie*, &c. 6me ed. corrigée
&c., Paris, 1820) as quite the ideal *contemporary* memoir-writer.   His record of
events was written up, he tells us, day by day; the knife that helped him to his
horse-flesh dinner served also to cut his crowquill pens.   The sack of Moscow he
described by the light of the conflagration, and for ink and inkstand he had often
but a *handful of gunpowder mixed with snow water!*

the well-known letter in the tenth book, Secundus writes to Trajan of the early Christians (from Bithynia late in 112 A.D.) much as an Eastbourne magistrate might communicate with the Home Secretary on the subject of the "Salvation Army."[1] And as an intimate and finished personal record these letters surpass anything in Latin literature. Interspersed with every variety of detail of common life, social, professional, and even sporting ("we shall laugh," he thinks, "to hear that he has killed three wild boars;" and so we do), with capital stories told with equal gusto and good temper, they give us the whole tone of a civilisation, the standard of its morality (Pliny's slaves we may be sure were better off than many servants in the eighteenth century), and in fine the picture of an age surprisingly like our own, when post-horses were a government monopoly (as they are still in the "Playground of Europe"), and fire brigades were regarded in the light of dangerous political associations, as they quite recently were in the United States.[2]

We are not forgetting Cicero, the greatest writer of the greatest age in Roman history, of which his long series of *Epistolæ ad Familiares* (sometimes miscalled *Epistolæ familiares*) and others, should have provided us with the most complete and intimate picture. It was M. Philarète Chasles[3] who first discovered Cicero to be an "overrated man." Ought we to regret that a man so refined, so wanting in brute courage, lived in an age when decision of character was so

---

[1] The history of the MS. of Pliny's celebrated letter is very remarkable. Discovered at Paris in 1500, used by several persons and then lost (apparently in Italy) in 1508, it has never been seen since. *V.* Professor Ramsay's *Church in the Roman Empire*. 1894. Ch. x., note.

[2] A good example, perhaps, of history repeating itself, see Nichols, *Forty Years of American Life* (the author's own time). Longmans, 1874, p. 312. "This position (that of the Irish 'boss' of a volunteer fire company) as leader of a hundred rough and ready young men was not without its influence. They all had votes; and in case of need could vote more than once. What was more important they could show fight, and keep others from voting."

[3] *Etudes sur l'Antiquité . . et sur les phases de l'hist. littéraire* (a most entertaining miscellany), Paris, 1847.

M

imperiously necessary, and when to be decided meant, most probably, to be unscrupulous? "Political exigencies" such as that which rendered the greatest of orators so ready to become the ally of Catiline and to defend the latter against his own charges of "rapine and plunder" might have pursued the painfully self-conscious, the "verbose and sophistical" rhetorician even into our own peaceful days. It is inevitably matter of regret that his vanity, his acute sense of his own merits and of his own sufferings prevented him seeing clearly even all that was going on around him ; and that he was more grieved, as M. Chasles complains, by the loss of a Greek curio than by the death of his *bourgeois* father.

But let us rather be thankful for what we have, for these inevitable confidential effusions of a cultivated gentleman, fallen among a generation of brigands and cut-throats, of a humanely sociable man torn this way and that by human ambitions and human weaknesses, for these confessions ranging from the highest to the meanest of human interests, nor regret that the self-revelation, always interesting and often absorbing is now and then so acutely pathetic.

If a great, a strong man would never have confided to us his vacillations between heroism and chicanery, his half-hearted decision at a very critical moment, to make friends with Cæsar, in order to make him less dangerous (*si eum mitiorem reddo . . num obsum ?*) let us remember that a great and strong man would have perhaps left us nothing more expansive, nothing more satisfying to human curiosity than—Cæsar's Commentaries.

And the "First Napoleon" (*pace* Dr. Mommsen), did he smile to himself when the greatest, or at least the most eloquent statesman of the day addressed him, in one of those eloquent letters, as his "second self"? When he returned Cicero's verses with the complimentary assurance that he "had never read anything finer in Greek," was he aware that the effusive *littérateur* who strove so hard to oppose "arms with words," described him alternately as a "d——d brigand" (*perditus latro*) and "the noblest and best of men," according to the fluctuations of that epidemic of the day, the *terrores Cæsariani*? An answer may be conjectured from the few words of his dropped about the pages of this voluminous correspondence.

But whatever the agonising exigencies of the greatest crisis in the world's history made it advisable or inevitable for the man of words to express, from the proudest and vainest exultation to the bitterest remorse and despair, how perfect throughout is the wondrous style, —the model of all subsequent generations—lucid, racy, fluent, never deranged, and if sometimes condensed (*breviloquentem me tempus ipsum facit*) by the acutest suffering, consoling itself in the torments of anxiety by a line or two from Homer, and when most panic-stricken by the Napoleonic celerity of Cæsar, finding time to discuss in a Greek exercise the question whether a patriot might or might not desert his country when under the heel of a despot! . . . .

For several centuries after the classic age, there is a plentiful lack of communicative and confidential literature. Not that such epithets are inapplicable, for example, to the miscellanies of Aulus Gellius (143), or Macrobius (*ob.* 420). But these classical and justly popular works, if not absolutely devoid of contemporary anecdote and history,[1] draw most of their subject-matter from earlier original sources. The horny Latin of Sidonius Apollinaris (436–488 A.D.) which it is yet a pleasure to read in Sirmond's splendid library edition (4to, 1652), conceals much interesting details of Saxon pirates and country life of Gaul in the fifth century when, after all, men studied, hunted, dallied with classics in the library, and dined sharp by the clepsydra quite unconscious that they lived in one of the "dark ages." Such darkness is, however,

---

[1] Such *e.g.* as the story told by Gellius of the two grammarians he left arguing (*Noctes Atticæ* xiv.) about the vocative case of *egregius*. Macrobius tells some good stories of the wit of Augustus and other persons, mostly at second or third hand. Both the *Noctes* and the *Saturnalia* (which borrows a good deal from it) are chiefly literary and critical. Of the first there is a good Elzevir (1651) and of the latter a particularly fine "Variorum" ed. Lugd. Bat. 1670.

especially among the ruins of the Western Empire, none the less
real.   The curious and sociable reader wanders about in its gloomy
shades finding scarce a "soul" to talk to but fierce ascetics denounc-
ing the world, and the flesh, and pious monks prattling of Blessed
Martin's miracles, or the absurd conceit of the Donatists.[1]

---

[1] See for example the correspondence of Nilus, an Eremite of Mount Sinai and
pupil of St. Chrysostom, edited in a sumptuous quarto by Pierre Possin, Jesuit (Gr.-
Lat.   Paris, 1657).   In these lucubrations (see Ep. 48) asceticism is almost carried
to the point of a *preference for* temptation and misery.   If such letters are almost
devoid, vulgarly speaking, of human interest, they show a far more intimate knowledge of the habits and principles of the Evil One than was ever attained by his
pretentious biographers of later times.   On the other hand Sulpicius Severus (who
died about 410 A.D.) is a charming writer of gentle and humane sensibilities.   See his

From title-page of *Delibatio Hist. Africanæ Ecclesiasticæ.*   Parisiis ap. Mich. Sonnium,
sub scuto Basiliensi, via Jacobæa.   1569.

Opera (*Life of the Blessed Martin*, &c.).   8vo. Elzevir. 1665.   Synesius, the sporting
Bishop, is known to every reader of *Hypatia*, and his letters (Paris, 1605) deal
as much with weddings, funerals, worthless servants, and valuable horses, as
might the memoirs of a modern Dean of good family.   As to the Donatists, let
us recommend to the reader a delightful little volume published by Sonnius at
Paris in 1569, entitled *Delibatio Historiæ Africanæ*, and containing the celebrated

The materials for history, even of private life, are not perhaps so very deficient in the third, and still less in the fourth century, A.D., but their unearthing requires more varied research. We turn of course in the first instance, to professed historians such as Ammianus Marcellinus (320–390), and the minor authors collected under the title of "Augustan" writers. But poetry, panegyric, and religious controversy (not too rigidly confined to their own subject-matters) disguise, in these ages of the world, matters of more real human interest. Thus the eight books of Salvianus of Marseilles (390–484) *De Gubernatione Dei*, consist largely of indignant diatribes on the corrupt civilisation of the great cities of the Empire.

Poetry, the reader might naturally be tempted to study for its own sake—Ausonius, Prudentius, and above all Claudian, from whom Mr. Bryce borrows those few eloquent lines (*Ode on Stilicho's Second Consulship*, v. 129) which paint the imperial feeling of the day, almost as well as Dante's famous letter[1] does for a period nine hundred years later.

Cecilius, author of that curious memoir *On the Deaths* (not to

works of Optatus (*ob.* 384) and of Victor of Utica (*ob.* c. 487) upon the religious controversies and the persecutions of the time.

A propos of such early *collections* of contemporary chronicles and memoirs, one of the best and most useful, a little volume rarely to be found, and well worth a few francs, is the *Annalium & Historiæ Francorum Scriptores coetanei XII.* &c. ex Bibliothecâ P. Pithæi. 8vo. Francofurti. 1594. This contains a most valuable selection of records from the eighth to the tenth century, several important accounts of the life and coronation of Charles the Great, Abbo Levita's metrical history of the Siege of Paris by the Northmen in 886, and the chronicle of Nithard containing (p. 473) the well-known forms of oath sworn (842 A.D.) by Louis of France and Charles of Germany respectively, which supply such invaluable specimens of the nascent French and German languages. "*Annales Francorum Pithæi*," says a redoubtable critic, "*le bon livre*, si vous voyez le mien vous verriez comme je l'ay manié."—*Scaligerana*, p. 266.

[1] See *Epistole edite e inedite di Dante Alighieri*, edited, with the treatise "*Dell' Acqua e della Terra*" by Alessandro Torri. 8vo. Livorno. 1842 (an edition not to be found in the British Museum, 1894).

mention the abominable and wicked lives) *of Persecutors*[1] (the completeness of which is secured by the omission of persecutors *who didn't die*), and Libanius, the eloquent orator, and popular lecturer, contribute, in spite of much dull and formal waste of words, to make real for us certain societies and individuals. Among early letter-writers, and from our present point of view, a respectable place must be given to Quintus Aurelius Symmachus, the contemporary of Augustine, Jerome and Ambrosius, Prefect of Rome, and last of the professed defenders of Paganism. The ten books of Symmachus, whose contemporaries regarded him and who seems to have regarded himself as a second Pliny, were reprinted and still circulated in an attractive Elzevir edition, 12mo, 1653.

The first great "Secret History," prototype of so many a suppressed or unpublished "original authority," appeared, as we might expect, at the great centre of civilisation in the sixth century, Constantinople, and remains, as every reader of *The Decline and Fall* is aware, about the most astonishing memoir ever given, even by private circulation, to a shocked and delighted public. This work known as the *Arcana Historia*, or *Anecdotes*, of Procopius might well have been called "The Scandalous Chronicle of Justinian and Theodora," the celebrated Emperor and Empress whom it has branded with something like eternal ridicule and infamy. Procopius of Cæsarea (who was secretary to the ill-fated Belisarius, and died in the same year as Justinian, 565 A.D.) had published a whole series of historical works treating in a complimentary, nay, flattering style, the military and civil achievements of the world-renowned lawgiver, but it was known that there existed or had existed an important supplement to these in the form of a secret history. Baronius, in his *Ecclesiastical Annals*, regrets its loss, but the manuscript was

---

[1] *Liber de Mortibus Persecutorum, hactenus Lactantio ascriptus*, with facsimile of MS.—another excellent "Variorum" ed. 8vo. Parisiis. 1710. For citations from the interesting works of Libanius (314–390 A.D.) *De vitâ suâ* and *Pro templis* an appeal against Christian persecution) see Lecky's *Hist. of Rationalism*, vol. ii.

then actually lying on the shelves of the Vatican library of which the
annalist himself had charge, and was first published some years after
his death (*Lugduni*, fol. 1623). Our own copy of this fine edition,[1]
edited by the learned Nicolo Alemanni, belonged to Alexander
Boswell, who bought it at Paris in 1729 for £3. The printer's
device is, by a curious coincidence, an immense rising sun.

No sun that ever rose diffused a more startling light upon imperial
affairs than this work. "The *Anecdota* of Procopius, compared with
the former works of the same author, appears," to one of Gibbon's
latest editors, "*the basest and most disgraceful work in literature.*"
But the horrified reader can hardly repress a smile, so complete is the
dichotomy of the author.

The "glorious wars" (of the history circulated under the august
nose of Justinian) here become "useless and wanton massacres."
The "buildings" so belauded as monuments of the great emperor and
his admirable queen become works of vain prodigality and useless
ostentation. "I doubt," concludes Dean Milman, "whether Gibbon
has made sufficient allowance for the malignity of the *Anecdota*."[2]
But although it may be literally true that the appalling profligacy of
Theodora's early life "rests entirely on this virulent libel," and
although the scoffing Gibbon is certainly prone to think evil, there
is really no evidence to answer an author who, whatever his motives,
was clearly himself acquainted with a generation of which hardly any
"libel" can be accounted incredible. Assuming so much, even if the
author of the *Anecdota* writes now and then in a tone of passion,
does that much affect his credit? There were facts of which, we can
well believe, he could not have survived the publication, and which

---

[1] Purchased for 2s. 6d., which shows that not all "first editions" continue to rise in
price. Engravings of a medal, and a portrait of Theodora will be found in the notes.
Alemanni (see note in *The Decline and Fall*) expurgated a few lines of the text.

[2] The editors of Gibbon, however, do not suggest, as at least one eminent
historian has since suggested, that the work is a (contemporary) forgery, which
however, it is admitted, would little affect its credit as an account of social
(and theatrical) manners.

yet deserved, as he tells us, to be recorded, for the instruction and warning of all future tyrants.   The anecdotist, with whom the cynical historian chuckles up and down his scandal-laden page, accordingly proceeds to tell us among infinitely more shocking things that Justinian was a "stupid ass" whose silliness was only equalled by his wickedness.   He represents the great lawgiver and his consort, "Dæmonodora," as "two fiends who had assumed human form for the destruction of mankind,"—which is very much the sort of thing that Shelley felt and wrote about Lord Castlereagh.   At the same time he has the fairness—or, must we say the malevolence ?—to mention that the renowned jurisconsult (and atheist) Tribonian when sitting on the bench at the emperor's side expressed the gravest anxiety lest his imperial colleague "should be snatched up to Heaven without a moment's warning, on account of his unique piety ! "

Both the above estimates of the great lawgiver cannot be correct, and if imperial courtiers were in the habit of saying that sort of thing, we can hardly wonder at a few exaggerations on the other side. The author, even when recounting that a monk once observed Satan himself in the likeness of Justinian, occupying the imperial throne— assures us that he and his friends quite believed this and all the other stories.   If so, one can only say that (whether we believe them or not) he was quite right in committing his impressions to paper.   In one way or another they cannot fail to be instructive.

Fortunately for poor human nature, the best as well as the worst of monarchs have had attentive biographers.

The faithful Eginhart, whose plain unvarnished tale of the disastrous retreat from Roncesvalles (celebrated from the opposite point of view in one of the most ancient Basque ballads),[1] is the kernel of all the

---

[1] See Fr. Michel, *Le Pays Basque*, 1857 ("rare, 20 fr." *Claudin*), where the text (in which many intelligible Romance words occur) and a French translation are given (p. 233).   The famous *Historia Caroli Magni*, long attributed to Arch- bishop Turpin, or Tylpin (*ob.* 753) is now discerned to be a composition of the eleventh or twelfth century.

elaborate fictions which afterwards clustered round the name of Roland, did for the founder of the "Holy Roman Empire" what Asser, the Bishop of Sherborne, did for the first maker of England. The well-known anecdotes of the Great Alfred's proficiency in reading and indifferent cooking rest upon this contemporary authority, whose name, with that of Camden, is also associated with an ancient controversy, which we cannot here discuss, as to the date of the foundation of the University of Oxford.[1]

Nevertheless the French texts recently published by Wulff (4to. Lund. 1881) are perhaps the most fascinating and excited pieces of ancient prose in the language. As the book is not on every library table, we here offer the reader a specimen—from the final episode of tragedy and treachery, when Roland tries to break his wondrous sword Durandal to prevent it falling into the hands of the Saracens.

"Et feri en la pierre de marbre par trois foiz, pour ce que brisier la voloit. Que vous diroie je plus? [This phrase 'Quid plura?' is of frequent occurrence.] En ii. moitiez fendi la pierre, que onques l'espee mal en ot.

"Dont commença Rollant a sonner son cor . . . . (that Christians might come at least in time to receive his horse and sword) lors corna son cors par tel vertu que si grant alainne en issi, que le cor fendi par mi, et si dist en et cuide que les veinnes dou col Rollant li rompirent"; and Charlemagne heard it from his camp eight leagues off and would have returned. "Mes Ganelon (the villain of the piece) said, Sire, ne retournez mie, que Rollanz [text i.] sone tote jor son cor por petit de chose . . . . sachiez qu'il na ore mestier de vôtre aide, ainz chace a aucune beste par cel bois, et pour ce va il ore cornant." Ha, Dex [elsewhere 'Diex' or 'Dieu'] tant son mauves et felon li conseil de Judas!"

The better known Chanson de Roland (8vo, 1870, with Fr. translation by A. Lehugeur) is earlier in date, probably belonging to the time of William the Conqueror.

[1] In Amhurst's curious Secret History of the said home of learning (3rd ed. 8vo, 1754), the author describes it as "a place so noted for faction and turbulency of spirit that it became 'a monkish proverb,

"'Chronica si penses, cum pugnant Oxonienses,
Post paucos menses, volat ira per Angliginenses.'"

The scholastic disturbance which King Alfred, accompanied doubtless by the necessary "troop of horse," is said, in a certain questionable passage of his biography, to have gone to Oxford to suppress, may never have occurred at all; but, assuming the existence of the University, the fact does not seem improbable.

But first among royal biographers should surely come the sweet and pious Joinville (1224–1317) and his intimate and pathetic memoir of Saint Louis—perhaps the most perfect work of its kind in any language, certainly unique as the complete journal of a crusade.

"On they came," he writes of Damietta, "a good thirty of them with their drawn swords in hand, and Danish axes. I asked my lord Baldwin of Ibelin, who knew well the Saracen tongue, what they were saying; and he answered that they said they were coming to cut off our heads." All about him French Knights were busy confessing their sins to one of the Brethren of the Trinity, of the household of William of Flanders. But Joinville could not think of a sin to confess—only that it was no use trying to defend himself or run away. And when one of the terrible axes was raised above him he could only kneel and cross himself thinking, "Thus died St. Agnes." But the Constable of Cyprus, who knelt, in that awful moment, at his side, insisted on confessing to him. "I absolve you," murmured Joinville, "with such power as God has given me. *But when I rose up I could not remember a word of what he had said.*" All which is unheroic, but very human, illustrating indeed the childlike Greek sensitive side of French nature; in a simple age when theologians were gravely debating whether two angels could occupy the same space, and mathematicians were morbidly anxious, as a learned wit assures

---

The most singular of all disturbances at Oxford is that described in the *Chronicle of Adam of Usk* (ed. E. M. Thompson, 8vo, 1876, p. 109) and which lasted for "*two years*" (1388-9). This was a conflict between the Northerners, and the Southerners and Welsh. The former held the streets as a camp, and shot arrows at their antagonists crying "War! war! sle, sle the Welsh doggys!" Several Halls were "broken and plundered," and many lives lost. And certain of the most distinguished colleges at Oxford have exhibited, in our own days, a quite mediæval laxity of discipline. . . . . On the other hand, do we not still get many of our Revolutions from that "home of the inexact and the effete," as Mr. Stevenson calls it, or, let us rather say, from "the Paris," as a kindlier critic has it, " of Great Britain " ?

us, lest the acute angles of a triangle should be injurious to religion. Quite different is our feeling for that flower of chivalry Bertrand du Guesclin when he tells us of the Battle of Poictiers, and of the wrath of Marshal Andreghen, when accused of fear because he counselled concession of the English demands. "Clermont," he swore, "the *rest* of my lance will be before the point of yours." With Du Guesclin's little volume (he died in 1380) we are already passing into the more conventional domain of the Chronicle, *par excellence*, as distinguished both from the early annalist, and the later "historian" (the ideal *Chronicle* by the way, is printed in black letter by Vérard, and the heading of every chapter begins with "Comment" in a fashion fatiguing to the eye) of Froissart, that is, and Jean le Bel, continued by Monstrelet.

Villehardouin, Joinville, Froissart, Monstrelet, the biographer of Du Guesclin, and the loyal servitor of Bayart, what a brilliant series do they not present of naive and fascinating original materials for history ! Perhaps no names but those of Matthew Paris in England and the three indispensable Villani[1] in Italy, are equally famous. Italian history in the days of the Republics is, of course, a vast and complicated tangle, which few writers even pretended to describe. Among isolated memoirs of the most stormy and factious period

---

[1] It is Giovanni who describes the "odious and appalling spectacle" which possibly owed its origin to the earliest circulation of Dante's *Inferno*, when upon a sort of bridge of boats erected over the River Arno all the horrors of Hell were enacted (May, 1304) by men dressed up as devils, and others stark-naked (?) representing souls in torture, amid a hullabaloo of yells and screams. "*The novelty of the entertainment*," we are told, drew vast crowds on to the wooden bridge which finally gave way, many of the spectators being killed, or drowned in the river. Thus was verified what had been promised in the previous advertisement of the entertainment that they should learn something of the other world. (*Storia*, lib. viii. 70.) An incident more peculiarly characteristic of Italian mediæval history is the disastrous failure of the great Bardi bank in 1345. (Lib. xii. 54.)

The small Chronicle of Compagni was published in 1728, and an excellent modern edition with index, forming part of the *Scrittori Italiani*, 8vo, Pisa, 1818, with Nardi's Life of Ant. Giacomini.

there is none more deserving of mention than the short *Florentine History* (from 1280 to 1312) of Dino Compagni, the contemporary and political associate of Dante *Aldighieri*, which plunges the reader at once into the very midst of the barbarous and bloodthirsty quarrels of Guelfs and Ghibellins, Blacks and Whites, Cerchi and Donati, and is none the less attractive for the all-pervading passion of the writer. Small histories, of one State or another, are numerous in the following centuries, and of very various interest, but many of these as well as more special works such as Petrarch's Letters, and *Res Memorabiles*, Politian's account of the Pazzi conspiracy (4to, 1769) belong strictly to the literature here considered.

England, if not so rich as Italy in histories, nor as France in memoirs, possesses at least one unique national monument in the famous *Paston Letters*, extending as they do in almost unbroken series from 1422 to 1509, and exhibiting to us the administrative darkness, local irresponsibility, and rough-and-tumble social savagery of the late (and stale) middle ages. But the *Paston Letters* are not exactly attractive reading. Not sufficient taste or capacity for writing has been developed at their date to make these records the enthralling work they might have been. Such taste and capacity hardly appear till half a century later, when the Renaissance has come, and its first merely literary and "book-making" enthusiasm has worn off. An excessive attention to literary form and style has an injurious effect upon literature the essential characteristic of which is vigorous self-expression. How often, for example, is the miscellaneous reader and book-hunter disappointed to find, on taking up what are entitled (forsooth) the *Familiar Letters* of some celebrity born about the date of the invention of printing, that the volume is stuffed with Ciceronian phraseology *et præterea nihil!* Of the literary "miscellany" often the most "humane" production of such an age, we have given examples at an earlier date (see page 163). In such works a collection of maxims or platitudes are frequently illustrated by examples drawn from any age but that of the learned writer. But one never can be quite sure. The materials of actual contemporary history now and then lie hid amid scholastic exercises and dilettante trivialities, and a single passing reference, or a brace of anecdotes, may make such a volume (at even more than waste paper price) well worth having.

Miscellanies such as those of Estienne Pasquier[1] and Claude Fauchet are, of course, standard works of reference. The inferior sort we only consult, as a rule, in order to take up the spoor of some historical myth or obscure quotation. The scandal of the true "memoir" is fresh killed, and has a "gamey" flavour of its own; and, as has been observed elsewhere, the natural home of this literature is in France, where it obtained a diverse but unrivalled growth in the second half of the sixteenth century, during the period of the religious civil wars, and again throughout the splendid (but less actual) "Augustan age" of the "Grand Monarque." The grave historian De Thou—who is chiefly a judicious compiler and editor of the original records of his time[2]—the journalist L'Estoile, the Protestant leader De Rohan, the unscrupulous and candid Brantôme, the "iron-armed" Calvinistic captain La Noue, whose *Political and Military Discourses* comprise more than their title suggests, Palma de Cayet,[3]

---

[1] Pasquier's *Recherches de la France* stand by themselves, so their frequent citation would seem to show, as a comprehensive sort of introduction to a vast number of subjects and authors. From the most important fact in history to a fancy concerning the song of the nightingale there is nothing the reader can feel certain of not finding therein. With regard to its bibliography, the existence of the handsome 4to edition by Sonnius, 1615 (of which I possess a copy) has, if I recollect right, been "revoqué en doute" by learned bibliographers. (The true book-collector should wish this to be the case with all his possessions.) Its special interest consists in the fact that, amid so much merely literary and antiquarian matter here lurks (suppressed in some editions) the most enthusiastic of *Tracts for the Times*, Pasquier's striking appeal to the Jesuits (iii. 36 *sq.* and see in particular p. 408). *Since the last edition* had occurred an event of no small significance in relation to his case—the murder of Henry IV. As to *Fauchet* see p. 252.

[2] V. Ranke's French History of the sixteenth and seventeenth centuries. *Appendix.*

[3] Whose *Chronologies Novennaire,* and *Septenaire* 1589-1604 contain many

Pierre Mathieu, and a score of other memoir-writers and quasi-historians (of pamphleteers we have spoken elsewhere) throw a lurid and troubled light upon the former period. But it is hardly necessary to say that there is one memoir of memoirs, which either as a personal revelation or as a record of events, should by rights come at the head of such a chapter as the present, the Memoirs of Marguerite de Valois,

Device from title of P. Mathieu, *Hist. des derniers troubles de la France*. 8vo. Jouxte la copie imprimée à Lyon. 1604.

Device from title-page of P. Victor de Cayet *Chronologie Septenaire*. 8vo. Jean Richer. Paris. 1607.

Queen of Navarre. Whole volumes might be written upon this single book, upon its wit, its candour, its artfulness, the deep tragedy pervading it, and the extraordinary relations of its *dramatis personæ* to one another in that wondrous age of which "*c'était le propre*"— the characteristic of certain highly interesting ages "*d'allier la licence avec l'activité*." M. Charles Caboche has written one such volume in

details not found elsewhere, and in particular (not to mention the story of the Wandering Jew) a considerable account of the voyages and discoveries of the time, French settlement in Canada, &c. The "*Mercure François*" in 25 vols. (1605-1644) is a continuation of this work. La Noue's extremely sensible *Discours Politiques*, &c. are to be had in a good *cubical* 16mo ed. with index, 1614.

his copious but most useful introduction, biographical and literary, for the work is also important in both respects. "Tous les mots risqués ou rencontrés par cette princesse," he tells us in an extremely French note which it is impossible not to cite, "ne sont pas restés dans l'usage. *Philastie* est demeuré grec malgré elle. . . . D'autres [expressions] ont disparu avec l'action qu'elles rappellent, on ne dit plus 'après l'avoir dagué on le jeta par les fenêtres' (43); grâce à Dieu on ne le ferait pas davantage." The picture of St. Bartholomew's Eve, following this citation, at least rouses pity for the bride of nineteen, kept awake late by the thirty Huguenot friends surrounding her husband's bed, with whom she was imperfectly acquainted, "having been but a few days married," and roused from her first slumbers by the terrifying grasp of a victim of the massacres, who flings himself upon her, streaming with blood, and pursued by four cut-throats of the League! As to the biography supplied by M. Caboche in his edition (1861, the text alone first appeared corrected from the MS. in 1842), it may be said to comprise (inevitably) all the most scandalous passages from all the contemporary historians, one important source being the atrocious pamphlet entitled *Le Divorce Satyrique*, which finds a congenial place in that *Recueil de pièces servant à l'Histoire de Henry III.* (p. 187, ed. 1683) referred to above.

The great Bethune, Duke of Sully, and Baron Rosny, who escaped as a boy of thirteen from the massacre of St. Bartholomew's, should by rights have bequeathed to us the most valuable record of all. But he did not, and thereby hangs a mysterious tale. The memoirs of Sully, in French and English, are most commonly known in a modernised version, revised and "arranged" (not so unfairly as has been alleged) by the Abbé L'Ecluse, at the suggestion of the Marquis d'Argenson (as the latter tells us in his own memoirs), and first published in three volumes, quarto, 1745. Whatever may be said of this text (and a whole volume of strictures upon its Jesuitical bias appeared soon after, and was reprinted in 1762), the "original" is, as near as may be for a book teeming with valuable information, absolutely unreadable. The subject is a painful one, and what fad or vanity induced the great economist to have the narrative of his life and doings addressed to him by a quartett of secretaries, who are

LIBRI TRE.

AL GRAN DVCA DI FIORENZA
ET DI SIENA.

IN VENETIA.

Device from the title-page of the History of the War in the Low Countries, of Ludovico Guilliardini (1523–1589), nephew of the historian ; *Commentari delle cose piu memorabili seguite in Europa, specialmente in questi paesi bassi* (the original edition dates from Antwerp) *dalla pace di Cambrai* 1529, *inf. a tutto l'anno* 1560. In Venetia, appr. Nicolo Bevilacqua. 4to. 1565. For some reflections made in this work, the author (who also wrote a topographical description of Belgium, *Totius Belgiæ descriptio*, 12mo, 1652) was imprisoned by the Duke of Alva.

endlessly employed, like characters of conventional drama, in telling
him what he already knows, who repeat themselves and confound
their subject-matter, and who were guided as to the amount they
wrote by the probable size of the volume to be filled!—passes comprehension. "You did this," chatter these fatuous officials, "and
then you said that," and "having, with your usual astuteness,
extricated yourself from the above-mentioned dilemma, you next
proceeded with characteristic tact to, &c., &c." The mere fulsome
flattery of the production, however concocted, is enough to sicken
any reader. Nor is it reliable, sad to say, as to many details. Where
the change of a date, for example, could give Sully the credit of an
additional diplomatic or political service to the great king his master,
the secretaries—or must we say the author?—scrupled not to change
it. Yet the work is truly indispensable, and, as Walpole observes
after perusing the first edition, will repay occasional prying excursions
into its chaotic contents. Only beware of the *Index*. Indices in
those old days were composed by trained lunatics who did nothing
else. Witness the following "prize entry" which we once found
under Q, after fruitless inquiry of all other letters, in the "table" of
a famous and valuable history of the sixteenth century, "*Quæ uno
die diversis locis acciderunt*"!

It should be added in common fairness that the day referred to
was a very remarkable one, even for the sixteenth century.

It is hardly possible, we think, for a reader not to find this active
and agitated period of more interest than any other. Every century,
every great epoch, has indeed a peculiar interest and "colouring," so
to speak, of its own, an interest and colouring expressed to a surprising extent, since the invention of printing (and most notably in
the case of the Renaissance), by the very appearance and typography
of its productions, a fact borne in upon all who have systematically
examined many thousands of old books.

But to come to a more practical point, if we recall the number of
striking, dreadful and significant episodes that star the surface of the

N

sixteenth century, the incidents of the Reformation, and the Council of Trent, the sack of Rome, the sack of Antwerp and other tragedies in the Netherlands, the Anabaptist rising in Germany, the execution of Mary Queen of Scots, the defeat of the Armada, the massacre of St. Bartholomew (and the other massacres and murders that mark the course of the religious civil wars in France), the Turkish victories in Europe, and the battle of Lepanto—if we consider such events, and the prevalent literary enthusiasm of the time, it is easy to understand how vast a number of what may be called local and *episodic* memoirs of this period (besides the larger works of professed historians) have come down to us, in many cases already collected for our use by contemporary editors, and in many others bound up together by judicious collectors of later date.[1]

It may be doubted if the celebrated Agrippa d'Aubigné did not rival Sully both in vanity and capacity. This gentleman of France died in 1630. *His* memoirs, which also supply a key to his *Universal History*, in which latter work he clearly considers that he had not

---

[1] For an example of the first one might refer to Goulart's celebrated *Mémoires de l'Estat de France sous Charles IX.* referred to above, which comprise not only a mass of details concerning the period, with documents, decrees, edicts, and harangues, &c., but also a selection of important tracts of the time,—or to such a collection of contemporary narratives as that put together by Lonicer in his useful "Turkish Chronicles," *Chronicorum Turcicorum, tomi duo.*" 8vo, 1578.

As to the second, as good an example as any I have to hand would be a *Recueil factice* in small 8vo (a sale duplicate from the British Museum, 1787) containing the following four pieces, the first three in the original Latin :—

(1) *An Account of the Turkish Attack on Malta* (1569, probably the most remarkable siege known to history), *with documents.* Venice, 1566.

(2) *An Account of the Turco-Polish War in Wallachia*, &c., &c. (1574 A.D.) Frankfort, 1578.

(3) *An Account of the Sack of Dantzig* (April 17, 1577), with a *contemporary satire. Ib.* 1578.

(4) Last, but not least—*An Account of the African Expedition, and death* (Aug. 4, 1578) *of King Sebastian of Portugal.* Nuremberg, 1581, which is (to indicate the popularity of the work) a Latin translation of the French translation of the original Portuguese account.

said quite enough about himself, are written in the very first person, and with that irresistible frankness and *abandon* which, one must admit, often characterises the most appalling mendacity. His single volume, which no one would think of laying down unfinished, reminds one constantly of George Borrow, not to say of "Terence D'Euville" in Mr. Bret Harte's "condensed" Sensation Novel. "At the age of four," says the latter hero, "I was the best shot and the boldest rider in the county." "At the age of six," writes M. Theodore Agrippa to his admiring descendants, "I could read Latin, Greek, and Hebrew without points, besides French."[1] "At seven-and-a-half I translated Plato's *Crito*, on my father promising that the work should be printed *with my infantine effigy on the title-page.*" Does any modern collector possess this volume? We should be glad to see it.

At the age of fifteen D'Aubigné was of course in the saddle performing prodigies of valour. To say that he was the wisest counsellor of Henry IV. and yet the staunchest of Huguenots; that in wit, intelligence, and heroism he surpassed all persons with whom he came in contact, is not to sum up his brief memoirs too favourably. His own repartees, recorded by himself, are really first-rate; and his "assurance" on many points convincing enough; and how excellent, for example, is his story of the gentleman who, joining the royal cavalcade, and assuming Roquelaure, as *le mieux doré* of the party, to be the king, took his place by the side of Henri Quatre,

---

[1] *Mémoires écrits par lui-même*, otherwise called *Histoire secrète*. The text of the common eighteenth century edition (1731) is modernised, and (?) corrupt. D'Aubigné was the grandfather of Madame de Maintenon. Upon his memoirs, and his satirical romance *Le Baron de Fœneste* see some remarks on p. 426 of Bayle's *Lettres Choisies* (3 vols. 8vo, Rotterdam, 1873) which letters, by the way, are a sort of pocket edition of the Dictionary, and crammed with entertaining details, literary and critical.

D'Aubigné, like a still greater satirist and memoir-writer, found a refuge from persecution at Geneva, in which neighbourhood he purchased an estate and built a castle to protect himself against the persecutions of the court of France, and the "ten assassins" employed by his political opponents. See La Beaumelle, *Mémoires de Mme. de Maintenon*, ed. 1789, i. 83.

and entertained that monarch with the latest scandals about the
" Reine Margot." [1] To this class of work, freedom of style and a
strongly-marked individuality give the greatest value. Brantôme is
free alike from prejudice and good taste, but his works are too much
a mere congeries of details, too frequently of the sort which merely
amuse or disgust. D'Aubigné is a real character for whom we feel
a sincere regard; nay, in his capacity of soldier, diplomatist, historian,
satirist—for he contributes the important " Confession Catholique du
Sieur de Sancy " to that celebrated *Recueil de Pièces diverses servant
à l'Hist. de Henry III.*, &c., which had such a vogue in the seventeenth century—one of the leading men of his time.

The mention of Henry III. recalls a rarer work—the *Mémoires très
particuliers*,[2] in which Charles de Valois, Duc d'Augoulême, describes, with much pathetic detail, the death of that monarch at the

[1] Busbec's little volume, so familiar to all book-hunters in the diminutive but excellent Elzevir edition of 1633 (Willems, 380)
is usually cited on Turkish affairs. Among the
Letters from Paris (Ep. xxiii. p. 517) is described
the scandalous scene between Henry III. and the
Queen of Navarre.

The mention of this excellently printed work
recalls the number of valuable histories and
records published by the Elzevirs. Of all these
the most beautiful I have ever seen (and quite
one of the best productions of the century) is
Cardinal Bentivoglio's *Hist. della guerra di
Fiandra*, 3 vols. 8vo, in Coloma, 1635–6 and
1640. Equally attractive is the (less valuable)
Memorie ovvero Diario, 1648, and the (highly
interesting) *Lettere* (from France and Flanders),
1646 (Crawford copy). All are in large clear
type, on fine paper. The device (Palm) here
reproduced is said to have been purchased
by the Elzevirs from Erpenius.

[2] 12mo, Paris (wood-cut title, view of the Seine) 1667. A curious fact, of which
I find a MS. note on my copy is that the (second) wife of Angoulême, himself a
natural son of *Charles IX.*, only died in 1713 !

hand of Jacques Clement. Angoulême—a boy of sixteen—himself saw the "demon of a monk," and held the feet of the king as he lay in his mortal agony.

With D'Aubigné, again, we may compare another lordly narrator of his own exploits, belonging to a yet more famous family. The *Mémoires d'Henri de Lorraine, Duc de Guise*, "le Guise Napoletain" (fifth duke, and great-grandson of Le Balafré, assassinated in 1582, and who also left memoirs), were first published in 1668, twenty-four years after the author's death, and reprinted in 1681, with supplement, 1687. Madame de Motteville tells us a good deal about the author of these memoirs. Apart from their value as a detailed account of the Neapolitan Revolution and the struggle with Spain by the generalissimo who directed it, the dry humour and despotic *verve* of the writer is peculiarly characteristic of one of those histories written by people *qui commandoient aux affaires*, of which Montaigne thought so highly.[1] "I replied, with a smile," writes the Duke, after one of his adventures, "that I was not the sort of person to be afraid of the *canaille* [ed. 1681, p. 138], since, when God made a man of my condition he put something (*un je ne sçais quoi*) between his eyes which the rabble could not face without trembling." This something and the promptitude with which he orders ill-disposed and impertinent individuals to prison or execution, affect the reader strongly. '*Fort sensés*,' is the comment of a French critic on these memoirs, the action of which is brisk, with no waste of words. It should be added that the Duke's confessor also contributed an interesting "account of the state of Naples" under his government, which does not in all respects accord with the Guise version.[2]

To return a little in time and to cross the Channel, perhaps it may safely be asserted that the most striking autobiography in the English

[1] See the excellent criticisms of historians in the chapter on Books. *Essais*, ii. 10.

[2] *Relation de l'Estat de la Republique de Naples sous le Gouvernement de M. le Duc de Guise*, traduit de l'Italien (de Francesco Capecelatro) par M. Marie Turge-Loredan (a French lady who apologises for appearing as an author). 12mo. 1680.

language is from the pen of the famous Lord Herbert of Cherbury
(1581–1648), a contemporary to some extent of D'Aubigné, since he
died but eighteen years later, and quite equally remarkable as a distinguished and original personality, a wit, a philosopher, a soldier,
and an author.[1] Moreover, he spent a considerable time abroad, and
came much under French influence.   Whatever the cause, Herbert's
superiority to an affected generation is as remarkable as the diversity
of his interests.

Fencing, hunting, duelling, travels in France and Italy, music,
racing, politics, captures of outlaws in the mountains of Montgomery-
shire, all interspersed with acutely sensible and highly moral reflections, make up his excellent little book.   The style is a trifle too
conscious, perhaps, even boastful, but thoroughly entertaining.   How
sharp is his retort to Condé's attack upon "the King my master's"
awful habit of "cursing."—It all came of his majesty's "gentleness"
of disposition.   How so?   Because *those whom he could have punished
himself* he left to the Almighty to punish.

With his *Life and Raigne of Henry VIII.* (as the author was
born nearly forty years after that monarch's death) we are not
here concerned ; but only a few years before the date of the memoirs,
which conclude with a mention of the first publication of the aristocratic author's *magnum opus* on the foundations of belief (*in
French*, Paris, 1639, 4to), was written by Sir Robert Naunton what
should by rights have been the best contemporary record of the court
of Queen Elizabeth.   Naunton was born some twenty years before
Herbert, yet his *Fragmenta Regalia*[2] was not published till 1641,

---

[1] For his great religious treatise see Hallam.   The Memoirs were nearly lost to
posterity.   A MS. could not be found in 1741, as Walpole tells us in the preface
to his first edition of them in 1764 (4to, 200 copies).   They were excellently
reprinted (8vo, 1824) by J. Warwick, Brooke Street, Holborn.   In my copy is a
fine portrait dated Saunders and Otley, 1826.

[2] No editions are worth having till Arber's annotated reprint of 1870 (see that
editor's preface), all the earlier issues 1641-42-53 (and the edition of 1814 is a
mere reprint of that of 1641) being more or less hopelessly corrupt.

six years after the author's death. The work—a "little draught of the great princess and her times," is of great value, but its defects (apart from the affectation of the style) are summed up in the fatal editorial comment—"Naunton lived too near the times he wrote of to write all he knew." Modesty and other regrettable characteristics made him prefer even the "censure of abruption" to the "deface-ment of persons departed, whose posterity yet remain." The work was therefore deliberately left in an obscure, imperfect, and unfinished state—a mere collection of notes on Queen Elizabeth's favourites—but is, needless to say, a booklet which every one should read, especially as it will not occupy the time usually given to an evening paper.

To English memoirs of the later seventeenth century the reader is pleasantly introduced in the interesting footnotes of Macaulay, who, whatever his defects, was more deeply saturated with the popular literature of his period than any historian living or dead, who draws "human interest" or local colour from the obscurest literature of libel, drama, and fiction, from Hamilton's Zeneyde or the gossip of Corporal Trim. From the mass of contemporary records of this time one naturally puts aside as works unique of their kind (like the *Paston Letters* aforesaid) the Diaries of Evelyn and Pepys, of which the latter, as the reader is usually reminded in the preface, is for the single decade which it covers (1659–69), of the more intense and exact contemporary interest; while the former, a more cultivated and leisurely work, covering a larger as well as later period (up to a month before the author's death at the age of eighty-five, February 27th, 1706), "partakes more of the nature of history." Dismissing these, which are in every reader's hands, perhaps it may be said that the English seventeenth century memoir suffers largely from its peculiar nature. Military memoirs and the analysis of cam-paigns are of course of a "special" interest, essential indeed to history, but generally appealing to something much smaller than "humanity." To many "voracious" book-hunters there is something almost terrifying in the very appearance, the ugly binding, the

common paper, the meaningless capitals, the crooked yet rarely
picturesque typography of an English volume of the seventeenth
century; the secret being that such literature is almost all in an
"atmosphere" of political, or still worse of theological, controversy.

In England, as in France, it may perhaps be said generally that
the transition from the sixteenth to the seventeenth century marks a
decline in interest. In France the civilisation following upon the
final settlement of the most absolute of absolute monarchies rather
represents a period of splendid but insecure repose. It was the
triumph of Mme. de Sévigné to show how high, how near to the level
of modern days such a civilisation could be carried in a society
where political and intellectual liberty were practically unknown.
In England there was more serious work to be done, and those
who did it, or resisted its doing, are often, from the point of
view of general and humane interest, too busy to be entertaining.
Puritanism, Political Theory, and Civil War, these make an atmosphere
which seems, for the time, to stifle in most writers all freshness,
freedom, and vivacity. Of the terrifying problems of theology we
need not here speak, but the tolerably plentiful and somewhat con-
fusing records of the Civil War in England, seem in their modern
"actuality" and seriousness[1] to have lost the touch of old world
romance that hangs about the struggles of the previous century.
The seventeenth century was, moreover, according to one of
our historians, the age when the "misrepresentations of Faction"
chiefly began.[2] Welwood's useful little *Memoirs of Material
Transactions in England for the Hundred Years preceding the*

---

[1] A seriousness curiously contrasted with the tragi-comic triviality of the
"Fronde," which hardly acquires a "dignity of history" in the commentaries of
the cold and sententious Rochefoucauld. To the French memoirs of this age
should be added the collection of epigrams and satires included in the *Tableau
de la vie de Richelieu, Mazarin, Colbert, and Fouquet*, 12mo, v. ed. 1694, *chez*
P. Marteau.

[2] David Hume, *History of his own Life*, sm. 8vo. Lond. 1777, p. 27 (with
the *Apology for his Life and Writings*, by Adam Smith. *Ibid.*)

Revolution of 1688,[1] (in part a memoir as well as a compendium) was written, he tells us, on account of the difficulty experienced by Queen Mary in "knowing truly the events of her grandfather's reign," and confided to her on the understanding that it should be shown to no one else without the author's consent. Queen Mary could not trust to a letter of General Ludlow (whose memoirs have just been re-edited by Mr. C. H. Firth) in which the character of Charles I. seemed to have been "strangely blackened," and thought that most histories of the time were either "Panegyricks or Libels." Probably she would not have been satisfied even with the letters and speeches of Oliver Cromwell,—although these, surely, if anything, bring back to us "that Puritanism" which, as Mr. Carlyle remarks, "is not of the nineteenth century but lieth buried in long rows of dumpy quartos (the very titles of which are wearying to the flesh) in huge indexless folios," and last but not least in the "fifty thousand unread pamphlets of the Civil War, which lie mouldering in the British Museum alone." Not that all the literature is so bulky (although the mere relation of sieges and battles, and of political chicanery is in any form apt to pall), for who has not read with delight the *Short Memorials of Thomas Lord Fairfax*"[2] that Fairfax to whom Buckingham's epitaph assigned (besides his other virtues) that

> "other thing quite out of date,
> called Modesty."

In these 128 octavo pages have we not the whole history of a Civil War, and what is still more interesting to all but the "Dryasdust," of the feelings it roused in a conscientious man supported only by a religious fervour to which our age is a stranger, through all the weariness and the "vexation of spirit"—kings cherishing

---

[1] See author's preface (7th ed. 8vo. 1749).

[2] Sm. 8vo, R. Chiswell, 1699, ed. Brian Fairfax. At the end is Chiswell's advertisement of the fourth and last part of Rushworth's Collections, and his catalogue (9 pp.) almost exclusively theological.

miserable delusions, soldiers who would be statesmen, "arch-agita-tors," "Hydra-head petitions," "private Juntos," and "levelling Factions," crowned by the loss, let us remember, of a beloved brother in one of the fierce charges on "Marston fields."

Students of Macaulay (and there is surely no writer whose refer-ences so well repay verification),[1] will know that there is one memoir writer—perhaps more often cited than any other—who is of continuous interest from the Restoration to the Revolution—but whose complete text was not published till some years after the historian's death. Among the numerous minor records of the latter half of this troubled century, the age of Evelyn and Pepys—the *Memoirs of Sir John Reresby*[2] supply, perhaps, a more useful and readable narrative than any, and, in particular, a quite pathetic picture, of the deep anxieties undergone by the average gentleman, of no particular principles or enthusiasm, lest he should be

"Off with the old love"

(constitutionally, of course, and revolutionally speaking)

"Before he was on with the new."

---

[1] Among the less obvious sources cited one may note—Halstead Robert, *Succinct Genealogies*, 1685, in folio, "a work probably known to few even of the most curious and diligent readers of history," and that for obvious reasons, the title being to some extent delusive, and the name "Robert Halstead" fictitious, the real author being the Earl of Peterborough. *Macaulay*, i. 269 (ed. 1858); *Inghilterra descritta dal P. D. Bartoli*, 1684; *William Fuller* (spy, double traitor, &c.) *Life of himself*, which one can believe to be very curious.

A perfect feast of criticism upon the great "*Quellen*" of the period, as well as a large assortment of invaluable original texts and extracts in half the languages in Europe will be found in the appendix to Ranke's great history, in which the personal and local "equations" of authors such as Burnet and Clarendon, the corruptions of individual character, the corruptions of texts, the deranging effects of exile and of office, of London and the Hague, are scientifically weighed and adjusted.

[2] 1734. 8vo. An abridged and imperfect edition (? from a MS. since lost). Complete text with notes by J. Cartwright. Longmans, 1875. If any other single work (apart from Evelyn and Pepys) supplies material of equal interest, it is the Diary of Narcissus Luttrell.

Reresby, at least, strikes one less as being in a particular clique or "faction" than other writers—most notably the pious authoress of *The Life of Colonel Hutchinson*, which famous work, however interesting the military exploits therein narrated, is most valuable as the picture of a particular religious atmosphere, of that "manner of life and conversation" which gave perhaps an unnecessary amount of pain to the late Mr. Matthew Arnold and rendered him seriously anxious about the social salvation of Mr. Goldwin Smith in the "long winter evenings of (colonial) Toronto."[1]

The oppression, social and religious, in the air of the seventeenth century is perhaps nowhere better expressed than in some chapters of that immensely popular little work of Bishop Earle (who died in 1665) *The World Display'd*.[2]

Who could forget his *She precise hypocrite* (!), "a Nonconformist in a close stomacher and a ruff of Geneva print," who "doubts of the Virgin Mary's salvation, and dares not saint her, but knows her own place in Heaven as well as the pew she has a key to," and is "so taken up with faith that she has no room for charity"?

Or to turn to that most important source of history of the period, Roger North's *Life of the Lord Keeper Guildford* (3rd ed. 2 vols. 8vo. 1819), which, like the author's other works, and his celebrated "Examen" of Kennet's History were put forward as an antidote to certain "solemn writers of English affairs." The young Francis North, son of Dudley Lord North was first put to school, we are told, at Isleworth under the "indifferent tutorage" of a Mr. Willis. The man was a rigid Presbyterian and his wife a furious Independent. "These two sects at that time

---

[1] See a characteristic passage, of perhaps rather forced irony, in the *Mixed Essays*. Ed. 1880, p. 83. To Mr. Goldwin Smith's exaltation of the Puritan ("Middle-class") ideal, the critic replies with Chillingworth's summary of the matter, "Scribes and Pharisees on one side, publicans and sinners on the other."

[2] Which had six editions (in its anonymous form) between 1629 and 1633, and perhaps an eighth in 1664 (preface to edition of 1740). See also *A Church Papist*, p. 28. Both these objectionable characters appeared in the first edition.

contended for pre-eminence in tyranny, so that they hated one another more than either the Bishops, or even Papists themselves"
—a result regarded by the biographer (who died in the year 1733)
as "the ordinary curse of God upon men permitted to prosper in

This Helmet was a Crown by Revelation :
This Halbert was a Scepter for the Nation.
So the Fifth-Monarchy anew is grac'd,
King Venner next to Iohn a Leyden plac'd.
        Pagitt's Heresiography, ed. 1662, p. 280.

wickedness." Mrs. Willis instructed her babes in praying by the
Spirit, especially for their "distressed brethren in Ireland." These
"fanatic schools" produced in the pupils, as we can imagine,

"violent reactions." But when the future Lord Keeper emerged from this discipline it was only to be subjected to a "Cavalier Master" (!) at the Grammar School of Bury.

When we consider how disturbed all social existence seems to have been, not only by the actual dangers of war, but by such pedantic factions, religious [1] and political, it is impossible not to feel some sympathy for that eccentric Marquis of Winchester described by Reresby, who usually dined all night and slept all day, yet was not really mad, but on the contrary "had good sense," in fact "most thought he counterfeited this *that he might be free and unconcerned from the affairs of that age.*"

The most striking, and historically significant antithesis to the pious Hutchinson memoirs would be those concerning the Comte de Gramont bequeathed to us by his illustrious brother-in-law, Anthony Hamilton, Hamilton the one French Briton, the one Irish Scot (for he inevitably recalls the liveliest Hibernian romance) who is by common consent, not only a master of classic French, but the absolute embodiment of *l'esprit Français.* The merits of this wondrous study in what may be called the later chivalry (for it is no more that of Henri Quatre than that of Bayard), this trivial, yet finished tableau of a society which recognised only one evil—boredom,[2] of this elaborate and complicated farce which concludes rather tamely by the usual *ne plus ultra* of romance, the marriage of all the

---

[1] In Ephraim Pagitt's *Heresiography*—"a description of the Hereticks, &c., *sprang* up in these latter times . . . . together with brasse Plates of the most eminent sectaries" about sixty species, from the Plung'd Anabaptist to the Grindletonian, are enumerated. This little volume (which I possess in the 1662 edition, containing the account of the Fifth Monarchy rising, and portrait of Venner) is in considerable demand among the numerous descendants of the passengers in the *Mayflower*.

[2] John Evelyn is surely to be thanked for preserving a portrait of the one virtuous and yet sociable individual who adorned the said court, wondering only "that any one could like her," and enjoining her younger friends to avoid the society of men. It is curious that the *Life of Godolphin*, 8vo, 1848, quite one of the finest productions of Pickering, should be seen so often "lying about the streets."

principal characters, have perhaps been overrated. In truth "le fond en est mince," but as Sainte Beuve proceeds to remark, though there may have been two or three such gallants as De Gramont, there is but one Hamilton, and this is the only work of his which is worth reading, and re-reading, as another French critic insists, once a year.

It is moreover—let us jealously assert—in so far as it is not a novel, an English memoir, since when we read it, we think less of such events as the siege of "Trin," or Lerida, of which we can read elsewhere, as of Buckingham dandling the Princess of Babylon's "baby," its squalls drowned by the hysterical laughter of the beautiful Frances Stewart and the whole uproarious court of St. James's.

French life is undeniably duller, if grander, under the settled despotism of Louis XIV. than in the more romantic age preceding it; for who could write about the "Grand Monarque" as Bassompierre does of Henry of Navarre? In the memoirs of Mme. de Motteville (ed. 1783, vol. i., p. 386) is a mention of him (*sub anno* 1646) which seems to note the passing away of the old *régime*.

The poor man had just died, quite suddenly. Having apparently recovered from an attack of fever, he was returning to court, and at the first hostel where he put up his servants found him the next morning dead in his bed. "He who had been so beloved by Henry IV."—as one knows from Bassompierre's touching picture of the familiar incidents preceding the dreadful tragedy of the assassination [1] —"and so favoured by Mary de Medici, so admired and famous in the days of his youth, *was scarce regretted in ours*." He was still handsome, courtly, obliging, and liberal, "*but the young fellows could not bear him*. They said that he was not the fashion now, he was too fond of his stories, of talking of himself and his time. I have known some so ungrateful as to ridicule him for his readiness to offer them hospitality when indeed he had scarcely wherewithal to dine himself." Besides, the marshal had an old-fashioned courtesy

[1] *Mémoires de Bassompierre.* Ed. 1665, I. p. 222. In this attractive little edition the "Journal de ma vie" forms three volumes, four in the reprint of 1723

towards women, and manners of a past school which he could not
be persuaded to abandon, and which seemed out of place in an age
when "unbridled ambition and avarice"—the change in moral and
social tone is ascribed largely to Mazarine influence—"passed for the
greatest virtues among the highest nobility." The new generation,
ripening for the "grand" gilt and stucco reign, was doubtless harder
and more artificial, and in a way, less communicative than that from
which Henri Quatre chose the familiar companions, upon whose
shoulders he hung while rallying them upon their superstitious
timidity.

Not that the materials of history, the history of an age in which
literature became "a chorus in praise of royalty"—were ever more
plentiful. De Motteville herself, the patient lady in waiting—first of
the numerous series of domestic chroniclers of French monarchy and
empire, continued to our own time in the persons of the Duchess
d'Abrantes, wife of General Junot and intimate of the great Napoleon,
and de Gontaut, whose memoirs have just appeared in English
(1894)—de Motteville, with her mild wonder at the caprices of her
distinguished employers, what would she have thought of the scenes
reserved for Mme. de Campan! Then again we have the dignified
and classical Rochefoucauld,[1] the light-hearted and theatrical De
Retz, now saving the state, now escaping from prison or assassination, the Marquis de La Fare with his sensational account
of La Brinvilliers and the "Poison chamber" (8vo, 1734), the
conspirator Montrésor (well known in his two Elzevirian "twelves,")
and the confidential Pierre de la Porte (1603–1680) *valet
de chambre*, and—one could have wished—tutor and governor
of the spoilt little "Grand Monarque"—for what a picture is

---

[1] Who is to be read in Renouard's beautiful edition, with the portraits of
Mazarin, Condé, and the rest. Sm. 8vo, "*papier fin*," 1804 (*imprimerie de
Crapelet*). The *Mémoires de M. D. L. R.* (not to be confused with the *spurious*
memoirs of the Comte de Rochefort) dated *Cologne* (*i.e.* Foppens, Brussels,
1662—in which form the work first appeared—are of no value, and full of mis-
prints owing, as we are told, to "the impatience of the public."

his of the poor lonely child craving for affection, and as yet so amenable to reason, growing up in that malarious atmosphere of flattery, corruption, and espionage in which "good books were regarded with as much suspicion as honest people"![1]

Such was the court atmosphere of that long reign. When the profligate Abbé de Choisy (Fénelon's contemporary) was writing one of his moral and improving manuals of history about Charles IX., the little Duke of Burgundy confronted him with a puzzling inquiry "*How will you manage to say that the king was mad?*" There was, however, at least one individual living through all this period, and at court, who literally did not mind making any observation suggested by its singular phenomena, and this was Charlotte Elizabeth of Bavaria, Duchess of Orléans, and mother of "the Regent," who, dying in 1722 at the age of seventy, saw enough both of the Most Christian King and of her own son to appreciate the general drift of French life and politics. She was, as we are told by St. Simon—the gossipping St. Simon whose inaccuracies she once or twice corrects—a coarse, rough, unsociable, and unpolished, but good-hearted creature, and what remains of the immense budgets of news she was always writing to her distinguished relatives in Germany, is not in all cases suited to the drawing-room table. The reader who is anxious to know the worst, should consult M. Brunet's admirable (French) edition (Paris, 1855) the German collections of the eighteenth century being all imperfect. It is she, by the way, who tells us, at second·hand, not content with blackening the character of her own generation, that Saint Francis de Sales *used to cheat at cards!* Possibly he never did, although Victor Hugo in a coruscating paragraph of *Les Misérables* avers that it was the great secret of his popularity.

The papers of the excellent Marquis d'Argenson, who discovered to the French court of 1744 the "entirely original and undeveloped business" of honesty, consist of most valuable political and literary notes on the events of his time (1694–1757), a work to be studied of

[1] *Mém. de La Porte.* 12mo. Genève, 1756, p. 253.

course in connection with Duclos, the vast St. Simon, who really
wastes a good deal of the reader's time, the correspondence of
Grimm, Diderot & Cie., and the ubiquitous Voltaire. Besides
the remark cited above, concerning Sully, he tells us (ed. 1825,
p. 233) that the Choisy Memoirs as printed at Utrecht, 1747, are really
only excerpts ("*la fleur de mon manuscrit*") from a larger collection
of his own, taken down from his kinsman the Abbé's dictation by
d'Argenson himself, and stolen by Olivet, the historian of the French
Academy.

The authorship of the memoir, it may here be observed,
especially of that which has no preface, is too often a matter of
mystery and fraud. The atmosphere of absolute monarchy was
frequently found insalubrious to authors of an inquiring spirit. They
wielded the pen in unwholesome dread of one of those upper cham-
bers in the Bastille where, nevertheless, Bassompierre found a quiet
place for writing, though Bussy-Rabutin could only read or think of
"horrors." Hence at the close of the seventeenth century the Dutch
press became, as Macaulay says, "the most formidable engine by
which the public mind of Europe was moved"; and many a more
veracious record than those of M. d'Artagnan (utilized, so Alexandre
Dumas assures us, in the production of his never-dying *Musketeers*),[1]

---

[1] Possibly more than one reader of the preface of *Les Trois Mousquetaires*—
"dans laquelle il est établi que les héros de l'histoire . . . . n'ont rien de
mythologique" may have concluded that the work there referred to, *Les
Mémoires de M. d'Artagnan—Amsterdam. Chez Pierre Rouge* (no date given)
was apocryphal. The full description, which M. Dumas perhaps quoted from
memory, we here give from the catalogue (1894) of a Parisian bookseller. *Mémoires de M. d'Artagnan, Capitaine-lieutenant de la 1re Compagnie des Mousquetaires du Roy, contenant quantité de choses particulières et secrettes qui se sont
passées sous le règne de Louis le Grand. 1700. 3 vols in 12.* (Anglice, 8vo. ?)
Veau pl. Rare. 25 fr. An order despatched by return of post failed to secure
this treasure. Charles de Bats, Comte d'Artagnan (*ob.* 1673) "a creature of the
ate Cardinal" was the officer who arrested Fouquet. *Mém. de Motteville.*
Ed. 1783, vi. 82. *Mém. de Choisy*, p. 177. Prosper Marchand in a note to Bayle's
Lettres Choisies (p. 653) classes the Memoirs with those of Rochefort as one of

O

found a publisher, and a more or less "Elzevirian" printer in Amsterdam or the flourishing suburbs of "Villafranca" and "Alethopolis." [1] Later in fact, the thing became a nuisance, one Courtilz de Sandras (1644–1712) having established somewhere in the Low Countries, a sort of memoir-factory, and inundated Europe (when not imprisoned in the fortress above mentioned) with the productions of his all too facile pen. So we read in the *Siècle de Louis XV* To such reproaches an obvious reply would be that Coligny, Turenne the C (omte) de R (ochefort), and the other victims of these outrages in duodecimo really lived and had adventures of their own. If they did not choose to record them, was that the fault of M. de Sandras (who was very likely the first personal interviewer), or a reason why he did not slake the public thirst for information?

Anonymous or pseudonymous libels of the eighteenth century are more easily classed, the onus being, so to speak, upon all such to prove to the reader that they were not written by Voltaire, who appears in as many countries and under as many names as the great twin brethren, though content, while printing his *Lettres sur les Anglois* (about which the Basle and London booksellers quarrel so) at a "small town in Normandy," to venture on occasional visits to Rouen in the disguise of the "Comte de Revol," or of a Milor Anglais.

those historical romances the nature and quantity of which were becoming a serious danger to history.

[1] Bayle's great work on tolerance (*Commentaire Philos. sur ces Paroles de Jésus Christ contrains-les d'entrer*, &c., which, according to the best authority, represents more than any other "the foundation of modern Rationalism," and about which he was naturally rather nervous, hails from "Cantorberry: traduit de l'Anglois de Sieur Jean Fox de Bruges par M. J. F.," and he even alludes to it in a letter to l'Enfant (Mar. 3, 1688) as a curious result of the "*démangeaison d'imprimer*" affecting the London press. See the *Lettres Choisies*, pp. 238 and 513. The second edition (Rotterdam. 2 vols. 8vo. 1713), bearing the author's name, is far preferable to the first (which is very incorrect) and contains also the important introductory tract—"*Ce que c'est que la France toute Catholique sous le règne de Louis le Grand.*"

And of *his* Memoirs (though equally concerning Frederick the Great and the principal powers of Europe) *écrits par lui-même*, in that fascinating thin 8vo. volume of 1784, on *papier bleu*, with their cosmopolitan jokes, their three "*suites*" dated from the "Délices," and their parting shot at the ecclesiastical order—may we not say that their perusal is a liberal education in—the last century? With these should be taken Duvernet's charming *Vie privée et politique*

Portrait of Voltaire—*D'après nature par Joseph Vernet à la séance de l'Académie Française.*
ou Voltaire est venu siéger pour la dernière fois en 1778. Frontispiece to *Lettres inédites*,
1818. To the Life by "T. J. D. V." is prefixed a facsimile of Voltaire's extremely clear
and regular handwriting.

de M. de Voltaire, suivie d'anecdotes (8vo. 1797), and the *Lettres inédites* (1818)[1] containing that excellent crayon portrait of the old

---

[1] It is excusable perhaps to prize these two library editions (uniform in respectable half morocco) more than any historical work in one's possession, even of the completest modern type. A special attraction of the letters here printed is that several contain in brackets passages excised " by order " from the Kehl edition.

Of Voltaire's goodness of heart one "anecdote" may be recalled, that of the proud but impecunious young officer staying with the wealthy proprietor of Ferney,

man they compel us to love, as he last appeared at the Academy
séance of 1778.

The thought of the eighteenth century and the reflection that some
one is (we believe) about to publish a new life of the Chevalier
d'Eon, revives our regret that Caron de Beaumarchais, the greatest
"character" of the pre-Revolutionary period, did not leave us
Memoirs of his "*Life and Times*,"[1] as distinguished from the *Memoir*
or two (a different matter) which he has left, and in which, as one
critic observes, "all his enemies appear exactly as ridiculous and odious
as he pleased, being led upon the novel platform of a quasi-legal
manifesto like so many strange animals merely existing for the reader's
diversion." One contemporary even observed, with a malign admiration, "If Beaumarchais demanded half my fortune, threatening as
alternative to write a memoir about me (in the style, that is, of
L'affaire Gœzmann) I should give it up to him *sur le champ*."

But let us keep to the subject in hand. Voltaire, not to dwell

---

and practically unable to return to his regiment. "Permettez," said M. de V.
"qu'un de mes chevaux *pour se former*, fasse la route avec vous," and, slipping a
purse into his hand, "je vous prie de vouloir bien vous charger de sa nourriture"
(*Vie*, p. 393).

As to the omissions the following is an extract from a letter addressed to Mme.
la Comtesse de Lutzelbourg," and dated "Aux Délices, près de Genève, 23 Juillet,
1759": "Je plains fort ceux qui ont les maisons de campagne à Louisbourg. Ils
s'en sont défait, comme vous savez, en faveur des Anglais qui sont maîtres de l'Île
[de la ville, de la garnison, de nos vaisseaux] &c. Il ne nous restera bientôt plus
rien dans l'Amérique septentrionale. Mais afin de ne point faire de jaloux, ils
vont caresser toutes nos côtes de France, les unes après les autres. Vous savez que
la désolation de Paris est grande non parceque Louisbourg est pris : non parceque
nous sommes battus partout et que nous allons l'être encore ; mais parcequ'on
manque d'argent et qu'on craint de nouveaux impôts. On a du moins le plaisir de se
plaindre et de crier contre tous ceux qui conduisent notre mauvaise barque "—but
even this pleasure could not always be enjoyed in public.

[1] The defect is to some extent supplied by Cousin d'Avallon's entertaining *Vi
privée, politique littéraire de Beaumarchais, suivie d'anecdotes, bon mots, &c.* (with
a fine portrait by Cochin) sm. 8vo. "*papier bleu*." 1802. Not a very common
book, and only recently added to the Library of the British Museum.

upon an inexhaustible subject, sums up in a unique degree the greatest interests of his time, but, for reasons beside what he himself tells us of the precarious arrival of MSS., &c., we do not pin our faith to such works as his *History of Russia*. Rulhière's *Anecdotes of the Revolution of* 1762, appended to his *Histoire de l'Anarchie de Pologne* (4 vols. 8vo. Paris, 1807) are better worth reading, for Rulhière was on the spot, at the French Legation.

To realise the true inwardness of any great epoch or incident the student should run his eye over a chronological chart, and inquire first who was living at the time who *could* have known, and of these who *did* know the facts, or even bore the same relation to them as Æneas did to the Trojan War.

Among these a high place must be given to those writers (including many a retired statesman and politician) who knew "every one worth knowing," and viewed things in general from a familiar and independent point of view, of whom the most famous in English history is beyond doubt Horace Walpole, fourth Earl of Orford (1717—1797), who, to the superficial eye often appears a mere "person of quality" dallying elegantly, as indeed he did dally, with "Letters," remaining none the less a man of wide culture and acute observation, perhaps "fit to live," according to the Chesterfield standard. At the bottom of a particularly entertaining page of eighteenth century history it is five to one that we find the familiar reference " *Walpole to Mann*." Posterity has reason to be thankful that Sir Horace Mann (whose answers were too dull for publication) was so frequently away from England as to appreciate the smallest details of social and political news. And what with the *Memoirs of George II.* (first published 1822) and of George III., edited by Sir D. Marchant in 1845, the nine volumes of correspondence ("Walpole's incomparable Letters" as Byron calls them) with Mann, Lord Hertford, and others published by Mr. Cunningham in 1857 (and covering a period from 1735 to 1797!), the *Reminiscences*, the journals, the *Hasty Productions*, the *Occasional Thoughts* and the polemical tracts, it may be doubted if Mme. de Sévigné and Saint Simon together could have left a livelier picture of half a century of national life, though we may regret that it is diffused over so many spacious volumes.

But one cannot quite agree with the great essayist (who asks in the chapter cited above—"What can we expect of a doctor writing on war?") that specialists of any kind are the best memoir-writers. His admired Froissart had little special knowledge, but an omnivorous curiosity, and there is many a volume of "lay" journal or biography the author of which at least admirably hitches on the Events of History to his own private affairs, interests, and amusements, which, like the Lucretian hooked particles, serve to attach them to our own minds.

Can we not "see from here" that immortal *trovatore* Cellini coming home from shooting on that day in Epiphany, 1537, with the gun ("same which I shot Captain Bourbon," perhaps) that never missed, across his saddle, and the excellent hound Barruccio at his heels, chatting cheerfully to young *Felice Guadagni-poco*? Messer Benvenuto is a little worried, it is true, about the medallion he is busily executing for Alexander Medici, Duke of Florence by the grace of Charles V. Lorenzino (and here the reader shall open his *Comedies et Proverbes* of De Musset, 1st ed. p. 53.) had repeatedly undertaken to send him the design for the other face of the work, and not sent it, and Cellini is impatiently expecting each day the long promised "reverse of the medal."

Meanwhile, the hard-worked artificer must have air and exercise; having enjoyed which this evening, he intends to shoot no more. But up get those two irresistible geese out of the ditch, bang goes the unerring weapon, and both fowls are bagged, of course, with a little trouble and the help of Barruccio. But this takes time; moreover, the sportsman gets into a dyke and sticks in the mud, and one of his high riding boots is filled with water, and he has to sit down, as incautious waders do, and wave his foot "in the air" to let the water run out. Then riding home he catches rheumatics, must needs stop and get Felice to light a fire to dry him. In fine, it is evening as they ride into Rome; and what is that strange fire in the sky over Florence? (This one presumes to have been a vision.) Ah! He will know the next day when couriers come in, post haste, to tell that the cry in Florence is "Down with dukes!" that young Lorenzaccio has "executed" the tyrant Alexander *himself*, who will therefore not need to be immortalised by the cunning hand of Cellini, and that *this* is the promised "reverse of the medal!"

It would be idle to inquire how many of these intensely interesting details are positively authentic, whether Benvenuto really saw sala-manders in the fire, or actually wounded the Prince of Orange—unless, perhaps, we could have approached the author in one of those rare moments of penitence and depression when, after reading "the Bible and the Chronicles of Villani," nothing less than an angelic mes-senger dissuaded him (ii. 18) from committing suicide![1] How many such *tableaux vivants*—so easy to observe, so difficult to forget—have not these interesting and confidential persons pre-sented to us in their passionate desire not to go to the grave forgotten and unknown! How varied in colouring and interest are the life-scapes preserved in their gallery—from the nameless iniquities of a Borgian Palace so respectfully recorded for us in the diary of the Grand Chamberlain of Alexander VI.,[2] to the latest Frenchified gossip of a court lady of our own respectable

---

[1] It is a singular fact that this most famous of autobiographies was never pub-lished till a century and a half after the author's death. Begun in 1559, as he tells us (iv. 10) and carried as far as 1566, it first appeared in an (incorrect) undated quarto, bearing the well-known imprint "Colonia. Pietro Martello." Of this a counterfeit was produced at Florence 1792.

[2] The complete Latin text of *John Burchard's Diary of the Times of Innocent II., Alexander VI., Pius III. and Julius II.*, of which Leibnitz gave the public a taste in his *Specimen Historiæ Arcanæ, sive Anecdota de Vitâ Alexandri VI. Papæ* (a title doubtless suggested by Procopius). 4to. Hanoveræ, 1696, has now been published. Florence, 1854. Ed. A. Gennarelli. For other contemporary accounts of the final tragedy in the Vatican garden (Aug. 17, 1503) see *Guiccardini*, and *Paolo*

century; from the letters of the suffering but hopeful Galileo[1] to the memoirs of a persecuted modern Radical;[2] from the casual notes of the vivacious and cosmopolitan Howell to the domestic and political register cyphered up every evening by the unfortunate Mr. Samuel Pepys, of whose private character we have now, it may be hoped, deciphered the worst. Historians of their own, and more or less of other people's "own times," like the Emperor Tiberius Claudius, whose work (in eight volumes, as Suetonius tells us) has unfortunately perished, or Frederick the Great,[3] or Leonardo Aretino,[4] or Mr. Justin McCarthy, biographers and autobiographers, writers of memoirs proper and familiar letters, social, political, personal, and topical,[5]

Giovio. The latter mentions the wine treated with the Borgian white powder which was handed to Alexander VI. by the mistake of an under-butler. Guicciardini, with an awful impartiality, gives a similar account as that which "was generally believed," the practice of poisoning superfluous cardinals and rich people being so notorious.

[1] *v.* Fabroni, *Lettere inedite di uomini illustri.* 2 vols. 8vo. Firenze, 1773-5.

[2] Bamford's *Passages in the Life of a Radical* first printed *by* and *at* Heywood. n. d. (1841-2).

[3] *Histoire de mon temps,* and (to some extent) the better known *Mémoires de Brandebourg* (avec suite "de main de maître," 1750). Voltaire by the way tells us (*Mémoires,* ed. 1784, p. 24) that the thankless author inserted a libellous portrait of his preserver Seckendorf *into some thirty copies* of this latter work. Does the reader possess one of these? M. de V. made a present of his to the Elector Palatine.

[4] Note that the work entitled in the Italian edition (4to, Venet. 1561), *Istoria universale de' suoi tempi* is the "history" and not the "memoir" left us by Leon. Bruni d'Arezzo (1364-1444). The latter is a minute work entitled "Commentarius rerum suo tempore gestarum," or in the rare Ital. sm. 8vo. (Venet. 1545), *Delle Guerre fatte nelli suoi tempi, e degli huomini famosi.*

[5] Under this head would fall for example that singular work (unique as a picture of signorial tyranny and provincial misery) Esprit Fléchier's *Mémoires sur les Grands Jours d'Auvergne en* 1665 (ed. Chéruel, with notice by Ste. Beuve, and index, 2nd ed. 8vo, 1862)—or Edmund Spenser's invaluable "View of the State of Ireland" (cir. 1596) first published 1633 (8vo, Dublin, 1767), and in some modern editions appended to his poetical works. His reflections on "the

who shall enumerate their infinite variety? Besides the memoir
strictly so called, would there not be something to be said of the flitting
and birdseye view of men and things preserved for us in those records of
travel which when well written (and illustrated) are perhaps the most
attractive of all reading? Unfortunately they run to bulk. In the
mind's eye one sees them, long shelves of folios and quartos—extra
volumes stuffed with maps and plates; the classics of Cook, Anson,
and the other industrious navigators of the eighteenth century, the
earlier records stored up in the vast and costly collections of Hakluyt, Purchas, and Ramusio;[1] all varieties of character and country,
from the romantic and entertaining letters of Pietro della Valle, to
the business-like travels in (and all round) Revolutionary France[2] of

successive governors *adopting different policies out of jealousy of one another"*
have quite a pathetic interest for the nineteenth century reader.

[1] The most famous collections would seem to be the following :—

*Hakluyt Richd.—Principall Navigations, Voiages and discoveries of the English
Nation.* 3 vols. fol. 1598-9. 1600.

*De Bry.—Collectiones Peregrinationum in Indiam Occidentalem et Orient-
alem.* 7 or 8 vols. fol. 1590-1634 (a work the full description of which occupies
50 columns of close print in Brunet's Manual of Bibliography).

Purchas.—Hist. of the World in Sea Voyages and Land Travells, &c. 5 vols.
fol. 1625-6.

Ramusio.—Raccolta delle Navigationi e Viaggi. 3 vols. fol. 1563-5 and 1583
(and a supplement of 1606).

In historical interest however these are perhaps surpassed by one little volume,
the *Historia Vinlandiæ Antiquæ seu partis Americæ septentrionalis* (sm. 8vo,
Havniæ, 1707 : priced £8 by Mr. Quaritch), which contains an account of the
discovery and colonization of part of North America by Norsemen at the end of
the tenth century. The fact is also mentioned by Adam of Bremen.

The correct text concerning Cook was never printed till a year or two ago.

[2] Cited in Disraeli *Curios. Lit.* for the early account of coffee as a beverage.
These letters, though their form, chronology, &c. (like that of Howell's) is doubtless
unreliable, are of considerable value and interest. They were first published at
Rome, 4 vols. 4to, 1650-63, and there is an 8vo ed. of about the same date,
also a recent and readable reprint (of which I have a copy) printed at Brighton !
2 vols. 8vo, 1843.

the agricultural Arthur Young. All these, all first-hand records of original observation and experience, are in their way to be classed as memoirs. Alas! that the same cannot be said of that monument of early English, the "Voiage and Travaile of Sir John Mandeville." The author or compiler—for Sir John himself is now dismissed as a not merely imaginative but imaginary individual—probably never travelled further than to the nearest bookseller's shop, where, having secured a second-hand MS. of Pliny (and there can be no doubt of this fact) he sat himself down to indite a work destined to prove that the "mynde of man," at least of mediæval man, "may not," as he mysteriously assures us, "be comprehended or withholden."

The mention of travels suggests another and a rarer class of personal record. At least one famous author and general, Don Alonzo Ercilla y Zuñiga (1525–1595), has left us a contemporary account *in verse*—thus reverting to mediæval fashion—of his exploits and discoveries. The "Araucana,"[1] which Cervantes thought one of the finest poems in the Spanish language, was, as the author expressly tells us, written up nightly like the Pepysian Diary, and has doubtless an importance to students of the early history of Chili. Yet, however wonderful as a literary feat, the book cannot be recommended as an entertaining work.

Isolated epigrams, indeed, short topical poems, and what may be called "metrical tracts," often possess in a high degree the virtue assigned above to the ideal epistle, and arouse proportionate interest. Such, for example, are the verses of the enlightened Chancellor L'Hospital upon various incidents in the civil wars of his time, the

---

[1] It was first printed 1578-90, and there is an excellent edition with portrait and plates, 2 vols. 8vo, Madrid, 1776. Of the works of Camoëns a "fort jolie édition" was printed by P. Didot, 5 vols. 12mo, 1814-5. The *Lusiads* is of course a work of greater historical (and indirectly autobiographical) interest, poetic beauty in fact being often sacrificed to precision.

capture of Metz, of Calais, or of Thionville, and the marriage of Mary Queen of Scots to Francis II.[1]   But the practical reader can content himself with the complete edition of only a few years later—*Epistolæ seu Sermones*, 8vo, 1592 ; and the best are to be found with the " Franciscanus " of Buchanan, and the epigrams of Turnebus in other contemporary collections (*e.g.*, Basileæ, 1572).   These opuscula, like prose pamphlets, are usually of moderate length.   But if an epic poem can ever take the place of a memoir or journal, it is no natural example of the genus, which should be untrammelled by artistic or other conventions, and, as has been said, pre-eminently readable.

This does not mean that it is our duty, even when it may be our pleasure, to devour them whole.

There are of course books to be gnawed like bones, books to be swallowed whole, and books of which the cream should be judiciously skimmed.   In our privileged dialogues with the great, the virtuous, and the wicked dead, we need not choose to hear all they have to say. But to know people we must go among them.

The memoir is essentially a rich pasture ground for intelligent grazing.   That study of individual lives, of social atmospheres, which does so much to " people the centuries " easily and effectively for us, has for its object the priceless, but not superficially demonstrable knowledge of the great "might have been," ancestor, after all, of the greater "may be"; the philosophy of what we will call "the imperturbably probable."   Children, and schoolboys who have not shaken off the severe candour of infancy are often secretly exasperated at the importance assigned by historians and preceptors (who appear too much to have the political game—the sum and the answer—in their

---

[1] Five or six of these pieces, in 4to, of from five to ten leaves apiece, in one volume I see priced in a Parisian catalogue at 30 and 40 fr.   All are described as very rare, and the four leaves " *In Francisci Delphini et Mariæ sereniss. Scotorum Reginæ nuptias amplissimi viri M. H. carmen*," (1560) as "the rarest tract in existence concerning that unfortunate princess."

own hands) to " events " which succeeded in happening only, so to speak, " by the skin of their teeth." Upon such minds is keenly borne in, in after life, the joy of hammering and chipping for themselves in what, in spite of its complex "faults " and delusive varieties, is after all, the bed-rock of history, of grubbing and quarrying in that ground-soil of human nature out of which " events," "institutions," and "systems" arise, and into which their *débris* are eternally decaying.

VI.

WITH RABELAIS AT ROME.

(1536.)

WITH RABELAIS AT ROME.

(1536.)

"Ist irgend eine Hoelle so muss Rom darauf gebaut seyn."
MARTIN LUTHER.

ERHAPS it might safely be asserted that few of the readers who now and then unbend (like the late Mr. Browning) over a jolly chapter of Rabelais, are equally acquainted with that humorous author's correspondence, which has indeed not descended to us in proportions sufficient to command attention.

But these few familiar epistles—addressed almost exclusively to Geoffrey d'Estissac, Bishop and Baron of Maillezais—have always been prized by the curious, more especially since the appearance in the year 1710 of Sainte Marthe's profusely annotated edition,[1] which has supplied such a mine of wealth to modern editors.

The letters of an original writer in his native tongue are generally worth reading, and those of Rabelais, besides the usual details of " human interest," give a sort of back view of various events and negotiations not beneath the dignity of history. One could wish for such a correspondent in every great capital, at every great historical epoch. But that would be intellectual luxury. The present work

---

[1] *Lettres de François Rabelais* écrites pendant son voyage en Italie, avec observations historiques, &c. 8vo. Paris. 1710. Earlier editions are very incomplete. A few more letters (mostly in Latin and of less general interest) will be found in the editions of Rabelais's complete works by MM. Burgaud Desmarets and Ralhery. 2 vols. 1857. &c. Passages here italicized are so given in the text of 1710.

constantly rouses a keen regret that we have not more of it, nay, an ardent desire to be allowed to cross-examine a writer whom we find in so thoroughly responsive a mood. . . . .

Rome is crowded at the time the correspondence begins, with princes, ecclesiastics, ambassadors, and their suites, each concerned with their several interests and intrigues, and all alike (including his Holiness Paul III.—Alessandro Farnese, who had in 1534 succeeded to the unhappy Clement VII.) awaiting with very mixed emotions the arrival of the Emperor Charles V., who is approaching tardily by way of Naples. Among the ecclesiastics is Rabelais's patron, the Cardinal Jean du Bellay, littérateur, and Minister of Francis I., first at the court of Henry VIII. (1527–33), and for the next two years in Rome, brother of the memoir-writers Martin and Guillaume, and uncle of the more famous Joachim, poet, and author of the *Défense de la Poésie Française*. Rabelais himself has private business of an important nature in the Papal court, no less than his absolution from the ecclesiastical censures incurred by his desertion of the abbey of Maillezais, and subsequent irregular life.

He writes, for the rest, as the casual spectator of a period crowded with interesting events and personalities, touching with tantalizing lightness the surface of matters of deep and often tragical significance, in which one only regrets that the worthy bishop,—to whose letters Rabelais, here on his good behaviour, pays such business-like attention—was not more interested. The celebrities of the period would swell a long list. Guicciardini, Paolo Giovio, Jerome Vida, Cardinal Bembo, and Michael Angelo were at this date elderly men. Ariosto, if alive, would have been a little more than sixty, Machiavelli but a few years older. Benvenuto Cellini, Pietro Aretino, and Teofilo Folengo ("Merlino Coccaio") were yet young or in the prime of life. Luther was still a hale and hearty man, and "Protestantism" just become (by the Peace of Nuremberg in 1532) an established political power in Europe; while an inevitable "Council" looming in the air terrified and embarrassed the Romish court.

Italy lay in misery and confusion a helpless victim of the ravages begun by the invasion of Charles VIII., and culminating in Bourbon's atrocious sack of Rome in 1527,[1] the prey of petty despotisms tempered alternately by assassination and foreign intervention. European diplomacy—at this moment centred in the Italian capital—presents a monstrous tangle of greed and treachery. Francis I., whose crushing defeat and shameful recovery of his liberty were yet fresh in the public mind, allied with the great Solyman—invader of Hungary and terror of Christendom—negotiating with Lutherans in Dresden, and burning them, to advertise his orthodoxy, in Paris ; Henry VIII. (whose assistance Francis sought against Charles V.) now divorcing that Emperor's aunt in open defiance of Papal interdicts, now defending the Catholic "Faith" and inaugurating Reformation by the impartial persecution of both religious parties ; Charles the Great, whose armies had plundered Italy and outraged the very Head of the Church, returning "at the pinnacle of his glory" financially insolvent from an unimportant victory over the infidel, and making triumphal procession to the Holy City as the saviour of Italy and Christendom, and announcing to the assembled powers his confident defiance (so soon to be falsified) of the arms of France ; and, in the background, the business-like Andrea Doria—"of whom," Montluc tells us, "the sea seemed to be afraid"—played off, by whichever European potentate could contrive to pay him, against Barbarossa, or the Catholic King of Spain.

It is under these circumstances that we find Master François Rabelais writing to his friend the Bishop (December, 1535) on the interesting but not historically important subject of vegetables for salad. He had despatched already "all the kinds which are eaten

---

[1] The letters of Sadolet (1477–1547) should also be consulted on this period. (8vo. Lugduni, ap. Seb. Gryphium. 1554.) He was a correspondent of the Cardinal Du Bellay, and barely escaped, as he tells us (p. 201) from the "fearful destruction" at Rome with the loss of all his possessions. See p. 7 *ante*.

at Naples except the pimpernel, which I could not get.   I send some,
but not a great quantity now, as I cannot give the courier any
more to carry. . . . .

"The Cardinal Du Bellay and the Bishop of Maçon have both
assured me that the settlement (of the little affair about the absolution) will be granted me *gratis*, although the Pope as a general rule
only gives gratis what is granted *per cameram*.   I shall only have to
pay the referendaries, proctors, and other such 'messers of parch-
ment' (*barbouilleurs de parchemin*).   If my money runs short I shall
appeal to your charity, as I don't expect to leave here till the
Emperor does."

"The thirty crowns you sent me," he adds in a subsequent letter,
"have almost come to an end.   Dress and lodging ran away with so
much money."

He had spent nothing on "*meschanceté*," nor on food, for he
usually dined with the Cardinal [1] or the Bishop of Maçon ; in fine,
would his patron kindly send him a letter of exchange?

By the Pope's advice Rabelais had carried his case into the court
as *contentious matter* (contradictorium), because, if so decided, the
sentence could not be questioned in France, as might be the case
with a decision *in camerâ*.

"The Emperor is at Naples, and will leave, as he has written the

---

[1] In a note (vol. i. p. 293) to the *Voiages de Montaigne* (8vo, Rome, 1774),
it is stated that Rabelais "carved and handed" the food at the Cardinal's table,
also that on one of these occasions he made a severely satirical retort "omitted in
Perau's *Life of Rabelais*" to one of the guests, a prelate who had indulged in some
rather free abuse of the French nation.   This, the editor says, is recorded of
Rabelais *by his friend Estienne Tabourot in the edition* (of his well-known
"*Bigarrures*"?) *called the "Little Jesus" edition*, ch. vi. p. 128.   The bibliographical reader may be able to verify the reference.   I cannot find it in the
edition of Rouen, 1591, and *Estienne* Tabourot (1547-1590) was certainly not a
friend of Rabelais's, who died when the latter was only six years old.   Perhaps the
Jean Tabourot referred to in the works (i. 145, ed. 1711) may be the original
authority.

Pope, on the 6th of January. The city is full of Spaniards. His Holiness gives him up half the palace, and the whole township of S. Peter's for his people, and is having 3,000 beds got ready in the Roman fashion, *that is to say, mattresses.* For the town is absolutely unprovided with them since its sack by the Landknechts. Also he is providing hay, straw, oats, rye, and barley; and wine—all that is on the wharves. *It will cost him a pretty penny, which in his great and obvious poverty, worse than that of any Pope for 300 years past, he would be glad to avoid.*

"The Romans have not yet settled what attitude they had best adopt, and there have been numerous meetings of the senators, conservators" (a sort of Board of Works), "and governor, but they cannot come to an agreement.

"The Emperor has notified them by his ambassador that he does not at all mean his soldiers to live at free quarters,—that is, without paying,—but just as shall please the Pope. *This greatly vexes his Holiness, who sees that the Emperor only wants to see with what consideration he means to treat him and his people.*

"By the advice of the Consistory the Holy Father has also sent two legates, the Cardinal of Sienna (Giovanni Piccolomini) and Cardinal Cesarini. Salviati and Rodolfo also have gone, and M. de Saintes with them, on account of the Florentine affair, I understand, and the difference between Alessandro de' Medici and Filippo Strozzi, whose property the said Duke wanted to confiscate. It is very considerable, for next to the Fuggers of Augsburg in Germany,"[1]

[1] In a letter to Jerome Froben of Basle, Roger Ascham writing from Augsburg a little after this date says, "I have seen the Greek library of Jacob Fugger and have a catalogue of the manuscripts." It contained many works which had never been published, and Ascham expresses a regret that the owner should not have made a more generous use of his property, stigmatising the celebrated bibliophile as a "*Bibliotaph,* or book-burier." *Aschami Epistolæ.* Oxoniæ. 1703. p. 253.

Having mentioned this, it is only fair to add that our own copy of Cassiodorus (Variarum Epp. Libri xii. Folio. Augsburg. 1533.) bears the inscription in a bold cinque-cento hand—"Ex liberalitate M. & Q. T. *Joannis Jacobi Fuggeri*

--the firm celebrated for their connection with the sale of indulgences
—"he is considered the richest merchant in Christendom. Strozzi
had placed agents in Rome to poison or assassinate the Duke at all
hazards, who hearing of this obtained leave of the Pope to carry arms
and went about with a guard of thirty soldiers armed to the teeth."

At this date—the age of Lucrezia Borgia and of the Thyestean
horrors of the House of Este (the patrons of Ariosto and Boiardo) at
Ferrara,—poisoning and assassination had perhaps by a few years
(seeing that Alexander VI. died in 1509) passed the very apogee of
their popularity. As to the general *morale* of the upper classes, one
may doubt if it was not worse in the self-conscious staleness of its
crime and vice, than the simpler darkness of the feudal Middle Ages.

To this consideration, and to the affairs of the House of Este, the
gossip of Rabelais will again draw our attention. In the reference to
Florence we touch upon a subject-matter to which we have elsewhere
referred.[1] The young Alexander Medici, first Duke of Florence, and
affianced to the daughter of Charles V., was murdered two years
later by his cousin Lorenzino, who himself was assassinated by order
of Cosmo I. in 1548. At the present date Strozzi, the freethinking
millionaire-conspirator, who had helped to restore Alexander and
been expelled by him, was attempting to return at the head of a
faction of "fuor-usciti." Failing in this attempt, he was subsequently imprisoned, tortured, and, as some say, privately put to
death.

"Hearing that Strozzi was gone off with the Cardinals to the
Emperor, and was offering 400,000 ducats to any one who would
inform against the Duke, the latter set out from Florence, leaving
Cardinal Cybo as governor, and arrived here about 23 o'clock the
day after Christmas Day, entering by St. Peter's gate with fifty light
horse, in white armour, lance in hand, and about 100 arquebusiers."

et Hieronymi Wolfii." (?) Jerome Wolf (1516-1581) philologer, editor of Demos-
thenes, Suidas, &c., &c.

[1] See ch.v., p. 197.

There was no ceremony on his arrival, only "the Emperor's ambassador" went to meet him. The Duke had a short audience of the Pope, and went off next morning. We then pass off, in a provoking manner, to the great news of the day.

"During the past week the Holy Father has received letters describing the defeat of the Turk by the Sophi, King of Persia." The Cardinal Du Bellay had the report confirmed from another (French) source. It was the greatest slaughter known for 400 years. On the Turkish side were killed 40,000 horses. *And think what a number of footmen must have fallen on both sides!* For among soldiers not given to running away *non solet esse incruenta* victoria. The principal defeat was near a little place called Koni (Khoi), not far from Tauris, for which city the Turk and the Sophi are at strife. The other near Betelis (Bitlis in Koordistan)."

The Turk had divided his army; "a bad plan," adds the sage Rabelais, "before you have conquered. *The French could have told you that, when the Duke of Albany (i.e.* John Stuart, son of Alexander the brother of James III.) *took off the flower and strength of their army before Pavia.*"

At the news of this defeat Barbarossa has withdrawn to Constantinople to secure the safety of the country, but swearing by his good gods that it is a mere nothing to the power of Turkey. But the Emperor is relieved from the necessity of preparing to meet a Turkish invasion of Sicily intended in the early spring. *This may give Christendom a good long rest, and those who exact tithes from the Church,* eo pretextu, *of providing resources against the Turk, will be hard put to it for cogent arguments.*"

Solyman the Great after the capture of Belgrade, of Rhodes, and the defeat of the Hungarians at Mohacz, had become involved, about 1530, in a struggle against Charles V. and the Republic of Venice. But a month later we find Rabelais writing : "I told you of the Sophi's victory at Betelis. The Turk has not been slow in avenging it. Two months later he fell upon the Sophi with such fury as never was seen, wasted a large district of Mesopotamia with fire and sword, and drove him back beyond the Taurus. He (the Sophi) is now having a fleet of galleys built on the Tanais for the purpose of a descent on Constantinople. Barbarossa is still there, having garrisoned Bona and Algiers in case the Emperor should attack him.

"I send you his portrait, drawn from the life; and a plan of Tunis and the maritime towns of the neighbourhood."

With a letter begun on December 30, 1535, he forwards to the Bishop another present (which many a bibliophile would be glad to possess), "*a book of prognostications*, about which all Rome is occupied. It is entitled *De Eversione Europæ*. For my part I don't place the least confidence in such things. But one never saw Rome so given over to these vanities and divinations as at this moment. I take the reason to be—

> Mobile mutatur semper cum principe vulgus."

Upon such "vanities and divinations" the author (or editor?) of the *Prognostication Pantagrueline*—a black-letter edition of which appeared at Lyons in 1535—speaks of course as an expert.

He also sends the good bishop an almanack for the coming year 1536; a copy of the Papal Brief directing the necessary preparations for the arrival of the Emperor (of which more anon); a copy of the "Entry" of Charles V. into Messina and Naples; and the funeral oration delivered at the burial of the late Duke of Milan.

This latter may have been of an improving nature, for the said Duke, F. Mario Sforza, a son of "Louis the Moor," died universally detested by his subjects for the exactions he imposed in order to pay tribute to the economical Emperor who had placed him on the throne.

January 1536 we return to the Florentine intrigues. Rabelais is unable to deliver M. d'Estissac's letter to M. de Saintes because the latter, with the Cardinals aforesaid, is still at Naples.

" I understand their business with the Emperor has not terminated as they wished. In fact he told them peremptorily that having established Alessandro de' Medici in the duchy of Florence at their express request and instance, and that of the late Pope Clement, and contrary to his own intention, to depose him now would be to act like a fool, doing one moment what one undid the next ; therefore they had better make up their minds to recognise him as their lord, and obey him loyally.

" As to their complaints against the Duke, he would take cognizance of them."

So the matter of the Grand Duke was left to be settled, a little later, by the dagger of Lorenzino.

Meanwhile the Pope's ambassadors had succeeded in inducing Charles to defer his coming till the end of February. (As a matter of fact he did not enter Rome till the middle of April, according to a MS. account of his peregrinations cited in the notes of Sainte Marthe.) "*If I had as many crowns,*" Rabelais mischievously remarks, "*as the Pope would give days of pardon and other such favours* proprio motu, de plenitudine potestatis, *to whoever would defer it for five or six years, I should be richer than Jacques Cœur!* They have begun great preparations here for his reception, and, by order of the Pope, made a new road by which he is to enter, that is to say, from the gate of S. Sebastian, towards the Campidoglio, the Temple of Peace and the Amphitheatre ; and he is to pass under the ancient triumphal arches of Constantine, Vespasian, Titus, Numatianus, and others, thence along by St. Mark's and by the Campo di Fiori in front of the Palazzo Farnese, where the Pope used to live" (the Palazzo Farnese was built by Paul III. out of the ruins of the Colosseum), "then past the Banks (via de' Banchi), and under the walls of the castle of S. Angelo.

" In order to prepare and level this route more than two hundred houses and three or four churches have been demolished to the very ground, *which many people take as an ill omen.* The day of the Conversion of St. Paul the Holy Father went to hear mass at St. Paul's, and feasted all the cardinals. Afterwards he returned by the above-mentioned route and lodged at the Palazzo San Giorgio. *But it is pitiful to see the ruins of the houses that have been destroyed; and no payment or compensation made to any of the owners!"*

These "preparations" for the coming of Charles V. seem incredible to modern ears, and considering the deplorable state of Italy, we can well imagine with how sincere a welcome that greatest of earthly monarchs was received. The statement of various historians, quoted by Prescott, that "it was found necessary to remove the ruins of an ancient Temple of Peace," presumably the one supposed to have been built by Vespasian and destroyed by fire in the time of Commodus), and that *this* was an ill omen, would appear (if we are to believe Rabelais) to give a very insufficient account of the matter. Such an appalling destruction of property may give us an idea of the respect it was thought necessary to show at this date to the head of the Holy Roman Empire.

"To-day the Venetian ambassadors have arrived, four fine old fellows, quite grizzled. They are on their way to the Emperor at Naples. The Pope has sent all his household before them; cubicularies, gentlemen of the chamber, Janissaries (*Giannizzeri*, solicitors of the court [1]), and Landknechts; and the cardinals have despatched their mules in pontifical state.

"On the 7th the ambassadors of Sienna were likewise admitted to a state audience, and made their harangue before the Consistory. The Pope replied in excellent Latin, and they left soon afterwards on their way to Naples. *I have no doubt all the Italian States will send embassies to the Emperor, who knows well enough how to play his game of getting money out of them, as has been discovered in the past ten days."* Of these imperial "devices" Rabelais promises to tell us more later on. Meanwhile he mentions the death at Naples,

---

[1] A college of one hundred "Janissaries" was among those established (for purely financial purposes) by Alexander VI.

"a fortnight ago," of the Prince of Piedmont. Louis of Savoy, a nephew of Charles V., was being educated with Philip II. when cut off by fever at the age of thirteen.

"The Emperor has given him a splendid funeral" (we may presume at the expense of the Neapolitans), "at which he was present in person."

The King of Portugal (John III., son of the famous Emmanuel, and also a nephew of the Emperor) had suddenly recalled his ambassador from Rome, who came "all booted and spurred to say good-bye to the Cardinal Du Bellay." Moreover a Portuguese gentleman who seemed to have made himself obnoxious by pleading the cause of the Jews baptised in Emmanuel's reign, and persecuted, for the usual financial reasons, by the present King, had been "assassinated in open day, close to the bridge of S. Angelo." From which two events Rabelais *doubts but there is some insurrection on foot in Portugal.*

It is in a short note dated January 28, 1536, that we learn the Turkish victories in Mesopotamia, and (incidentally) that the Emperor was then occupying the Duchy of Milan, the subject of so much contention and evasion on the part of Charles and the French king. Twelve hundred Landknechts despatched for that purpose had, Rabelais tells us, wearied of being at sea, and, on suspicion of treachery, murdered their pilot and crew. Being, however, unable to manage the vessel transporting them, all were drowned within a stone's throw of port !

So we revert to the all-absorbing topic.

"The Emperor (February 15, 1536) is still at Naples, and expected here at the end of the month. Great preparations are being made for his coming, and lots of triumphal arches. His four marshals of apartments are already here, two Spaniards, a Burgundian, and a Fleming.

"It is pitiful to see the ruins of churches, palaces, and houses

which the Pope has had pulled down and demolished to make a level
highway for him. And for the expense besides he has taxed the
College of Cardinals, officers of the court, artisans, even the very
water-carriers.

"The whole city is full of foreigners.

"On the 5th arrived the Cardinal of Trent in Germany (Bernard
de Clos) in full state, more sumptuous than that of the Pope. In
his train were more than a hundred Germans in gala costume, red
robes striped with yellow, and embroidered on their right sleeves a
sheaf of wheat, bound, bearing the motto *unitas*.

"I gather that he is most anxious for the peace and settlement for
all Christendom, and for the Council in any case." The Council of
Trent, one may observe, was convoked in 1542. "I was present when
he (De Clos) observed to the Cardinal Du Bellay, ' *The Holy Father,
the Cardinals, Bishops, and Prelates of the Church shrink from the
Council*[1] *and will not hear of it, in spite of reproaches from the secular
arm ; but I see the time approaching, and not far off, when the
Church will be compelled to demand it, and the laity will refuse to
listen to them. That will be when they have taken from the Church
all the wealthy patrimony given in days when the Church authorities by means of frequent councils, used to preserve peace and unity
among the secular*' "—a "disestablishment" to some extent carried
out by Henry VIII. ; but we do not know that the Catholic Church
ever showed the predicted appetite for councils.

Rome, it would seem, must have been quite occupied in watching
the arrival and departure of distinguished guests.

On the 3rd arrived no less a personage than Andrea Doria, whose
judicious patriotism had now raised him to the height of his renown ;
but he arrived, as Rabelais confides to us, "at a somewhat awkward
moment. No honours were paid him on his arrival," except that

---

[1] In the fifteenth century it was a crime (of *lèse-majesté*) to speak of councils.
See Platina's singular account of the persecution he suffered at the hands of
Paul II. *Vitæ Pontificum.*

Signor Pier Luigi (of whom we hear more presently) "conducted him to the palace of the Cardinal Chamberlain, a representative of the celebrated Genoese house of Spinola. The next day he visited the Pope, and the next departed for Genoa, the Emperor having given him instructions 'to see what way the wind blows, in France, in respect of a war.'

"Certain news has been received here of the death of the late Queen of England, and they say also that her daughter is very ill."

At the decease of the divorced Catherine of Aragon, Mary was twenty-one. We here stumble on a detail of English history. "The Bull preparing against the King of England to excommunicate him and proscribe and interdict his kingdom," which purported to render void even mercantile contracts with a heretical people—a provision obviously affecting not only Englishmen—"has nevertheless, as I wrote you, not yet passed the Consistory, on account of the articles *De commeatibus externorum et commerciis mutuis*, to which his grace the Cardinal Du Bellay and the Bishop of Mâcon made opposition on behalf of the King (*scil.* Francis I.) by reason of his interests in the matter. It has been postponed till the arrival of the Emperor;" an epoch almost as important, in these letters, and as vaguely determined as the coming of the Coquecigrues, when kingdoms, we know, were to be redistributed, and all diplomatic matters straightened out.

Before that, however, Rabelais's own little business was brought to a happy conclusion.

"I have, thank Heaven, settled all my affairs, and it has only *cost* me the drafting of the Bulls, the Holy Father having of his own free will accorded me the composition. I think you will find the means quite satisfactory. I have got nothing by the said Bull which is not legal and right. But as to the formalities I have been put to a deal of thought. I can assure you I have hardly made any use of the Cardinal or of the Ambassador" (Du Vely, Francis's representative at the Imperial court) "though they offered very kindly to employ not only their own recommendation but even the very name of his Majesty."

Rabelais's offence, as appears from the absolution granted him on the 17th day of January, 1536, was that he had deserted the abbey of Maillezais to which he had been attached, and led a vagabond life in the habit of a secular priest, to the great scandal of the Church, finally taking up the profession of medicine. The "composition" accorded by Paul III. allowed him without prejudice to his ecclesiastical profession, to practise as a doctor wherever he pleased, but for charity, and gratuitously. But his generous patron, the Cardinal Du Bellay, having about this time found his services useful, presented him with a competent living and the cure of the village of Meudon.

This was the second of at least three occasions on which Rabelais was near coming into dangerous conflict with supreme authority. On the third and last, when that authority was audaciously derided, the reputation for good and evil of the learned satirist was such as to require and justify the protection of a powerful monarch, while more than one kindred spirit expiated the Rabelaisian freedom of their opinions at the stake.

At this date a few unsuccessful editions of medical works (such as the selections from Hippocrates and Galen, printed at Lyons in 1532), had ushered in the first absolutely anonymous sketch of the great satire destined to set all the monastic world by the ears, and warranted by the pious author himself to sell fifty-four times as fast as the Bible !

But to return to the letters. Besides his employment about the eminent and enlightened Du Bellay, Rabelais, as we see, was also rendering some kind of services to the Bishop of Maillezais, his ecclesiastical superior. Among other things he had been searching the registers of the palace to find a record of the resignation of a certain Dom Philippes (of the aforesaid abbey) in favour of his nephew. " I have had diligent search made," he writes "under the

years 1529, 30, and 31." Moreover he had "tipped" the clerks
of the registry two gold crowns, as it was troublesome work. The
Bishop, moreover, does not specify exactly enough what is wanted.
"You must tell me the man's *diocese ;* and whether the resignation
was supposed to be made by way of exchange (*permutationis causâ*)
or absolutely (*pure et simpliciter*)." Anyhow the clerks could find
nothing. "So I think there must be something suspicious about the
case."

As to the vegetable seeds, D'Estissac should clearly have been
satisfied. Those despatched were "the very best known in Naples ;
what the Holy Father has sown in his private garden at Belvedere."

Device on last leaf of *M. Hieronymi Vidæ Poemata.* Lugduni. 8vo. 1533. Ap. *Sebast.*
Gryphium, for whom Rabelais had a few years before been employed in correcting proofs.

Other inquiries of the Bishop, Rabelais, we can well understand,
could answer without any research into the records of the time. But
the genealogy of papal families was a complicated matter requiring
infinite tact for its elucidation.

"You ask me," says the Secretary, "*what relation is Pier-Luigi*
(Farnese) *to the Pope.*"

This injudicious conundrum lets in by a side-door to what might
be a voluminious *chronique scandaleuse.*

"*Sçachez que le Pape ne fust jamais marié.*" There was not much

in that, but we may follow the matter a little further, turning from
the letter thus prefaced, of Rabelais's, to Bernardo Segni's precious
Istorie Fiorentine, which cover all this period.   Pier-Luigi, afterwards Duke of Parma and Piacenza, but of whom more must not be
said, poses as the blackest figure of a by no means mezzotinted age.
Borgia, Este,[1] Sforza, Medici, **Farnese**! What a criminal calendar
might be composed of these great names if one knew but where, in
common fairness, to begin !

Roderic Borgia, better known as Alexander VI., who purchased the headship of the Church in 1492 with several mules'
burdens of silver, first began the practice of calling the "Pope's
nephews" by something like their right name. His virtues, Guicciardini naïvely tells us, were "considerably surpassed" by his vices. It
was his practice to make cardinals (he appointed forty-three in the
eleven years of his Papacy) at fees varying from 10,000 to 30,000
crowns, and then to poison them off, until, "hoist with his own petard,"
he perished by the inadvertence of a servant in 1503.[2] Among the
cardinals surviving him was Alessandro Farnese, afterwards (as in
these letters) Paul III. The good fame of this dignitary was sullied,
Segni tells us, by the suspicion aroused in many minds (the sudden
death of Cardinal Contarini in 1515 was a case in point) that he also
practised the Borgian art, had in fact *been taught it* by Alexander, who
conferred on him this favour in return for the love of his "beautiful
sister." The sister was, it is hardly necessary to say, married to
some one else. Her husband heard of the Spaniard's intrigues and
disapproved of them ; "*somme toute*," as Rabelais tells the story, "*il
la tua*." Pope Alexander was grieved, and gave young Farnese a
cardinal's hat and other desirable things "to console him." When
the latter attained the Papacy in 1534 at the age of sixty-eight, he lost
no time in providing for his family. This and, a little later, a per-

---

[1] A fund of interesting and curious information upon this subject and period will
be found in L. Cappelli's excellent edition of the Letters of Ariosto. Bologna. 1866.

[2] See p. 198 *ante*.

sistent hostility to the power of Spain, were his leading motives of action.

Behind the festive preparations above described for the coming of Charles V., we discern in the letters, and yet more clearly in Segni's chronicle, the Pope, hesitating whether or no to fly from Rome, and finally deciding to arm such force as he could collect and remain to welcome " Cæsar."

Rabelais has mentioned the visit of the Duke of Florence ; but he does not tell us that when Alexander Medici, scarcely announced, hurried up the Vatican stairs and suddenly appeared in the Papal presence, Paul III.'s first thought was that an attempt was being made to seize his sacred person. Paul was strongly suspected of having had a hand in poisoning the Cardinal Hippolyto Medici. Alexander was more probably himself guilty of this crime, not to mention others. The Cardinal had previously tried to blow up his cousin the Duke with gunpowder (novel means which must have seemed an agreeable relief to the dreary interchanges of "veleno" with its painfully familiar symptoms) and failed. According to another account Francesco Berni, a true compeer and contemporary of Rabelais, famed as the licentious inventor of burlesque, was employed by one of these two noble villains to poison the other, and having declined the task (which shows that he was not altogether devoid of scruples), was very naturally poisoned himself, by way of closing an unpleasant family episode.

The Cardinal Medici may have been a cardinal too many, obstructing the advancement of the Farnese family. At any rate, all the Pope's *nipoti*,[1] including the infamous Pier-Luigi (who, after holding

---

[1] Upon the vast and dark subject of Papal family jobbery and personal iniquity the reader may refer to Gregorio Leti's work *Il Nipotismo di Roma*, 12mo, s. l. (Amsterdam), 1667, which (besides being one of the rarest and most beautiful productions of the Elzevir press) is full of curious anecdotes, and I suppose the most valuable composition left by its author, although the *Dialoghi Historici dell' Academico incognito* (Geneva, 1665) are worth having, which can hardly be said of the *Vita di Donna Olimpia Maldachini* (sister-in-law of Innocent X.) published

the "apple of the world" at the solemn reception of Charles V. in St. Peter's, and some ten years of despotic iniquity, was finally assassinated with every horror known to long-stored revenge in 1547), received the hat, and there was even, Rabelais adds in his own style, a little "cardinalicule" of the second generation. Whether the Holy Father did or did not cause the death of Hippolyto, his assistance to the Strozzi party against Alexander Medici seems to have availed the latter very little.

The efforts of the Cardinals Salviati and Rodolfo in what Rabelais has called "the Florentine affair" were, as we soon learn, quite unsuccessful.

On their return from Naples we hear the story in detail. Strozzi and his friends offered the Emperor a *million in gold*, which must have been a considerable temptation to the impecunious Charles, and undertook to finish the fortifications of the citadel, "La Rocca," at Florence, to have it garrisoned by competent troops in the Imperial interest, and to pay the Emperor an annual tribute of 100,000 ducats. Such was the market price of the right to oppress Florence.

The exasperating Charles, however, received Duke Alexander on his arrival among the political competitors at Naples very favourably; and the latter, now the affianced husband of Margaret of Austria (marriage being clearly as important a diplomatic agency as assassination) seems to have played his cards well.

Having lavished vast sums on the fortress aforesaid, he had judiciously caused to be painted on its portals the Imperial Eagle with wings, Rabelais assures us, "as big as the windmills of Mirebelais, *to show that he holds only of the Emperor*"—an elaborate piece of flattery.

under the name of L'Abate Gualdi, 1666. See a notice in Appendix to Ranke's *Hist. of the Popes*. In the first-named work (Pt. ii. p. 8) we are told that "Duke Valentine (Cæsar Borgia), robbed, murdered, outraged, and trampled on all laws human and divine at his own pleasure, without thought or scruple, but *what was worse* was that he covered these monstrous vices with the mantle of the Papal authority, and commonly excused them with the remark *ch'egli sapeva benissimo quel che faceva perchè il suo padre che gli lo permetteva haveva seco lo Spirito Santo!*

Alexander Medici had also "tyrannised so adroitly," in the family style, as to get up a popular demonstration "*nomine communitatis*," in his own favour. In fact, as the historian Francesco Guicciardini himself argued the Duke's cause, we might presume that there was something to allege in his favour besides the heraldic work of art above mentioned. Guicciardini, however, defended his vices, which, as in the case of Pier-Luigi, were of a kind to affect the happiness of other people, by pointing out that he was very young, which may not have satisfied every one.[1]

"Intrigues"—or what is briefly summarized under that favourite term by many a modern historian—seem often a mere conventional stepping-stone from one state of things to another. To the Bishop of Maillezais the "true inwardness" of certain contemporary events must have been clearly apparent.

Thus, in one Rabelaisian epistle we have a complete cameo of another historic "affair," not unimportant in its day, of which Ludovico Ariosto could also have told us something. The Duke of Ferrara was engaged in a long dispute with the Pope as to the amount of the fine to be paid for his investiture to the estates held in fee of the Papacy. Paul III. had reduced his demand to the sum of 50,000 crowns. The Duke offered 35,000, and there they stuck. A representative, one Jannet, came from Ferrara to argue the case.[2]

In cash the only difference between the exalted disputants was 15,000 crowns; but there was a further point. The Pope wanted to be recognised as feudal lord of *all* the Ferrarese territories. The Duke would only do homage for those parts for which his father had

---

[1] Alexander Medici is usually represented as a youthful monster of iniquity. That he was not devoid of justice and humanity, or at least of a considerable sense of humour, may be inferred from an entertaining record of him which ran through four or five editions before the end of the century. *Attioni e sentenze del S. Alessandro Medici, primo Duca di Firenze.* Venezia. Giolito. 4to, 1564, by *Alessandro Ceccheregli.*

[2] *Lettere di Ludovico Ariosto. Bologna,* 1866 (cited above).

Q

rendered it in accordance with a decision of Charles V., in the time of Clement VII.

"The point (*la finesse*) of this lies in the fact that the Emperor has no money, and is looking for it in every quarter. He borrows of everybody, and *taille tout le monde qu'il peut.*

"When he arrives here he will of course try it on the Pope. He will argue that he has engaged in all these wars for the sake of Italy and his Holiness, and that *he* (the Pope) must contribute to them.

"The Pope will answer that he hasn't a penny ; nay, he will produce proof positive of his poverty. Then the Emperor will ask him for the Duke of Ferrara's money, *which he might get by a stroke of the pen* (lequel ne tient qu'à un fiat).

"You see how mysteriously these matters work." We do.

A word upon postal arrangements may conclude this *réchauffé* of the gossip of a special correspondent of the sixteenth century.

The transmission and delivery of the letters was a matter of some care and anxiety. There was no organised post, and it was a far cry even to such irregular facilities as were enjoyed by Mme. de Sévigné. Rabelais's own replies, he thought, were tolerably safe as far as Lyons, for so far they were carried "in the sealed packet which is for the business of the King." This was there opened by the Governor, whose secretary—"a friend of mine"—kindly distributed them to certain merchants, of Poictiers and others, by whom the rest of the forwarding was effected.

Rabelais addressed his letters thus "under cover" to the care of Michel Parmentier, a bookseller (is he otherwise known?) living at "the crown of Basle," whom he advises D'Estissac, when sending anything important, to propitiate with an occasional crown enclosed. Rabelais himself had found presents of little knicknacks from the Roman shops of considerable use for this purpose. "A little," he sagely remarks, "often goes a long way with these good people." Of bankers—and this is rather strange news—he writes to the Bishop :

" I agree with you that they are not to be trusted." They were as likely as not to open the packets for themselves and appropriate the contents—gratuity, we presume, and all ! Gentlemen, he calls them, of " *peu de foy.*"

In this respect, if we may believe Rabelais's brief chronicle of the time, perhaps they were not much worse than their most distinguished customers.

VII.

THE WIT OF HISTORY.

THE WIT OF HISTORY.

HOULD we ask of the idlest and most discursive of readers what it is that on the dullest of pages most surely arrests his vagrom attention—he would probably reply—"Short sentences in inverted commas." Personal remarks, epigrams, apophthegms of wit or wisdom—for this is what such quotations usually mean—do they not often furnish the best *memoria technica* of past episodes, or at least the most piquant source which flavours the solid joints of historical "information"?

Of the memoir and the pamphlet we have spoken elsewhere. The "Wit of History," in the best sense of the words, should represent the quintessence of an ephemeral tract, the most "instantaneous" of memoirs, the few words smacking of the time, the place, the occasion in which dazzling genius or rude common sense catches and preserves for us a memorable scene, a long-lost point of view, or collects and throws into artistic and imperishable form

"Le bon gros sens qui court les rues."

Or again it may be taken to comprise all these isolated utterances of distinguished people, works of art more or less venerable, set and framed, as it were, in the interest or admiration of average humanity. Both species are of unfailing interest to the class of persons vaguely known as "Posterity."

Alas! that the ideal specimens of the genus are far from being as common as they should be, that the best, the most inevitable have unfortunately not always been the most popular, while, on the other hand, very inferior specimens—corrupted, badly "stuffed" and "restored" by Vandal taste, have often found and long retained a place in the museums of history.

Great, however, in any case is the force of the traditional *bon mot*, or even the simplest remark bearing upon a great occasion.

In early boyhood—the season when faith is green—it gave many of us a simple pleasure to believe that the Duke of Wellington, at a crisis in the Battle of Waterloo exclaimed—"Up, Guards, and at them!" It seems an obvious enough thing to have said. Yet at a later stage of our education, this romantic belief is sapped by the gradual conviction that the "Iron Duke," with his natural reserve, merely observed—"Now, gentlemen, if you please."

Lastly, as even this splendid vision fades on our riper manhood, we learn with pain from some scornful writer in a newspaper (who has that very moment acquired the knoweldge—and this is what makes him so scornful—from the latest specialist on the subject) that the general in question never made either of these observations, was, in fact, in a different part of the field, and gave his orders through an aide-de-camp, who perhaps merely waved his sword, pointed, and uttered, in his impatience, an imprecation devoid of literary interest which no one distinctly heard, or has accurately remembered.

These things, which we merely take as types, may or may not be so. It matters very little. Such exclamations throw but little light upon the facts, which are tolerably well known.

At any rate, the reader acquainted with the works of M. Victor Hugo[1] will not ask if the dramatic *La Garde meurt mais ne se rend pas!* has any foundation, recorded though it be in the contemporary epistle of Mrs. Col. Rawdon Crawley, C.B.

General Cambronne used to blush when he was asked the question, seeing that he not only surrendered, but survived till the year 1842

---

[1] *Les Misérables*, Pt. ii. 1.

The famous phrase, apparently invented by one Rougemont, a journalist, is to British ears a turn "too French."

If Frenchmen have said as many good things as other people, they have probably, in their self-conscious moments, spoilt or invented many more. It was Barrère who concocted what may be called the maritime *pendant* to "La Grande meurt, &c." in that episode of the *Vengeur*, captured June 1st, 1794, in the engagement between Lord Howe and Admiral Villaret-Joyeuse. The story supplied a whole page of rhapsody to Carlyle.

"Ocean yawns abysmal. Down rushes the *Vengeur* carrying 'Vive la République' along with her unconquerable into eternity."

It is interesting to note that an officer of H.M.S. *Brunswick*, the vessel engaged with the *Vengeur*, survived to set the excitable historian right. For the *Vengeur* sank as a British prize, and with British seamen on board her, her own captain and half her crew being safe in one of Howe's men of war. The page of rhapsody was accordingly cancelled, or rather ironically explained away in subsequent editions. The survival of the truth seems here, as elsewhere, rather a happy accident. A "good thing," and in particular a good saying—for sayings leave less trace in the phenomenal world than doings—whether authentic or not, once reported is sure to live, and very likely to grow and multiply until the serious historian comes round and prunes the plant severely, or digs the weed up by the roots. The Duke of Buckingham and other courtiers never wearied of hearing King Charles II. tell his stories ten times over, because they were always "enriched by some new circumstance," but one feels sure that none but the dull and prosaic circumstances were ever omitted.

The same monarch, whose conversational wit was, as we know from an equally respectable source, exactly proportioned to the unwisdom of his general conduct, has bequeathed us specimens of the "historic witticism" in the celebrated anecdote of the Duke of

York, which, as Dr. William King tells us,[1] the old Lord Cromarty used often to repeat.

Charles, attended only by the last-mentioned peer and the Duke of Leeds, habitually took a turn up Constitution Hill as far as Hyde Park. It was there that one morning the Duke of York—who had been hunting on Hounslow Heath, and was returning in his coach—as the guards surrounding the vehicle stopped at sight of the King, immediately got out and rallied his royal brother on the danger to which he exposed himself by such lonely promenades. "No kind of danger, James;" was the King's answer, "for I am sure no man in England will take away my life to make you king."

Nothing could be better than this, as a sample of the simple, lucid, and popular *bon mot historique*, which for earlier and less reticent generations did what a cartoon in *Punch* does for the modern Englishman.

The member of Parliament who has just written a book upon "Personality in History" (an ambiguous title which, however, does not refer to rude observations like that of Philip II. to William of Orange—" Not the States, but *you, you, you* ") should have devoted a chapter to historic wit. M. Edouard Fournier did this for French history in a fascinating little volume published some thirty years ago,[2]

---

[1] King, W. (1685–1763), *Political and Literary Anecdotes of his own times* (8vo, Murray, 1818), p. 62; and see *Buckingham's Short Character of Charles II.* Works. 1714. Vol. ii.

Some interesting details upon this period will be found in [B. L. de Muralt's] *Lettres sur les Anglois, les François et les Voiages.* 8vo. Cologne. 1725. It was the fashion, this author tells us, for all sorts and conditions of people to row about on the Thames and *chaff one another* (" se dire des injures en passant "). The boatmen told you how they "scored off" the King by calling him a " *chimney-sweep* "—a delicate allusion to his complexion.

[2] *L'Esprit dans l'Histoire, recherches sur les mots historiques.* Paris. 1857. The author cites Brotier's *Paroles remarquables* (1790); Lancelotti, *Farfalloni degli antichi historici* (Venet. 1736: French transl. 2 vols. 1770); and other similar works. M. Charles de Rozan's modestly entitled work *Les petites Ignorances de la Conversation* (6th ed. Hetzel, 1872) will also be found useful to the

which the student will find an invaluable addition (and introduction) to his "original authorities." If M. Fournier erred, it was on the side of scepticism, but his work shows extensive research coupled with the necessary sense of humour.

It is painful to many of us to have our fondest illusions dissipated for the sake of what sometimes seems a pedantic accuracy. But to jump at once to the most famous of all French "mots historiques," there seems to be no authority for the celebrated constitutional dictum of Louis XIV. The story usually runs as follows :—

On a celebrated occasion in 1655 that monarch, then aged seventeen, entered the Parliament in red coat, grey hat, and hunting boots (later writers give him a whip, which doubtless adds to the effect), and in a brief altercation with the *soi-disant* representatives of the nation exclaimed curtly (according to the tradition), "*L'état ! l'état c'est moi !* The remark, which is not recorded by the journalist of the Parliament, is probably an anachronism of a species not uncommon. *At the date,* that is, it did not correspond with fact, although there is no reason to doubt that the young king spoke as the well-drilled pupil of Mazarin, to whom he returned immediately after the incident.[1] About the personality of the "Grand Monarque" of later days flattering fictions cluster thickly and luxuriantly, witness all the

general reader. In the examples here selected I have found it interesting and instructive to verify Fournier's numerous references : one of which however I must leave to the reader. It concerns the account found in modern histories of an incident in the battle of Brenneville (1111 A.D.), between Henry I. and Louis le Gros, when an English knight, having seized the French monarch's bridle, called out that he had taken the King ; upon which Louis felled him to the earth with a blow from the royal mace, and exclaimed " *Kings are not taken even at chess.*"

This remark, which is not in the *Vita Ludovici VI.* by the Abbé Suger, M. Fournier found, he tells us, by chance in Bk. i. ch. 5 of the *Polycraticon* (meaning the Polycraticus) of John of Salisbury (ob. 1180), whose authority, though so nearly contemporary, he considers insufficient for an anecdote which certainly sounds too epigrammatic to be true.

[1] Bazin. *Histoire de France, &c.,* t. 4, 347. The King spoke, according to the gazette, " *avec une gravité vraiment royale.*"

bombast written by Court poets about the " Taking of Namur " and the " Passage of the Rhine "—which flattery 'tis pity Prior was not alive to ridicule,[1] and for which the reader need only be referred to Voltaire's Louis XIV. and the numerous memoirs of the period. But the great Louis did *write*, some years afterwards, for the instruc· tion of the Duke of Burgundy, the significant phrase : " The nation in France has no corporate unity (*ne fait pas corps*), *it resides altogether in the person of the King*." Thus, " l'état c'est moi " may stand as the " abstract and brief chronicle " of a (little later) time. James II. is said by some authorities to have hazarded a similar, but less epi- grammatic, definition of his place in the constitution—" Don't you know I am above the law ? " To which the Duke of Somerset *aura répondu* (the French idiom is sadly wanting in our language), " Your Majesty may be, but I am not."[2]

To the same genus belongs La Pompadour's immortal "Après nous le déluge "—the expression either of abandoned epicureanism or of a sense of coming judgment. And just so does the sagacious Mme. de Staël characterise the whole day-to-day existence of the pre-Revolu- tionary generation. The kind of happiness they enjoyed resembled the sensations of the man falling out of the third-floor window. " *Cela va bien pourvu que cela dure*."[3] And a score of brilliant and " epoch painting " reflections of Disraeli will recur to the reader.

---

[1] As to this see the *Mémoires du Comte de Guiche conc. les Pais-bas*, &c. 8vo. Londres. 1744. The Count, who once, when drunk, called the King a poltroon ("un faux brave :" His Majesty pretended not to hear) commanded a regiment of cuirassiers on the occasion, but though he and his troopers seem to have made the passage easily, in the face of an enemy and under fire, it does not seem to have been devoid of danger. Bossuet called it " *Le prodige de notre siècle*." Voltaire " knew an old woman who had made the passage scores of times (*on horseback*), merely to defraud the custom-house."

[2] So Macaulay, ed. 1858. iii. 2 (misprint in index) citing *Burnet, Hist. of his own time :* but *cf.* appendix to Ranke, *Hist. of England*.

[3] Fournier does not mention this. It will be found in the *Considérations* (ed. 1818, iii. 386), where, it need hardly be said, numerous almost equally incisive criticisms are to be found. Voltaire's " Les jeunes gens . . . . *verront de belles*

The exact authenticity of such **sayings** does not always interfere **with** their practical value. If Sir Robert Walpole did not say (as Horace rashly assures us, *Walpoliana*, **I. 90,** that he did not) that "**every** man has his price," we **know, if only from** his son's letters, **that he** must have said something very like it.[1] To learn **the main**

choses, &c. (1764), may be compared with even more distinctly **prophetic words of** Lord Chesterfield.

[1] It is hardly necessary to say that Walpole's letters, in spite of their diffuseness, and apart from their sober sense, are a perfect mine of historic wit and international badinage, which might form the subject of many a useful examination paper. **For** example :—

1. What eminent poet is described **by** what eminent **divine as** "*Mens curva in corpore curvo*"?

2. To what Royal Duke was it proposed to offer the freedom of "the Worshipful Company of Butchers"?

3. Who was "the new Fabius '**qui** *verbis* restituit rem '"?

4. Explain the following allusions, **giving approximate dates**—
    (*a*) "The earthquake . . . . **they say, is landed at Dover.**"
    (*b*) "*Les Anglois viennent nous casser les vitres avec des guinées.*"
    (*c*) "The French do not improve, like their wines, **by crossing the sea.**"

5. **To** whom, and of what country, did what monarch observe—"*My lord, I wish it were* 100,000 *miles away, and that you were King of it*"?

6. **Which is the** religion that "lets you eat nothing, but **makes you swallow** everything"?

7. Explain **fully the two following** extracts from **Walpole and a contemporary** French historian :—
    (*a*) "The twelve judges . . . . have made law of that of which 'no one else could make sense."
    (*b*) "Il a livré un combat à **un amiral** français et on a trouvé qu'il n'était pas assez près de lui"—mais l'amiral français était aussi loin de l'amiral anglais que celui-ci était de **l'autre?** "Cela est incontestable," lui repliqua-t-on ; "mais dans ce **pays-ci, il** est bon de tuer de temps en temps un amiral pour encourager les **autres.**"

(See *Letters to Sir H. Mann*, 1741–1760, 3 vols., **1833** ; and *Candide*, ch. xxiii.)

If the above questions were considered too easy, **obscurer** historical *jeux d'esprit* (in which few students could not be "ploughed") might be found in the *Catalogue of new French* **Books** ("*L'art de chercher les* **ennemis** *sans les trouver, par le Maréchal de Maillebois*," &c., &c.) transcribed **by** Walpole for the amusement of **his** "dear child," Sep. 11, 1742 ; **or in the satirical** advertisements appended to

outlines of history in the easily digestible form of such "good things" one must frequent the society of the great ones of the earth, of generals, statesmen, cultivated "persons of quality" like the connoisseur of Strawberry Hill, or cosmopolitan *littérateurs* like the author of *Candide*.

The Prince Eugène in what are called his memoirs [1] has left more than one or two. Thus he called England—of which he had some practical knowledge—"the land of contradictions," with an opposition of "faction," and a diplomacy of bad faith. Thus may we see ourselves as others, and friends too, saw us some two centuries ago. The same great general has left a still more famous professional reflection on the House of Savoy (who have been accused by other authorities of always conspiring with their enemies against their allies)—"*La géographie les empêche d'être honnêtes gens.*"

The mention of geography naturally recalls a royal observation almost as famous as "*L'état, c'est moi.*"

According to Voltaire (*Siècle de Louis XIV.* ch 28, which chapter with the two preceding it are devoted to anecdotes of the reign), when the Duke of Anjou departed to take the crown of Spain, the King observed to him, in order to mark the union which was now to prevail between the two nations: "The Pyrenees are no more" (*Il n'y a plus de Pyrénées*).

Voltaire, as Fournier points out, must have been acquainted with the

certain numbers of the *Craftsman* ["Old Franklyn," by the way, the printer of this periodical "under Tom's Coffee House, Covent Garden," 3rd ed. 1727, was afterwards a tenant of Walpole's at Twickenham, and told him that Pulteney never *wrote* in the paper—only suggested ideas. *To Mann*, Ap. 27, 1753]; or, to go back further still, in *Agrippa D'Aubigné's* comic catalogue (*Inventaire des livres trouvés dans la Bibliothèque de M. Guillaume*), written early in the seventeenth century. See Duchat's notes to the Memoires, &c. of D'Aubigné, 1729.

[1] The well-known *Mémoires* du Prince Eugène de Savoie, écrits par lui-même (2de reimpression de l'éd. de Weymar, 1809, with fine portrait, 8vo, 1811), were apparently compiled or edited by the Prince de Ligne, whose *own* Letters (published by Mme. de Staël, Genève, 1809) are full of entertaining gossip upon the sovereigns and celebrities of the day—Frederick the Great, Jean Jacques, Voltaire, &c.

authentic version of the story, which is contained in that very journal of Dangeau of which he had himself published extracts.[1] But Voltaire's taste for accuracy and authenticity was arbitrary and irregular.

Thus when the poor Abbé Velly wrote to ask him where he found authority for his statement in the *Essai sur les mœurs*, that the French crusaders, after the capture of Constantinople in 1204, "danced with women in the sanctuary of the Church of St. Sophia" —a detail which would naturally strike the student of manners—the historian naïvely replied, "Nowhere. I invented it out of my own head (*c'est une espièglerie de mon imagination.*") The present case is not so bad, but what Dangeau actually records (under date Nov. 16, 1700; the complete journal is now published) is that the *Spanish Ambassador* very appositely observed that the journey (into Spain) was an easy one now: *the Pyrenees were melted*—a metaphor thoroughly Spanish in its hyperbole.

M. Arouet preferred to improve and Frenchify it, which was the more inconsiderate since he himself tried to expunge from the inaccurate but still useful work of President Hénault [2] an epigrammatic remark which has hardly less authority.

The clever or otherwise remarkable utterances of Royalty, to some of which we have referred, would of course fill a book, and a very entertaining one, by themselves. It is certain that Louis XI. (of whom

---

[1] Londres. 8vo. 1770. Voltaire, however, remarks (on p. 178, vol. ii. of the sumptuous edition of his history printed by P. and J. Didot, 4 vols., 1820) that these Memoirs "which people regard as a precious monument" were only backstairs gossip, a pack of absurdities and inaccuracies.

[2] See *Nouvel Abrégé Chronologique de l'Hist. de France*, nouv. éd., revisée, corrigée, etc. (with a copious index), 3 vols., 8vo, Rouen, 1789. This "skeleton history" contains an immense mass of details arranged in a lucid and readable form. On p. 937 of vol. 3 will be found italicised the reply of Louis XIV. to the English Ambassador's complaints about the fortification of Mardyck. "*M. l'Ambassadeur, j'ai toujours été maître chez moi, quelquefois chez les autres,*" &c. "Le Président," writes Voltaire, "m'avoua que cette anecdote était tres fausse"— but, as it was printed, would not withdraw it.

M. Fournier says nothing) made many good, if not highly polished, observations. It was he who replied to the Genoese when the Republic offered itself to his protection : " *Vous vous donnez à moi, et moi je vous donne à tous les diables.*"

With his humorous actions we are not here concerned, and therefore leave the story of the " turnip " (which might be regarded as a " chestnut ") for the reader to look for in Comines, and find with others in the *Convivium Fabulosum* [1] of Erasmus. But a word may be said here upon the historic practical joke alleged to have been perpetrated by Charles V. upon the Landgrave of Hesse, by the substitution of the word *Ewiges* (lifelong) for *Einiges* (short or light) in the official description of the imprisonment which the latter Prince was to undergo.

When the Elector had smiled, while making his submission, on the same occasion, Charles certainly observed "Good, I will teach you to laugh " (*Wel, ik zal u leeren lachgen*).[2] Did he, then, do so in the manner supposed ? The story has always been current. We have read an odd version of it in that curious repository of wit, the *Bigarrures* of Tabourot, Seigneur des Accords (ed. Rouen, 12mo, 1591, p. 46), where the author observes that the two German words " enich " and " ewich," meant respectively "*with*" and "*without*" ! But that is a detail. The traditional version may be found even in Motley's *Dutch Republic*, yet later authorities say that unfortunately *neither* of the two similar expressions (*ewiges*, or *einiges—Gefängniss*) appear in the document referred to at all ! How then did so distinct a good story originate? *Quien sabe?* " Revenons à nos moutons "—remembering always that "à ces moutons" is the original fifteenth-century text.

That charming writer M. Augustin Thierry dwells in one of his letters on the " different manners of writing history." Their variety

---

[1] *Colloquies*, ed. 1664, p. 367. This chapter contains other anecdotes well worth reading, and of some contemporary interest. Erasmus was born sixteen years before the death of Louis XI. [2] *Dyer's Mod. Europe*, ed. 1861. II. 50.

once so considerable—ranging from that of the genealogical annalist who traced the Frankish descent from pious Æneas, to that of the modern French historian who fancies that his language was the "native tongue" of Charlemagne—is nowadays being toned down. It is indeed curious that quite respectable writers should have gone on, even up to the eighteenth century, repeating accounts of incidents which never occurred, and stuffing their columns with eloquent orations which were never delivered.

The "solemn quarto" historian of the age of Hénault and Voltaire is sometimes more trying than the early chronicler of whom we have spoken elsewhere.

Hear Lord Orford (once more) upon this very matter. "I shall like, I dare say, anything you do write; but I am not overjoyed at your wading into the history of dark ages, *unless you use it as a canvas to be embroidered with your own opinions and episodes*, and comparisons with more recent times. That is a most entertaining kind of writing. (Sep. 30, 1785.)

"In general," adds the person of quality, "I have seldom wasted time on the origin of nations, unless for an opportunity of smiling at the gravity of the author, or at the absurdity of the manners of those ages; for absurdity and bravery compose most of all the anecdotes we have of them, except the accounts of what they never did, nor thought of doing." There is much good sense in this. But it smacks of irreverence to the ear of the serious modern historian. He does not think that he confers a favour on early history by "embroidering" thereon the "opinions and episodes" of the nineteenth century!

As to fictitious discourses, and witty sayings, these are foibles derived from the ancient classics which accordingly received new life at the Renaissance. Thus the historiographer of Henri Quatre informs us in the preface to one of his volumes, how such a functionary ought to set about his business. His work, we read, was to be adorned with a mosaic of good things drawn from the best Greek

R

and Latin authors. Needless to say, this artificial habit reacted upon the history. Its heroes would soon be found doing the things best described by Livy, illustrating the moral maxims of Sallust or Tacitus, and uttering eloquent reflections, not because they did make, but because with a proper regard for the entertainment of posterity, they should have made them.[1]

This, in fact, is one of the reasons for regret that such a large proportion of our early histories are written in what was till Johnson's time the language of humanity, and is still perhaps that of the scholastic world.

For so many distinguished authors, especially in the sixteenth century, were so carried away by the newly invented pleasure of writing Latin, so intoxicated, in the worst cases, with the exuberance of a Ciceronian verbosity, that style often occupied their attention to the exclusion of fact. Hence we come to regard with suspicion and alarm any early historian who, like Cardinal Bembo, is lauded by

---

[1] It is a different matter when a historic personage himself takes to imitating one or other of the heroes of antiquity Since of all nations the French are probably the most imitative, and of all generations that of the French Revolution was the one most anxious to find respectable precedents for its conduct, one is hardly surprised to find what seems a remarkable example of this tendency in the harangue addressed by General Dumouriez to his disaffected troops at Grand-Pré :—

"As for you, *for I will neither call you citizens nor soldiers*, nor my men (*mes enfans*), you see before you this artillery, behind you this cavalry. . . . I know that there are scoundrels among you charged to encourage you in crime ; *dismiss them yourselves, or denounce them to me. I hold you responsible for them.*"

It seems hardly possible that Dumouriez, whose mind was saturated with the classics, and who, when not engaged in war or travel, lived, as he tells us, among his books, and re-read Plutarch every year, should not have been thinking of the most celebrated passage in Tacitus, if not in all Latin prose, the speech, that is, of Germanicus to the mutinous legion—"Quod nomen huic cœtui dabo? Militesne appellem? . . . . an cives? . . . . discedite a contactu, et dividite turbidos ; id stabile ad pœnitentiam, id fidei vinculum erit." See Tacitus, *Annals*, i. 42 ; *Vie de Dumouriez* (1794), iii. 157. *Mémoires* (1794) pref. The three volumes of the *Vie* are completed by the (previously published) two volumes of the *Mémoires*.

contemporaries for his classical taste. One always wishes that these authors had written in their native language, or that like Mariana, who first wrote his history in Latin in order to acquire a prose style, they had had the industry to translate their own works, and thus leave an original text in the vulgar. The idols of epigram and antithesis (apart from other temptations) have, even in our own enlightened days, now and then distracted a historian from the paths of candour and self-restraint; and certainly the attractions of a fluent and effective style had a far greater influence in the eighteenth century. We all remember how Gibbon tells us that "he arrived at Oxford with a stock of erudition that might have puzzled a doctor, and a degree of ignorance of which a schoolboy would have been ashamed"; but the fact is that Gibbon (and certain other writers who only resembled him in this respect) rarely arrived anywhere, even at the simplest historical statement, with (so to speak) only one bound, more particularly when uttering general reflections upon dark and distant ages "couched" in the subjunctive mood.[1] Even the pungent double-barrelled wit of Macaulay irresistibly suggests now and then to the reader's mind that the whole class of substantives in employment must have "struck" for equal adjectival wages, and got them. Not to consider such matters too curiously, the inexperienced historian will do well to remember the cynical and reticent Mr. Scrooge's reply to the improving discourse of Marley's Ghost—"Don't be flowery, Jacob."

An eminent professor recently published a series of lectures which he had delivered before a guileless university audience, in one of which occurred the following typical passage : "About this time the

---

[1] This way of writing is closely connected with that use of the "Broad A" ridiculed by the Rev. Sydney Smith—"Who, O gracious Heaven !" he asks, "are *a* Bennet, *a* Cyril Jackson, *a* Martin Routh?" But it would perhaps be less excusable to ask, "Who are *a* Theodoric, *a* Jovian, *a* Belisarius"—or whatever the names are which sound so well in certain familiar passages of what may be called historical declamation?

young Earl of ——, riding down the leafy lanes of ——, was met and cut down by a party of Roundheads," which, we take it, smacks as much of orthodox English history as the paragraph repeated by "Alice" in Wonderland, and beginning "Edwin and Morcar, the Earls of Mercia and Northumbria." But a truculent and hostile reviewer, entering upon the picturesque scene, pointed out with ill-controlled exultation that, apart from other inaccuracies, the Earl of Shrewsbury in question (whose title was, it seems, correctly given) being fifty-four years of age, was no longer young; that "the lanes"—it being January—were "presumably not leafy"; and, finally, that the Earl was not "met" or "cut down," but (though that is little matter to us in the year 1895) "shot with a musket ball as he was endeavouring to escape." Such is the conflict between "old-world" romance and nineteenth-century actuality: such the perils that environ the careless dabbler in history. Behind every leafy hedge lurks a specialist armed to the teeth with "original authorities," and ready to cut down the ill-equipped straggler.

A hundred and fifty years ago, if an author merely maintained a dignified tone, no one ventured to make rude remarks.

It has been seen what Voltaire could do in the way of adorning history. Paolo Giovio, a valued historian of an earlier epoch, took an even stronger line, as Guillaume Bouchet tells us. When taxed with fabrication, he replied that he did not care; for a hundred years hence no one would know any better, and every one would believe what was "couched in his history." Giovio was right, but he did not look quite far enough ahead.

"Mots" which have their origin in the corruption of the text, and not of the author, are obviously of less significance; and of these Fournier provides one example, drawn from Chateaubriand, a writer not much to be relied upon in matters of fact. In flowery language Chateaubriand described the dark and stormy night on which Philip of Valois, flying from the battlefield of Crécy, knocked at the gates of the Château of Broye, exclaiming, "*Open, open! 'Tis the Fortune of France !* " But he was wrong. It was only, according to what is considered the correct text of Froissart, " *the unfortunate King of France.*" We confess to a lingering hope that the former reading— "c'est la Fortune de la France "—which we find in the Sauvage edition of 1559 (vol. i. p. 154), may turn out to have some authority in its favour. If a trifle obscure, it is more dramatic, like a host of things which Cardinal Richelieu, Henry IV., Talleyrand, and other less famous personages on certain critical occasions abstained from saying.

All kinds of observations, from the Epigram of the Hundred Days —" c'est le commencement de la fin "—down to the most trivial of witticisms, were fathered upon Talleyrand, whose recently published memoirs seem rather to have disappointed the public. Sometimes the minister was surprised at his own wit. Sometimes the genuine author tried to assert his rights, but in vain.

It would be a pedantic reflection on the title of a popular novel of the day to repeat that there is no authority for "*Je couvre tout de ma robe rouge.*" Yet the original remark appears to have been, " Je *renverse* tout avec ma soutane rouge "—a different idea. It is to the cardinal, too, that we often hear attributed the ruthless response to the protest, " Monseigneur, il faut vivre " (or rather, " il faut bien que je vive ")—" Je n'en vois pas la nécessité." But, as a matter of fact, this was said by the Comte d'Argenson to the despicable Abbé Des Fontaines, whom he deterred by threats of prosecution from his favourite occupation of libelling Voltaire.[1] As to Henri Quatre, who has been victimised enough by the sententious Hardouin de Perefixe and others, he did not personally deal much in maxims of the copy-book order. One of the few genuine remarks recorded of him is that addressed to his staff at the battle of Coutras (where, as at Ivry, he wore long plumes), and recorded by Brantôme. " Get out of the light," he said, "*I want to be seen !*" (ne m'offusquez pas : je veux paroistre).

---

[1] D'Argenson, *Mémoires*, ed. 1825, p. 76. Fournier does not mention this.

How different is this kind of exclamation, which no one would have dreamed of inventing, from such apocryphal vanities as that attributed by Southey to Nelson *à propos* of the uniform " with four stars" which he did *not* wear at Trafalgar.[1]

Having mentioned Trafalgar, it would be impossible not to refer to the celebrated signal with which Nelson, when all necessary preparations had been made, "amused" the British fleet before his last and greatest victory. There seems to be no doubt as to the fact. But in the entertaining naval reminiscences of Rear-Admiral Hercules Robinson[2] (who was present as a midshipman on board Blackwood's vessel, the *Euryalus*) we read what seems a correction of the traditional account. "Lord Nelson's 'England expects,' &c., was sublime, but then here is the historical lie, ' *It was received throughout the fleet with shouts of acclamation, and excited an unbounded enthusiasm.*' Why, it was noted in the signal-book and in the logs, and that was all about it ; *we certainly never heard one word about it in our ship till our return to England.*" There were other signals of less historic interest which the author remembered well being addressed to the captains of his own and other vessels: "I—rely—upon—your—keeping—sight—of—the—enemy," and a "**sagacious** order" given before going into

---

[1] See Arnold's *Lectures on Modern History*, 1843, Lecture viii., which deals largely with the subject here considered.

" In honour I gained them, and in honour I will die with them," says Southey (*Life of Nelson*, Bohn's ed., 1861, p. 366). What Nelson did say was, as Arnold had it, through Captain Smyth, from Hardy himself, that *it was too late then to think of changing a coat*. But his language (v. *post*) was often less simple.

[2] *Sea-Drift* (with fine portrait of the author, plan of battle of Trafalgar, &c.) by Rear-Admiral Robinson—8vo, blue cloth, Portsea, 1858—a volume of miscellaneous yarns and reminiscences of the greatest interest.

In the review in the *Quarterly* (vol. 109, p. 308) of M. Fournier's work, entitled "Pearls and Mock Pearls of History," the author (Abraham Hayward) wanders into so vast a field as to be almost bewildering. But of " England expects," &c., he merely observes, "Doubt has been thrown upon the celebrated signal of Nelson," without saying where or by whom, but presumably referring to this account published only two years before.

action : " Paint—the—hoops—of—your—masts—white." The enemy's were black.

Admiral Robinson himself, by the way, makes some interesting reflections upon the " taste for orationising," imbibed, as he thought, from Roman history. The best speech he could remember was that of " Old Maples " when he took the *Argus* in the *Pelican* in 1814— " Send all hands aft! My lads, there's the *Argus*, no doubt about it ; and now, my lads, if you don't take the *Argus*, my lads, why then, my lads—why then, my lads—why then, my lads—*the Argus will take you*. Pipe down." " Old Maples " was perhaps ignorant to what an extent this theme might have been expanded by a classical orator. Some of the bravest and most practical of men (the Admiral acutely observes) wrote and spoke in a highly ornamented and even boastful style. " Wellington wrote like a log-book, but he was *sui generis ;* almost all other commanders affected fine writing or simplicity." Admiral Watson's " We fell in with the enemy's fleet, burned, sunk, and destroyed as per margin " seemed to the author as unnatural as Collingwood's " beautiful " description of the Battle of Trafalgar was, as a source of history, incorrect and misleading. " Old Cuddie " was, in fact, more at home walking the poop of his vessel, " a quarter of a mile ahead of her second astern," and serenely " munching an apple," before she glided into action (her first broadside killed 350 men), than when elaborating an *ex post facto* theory of " that irregular battle." Men of action have usually rather inclined to the style of " Old Maples " in moments of emergency, as appears from the example given above of Henry IV. He may or may not have estimated aloud the comparative value of Paris and a certain religious observance, but it was the faithful and economical Sully, and not the King, who made the reflection which should have occurred to our own James II. :[1] " *Sire, sire, la couronne vaut bien une messe.*"

---

[1] In fact, the Archbishop of Rheims, brother of the minister Louvois, did speak scornfully of the Royal exile as one who " lost three kingdoms for a mass."

Voltaire, *Louis XIV.*, ed. 1820, i. 299.

Historic sayings are difficult to classify; but of all the *dicta* directly connected with celebrated characters in history, probably none is more famous than the spontaneous outburst of the Hungarian nobility when, in the great hall at Presburg (September 1741), they rallied round the lone and heroic figure of the Empress, and, drawing their swords, exclaimed, " Moriamur *pro rege nostro*" (so we may read it italicised in Alison and elsewhere) "*Mariâ Theresâ*." There is a certain piquancy in the generic license of the Latin which has captivated thousands of readers.

It is to be noted that, for his estimate of the character of the pious and courageous Maria Theresa, Alison cites on the same page *Wraxall's Memoirs*,[1] which give a graphic account of the whole episode, on the authority of persons of the highest quality. "I never saw any," writes Sir Nathaniel (ed. 1799, vol. ii. p. 295), "who could mention it without emotion. All asserted that the scene was the most touching to be conceived."

So far, so good. The Queen, previously crowned as *King*, in evasion of the Hungarian custom which excluded females from the throne, addressed the Diet in excellent Latin.

"*Agitur de regno Hungariae, de personâ nostrâ*," she began. . . . . "*ab omnibus derelicti, unice ad inclytorum statuum fidelitatem, arma, et Hungarorum priscam virtutem confugimus.*"

---

[1] *The Memoirs*, that is, *of the Courts of Berlin, Dresden, Warsaw, and Vienna* (1777–1779), 2 vols., 8vo, 1799 : see vol. 2, p. 295. These volumes, which are of the greatest value and interest, and in particular give the most minute account of Maria Theresa and the Austrian Court, must be carefully distinguished from Sir N. W. Wraxall's *Historical Memoirs of my own time* (1772-1784), the first edition of which (with portrait, 2 vols., Cadell, 1815, containing the passages afterwards suppressed, i. 205—Bindley £1 5s., Strettell £1 18s.) lies before us. This work, containing an atrocious libel on Count Woronzow (Lowndes's *Bibliographer's Manual* says Prince Gortschakoff!) for which the author was prosecuted and imprisoned, met with a severe and apparently well-deserved castigation from both the *Edinburgh Review* (xxv. 178) and the *Quarterly* (xiii. 196) as a repository of slander, stale news, and second-hand gossip; but contains, of course, a good

" We all," continues Wraxall's informant, " as if animated by one soul, drew our sabres, exclaiming unanimously—(what does the reader expect ?)—'Vitam et sanguinem *pro majestate vestrâ.'* " There seems no reason to discredit this account. A German critic (cited in Dyer's Modern Europe) questions the sword-drawing, and seems to prove that the romantic details represent a confused account of several different scenes.

Such an inaccuracy in the account of a notorious episode in the last century leaves us little room for confidence as to the most celebrated dramatic utterances of the Middle Ages. Two or three examples of these—to dismiss specimens which have little historical interest—are worth discussing. If Edward III., when landing on the coast of France, is related to have made much the same observation as both Julius Cæsar and William the Conqueror did of Great Britain, this need not rouse much suspicion ; for like situations tend to produce like sayings and doings.[1] Nor perhaps is the inquiry of much importance whether Jacques Molay, the Grand Master of the Templars, when burning at the stake in 1314, did or did not utter the prophecy often attributed to him. " I have read," says Mézeray, in his ponderous abridgment of the History of France, " that the Grand Master, having only his tongue free, and half stifled with smoke, cried aloud,' Clement, cruel and unrighteous butcher, I challenge thee to appear in forty days before the Judge of all.' "

Neither the chronicler of St. Denis, nor Villani, who describes the execution in detail,[2] say a word of any such challenge. But lately a

many anecdotes which are worth reading. A third series, the commoner, *Posthumous Memoirs*, 3 vols., appeared in 1836.

[1] It is more amusing to learn, even at third-hand, that William of Orange when he landed, began a popular harangue (in which it is hardly conceivable he can have proceeded much further) with the suggestive sentence : " We have come for your good, *for all your goods.*" Spence's *Anecdotes*, ed. 1820, p. 337. Spence had this from Nathaniel Hooke, who was born in 1690.

[2] Giovanni Villani (a contemporary, for he only died in 1348) merely record Molay's exclamation that he deserved death for having been lured into a con-

rhymed chronicle, presumably Mézeray's only authority, has been unearthed which gives the story in detail.

The coincidence that both King and Pope died shortly after the Grand Master was exactly one of those facts strongly influencing popular imagination which a romancist was bound to deal with. A metrical chronicle, if we recollect right, was a principal "authority" involved in the controversy which raged during the past year in the pages of a contemporary review, and indeed seems to be not yet extinct, as to whether our Saxon ancestors at "Senlac" fought behind a palisade or in the open. The former hypothesis, which perhaps does not seriously reflect upon the national courage, seemed to be gaining the day, but to base such a fact upon a mere romance of the time would be little better than basing a fact in modern politics upon one of Disraeli's novels; not that the rhymed chronicle was not often more prosaic and less imaginative than the dullest modern prose. But while it is a common case that, as M. Fournier quotes from Beaumarchais, "anciens petits mensonges assez mal plantés *ont produit de grosses, grosses vérités*,"[1] all persons acquainted with the "Twins" and "Nova Scotia Sheep" myth evolved in the *School for Scandal* understand how a chance word or suggestion sometimes sets a complete story going. Thus, to take an example, stumbled on at haphazard, in *Murray's Guide* is an exciting note concerning the villa of Vedius Pollio, near Naples, and the huge lamprey kept in his fishpond and "*fed upon the flesh of disobedient slaves.*" This should make the modern reader's flesh creep. The story will be found, where we should expect to find such stories, in *Guyon's Diverses Leçons*, Lyon, 8vo, 1610; and further back still, in Pietro Crinito's treatise *De honestâ disciplinâ* (i.e., de omnibus rebus et quibusdam aliis), on p. 23 of the fine edition printed by Nicolas de Barrâ in 1518. The "original authority" is apparently the anecdote given by Seneca in the dialogue

fession by the flattering artifices of the Pope and the King—Philip the Fair. *Storia*, viii. 92.

[1] *Mariage de Figaro*, iv. 1.

De Irâ, where, by the way, a fund of entertainment is to be found. The Emperor Augustus was one day dining with Pollio, and a slave happened to *break a glass*, upon which Pollio in a rage conceived the idea of ordering him to be thrown into the fishpond. The slave, however, threw himself at the feet of Augustus, begging to be allowed to die any death—"*modo ne esca fieret*"—only *not* to be used as live bait. The Emperor, "struck by the novelty of such a punishment," ordered every glass in the house to be broken, and the fishpond to be filled up. And that was all.

But if insignificant and doubtful materials have often been evolved into "grosses, grosses vérités," on the other hand, a genuine fact or dictum once popularised runs considerable risk, if its original source be lost, of sharing the fate of the fictions with which it has become associated. It rather appears that the celebrated and touching scene of Philip Augustus before the Battle of Bouvines (1214) offering to give up his royal authority to any one whom the army might consider more worthy of it should be assigned to this class. Thierry devoted a whole chapter to the demolition of the theatrical narratives of Anquetil and the Abbé Velly, according to which the monarch laid his crown upon the altar, saying, "*Elle est au plus digne*," and the host responded with acclamations of "Vive Philippe, vive le roi Auguste." Thierry quotes at length [1] the account (of the preparation for the battle) given by the chaplain, Gulielmus Armoricus who stood "just behind the King and close by him"; and yet says not a word of the matter, which, in any case, is curious. But apparently Thierry had not seen the then recently published *Chronicle of Rheims*,[2] containing an impressive and far more credible description

---

[1] *Lettres sur l'Hist. de France*, L. i., 7th ed., 1842; and *Duruy, Hist. de Fr.* It must be remembered, of course, that the "Hellenically" emotional impulse which induces a native historian to prefer the most self-conscious and artificial version of such an utterance, also operated upon the characters in his history. For a curious and pathetic expression of "French" feeling (upon the Franco-Prussian War), see the preface to the work last cited (ed. 1873).

[2] *La Chronique de Rains*. Publiée d'après le MS. unique de la Bibliothèque

of the scene—a scene in itself, as Duruy thinks, deeply significant of the danger in which the French King and his army were placed—but which was embellished by later hands into an object of historic suspicion.

But there is another and more celebrated mediæval utterance which, embodying as it does the expression of a fanaticism and intolerance hardly intelligible at the present day, has a permanent historical interest. In our own civilised age, at a meeting of the Archæological Society of Béziers (in 1844), a certain M. Henri Julia was reading a paper upon the sack of that city at the outset of the crusade against the Albigeois (July 1209), and he had just quoted the atrocious words attributed to the papal legate Milo (words, by the way, which read perhaps better in English than in French), "Kill kill them all : *God will know His own !*" when a young priest rose in the audience and cried out, "That is false. It has been disproved"; and a "scene" ensued, of which it need merely be said that the chairman does not seem to have supported the lecturer.[1]

The interruption, if not an unnatural one, was not exactly correct. The best historians of our day repeat the allegation. "Then," says Dean Milman, describing the episode, "was uttered the frightful command, 'Slay them all. God will know His own.'" And Sismondi writes : "It was Arnold, abbot of the Cistercians, who, when

Roi, par Louis Paris, 8vo, 1837. See p. 148. "Quant li baron l'oirent ensi parler, si comencerent à plorer de pitié et disent : ' Sire, pour Dieu merchi. Nous ne volons roi se vous non.'" The author of this interesting chronicle has recorded a favourite oath of Philippe-Auguste which is, says the learned editor, mentioned nowhere else—"*Par la lance Saint-Jaque.*" (As to other royal oaths, *cf. Brantôme,* ed. 1740, vi. 277.) Here also will be found (ch. viii.) the original and full account of Blondel's discovery and rescue of Richard Cœur de Lion, which was previously known only from Claude Fauchet's *Recueil de l'origine de la langue et Poësie Française,* 4to, 1581, "ouvrages estimé et peu commun." Fauchet, the interest of whose book is due in part to his having had access (it is said) to various MSS. now lost, quotes a MS. version of the fifteenth century, in his possession, apparently copied from the above.

[1] *Fournier,* p. 62.

asked how heretics should be distinguished from Catholics, replied, 'Kill them all. God will know those that belong to Him.'"[1]

The remark, attributed to one person or the other, is recorded by several contemporary authorities. But, on the other hand, it is not mentioned by those whose authority would, *primâ facie*, be the best, that is the native chroniclers of the country, nor by Pierre de Vaux Cernay,[2] *the* authority *par excellence*, an eye-witness of the whole transaction, who would, it is urged, have been proud to record it. This to readers acquainted with the barbarous invective and blood-thirsty sarcasms of that orthodox writer will not seem at all incredible; but after all he might not have heard the words, and the inhabitants of the doomed city certainly would not have heard them if they were uttered *before* the attack. Therefore there remains little reason for doubt that one or other of the crusading leaders did utter a remark which, if not devoid of originality and wit, would at least have come more suitably from the mouth of a layman.

The subject of persecution naturally recalls another historical question which, except in so far as any striking fact supplies historians with material for a sensational statement, seems hardly to form part of M. Fournier's subject-matter.

---

[1] Sismondi, *Literature of Southern Europe*, i. ch. 6. Milman's *Latin Christianity*, ed. 1883, i. 429.

[2] *Historia Albigensium et sacri belli in eos anno* 1209 *suscepti, duce et principe Simone à Monteforte*, &c., 8vo, Trecis, 1615, ch. xv. This first edition of a work not more remarkable for the hideous tragedies it describes, than for the fanatical atrocity of the author's frame of mind, one has some difficulty in procuring. A French translation was published in 1569. And the short chronicle entitled *Præclara Francorum Facinora* .... contra *orthodoxæ fidei hostes*, sm. 8vo, n.d. (*Panzer, Ann. Typ.* iv. 132, 524) is a distinctly rare book. The anonymous history in Provençal prose (*Hist. des Guerres des Albigeois, etc., avec introduction par un indigène*, Thoulouse, 1863—some curious specimens of provincial animosity are preserved in the preface), which is probably a fourteenth-century reproduction of a contemporary chronicle (as Sismondi, who quotes the awful description of the sack of the city as a specimen of thirteenth-century prose, seems not to have noticed), certainly seems to assert (p. 6) that "Senhor Milo" died of a "certana malaudia" before the Crusaders reached Béziers.

It is said, to return to that age of excitement the sixteenth century, that **Charles IX.**, whether he did or did not write the poem assigned to him, upon the occasion of the massacre of St. Bartholomew's **Day**, "fired upon the flying **Huguenots** with an arquebus from the window of his apartment in the Louvre."

Where should we expect to find the origin of such a **story?** Scarcely in the life of that **pious monarch** by his chaplain Antoine Sorbin, misnamed *de Saincte Foy*,[1] **but** *of course* in the memoirs of Brantôme.

And there it will duly be found. Charles IX., Brantôme **tells us,** when once his consent to the proposed **massacre had** been obtained, took up the idea with enthusiasm, "so much so that whilst the game was going on at break of day, the King, seeing some Huguenots who were running about and trying to escape, took a **great** arquebus that he used in hunting, and discharged it right at them, **but** to no purpose. *The arquebus would not carry so far.*" This **last** touch has certainly the air of veracity. The objections of various French critics are based upon an architectural argument too long to be here rehearsed. **But if** that part of the Louvre to which popular tradition assigned the act, when, in 1793, an inscription was erected to commemorate the royal infamy, did not exist in 1572, this may surely mean only that popular tradition was wrong, as it constantly is. The particular room **or** window is hardly the essence of the story, as it is, for example, of the legend that **Henry III.** died from the poisoned **dagger** of Jacques Clement in the very apartment and on the **very day** in and on which he had **eighteen years** before[2] taken part in the council which

---

[1] *Abrégé de la vie, mœurs, et vertus du Roy très Chrestien et debonnaire Charles IX., vrayement piteux* (sic), *propugnateur de la Foy Catholique et amateur de bons esprits*, à Lyon, chez Ben. Rigaud, 1574. But this (*rare*) volume—my copy wants part of the preface—contains many curious anecdotes of the time, and details of the King's private life. See also *Brantôme*, ed. 1740, vol. ix. 427. *Mémoires de l'Estat de France*, etc., 3 vols., 1578, i. 294. This latter is, I believe, the most copious and circumstantial account of the massacre in existence.

[2] See a note of L'Ecluse's to Sully's *Memoirs*, vol. i. and p. 180 *ante*.

planned the massacre. And the central fact—the shooting—is supported by a good deal of contemporary evidence. L'Estoile, whom
Fournier does not mention, refers to the King, in his journal, as
"potting" (*giboyant*) at the Calvinist fugitives. The *Mémoires de
l'Estat de France* (mentioned above), which describe the Queen-
Mother's anxiety lest the King should change his mind, and the
accidental precipitation of the massacre, mention the report that the
King, seeing his guards in the street shooting, cried out, "Let us
have a shot, they are running away"; and fired an arquebus which
he used in hunting. They also state that Charles, looking out of
a window, and struck by the fineness of the Sunday and Monday,
remarked, presumably a little later, that the "weather seemed to be
rejoicing at the destruction of the Huguenots.' (i. 318.) De Thou
speaks of a gun or cannon being fired "by order of the King, as it
is believed," which may have had something to do with the story.
In fine, Voltaire, in a note to the second edition (1724) of the tiresome epic poem afterwards called the *Henriade*, says that ever so
many people had heard the story from the Marquis de Tessé, who
died in 1725 at the age of seventy-five, and who had it from the very
man who, as a boy, loaded the arquebus. What more could we ask
but the arquebus itself? Seriously, the substance of the story
required a good deal of invention.

It is interesting to note that the President Hénault, who, as we
have seen, deliberately recorded a *bon mot* of the Grand Monarque
for which he knew there was no authority at all, at first admitted this
anecdote of Charles IX. to his abridgment, qualified by a "*dit-on*,"
and finally excluded it altogether.

A discussion accidentally started the other day upon a far more
ancient subject-matter reminds one that there may be sayings in
themselves insignificant, or merely epigrammatic, which have become
traditionally famous through the consequences that followed them.

Among the isolated utterances which history has found cause to
remember, hardly any can be more celebrated than that immortalised

by Dante as the origin of the Guelf and Ghibellin factions in Italy —" capo ha cosa fatta," or, as it runs in prose, " cosa fatta, capo ha."

This is the reflection attributed to Mosca de' Lamberti on the occasion of the consultation held by the Amidei and their friends as to how they should revenge themselves upon Messer Buondelmonte de' Buondelmonti for the insult put upon their family by his contemptuous breach of promise of marriage. It is worth while to refer to the description of the incident, which occurred in the year 1215, given by Giovanni Villani in his chronicle, because a question was recently raised, or revived, as to the precise meaning of the remark, which soon passed into a now extinct proverb.

To the ordinary reader the sense in which Lamberti must have used the phrase will seem inevitably determined by the circumstances under which he spoke. It was a question whether the insulter of the family should be wounded or merely beaten (*o di ferirlo, o di batterlo di man vuote*), when Mosca de' Lamberti, breaking in on the discussion, exclaimed, " cosa fatta capo ha "; " *cioè* " (as the chronicler explains) " *che fosse morto* "—" e cosi fu fatto " : and then follow the details of the assassination.

What could have been the meaning of such advice, unless it were to reject both the suggested alternatives in favour of more drastic measures which would finish with the matter once for all ? What else could be the point of the exclamation prefixed by Dante to the " ill-omened word " in the lines.,

> " Ricorderati anche del Mosca
> Che dissi, *lasso !* capo ha cosa fatta,
> Che fu 'l mal seme per la gente Tosca " ?

It has been suggested that (since " *capo* " doubtless means a beginning, as well as a " head and crown ") the speaker must have meant, not that " a thing *done* is done with, completed," but that " a thing done paves the way for future action " (of some quite undefined nature). Could there be a more pointless, a less emphatic argument in favour of a decided course of action ? There is force in comparing an action "well begun" to one which is "half done"; but to compare an act completely executed "cosa *fatta*" to the beginning of something else unknown and indifferent, is surely neither witty nor forcible. The speaker in 1215 was not thinking of the long factions destined to rage between Guelf and Ghibellin in the unknown future, but of settling *finally* an account in the already past. It is argued that the question was whether *no action at all* should be taken, or some, cosa "fatta." But Villani's words show that this was precisely *not* the point in dispute, but whether half measures of some kind would or would not suffice, whereupon Mosca gave his vote for what all the early historians understood to mean "la mort sans phrase."[1]

And this latter dictum, which brings us back quite inevitably and unintentionally to M. Fournier and French history, this "mala parola" attributed to the Abbé Sièyes, is to be added to the vast catalogue of effective sayings which yet remain unsaid; except, that is, at second-hand. The Abbé Sièyes did indeed vote for the execution of Louis XVI., but merely, as he asserted, with the words, "*La mort.*" The rest of the phrase belonged, he thought, to the "indirect oration" of some reporter, who gave a more

[1] See *Athenæum*, April 20, 1895 (reviewing a recent work on Dante); *Inferno*, xxviii. 107; *Giovanni Villani Storia*, v. 38; and *Ricordano Malespini* (the almost contemporary authority whom Villani here, as often elsewhere, follows almost verbatim), ch. 104 (ed. 1598, p. 90). Volpi's invaluable *Indici di Dante*—Comino, Padua, 1727 (revised ed. Venice, 1819)—and the *Raccolta di Proverbi Toscani* of Giuseppe Giusti (the famous satirist), Florence, 1853.

The story as given by Bandello (vol. i. novel 2: I quote the edition of 1566, which is presumably reliable in this matter) is that at the family conclave, after certain proposals of violence and bloodshed had been put forward "vi furono alcuni che discorrendo i mali che ne potevano seguire, non volevano che tanta a furia fosse da correre, *ma da pensarvi più maturamente.* Era tra i congregati il Mosca Lamberti, huomo audacissimo e pronto di mano il quale disse che chi pensava diversi partiti, nessuno ne pigliava : e soggiunse quella volgata sentenza," &c. It is dangerous to attack a reviewer in his native fastnesses, but what ground is there for saying that "comes to a head" (a special and medical English idiom) is an impartial translation of "capo ha"?

picturesque turn, as Macaulay sometimes did to the remarks brought
on to his pages in inverted commas, to the original text.

We are here clearly declining from the historical to the purely personal "historic" saying. Among these none is more familiar than the
epigrammatic "All is lost but honour" (*Tout est perdu fors l'honneur*)
of the most light-hearted of French monarchs. But most people are
now aware that Francis I. appended to the famous phrase (in his
original letter, which has long since become public property) the
words, "*and my life, which is safe,*" an addition at once natural in a
filial epistle, and characteristic of the author, to whom, as is known
from subsequent events, honour was by no means everything.

Nor need we here rehearse examples of the common "supercherie
littéraire" such as that of M. Querlon (editor, by the way, of Montaigne's travels in Italy), who composed for an anthology of 1765, and
the mere fun of the thing, the "touching lines" by Mary Queen of
Scots, reprinted in certain conventional histories. Of such fictions
might it not often be said—

"Il n'y a dans de telles affaires que le premier pas qui coûte,"

an adage, by the way, which might seem as well entitled to
examination as many of those in M. Fournier's work,[1] though he does
not mention it. The story (concerning the progress of the martyred

---

[1] Fournier confines himself to French history. It is hardly necessary to say
that a chapter (of less general interest) might have been added upon the peculiar
wit of Italy, of the "Pasquino and Marforio" who, as Beckford said, "take the
place of Horace, Juvenal, and Persius." On this matter the reader might
consult the interesting preface to Giuseppe Belli's *Duecento Sonetti in dialetto
Romanesco*, ed. L. Morandi, Florence, 1870. Most of the satirical jests there recorded
concern local and papal abuses, an inexhaustible subject, but not all. At the time
of the French invasion, when Napoleon was busily transporting so many priceless
Italian MSS. and works of art to Paris, Marforio inquires of his colleague,
"Pasquino, che tempo fa?" E quello rispondeva "Uh! fa un tempo da ladri!"
and a few days later "Pasquino, e vero che i Francesi son tutti ladri?" "Tutti,
no : ma *bona-parte.*"

See also *Pasquino e Marforio* (containing original Latin and Italian texts of the
most famous pasquinades), 8vo, 1861, rare (by M. Mary Lafon), reprinted 1877.

St. Denis carrying his head in his hands) is quoted by Gibbon, and will be found in the correspondence of his friend Mme. Du Deffand.[1]

But a perfect example—and this shall be the last—of the evolution of a classical *bon mot* is supplied by that comparison of Racine and coffee which many readers expect to find in the immortal letters of Mme. de Sévigné. It was made in three stages [2]—

(1) Madame wrote in 1672: "Racine writes comedies for La Champmeslé (the popular actress), *not for the generations to come,*" and suggests that he has not much in him, ending with a cheer for " our old friend Corneille." And four years later she observes to the unsympathetic daughter: "So you have quite given up coffee? So has Mlle. de Méri."

(2) Eighty years later Voltaire (what should we do without Voltaire?) ran the two phrases together, with a slight variation : " Mme. de Sévigné always held that Racine will not go far : she judged of him as she did of coffee, of which she used to say people would soon get tired."

(3) Upon this preparation of materials enter La Harpe, conventional dramatist and popular lecturer on literature, who proceeds to coin an immortal phrase—at least it is scarcely dead yet—" *Racine passera comme le café.*"

But we must not wander further into the region of merely social and literary " good things."

Alas ! that the slightest research in this as in other departments should so often tend to convince one that the really good thing is too good to be genuine, or that, if not corrupted, it has at least been borrowed by the traditional or *soi-disant* author. It was ever thus with all authors, little or great, and at all periods of which we know anything. No need to tell the student of any modern edition of

---

[1] *Decline and Fall of the Roman Empire*, ed. 1872, v. 33. *Deffand, Corre pondance inédite*, Colburn, 1810, L. xxiii.

[2] See the *Notice sur Mme. de Sévigné* prefixed to the edition of her Letters 12 vols., 1818 (vol. i. p. 132).

Julius Cæsar, for example, how little Shakespeare was to be trusted
to poach only incidents or "materials" from the preserves of a
North's Amyot's Plutarch and the like. And every schoolboy (at
least every schoolboy who has read Lalanne's *Curiosités Littéraires*)
knows that the finest "flash of genius" in Molière—

> "Que diable allait-il faire dans cette galère?"—

is a barefaced crib from Cyrano de Bergerac.[1] In these inquiries
authenticity, like historic accuracy in the other, soon vanishes from our
straining gaze. To appropriate successfully the "good things" of
another man, there is but one successful principle, and that is—what
an early scholar is suspected of having done with a last treatise of
Cicero—*to destroy the original.* Hence the true maxim for the
pirates of historic wit—

> "Pereant qui ante nos nostra dixerunt."

---

[1] Just as the paradox about "talking prose without knowing it" now eternally
associated with the "Bourgeois gentil-homme," belongs in fact to the Comte de
Soissons. v. *Lettres de Sévigné* (June 12, 1686).

INDEX.

INDEX.

NOTE.—The names or titles of books (only) are in italics.